WHEELS OF TERROR

SVEN HASSEL

Translated by I. O'Hanlon

CASSELL

Cassell Military Paperbacks

Cassell
An imprint of the Orion Publishing Group
Wellington House, 125 Strand, London WC2R 0BB

First published in Great Britain by
Souvenir Press Ltd 1959
This edition published 2004

A CIP catalogue record for this book is available
from the British Library

ISBN 0-304-36633-1

Typeset at The Spartan Press Ltd,
Lymington, Hants

Printed and bound in Great Britain by
Clays Ltd, St Ives plc

With hell inside you it can be fine
To live a jester under God's spell,
Yet open heaven's gates divine
With the heavy keys of your private hell.

This book is dedicated to the three greatest jesters of the 27th (Penal) Panzer Regiment: Obergefreiter Joseph Porta, 'Tiny' and the 'Little Legionnaire'.

1

The air-raid screams, whistles, thunders. Fire falls from the sky. Mothers cry to God and throw themselves over their children to protect them from the rain of fire falling on the asphalt.

Soldiers, trained in murder and hate, soldiers carrying their arms, are to be the people's protectors.

When the enemy bombers are silent, the rifles of these protectors speak.

Ordinary decent people, whose last energy has burnt away in panic-stricken terror, are being murdered by the soldiers of their own country.

What is the meaning of it all?

Dictatorship, my friend.

Nox Diaboli

The barracks were silent and dark, wrapped in the dark velvet of autumn. Only the sharp heel-taps of the sentries' hobnailed boots could be heard as they walked their tedious watch on the cemented path in front of the gates and along the sides of the barrack buildings.

In Room 27 we sat and played cards, Skat, of course.

'Twenty-four,' Stege called.

'You bloody whore,' Porta rhymed, grinning ferociously. 'That's where I came in.'

'Twenty-nine,' Möller bid quietly.

'Sod you, you Schleswig spudpeeler,' Porta said.

'Forty,' came calmly from The Old Un. 'Who can beat that? Laughing on the other side of your face now, eh, Skinny?'

'Don't be too bloody sure. Even playing with sharpers like you, you old . . .' Porta leered at The Old Un. 'I'll see you off. Forty-six!'

Bauer started to laugh loudly:

'I'll tell you something, old Porta. Here's forty-eight, and if you can beat that—'

'Not too much talk, my lamb. Quite a few of you died from that. But if you want to play with experienced people, this is how it is done.' Porta looked very smug. 'Forty-nine!'

At that moment loud whistling came from the corridors:

'Alert, alert, air-raid warning!'

And then the sirens cut in with their rising and falling banshee wails. Bursting with malice and cursing fluently, Porta flung down his cards.

'To hell with these bloody Tommies – coming and mucking up the best hand I've had for years!'

To a recruit, who stood looking confused and fumbling with his gear, he roared:

'Alert, my pretty, air-raid warning! Down to the shelters with you, double-quick, off!'

The recruits stood open-mouthed listening to his Berliner guttersnipe bellowings.

'Is it really a raid?' asked one of the recruits nervously.

'Of course it's a bloody raid. You don't imagine the Tommies have come to invite us to a ball at Buckingham Palace, do you? And that's not the worst of it! Now my lovely game of Skat goes to hell! Just to think what a mess a damned war can make of quiet, honest people's lives . . .'

Wild confusion had broken out. Everyone was tumbling round each other. Lockers were torn open. Heavy boots thundered through the long corridors of the vast block of barracks and down the stairs to the assembly points. Those who had not yet properly learned how to cope with their new hobnailed boots fell flat on the slippery tiled floors. Those who came behind waded over the novices, who had all more or less gone wild with panic when they heard the sirens. Most of them had enough experience to know that in a moment the bombs would come screaming through the pitch-black night.

'Number four platoon – over here.' The Old Un's quiet voice sounded curiously penetrating through the dark so dense it could nearly be cut. In the sky we could hear the heavy bombers winging towards their target. And now the flak began to bark hollowly from here and there about the city. Suddenly a light flared, a sharp white light which hung in the sky like a beautifully lit Christmas tree. The first target-light. In a minute the bombs would be drumming down to earth.

'Number three to the shelters,' sounded RSM Edel's deep bass voice.

At once the company's two hundred men split up and rushed in all directions to slit-trenches or even just heaps of soil. We soldiers were afraid of what were called air-raid shelters. We preferred the open trenches to the cellars, which we regarded as rat-traps.

And then hell loosed itself. Round us the enormous explosions shrieked and thundered. The bombs fell like a blanket over the city. In a moment everything was lit by the blood-red light from the great sea of flames. Crouching in our trenches, it looked as though the whole world was disintegrating in front of our eyes.

For miles around, the explosive and incendiary bombs illumined the condemned city. No words could ever describe that horror. The phosphorus of the incendiaries spurted like fountains in the air and spread an inferno. Asphalt, stone, people, trees, even glass went up in flames. Then the high explosives followed, spreading the inferno even wider. The fire was not the white fire of a furnace but red, like blood.

New, blinding Christmas trees appeared in the sky, giving the signal to attack. Bombs and air-torpedoes shrieked down on the city. Like an animal marked for slaughter it lay there, and like lice people searched for wrinkles and crannies to hide in. They were finished, torn to shreds, suffocated, burned, broken, minced. Yet many, just for a moment, made desperate attempts to save their lives. The lives to which they clung despite war, hunger, loss and political terror.

The Firling Flak at the barracks stuttered and barked against the invisible bombers. Orders had demanded that it should be fired. Fine! The gunners fired, but one thing we knew: not one of the great bombers would be damaged by the ridiculous Firling Flak.

Somewhere someone cried so loudly that the voice penetrated the din. The hysterical and sobbing voice cried for the ambulance squad. Two bombs had hit a single barracks-block.

'God help us,' murmured Pluto who lay on his back in the slit-trench with his steel helmet pushed over his forehead. 'I only hope they've hit some of the Nazi high brass down there.'

'Funny how a city can burn,' added Möller as he lifted himself up and looked out towards the glowing sea of fire. 'What is it that burns so?'

'Fat women, thin women, beer-blown men, thin men, bad children, nice children, beautiful girls, everything mixed up,' said Stege and wiped the sweat off his brow.

'Well, well, children, you'll soon find out – when we go down and help with the clearing up,' The Old Un said evenly, and lit his old pipe with its period-piece lid. 'I'd rather see something else. I don't like seeing half or whole-charred children.'

'That's too bad,' said Stege. 'There's going to be no difference between us and a mob of slaughterhouse workers when we get going down there.'

'Isn't that what we are?' Porta asked, laughing evilly. 'What is this bloody army we have the honour of belonging to, but just a huge butchery? Still, never mind. At least we'll have a trade to fall back on, eh?'

He stood up and bowed sardonically to the whole gang of us as we lay there with our backs pressed against the sides of the trench:

'Joseph Porta, Corporal by the grace of God, butcher in Adolf's army, habitual criminal and death candidate, corpse-carrier and incendiary! Your servant, gentlemen!'

At that moment a new Christmas tree flamed up near us, and he dropped quickly back into the trench.

He added, sighing: 'Another party is off to hell. Amen!'

For three solid hours, without a minute's peace, the explosives drummed down from the dark velvet sky. The phosphorus containers poured on the streets and houses in close-knit showers, in one impenetrable hailstorm of death and destruction.

The flak had long since been silenced. Our night fighters were up there, but the big bombers were not bothered by their smaller brothers-in-hell. The huge steam-roller of fire crushed the city from north to south, from east to west. The railway station was a roaring ruin of flames with red-hot carriages and engines in one molten heap, as if it had been ground by a giant amusing himself. Hospitals and nursing-homes collapsed in a holocaust of mortar and fire. Here the many beds provided excellent opportunities for the phosphorus to sport. Most of the patients were in the cellars, but there were many left in the wards for the flames to devour. Screaming, amputated cases struggled to get up and away from the flames which licked hot and hungry through doors and windows. The long corridors provided chimneys with a splendid draught. Fireproof walls burst like glass under the devastating pressure of explosives. People got up, only to fall gasping to the ground, suffocated by the heat. The stench of singed flesh and fat floated across to us in our trenches. Between the detonations the last half-strangled screams reached us.

'Children, children,' gasped The Old Un, 'this is bad, this is. Any left alive will be round the bend after this bloody lot. Give me the front-line any time. There women and children don't get roasted and skinned. The damned swine who invented air-raids should have a taste of this.'

'We'll burn the fat off Hermann's backside when we have our revolution,' hissed Porta. 'Where's the fat slug now, I wonder?'

At last it looked like ending. Piercing whistles and words of command rang out through the barracks, which were still illuminated by the ocean of flames. In single file we doubled to our stations.

Porta leaped wildly into a Krupp diesel lorry. The engine whined, and without waiting for orders he swung the huge vehicle out and roared off. We clung on as best we could. A nineteen-year-old lieutenant shouted something, and ran at the roaring vehicle. A couple of big hands heaved him in.

'Who in hell's name is driving this!' he gasped, but nobody answered him. We had enough to do trying to hang on to the madly bucking truck which Porta with a deft hand steered between the deep craters in the road. We thundered through the burning streets where tramcars and other vehicles lay broken between mortar rubble and fallen lamp-posts. But Porta didn't take a fraction off his speed. At one point, he swung in on clear pavement, knocking down small trees like matchsticks. But near Erichsstrasse we had to stop. A couple of air-torpedoes had struck, and a building lay like a wall across the street. Even a bulldozer would have had to call a halt.

We leaped off the truck and with pickaxes, axes and shovels, worked our way through the rubble. Lieutenant Harder tried his best to gather us under his command, but nobody paid any attention. The Old Un took charge. Shrugging his shoulders, the young officer grabbed a pickaxe and followed the file behind. The Old Un, the experienced front-line soldier. Like all of us, he had changed his weapons for a tool which we handled with as much adroitness as when we used flame-throwers and machine-pistols in battle: the entrenching-spade.

Through the raw, nauseating smoke people bandaged with dirty rags came towards us. Grossly swollen burns spoke their own clear language. Here were women, children, men, old and young, whose faces terror had turned to stone. Madness shone out of their eyes. Most of them had had their hair singed off, so one could barely distinguish one sex from the other. Many had wrapped themselves in wet sacks and rags as a protection against the flames. One woman in her madness shouted at us:

'Haven't you had enough! Haven't you dragged out this war long enough! My children are burnt to death. My husband is lost. May you burn, too, you damned soldiers!'

An old man took her by the shoulder and drew her away:

'Now, now Helga, take it easy. You might make things even worse for us, you know . . .'

She tore herself loose and leaped at Pluto with fingers spread like a tiger's claws, but the big docker shook her off as if she had been a small child. She banged her head against the hot asphalt, burst into uncontrolled screams. She and the old man were lost to us as we worked our way forward to the gigantic cliff of ruins. Surrounded by flames it towered in front of us.

A policeman without his helmet and with his uniform nearly burned away stopped us and stammered:

'The Children's Home, the Children's Home, the Children's Home . . .'

'What are you drooling about?' The Old Un snarled as the policeman dragged at him and kept on stuttering:

'The Children's Home, the Children's Home!'

Quickly Porta stepped forward and slammed his iron fist two or three times in the policeman's face. This treatment had often produced striking results at the front when we had used it on somebody with shell-shock. It also helped a little now. With eyes nearly popping out of his head with terror the policeman gabbled a sort of explanation, words tumbling out.

'Save the children! They're trapped inside. The whole lot is going up like matchwood!'

'Stuff it, you Schupo swine!' bellowed Porta grabbing the man by the shoulders and shaking him like a mat. 'Get your fat copper's carcase moving to the Children's Home and bloody quick! In front of us now – *los mensch!* What are you waiting for? I'm no captain – just Corporal Joseph Porta by the grace of God – but I expect crap like you to take my orders!'

The policeman, who looked as if he wanted to run for it, started to dart about confusedly, but Lieutenant Harder clutched him: 'Didn't you hear? Get going! Show us the way, and don't dawdle or you'll be shot!'

Simultaneously he swung his Mauser under the nose of the half-crazed policeman. His lips were trembling violently and his cheeks were streaked with tears. Normally, as an old man he would have been pensioned off but for the war.

Pluto, his giant's body towering over him, gave him a brutal shove and growled: 'Shut up and march, Grandad.'

The policeman, half-running, staggered along in front through collapsed shells of streets, where flames danced heavenwards. Women, children and men lay pressed fast to the ground. Some were dead, others had been struck dumb, and the cries of some curdled our blood.

Where a few hours before there had been a street corner, a little boy came running to us, shouting and dribbling in his fright. 'They are all trapped in the cellar. Help me get Mummy and Daddy out! He's a soldier like you. He was just home on leave. Lieschen has lost her arm. Henrik has burned up.'

We stopped for a moment. Möller petted the boy's head: 'We'll soon be back!'

We had reached a mountain of fallen rubble. It was impossible for us to go on. As we turned to ask the policeman to lead us another way there were enormous explosions close by. Like lightning we dived for shelter. Experience of the front line helps.

'What the hell, is Tommy back again?' hissed Porta.

Still more metallic thunderclaps, missiles, stones and earth showered over us. When fragments hit our steel helmets they rang with a curious high-pitched scream. But the new onslaught could do little more than interrupt us. Soon it ceased.

'They're dropping them blind now,' said The Old Un briefly and stood up.

We pressed on towards our target, the policeman in front. He led us through a cellar. We smashed holes in the wall with our pickaxes to reach what looked like the remains of a big garden. Its trees had toppled and burnt and layers of rubble and twisted iron, the remnants of a building, were still burning furiously.

The policeman pointed and muttered:

'The children are underneath that lot . . .'

'God, what a pasting it's got,' Stege said. 'And what a hell of a stink! They must have had phosphor-bombs on top of the incendiaries.'

The Old Un looked quickly round, taking stock, and began to attack vigorously something that looked like cellar steps.

With feverish anxiousness we hacked, shovelled and dug through the rubble, but for every shovelful we shifted a shovelful of debris poured down. Soon we had to stop to draw breath. Möller said that the most sensible thing would be to make contact with those in the cellar, if any were still alive.

The policeman was sitting with dead eyes rocking himself to and fro.

'Listen, Schupo! Is this the right place,' cried Porta, 'or are you fooling us? And, damn you, stop playing rocking-horse! Give us some help. What do you think you are paid for?'

'Leave him be. He can't help it,' Lieutenant Harder said wearily. 'This is a Children's Home. Or it has been. It says so on that notice-board over there.'

Following Möller's advice, we knocked at what had been a doorpost and after what seemed eternity we got an answer, very faintly as it came through to us: *knock! knock! knock!* Hitting the post again with a hammer, we listened with our ear to it. There was no doubt: *knock! knock! knock!* We worked like madmen with our pickaxes and crowbars to smash through to the cellar. Sweat made furrows on smoke-blackened faces. Skin was torn off hands. Nails broke and palms blistered as we man-handled the hot, sharp mortar and brick.

Pluto swung round at the policeman who was rocking on his haunches as he mumbled incomprehensibly.

'Come here, you stupid old flatfoot. Help us with this shaft,' he shouted.

As there was no response the giant crossed to Schupo, grabbed him and carried him without effort to the shaft, where we worked on indifferently. The old man bumped down to us. When he got to his feet, somebody thrust a spade into his hand and said:

'Get weaving, chum!'

He started digging, and as the work brought him to his senses we didn't worry any more about him. The Old Un was the first to break through. It was only a tiny crack, but through it we could just see a child's hand scratching desperately at the cemented wall.

The Old Un spoke soothingly into the darkness. But instantly a chorus of children's screams drowned him. It was impossible to calm them. The hole was now bigger, and the little hand was thrust through, but we had to hit it in order to make it withdraw. As we got one hand to shrink away another fought to take its place.

Stege turned and burst out: 'It drives me mad! We'll break their hands if we have a real bash at this.'

From the other side of the wall we heard a woman's voice screaming for air, and another shouting: 'Water, water, for God's sake bring water!'

The Old Un still on his knees, spoke soothingly to them. His patience was enormous. Without him we would all have thrown down our tools and run away with our fingers jabbed in our ears to stifle the mad voices.

Dawn hardly penetrated the thick suffocating carpet of smoke over the burning city. We worked with gasmasks but were nearly choked. Our voices sounded hollow and far away.

We had managed to make a new hole. Desperately we tried to quieten the unhappy people in the collapsed cellar. The atmosphere of horror during the raid can be imagined, but only those who have experienced bombs know that they are not the worst. The human spirit's reaction to them is worst of all.

'Our Father, who art in Heaven,' a trembling voice rose. The pickaxes and shovels clattered on. 'Forgive us our trespasses' – a shrieking bang, splashing, and fire poured everywhere. New, ear-splitting bangs. Another raid? Another stray drop? No, incendiaries!

We pressed our bodies hard against the very foundations of what had once been the Children's Home.

'Thine is the Kingdom . . .'

'By God, it isn't,' Porta's excited voice answered. 'It belongs to Adolf – that swine!'

'Help, O God in Heaven, help us and our children,' cried a praying woman in the cellar. A child sobbed: 'Mummy, Mummy, what are they doing? I don't want to die, I don't want to die.'

'Oh, God, get us out,' another woman cried hysterically, as a white, well-groomed hand clawed at the hole and broke its polished nails on the cement.

'Take your hand away, my girl, or we'll never get you out,' Pluto bellowed.

But the long slim fingers still clawed desperately. As Porta hit them with his buckled belt the skin broke and blood oozed out. With another smack they lost their grip and slid like dying worms away from the crack.

New explosions. Cries and swearing. Timber hurtled down with stone and gravel into the sparkling phosphorrain. We were trapped on all sides. The policeman lay inert on his back, beaten by exhaustion. Pluto casually rubbed the toe of his boot on his face and said: 'He's had it. The Tommies have dished out more than the old bastard could take.'

'To hell with him,' Lieutenant Harder retorted impatiently. 'Germany is full of tough-guy policemen. How many poor devils has he put in gaol? Forget him.'

We got on with our work.

Then one big explosion, the biggest we had ever experienced, shook the ground under us. Then another and another and another. We flung ourselves headlong into cover and pressed ourselves flat. Those were no stray drops.

It was the start of a new raid.

The phosphorus streamed on to the asphalt. Petrol bombs spurted fire-fountains twenty yards into the air. Flaming phosphorus poured down over the ruins like a cloudburst. It whistled and whirled in a tornado of fire and explosives. The biggest air-mines literally lifted whole houses into the air.

Porta lay beside me. He blinked encouragingly through the gas-mask's large screen. I felt as if my mask was full of boiling water and steam. It pressed against my temples. A choking terror gripped my throat. 'In a moment you'll get shell-shock,' the words shot through my head. I half sat up. I had to get away, no matter where, anywhere, only away.

Porta was over me like a hawk. A kick, and I was in the hole again. He hit me again and again. His eyes gleamed through the screen of the gas-mask. I shouted:

'I want to go, let me go!'

Then it was over. How long did it last? One hour? One day? No, ten to fifteen minutes. And hundreds had been killed. I, a panzer soldier, had shell-shock. My friend had damaged my jaw. One tooth was broken. One eye was swollen. Every nerve screamed in wild revolt.

The city had turned into a furnace of foaming fire where people ran shrieking from the ruins which flamed like a gas-stove's blue burners. Living torches, they tottered, whizzed round and fell, stood up and went faster and faster. They kicked, shouted and screamed only as people *can* scream in death agony. In a flash a deep bomb-crater was filled with burning people: children, women, men, all in a danse macabre supernaturally lighted.

Some of them burned with a white, others with a crimson flame. Some were consumed in a dull yellow-blue glow. Some died quickly and mercifully, but others ran around in circles, or reeled backwards rolling head over heels and twisting like snakes before they shrank into small charred dummies. Yet some still lived.

The Old Un, always so calm, broke down for the first time in our experience. He shouted in a thin high-pitched scream:

'Shoot them. For Christ's sake, shoot them!'

He put his arms across his face to shut out the sight. Lieutenant Harder tore his pistol out of its holster, slung it at The Old Un and shouted hysterically:

'Shoot them yourself! I can't.'

Without a word Porta and Pluto drew their pistols. Taking careful aim, they opened fire.

We saw people hit by bullets aimed with deadly precision, fall, kick a little, scratch a few times with their fingers, and then lie still to be immolted in the flames. It sounds brutal. It was brutal. But better a quick death from a heavy-calibre bullet than a slow one in a monstrous grill. Not one of them had a chance of rescue.

From the cellar of that devastated Children's Home rose cries to heaven from hundreds of children's throats, the cries of suffering, trembling children, innocent victims in an infamous war such as no one had ever imagined before.

Time after time, Pluto, Möller and Stege crept down into the gloom and pulled them out. When the cellar at last collapsed, we had managed to get a quarter of them out. Most of them died shortly afterwards. Pluto was trapped between two granite blocks and only sheer luck saved him from being crushed. We had to prise him loose with crowbars and pickaxes.

Exhausted, we threw ourselves on the trembling ground. We tore off our gas-masks, but the stench was so nauseating that it was intolerable without them. A sweetish, all-pervading smell of corpses was mixed with the sour, choking stench of charred flesh and the odour of hot blood. Our tongues stuck to our palates. Our eyes stung and burned.

Glowing roof tiles whirled through the air. Smoke-blackened flaming joists sailed through the streets like leaves driven on an autumn evening.

We ran crouching between the banks of flame. In one place a huge unexploded air-mine, evil messenger of death, stood darkly against the sky. Several times we were blown along the streets by the gale which had developed. It resembled a gigantic vacuum-cleaner. We scrambled and waded through a morass of skinned bodies, our boots slipping in jellied, bloody flesh. A man in a brown uniform staggered towards us. The red and black of the swastika on his armband was like a mocking challenge, and our grip tightened on our implements.

Lieutenant Harder said hoarsely:

'No! Cut *that* out . . .'

A trembling hand tried to restrain Porta, but the motion was half-hearted. With an oath, Porta swung his pickaxe and sank the point into the party member's chest as Bauer swung his spade and split the man's skull.

'By Christ, well done!' Porta shouted, and laughed savagely.

People were twisting in agony on the ground. The tram rails were red-hot and curled into grotesque patterns which thrust out of the hot asphalt. People who had been trapped in their houses jumped in madness from what had once been windows and hit the ground with soggy thuds. Some shuffled along on their hands dragging maimed legs behind them. Men thrust away wives and children who clung to them.

People had become animals. Away, away, only away. The only thing that mattered was to save oneself.

We met other soldiers from the barracks who were out like us to do whatever rescue work was possible. Many of these parties had senior officers with them, but leadership had often been taken by an old front-line sergeant or corporal. Only experience and nerves of steel mattered here, not rank. As we dug and heaved to free people from the collapsed cellars terrible scenes met us in the hot, stinking rooms which had been shelters.

In one place five hundred people were crowded into a concrete shelter. They were side by side with their knees comfortably drawn up, or on the floor with their heads pillowed on their arms. Asphyxiated by carbon monoxide they had suffered no apparent injury.

In another cellar were scores of people lying on top of each other, burnt to a solid mass.

Screaming, sobbing, childish cries for help:

'Mummy, Mummy, where are you? Oh, Mummy, my feet hurt!'

Women's voices calling in anguish for their children – children who were crushed or burned or swept away by the gale of fire or who were tottering aimlessly down the streets stupefied with terror. Some found their loved ones, but hundreds never saw them again. God knows how many were sucked up in the hot breath of the giant vacuum-cleaner, or carried away in the river of refugees pouring from the stricken city into the dark fields, into the unknown.

2

Dead, dead, only the dead. Parents, children, enemies, friends, piled in one long row, shrunken and charred into fossils.

Hour after hour, day after day shovelling, scraping, pushing and lifting corpse upon corpse. That was the job of the burial commandos.

At the shout of 'Air-raid warning!' the children had run their last steps into the cellar. They had sat there, paralysed by fright until the hellish river of phosphorus reached them and ate the life out of their small twisting bodies. First quickly, then more slowly, until silence lay mercifully over them.

Such is war.

Those who have forgotten to weep, would have been taught anew had they stood beside the Ghouls' Squad, the panzer soldiers, and watched them at their work.

Furioso

The men from the penal units always got the dirty jobs both at the depot and the front.

We had newly come back from the Eastern Front to train with our new tanks and to make up our numbers. We were a penal regiment. All of us came from concentration camps, gaols, reform-camps or some of the other torture institutions flourishing during the German Millenium. Of our platoon, only Pluto and Bauer were convicted criminals.

Pluto, the huge docker from Hamburg whose civilian name was Gustav Eicken, had landed in clink because he had stolen a lorry-load of flour. He always insisted it had been a frame-up, but we were convinced he had pinched the flour. Bauer had been condemned to six years' hard labour because he had sold a pig and a few eggs on the black market.

The Old Un, our troop sergeant, was the oldest of us. He was married, with two children, and a carpenter. His political convictions had brought him a year-and-a-half in a concentration camp. Afterwards as a PU ('Political Unstable') he had landed in the 27th (Penal) Panzer Regiment.

Corporal Joseph Porta, tall, thin and unbelievably ugly, never forgot to say he was a Red. A red banner, planted on the top of St Michael's church in Berlin had sent him to a concentration camp and then the penal regiment. He was a native Berliner with a fantastic store of humour and cheek.

Hugo Stege, our only university man, had been mixed up in some student demonstrations. He had spent three years in Oranienburg and Torgau before being popped into the mincing machine of the 27th (Penal) Panzer Regiment.

Möller had been unwilling to write off his religious convictions which had cost him four years in Grosse Rosen. Later he had been reprieved with the right to die in a penal regiment.

As for myself, an *Auslander* German of Danish and Austrian stock; I had been condemned for desertion in the beginning of the war. My stay in Lengries and Fagen had been short but stormy. Afterwards I was branded a PU and sent to the penal regiment.

After the air-raid we were divided into rescue and burial parties. In five days we had shifted load after load of bodies from cellars and bomb craters. Now we paraded in a churchyard and put the corpses to rest in the big mass graves. Attempts at identification were hopeless in nearly all cases. The fire had done its work well, and most documents had disappeared. If the fire had not destroyed them, they had been stolen by corpse marauders who, like predatory fish, poured forth everywhere. When these human sharks were caught rifle shots quickly exterminated them. Curiously enough, they came from all classes.

Late one evening we caught two women. The Old Un had noticed them. As we wanted to make sure, we hid and took stock of their movements. They sneaked around the fallen walls and bent over corpses whose stench must have turned even their stomachs. With vulture-like avidness and clearly following an established routine, they searched pockets and handbags for valuables. When we grabbed them we found thirty watches and fifty rings and other jewellery on them. A wad of banknotes they protested belonged to them. They had a knife to cut off the fingers of the corpses to get the rings. Proof was as clear as daylight. After a few hysterical shouts they both confessed.

With our rifle-butts we forced them to a smoke-blackened wall and made them turn their backs. It was the quiet Möller who shot them in the neck. When the magazine was empty Bauer pushed them with his foot to make sure they were dead.

'Bloody hell, what cows!' said Porta. 'I bet they belonged to the party. Those are the boys for letting nothing go to waste. I wouldn't wonder if we were ordered to cut the hair off the corpses – those that have any left.'

Porta and Pluto stood in the open grave. We heaved the corpses to them from refuse-carts. Arms and legs hung over the sides. A head over the back wheel of one dangled to and fro. The mouth was wide open and the teeth bared like those of a snarling animal.

The Old Un and Lieutenant Harder kept yellow and red record cards on those we managed to identify. Otherwise we just counted like grocers' boys counting sacks in the store-room. The two of them made out list upon list: so many sacks – so many women and men.

Grain liquor had been issued to enable us to stand up to the job of handling the liquescing corpses. Every few minutes we drank deeply from the huge communal bottles which stood by an old gravestone. We were not sober one moment during that spell of work. Without the hooch we would have broken down.

Some Prussian pedant had decreed that bodies found in the same cellar should be kept together. That was why sometimes we got a water-trough or bathtub filled with a blackened, congealed porridge which had once been people. They had been shovelled and ladled into the same bathtub. On top lay a notice giving the number contained in the tub. Fifty people who had been in the phosphor bath hardly filled an ordinary bathtub.

A giant Russian prisoner-of-war who worked with our party wept the whole time. What filled him with such anguish was the number of children. As with utmost gentleness he laid them in their graves he prayed:

'Shallkij prasstaludina, malenkj prasstaludina!'

If we tried to put a few adults with the children he became distracted, so in the end we let him do as he pleased. Although he drank copiously he seemed completely sober. Gently he smoothed out the small limbs, and where any hair was left he patted it in place. From early morning till late at night all alone he tended his gruesome charges, and we did not envy him . . . The Old Un maintained that his apparently sober condition proved he was on his way to insanity.

It was a blessing to have Porta with us. His robust humour made us forget the human degradation we went through. As the arm of a big fat man came away from the body, Porta guffawed drunkenly and cried to Pluto who stood open mouthed with the arm in his hand:

'What a grip! Good thing the gentleman will never know how hard you shook his hand.' He took a large swig from the schnapps bottle and went on: 'Now put his arm nicely beside him, so that he'll be able to shake hands in heaven or hell, wherever he's going.'

Every time we arranged a row of corpses, we threw a thin layer of earth on top and then a new layer of bodies. Because there was little room in the mass graves we had to tread the bodies down. The gas from the corpses stank to heaven, and Porta balancing precariously on the edge of the grave cried:

'What backside cyclones! It stinks worse than you, Pluto, when you've been eating yellow peas. And that's saying something!'

When we had filled a grave we put on top of it a notice fastened to a pole for the information of those who later would be erecting crosses and gravestones.

Four hundred and fifty unknown. Seven hundred unknown. Two hundred and eighty unknown. Always a figure. Everything had to be in order. Prussian bureaucracy insisted on it.

As the days went by the corpses slipped out of our grip. Rats and dogs made off with great chunks of flesh. We were vomiting continually, but orders had to be carried out. Even Porta became subdued and silent. We growled and swore at each other, and sometimes fights developed.

One time, when Porta was about to bury a half-naked woman with her legs grotesquely drawn up, he tried to straighten them. The storm hanging over us was released by Pluto's impatient question:

'What the hell are you wasting time for? It's all the same to you, you don't know her.'

Porta, whose uniform like the rest, was covered in a greenish slime, frowned drunkenly at the huge docker:

'I do what I bloody well like without your permission.' He hiccupped loudly and raised the bottle of schnapps: 'Here's to you, you shower of undertakers!'

He held the bottle away from his mouth, bent his head backwards and we saw how the schnapps poured down his throat. When he had finished, he burped prodigiously and spat in a high arc to hit the newly emptied charnal-cart.

'Stop that, Porta!' Lieutenant Harder shouted in sudden rage, his fists clenched.

'Certainly, sir, certainly. But if you, sir, would yourself look at the girl, you would agree she can't be buried like this.'

'Get it over with.'

'What, sir?' asked Porta and eyed Harder malevolently. 'With straightening out the legs, or what?'

'Porta, I order you to shut up!'

'My God, I won't. Do you think I'm scared of you, you louse, because you have silver on your shoulders? And not so much Porta. I'm Corporal Porta to you.'

In one leap Harder was round the grave and down with Porta among the corpses, hitting him in the face.

Then Pluto and Bauer, who were the first to get over their astonishment, parted them. They hit each a terrific blow, so that both the lieutenant and the corporal tumbled back into the slush. We got them out and dumped them on their backs.

They rose scowling, and under our watchful eyes drank

deeply from the bottle of schnapps. Porta turned quickly and went back to the grave, but Harder followed, put one hand on Porta's shoulder while offering his other hand and said:

'Sorry, chum, nerves. But you are a shocking talker. I know you don't mean anything. Let's forget it.'

Porta opened his ugly face in a broad grin, his only front tooth shining benevolently at Harder:

'Fine, sir. Old Porta, Corporal by the grace of God in the Nazi army, doesn't bear grudges. But it was a real one you hit me. Where I'm damned if I know. I've only known one officer who could fight, my highly honoured old field commander Colonel Hinka. But watch that big swine Pluto there. He'll kill you or me one day if he gets a chance to butt in every time we have a fight. He's got a punch like a kick from a stallion.'

We got steadily more and more drunk. Several times one of us would fall on top of the bodies in the grave and make ridiculous apologies to the dead. From the middle of the grave among the beautiful churchyard willows and poplars, Porta suddenly bawled:

'He, he, he! Here's a bloody tart, card and all, and to beat the lot I know her!'

Still shaking with laughter he threw a yellow card at The Old Un.

'It's Gertrude! By Christ, it's Gertrude from the Wilhelmstrasse. So she's kicked the bucket! It's not eight days since I was in bed with her, and now she's bought it.'

Porta bent and examined the dead Gertrude with keen interest. With a great show of expert knowledge he said:

'It's an air mine. That's clear enough. Lungs burst. Otherwise intact though. Fancy her getting it, a first-class tart. Real value for twenty marks!'

Soon afterwards we heaved the body of a man dressed in a well-tailored suit down to Porta and Pluto.

'You're going to have posh company, Gertrude,' said Porta. 'Not just a front-line dog like me. There you are, boys, everything ends well. If I had told her eight days ago she was going to be buried with a gentleman in patent leather shoes and white spats she'd have thrown me out.'

Lieutenant Harder squinted over to the long row of waiting carts which ceaselessly rolled up filled with bodies.

'Hell, will it never end?' he said wearily. 'And we aren't the only burial party.'

'It seems like two new corpses come in for each one we load,' said a sergeant-major from No. 5 Company. 'Several other burial parties have broken down. We've had to get new troops.'

'Kids still wet round the ears,' snapped Harder and returned to his lists.

A little later we were sitting on some fallen grave-stones. Porta was going to tell us a story from his eventful life, but when he started describing his favourite dish of brown beans and pork we had to stop him. Even half-drunk we couldn't abide the subject of food.

We buried people for days. In our drunkenness we made the filthiest jokes about our horrible work. They kept us from insanity. For in spite of the impersonality of mass death each single person had gone through his own life and death agony. Mothers and fathers had worried about their children. They had had money-troubles, drunk beer from large tankards or wine from tall glasses, danced, had fun, slaved in factories or offices, wandered in sun and rain; enjoyed a warm bath or a quiet evening with friends talking confidentially about the end of the war and better days when they would have great times together. Instead, full stop. Brutally, evilly, violently, death had come. It may have lasted a fraction of a second, minutes or hours, to end by being buried by tipsy soldiers from a penal regiment, who spewed foul jokes as the only epitaph for men and women who had once striven and hoped.

Our last job was to go down into cellars where there was no chance of getting the bodies out. We, the Ghouls' Squad, in our black tank uniforms, with the laughing skull flash on the collar, used flame-throwers to destroy the last slimy remains of what had once been human beings. Where we advanced the living ran in terror.

Everything turned to ash where the red hissing tongue of

the flame-thrower licked along. The air trembled when our detonators were set off. In thick dust clouds the last remnants of houses crumpled. The only message from the army about this hell ran laconically: 'Several cities in North-West Germany have sustained terror attacks from enemy aircraft. Among others Cologne and Hanover were heavily attacked. Numerous enemy bombers were shot down by our flak and fighters. Retaliation will rapidly follow.'

3

A soldier's weapons are given him to be used. That's laid down in the regulations, and these a soldier must obey.

Lieutenant-Colonel Weisshagen loved regulations. He constantly reminded everyone: 'You learn only from regulations and by example.'

He was taught that despite regulations it is uncomfortable to get your cap shot off.

A Shot in the Night

For eight days we had trained with new tanks. We had returned to barracks from the infamous Sennelager, near Paderborn, the most hated of all Germany's hated training grounds.

The soldiers said that Sennelager had been created by God in his ugliest mood. Personally I thought there was something in that. Its equal for uncomfortable terrain with sand and bog, thick bush and impenetrable thorns, would be hard to find. It was surely more desolate and depressing than the Gobi desert. It had been cursed by the thousands who had trained on it in the Kaiser's time and who were later to fall in the 1914–18 war. The volunteers in the hundred-thousand strong Reichwehr, who had chosen the soldier's trade to escape from unemployment, came to long for the grey hopelessness of civilian unemployment rather than face daily the hell that was Sennelager. We, the Third Reich's soldier-slaves, got it tougher than any of them, and the legendary 'Unteroffizier Himmelstoss' in the Kaiser's time had nothing on our officers and NCOs when it came to the routine of military sadism. He was only a baby.

Many people condemned to death by court-martial in the Rhine-Westfalen command were executed here. But as The Old Un once put it, when you were brought here to die, death must be a blessed release if only to escape looking at the incredibly depressing soul-destroying stretch of country that was Sennelager.

Pluto and I were chosen for guard-duty the first night. We had to stand with our steel-helmets and rifles and stare enviously at our lucky friends who went to town, there to rinse away the taste of the training-ground with beer and schnapps.

Porta fairly danced past us, laughing his head off. We could count the last three teeth in his huge gob. The army had given him sets of dentures for the upper and lower jaws, but he carried them in his pocket, well wrapped in a piece of grubby cloth which he used to clean his rifle before parades. When he was eating he solemnly unwrapped the teeth and placed a set on each side of his plate. When he had stuffed himself with his own food and any leftovers he could scrounge, he would polish the teeth with his rifle-rag, wrap them conscientiously in the rag and put them back in his pocket.

'Mind you keep the gates wide open when Father comes home,' he grinned. 'I'm bound to be drunker than you've seen me for a long time, and my well-trained male organ's scared stiff already with all the work I've got cut out for him. Cheerio, soldier boys, and take great care of the Prussian barracks.'

'That stupid red-haired bastard!' Pluto growled. 'Off on the spree, and the best we can hope for is a game of pontoon with the snot-nosed recruits.'

Very lonely we sat in the canteen and ate our nettle soup – the eternal *Eintopf* which always made us slightly sick.

A few recruits were also there playing grown-ups because they wore uniform. A great deal of their self-confidence would vanish when they got their marching orders, and landed in a battle unit on the eastern front.

Sergeant-Major Paust was also present with some of the NCOs. He drank beer in his own special grunting, guzzling way. When he saw us in our guard-order eating the deadly *Eintopf* he guffawed and shouted in his barracks slang:

'You two sucking-pigs, do you like guard-duty? It's Daddy

here who looked after that. I fancied you needed a little rest. Tomorrow you'll thank me for not having a hang-over like the others.'

As we didn't answer, he half-stood up, leaning on his huge fists and sticking out his massive Prussian jaw:

'Answer me! The regulations lay down, that men must answer their officers! Not front-line manners. We still have lawful and civilized order here. Remember that, you cows!'

Reluctantly we stood up and answered:

'Yes, Herr Feldwebel, we like guard-duty.'

'Heavy in the seat, what, you swine? I'll bloody soon see to that. Either in 'Senne' or on the parade-ground!'

He threw out his hand and bawled:

'You are dismissed!'

We sat down slowly and I whispered to Pluto:

'Is there any lower form of life than a man with a rank who's everything with it and nothing without it?'

Pluto glowered at me across the nettle soup:

'It's the training officer. He's got to use the scrapings of the gutter to do his job for him. Let's get out quick before I puke.'

We stood up again quickly, but just as we reached the door Paust roared:

'Here, you tired heroes! Never heard of the regulation which tells you to salute your senior ranks when you enter or leave a room? Don't try to get away with anything, you bog-lice!'

Shaking with frustrated fury we went up to his table, clicked our heels together and stretched our hands along the seats of our trousers. Pluto roared out, insultingly loud:

'Obergefreiter Gustav Eicken and Fahnenjunkergefreiter Hassel humbly beg you, Herr Feldwebel, for permission to leave the room, then to proceed to the guard-room by gate number four, where we will execute our duty as commanded!'

Paust nodded condescendingly, at the same time lifting a huge tankard to his broad, sweating face.

'Dismissed!'

With a terrific bang of our heels we about-turned and marched noisily out of the steam and stink of the canteen.

Outside, Pluto stood cursing obscenely. He finished by lifting one leg and venting an enormous fart in the direction of the closed canteen door.

'I wish to God we were back at the front. If we stay here much longer I'm bound to screw the neck off Paust and pack him together so that he'll be able to wink at his own tail!'

Dully, we sat in the guard-room and played pontoon, but were soon fed up and packed it up. We threw ourselves back into high-backed guard-room chairs. Here we sat mooning over some strongly pornographic magazines, which Porta had lent us:

'What a fanny she's got!' Pluto grinned and pointed to a girl in my magazine. 'If only I could meet a lass like that I'd really show her what I'm made of. I want thighs I can embrace with both arms. How would you go for a great cow like that on a table with only her chemise on?'

'Not much,' I answered. 'I go for what you'd call the skinny ones. Now, look, that's something. If I had one like that turned over every six months I could last out a thirty years war.'

The guard commander, Sergeant Reinhardt, came across and leaned over our shoulders. He was drooling:

'Well! What do you know! Where do you get magazines like that?'

'Where do you think?' Pluto answered insolently. 'Every Wednesday the YMCA distributes them. Ask the girl in the reception. She's got a load under the issue-bibles.'

'Don't get fresh, Corporal, or you'll have me after you,' Reinhardt said angrily as Pluto burst out laughing. But in a moment he was mollified. His eyes bulged as he thumbed through pictures of the most fantastically unnatural erotic positions. Even Casanova might have gaped.

'No, by God,' breathed Reinhardt. 'As soon as duty's over I'm off to find a bit of frippet. This gives you an appetite. That's a bloody good one, I must try with Grete tomorrow.'

'Blimey. That's nothing,' said Pluto condescendingly. 'Just look here,' and he pointed to a picture showing a completely insane situation. 'I knew that one already when I was fourteen.'

The lower jaw in Reinhardt's peasant's face dropped in gaping astonishment, and he stared with admiration at the big Hamberger:

'When you were fourteen? That's a lie. When did you begin?'

'When I was eight-and-a-half. With a married bitch while her husband was out selling fruit. It was a sort of tip because I had got her eggs from the grocer in the Bremerstrasse.'

'Hell, stop making me randy,' Reinhardt groaned.

'Here, can you get me a married woman? You must know a lot of them.'

'Sure I can, man, but it'll cost ten opium-fags and a bottle of rum or cognac in advance. And when you've had your tart another ten opium-fags and another bottle – from France, none of that German stuff.'

'It's yours,' said Reinhardt eagerly, 'but God forgive you if you cheat.'

'To hell, if you don't trust me, get your tart yourself,' answered Pluto and turned the pages of his magazine indifferently. Not by as much as a glance did he betray how badly he wanted the opium-cigarettes and schnapps. He knew Reinhardt could get hold of them.

The sergeant was walking excitedly up and down the guard-room. He kicked the kit belonging to one of the recruits into a corner and then proceeded to reprimand the poor devil for his unsoldierly behaviour on duty. Then he came across and put his arm in a friendly way round Pluto's shoulders and mine.

'Never mind, my friends, I didn't mean it like that. One gets a little suspicious. All these depot stallions are nothing but a bunch of crooks and swindlers. It's different with you lads from the front. You understand the meaning of friendship.'

'I don't understand why you stick around here when you hate it so much,' said Pluto, blowing his nose in the old-fashioned way and flicking some of the snot on Reinhardt's chair. This Reinhardt chose to ignore. 'Come along with us where it bangs.'

'Good idea, I might at that,' replied Reinhardt. 'Soon it'll be unbearable in this town, unless you've got front-decorations up. Even old hags give you the bird. But what about this tart, can you fix one up, chum?'

'In next to no time, but first an advance,' answered Pluto and stuck out his palm.

The outstretched hand gave Reinhardt nervous twitches in his face.

'I swear you'll have ten fags to-morrow when duty is finished, and the cognac is yours as soon as I have been to town to see the bloke who lays it on for me. But can you raise the other thing for to-morrow evening?'

Pluto answered in a chilly tone:

'You'll get your tart, and it'll be to-morrow evening.'

The recruits, most of whom were not yet eighteen, glanced blushingly and shyly across at us. This kind of talk was every day speech to us. We would have stared completely uncomprehendingly at anyone who suggested it was immoral. The deal Pluto and Reinhardt had just made was to us just as normal as an execution was in Sennelager. We had learnt new values in the great mass production factory called the army.

At last darkness enveloped the huge barracks and its scattered outbuildings. Here and there behind the blacked-out windows lay a recruit who had fallen asleep crying soundlessly. Home-sickness, fright and many other things had broken him down and made him behave like the child he was despite the weapons and the uniform.

Pluto and I went out on our spell of sentry-duty. We had to walk along the foot of the high walls which surrounded the whole barracks area. We had to see to it that all the regulations were kept, that doors were closed at 10 p.m., that the ammunition boxes behind the parade-ground were properly stowed. If we met anyone in the grounds, he had to be halted and his papers examined. Our officers took a peculiar pleasure in wandering about just to make sure the sentries were alert enough to challenge them.

Colonel von Weisshagen, our commandant, had a special passion for this form of sport. He was a very small man with a much too big monocle screwed into his face. His uniform was a study in the fancy dress of a Prussian officer: green tunic in a half-Hungarian, half-German cut, very short like a cavalry-man's; light grey breeches almost white with the hide of half a cow sewn to the seat, typical cavalry style; black, very long, patent-leather boots. It was a riddle to us how he managed to bend his legs when he wore them. because of the breeches and the boots he was nick-named 'Backside and Boots' by the soldiers. His cap was high in front, of the kind particularly favoured by the Nazi bosses and heavily embroidered with eagle and wreath, and a chinstrap fashioned from an enormously heavily knotted silver cord. Naturally his greatcoat was of the long black leather kind, with those dashing broad lapels. Around his neck dangled a 'Pour le Mérite'. That was his decoration from the First World War when he had served in one of the Kaiser's horse guards regiments. He still wore the old cavalry insignia quite improperly, on the shoulder tabs of his Nazi army uniform.

The soldiers laid bets between themselves if the mannikin had any lips. His mouth was a thin line which literally disappeared in his hard-lined face made unsightly by a duelling scar. His ice-cold blue eyes dominated the brutal face. When you were up in front of the little commandant you became cold with fright as he addressed you in velvet tones while his cold unfeeling eyes sucked your stomach out. They were a cobra's eyes, Oberstleutnant von Weisshagen's eyes, commandant of the 27th (Penal) Panzer Regiment's depot. Nobody could remember ever having seen a woman in Von Weisshagen's company and small wonder. Any woman in his presence would have become stiff as a board when his eyes pierced her. When he was thrown out of the army at the end of the war he was a certainty for a governorship of an institution for particularly difficult prisoners. The man simply did not exist it seemed, whom he could not destroy or shape at will.

One other spectacular thing about this man. He always

carried his revolver-holster unbuttoned, the more easily to reach the evil shining black-blue Mauser 7.65. His batmen (he had two) said he carried as well a Walther 7.65 with all six bullets filed down to dum-dum heads. His riding-whip, hollowed, hid a long thin swordstick. He would whip it out in a flash from its beautifully plaited leather-covering. He knew he was hated and feared and had taken precautions against any persecuted wretch who might become desperate and light-headed enough to attack him. Naturally he was never sent to the front, his connections in high places saw to that. His red-haired mongrel, 'Baron', was a complete fairy tale in himself. The dog was included in the army list of the nominal roll of the depot and several times was degraded in front of the whole battalion. The adjutant, as proper in such circumstances, read out the punishment in the orders of the day. Somehow the dog never rose above the rank of corporal. At the moment he was a lance-corporal and locked in a cell as a penalty for dropping excrement under his master's desk.

Tough sergeant-majors sweated blood when Von Weiss-hagen's gentle voice whispered over the telephone about something they had overlooked. Less than five minutes after a man had dropped or lost a piece of paper in front of the company billets the commandant would know about it. Sometimes we were convinced that his gruesome eyes were able to see through walls, he was so well informed about everything that happened. He always imposed the strictest sentence among the thousands of rules the Third Reich had crammed into military law. Gentleness and mercy were to him sure signs of weakness and portents of the world's destruction. He loved giving nerve-racking orders to all his subordinates, privates as well as officers. He would sit behind his huge mahogany desk decorated with a miniature flagpole flying the armoured corps standard soldered on to a base fashioned from a hand-grenade. He would stare at one of the soldiers standing to attention in front of him and suddenly shout out:

'You, jump out of the window!'

God forgive the soldier who hesitated to run to the

window, fling it open and start climbing out. The office was on the third floor. At the last moment the little officer's voice would say:

'Good, good, get away from that window!'

Or he would come into a room silent as a cat (his boots were rubber-soled). The door would open, and, in a voice mild yet like a whiplash, he would say:

'Now then, hand-stands!'

The name of anyone unable to stand on his hands was carefully taken note of in the little grey-covered book he carried in his left breast-pocket. He wrote in beautiful script, using the culprit's back as a table. Next day the poor devil would get a week's punishment drill.

Pluto and I were chatting as we strolled carelessly on our long tour round the barracks area. Pluto had a cigarette in his mouth. It was short enough for him to tip backwards into his mouth – a trick at which he was adept – should sudden concealment be necessary. He kicked the lock of an ammunition box. To his great delight it opened. This would cause great trouble for No. 4 Company next day when we reported the lock out of order.

Behind the parade halls he spat out his microscopic butt-end. It landed on the dry grass. We stood awhile hoping that the grass would burst into flame and lighten the monotony of our patrol.

We walked on with slow measured steps. Our fixed bayonets blinked with evil flashes. We had not gone far when someone shot up in front of us. At once we both knew it could be nobody but Colonel von Weisshagen. He looked like a black teacosy in his hat and overcoat.

Pluto bellowed the password: '*Gneissenau*', and it rang all over the depot. Then there was a silence for a few seconds until Pluto roared again:

'Obergefreiter Eicken and Fahnenjunkergefreiter Hassel, detailed for sentry-duty carrying out patrol in the barracks area. According to regulations the papers of the Herr Oberstleutnant are required for inspection.'

Silence.

The leather coat rustled. One small gloved hand shot between the upper buttons and was quickly withdrawn. The next moment we were staring into the muzzle of his pistol. His well-known bland voice whistled at us:

'What if I fired now?'

At the same moment a shot cracked from Pluto's rifle, the bullet whined over the commandant's head knocking his hat off. Before he could recover from his surprise my bayonet was at his chest. Then Pluto placed his bayonet-point intimidatingly against the mannikin's neck. We took his pistol.

'The Herr Oberstleutnant is required to put up his hands, or we fire!' he said silkily.

I nearly started giggling. It sounded completely insane: 'The Oberstleutnant is required to put up his hands.' Only in the army could anyone behave so like an idiot.

I pressed the bayonet firmly against his chest just to show him how eagerly we were carrying out our orders.

'Nonsense,' he snapped. 'You both know me. Get your bayonets down and get on with your patrolling. Later I'll require you to make out a report about the shot fired.'

'We do not know you, Herr Oberstleutnant. We only know that we have been threatened with a firearm during sentry-duty. We ask the Herr Oberstleutnant to accompany us to the guard-room,' Pluto answered with merciless politeness.

Slowly we moved towards the guard-room despite heavy threats from the commandant. But we kept out bayonets at the ready.

Our entry into the guard-room caused great commotion. Reinhardt who had been sleeping, sprang up and arranged himself in the required position of attention at the three regulation paces in front of the commander. In a shaking voice he shouted:

'Attention! Unteroffizier Reinhardt detailed as guard commander humbly offers his report to the Herr Oberstleutnant: the guard consists of twenty men. Five on sentry duty with rifles. Two patrolling. Under arrest four prisoners. One Gefreiter from No. 3 Company on two days' detention. One tank gunner and one Obergefreiter from No. 7 Company on six days' detention. All three for staying out without night passes, And one Gefreiter dog on three days' detention for dirtying the floor. Report humbly to Herr Oberstleutnant that nothing special has occurred!'

With great interest the Oberstleutnant studied the purple-faced Reinhardt:

'Who am I?'

'You, sir, are the commandant of the depot of the 27th (Penal) Panzer Regiment, Oberstleutnant von Weisshagen.'

Pluto gleefully announced to Reinhardt:

'Herr Guard Commander! Obergfreiter Eicken, leader of the barracks patrol consisting of two men, humbly reports that we arrested the Oberstleutant behind No. 2 Company's parade-hall. As we got no answer to our challenge, and on request of papers were threatened with a pistol, we fired according to standing orders a warning shot from my rifle, model 98. The prisoner's hat was blown off and holed by the bullet. We disarmed the prisoner and led him unwounded to the Herr Guard Commander. Humbly awaiting further orders.'

Silence, long velvet silence.

Reinhardt gulped. This was beyond him. The commandant looked inquiringly at him. Everybody waited, but silence reigned. The blood came and went under the skin of Reinhardt's baboon face. Everyone waited for the bumpkin to speak. At last the commandant lost his patience, his bland voice sounding faintly hurt as he addressed the unhappy sergeant:

'We know now that you know me. You are the guard commander. The security of the 27th Regiment's barracks lies in your hands. What do you order, Unteroffizier. What are you going to do? We can't stand here all night!'

Reinhardt did not know what on earth to do. His eyes rolled in desperation. We could almost hear him search for an expedient. On the table the pillow and greatcoat were silent witnesses to his illegal sleep. They did not escape his attention either. His eyes came back to Pluto and me with the commandant between us. All three of us waited with badly concealed glee for what the base-hero would order. Fickle fate had suddenly against his will given him more power than he cared for. Before him stood a human being, an ordinary human being with a body, two legs, two arms, a face, eyes, ears, teeth made like all other human beings, but – a large but – a sinister but – this particular being wore a black leather coat, patent-leather boots, Sam Browne and gold stars on plaited silver shoulder-tabs. To Reinhardt he was God, Devil, World, Power, Death, Life, everything connected with destruction, torture, promotion, degradation and, last but not least, he was able to pronounce the few words which could send a certain Sergeant Reinhardt to a battle unit. Behind that, under its ghostly snow, waited the Eastern Front. Whether he was now to escape such a fate or not depended entirely on his not offending his God standing before him smiling mockingly.

Slowly Reinhardt's brain connected with his tongue and now bluster took over. Bellowing like a bull he roared at Pluto and me:

'Are you both mad! Release the Herr Commandant immediately. This is mutiny!'

A more relaxed and even satisfied expression shone on his face as he went on:

'You are under arrest! I'll call the orderly officer at once. You'll pay dearly for this. You must excuse them, Herr Oberstleutnant.' He addressed the commandant and clicked his heels together: 'They are only two stupid animals from the front. I'll see to it that a report is made out right away. Of course this is a court-martial offence . . .'

The commandant practically hypnotized the room with his eyes. This was better than he had hoped for. Just his opportunity to make one of his dreaded examples.

'Well, Unteroffizier, that's what you think!' He brushed an imaginary speck of dust off his big coat lapels as he received his pistol and holed cap from Pluto, who was openly grinning.

Without a sound the commandant walked on his rubber-soles across to the table, he pointed to Reinhardt's improvised bedclothes and ordered into thin air:

'Get it away!'

Ten recruits as well as Reinhardt flew forward to carry out his command. The coat and pillow disappeared like magic.

Slowly the commander unbuttoned his coat. His little grey-covered book came out from his left breastpocket. Ceremoniously dusting himself, he brought out his silver pencil with a flourish. The book was placed on the table at the angle prescribed in the junior schools when lessons in hand-writing are being given. As he wrote he thought out loud:

'Unteroffizier Reinhardt, Hans, serving with No. 3 Company, detailed as guard commander under special circumstances, was found improperly dressed on duty. His tunic was unbuttoned. His belt with pistol was beyond his reach, so it would have been impossible for him to use his own firearms in an emergency. This violates Regulation No. 10618 of April 22nd, 1939, concerning guard duty. Furthermore Army Regulation No. 798, same date and year, was grossly violated as he was found sleeping on the table in the guard-room. Still further, he used the army's greatcoat as a blanket. At the same time an instruction issued by Oberstleutnant von Weisshagen as a Depot Order on the 16th June, 1941, has been broken. It concerns the identification of persons found in the barracks area after 10 p.m. The guard commander takes no decision on such an occasion but sends instead for the orderly officer.'

With a jerk he turned to the gaping Reinhardt:

'Well, Unteroffizier, anything to report?'

Reinhardt was dumbstruck. The commandant adjusted his belt and polished his monocle on a snow-white handkerchief. Then he snapped:

'Obergefreiter Eicken and Fahnenjunkergefreiter Hassel! Take Unteroffizier Reinhardt to the cells! He is under arrest for gross indiscipline on guard duty. The matter will go forward as evidence for a courtmartial. To-morrow he shall be transferred in custody to the 114th Grenadier Regiment Standorts prison. Until relieved of duty Obergefreiter Eicken will serve as guard commander. The patrol carried out their orders correctly and with zeal.'

On his silent feet, he walked out of the guard-room.

'Come along,' Pluto grinned at Reinhardt. 'Any attempt to escape and I use my bayonet!' At the same time he noisily brought his rifle to the ready.

All three of us marched down the passage to the cells. Pluto enthusiastically dangled the big bunch of keys. The dog from cell No. 78 caused Pluto to bellow:

'Shut up! Silence after 10 p.m.!'

With unnecessary noise we shot the bolt back from cell-door No. 13 and pushed Reinhardt in.

'Undress, prisoner, and put everything on the bed,' ordered Pluto taking great pleasure in his role as prison warder.

A few minutes later the broad-chested Reinhardt stood before us as God had made him. A fat peasant of no consequence, robbed of the cords and ribbons without which he was what he had been created: a bewildered, thick-skulled farm labourer.

Pluto was determined to carry out every regulation in the book.

'Prisoner, bend forward,' he ordered, aping Sergeant-Major Edel's roar.

As carefully as any scientist he studied Reinhardt's upturned behind.

'The prisoner has nothing concealed up his backside,' he established with delight.

He then examined the ears of the lost and gaping Reinhardt and announced gleefully:

'Prisoner, do you know the regulation concerning personal cleanliness? This hayseed doesn't know how to shovel the muck out of his ears. Write: the prisoner was found on arrest to be in an extremely dirty condition. His earholes were bunged up with filth.'

'Do you expect me to write as you say?' I wanted to know.

'By God I do! Aren't I guard commander? Haven't I got responsibility for the prison register?'

'Oh shut up, you stupid swine,' I replied. 'As far as I am concerned I don't mind putting your tripe down, but you'll sign it.'

'Yes, sure. Why make all the fuss?' said Pluto.

We examined Reinhardt's uniform miscroscopically. His address book was read through. Pluto was also very interested in a round packet of cigarettes. He sniffed one or two. Then he bawled:

'The prisoner is bloody well in possession of opium-cigarettes! Shall I take care of them, you criminal? Or shall we make out a report? Then you can hear what the court-martial has to say about an NCO who carries narcotics about with him. Well, what do you want done?'

'Bloody well keep them, and stop blowing yourself up any bigger,' answered Reinhardt bitterly.

'Quiet, prisoner, and don't get fresh. Otherwise we'll have to see what the regulations say about obstreperous and difficult prisoners. When you address me it's 'Herr Guard Commander'. Remember that, you cow-pat!'

Grinning, Pluto stuffed the packet of opium-cigarettes into his pocket. Then he gathered up the fallen hero's effects. Everything except his underwear and uniform went into a bag. Pluto pointed to the list I had made out from his dictation:

'Sign here as witness that all your belongings are here. There'll be no nonsense then when in the distant future they turn you loose.'

Reinhardt wanted to check the list, but Pluto cut him short:

'What the hell, do you imagine you'll be allowed to study in prison? Just sign, at once. Then dump your rags outside the door so we can shut you in as the commandant ordered. What a bloody cheek!'

Without protesting Reinhardt did as he was told.

'If you want to use the bucket do it now,' announced Pluto.

'No, Herr Guard Commander,' came reluctantly from Reinhardt. He stood stark naked under the little cell window.

'I hope not for your sake,' said Pluto, 'and God forgive you if you ring during the night. We want peace to think over the serious events which happened tonight.'

'Certainly, Herr Guard Commander!'

Triumphantly Pluto peered into the bare cell before he ordered:

'Good, prisoner. Go to bed, and stay there till you hear reveille.'

He walked out of the cell, banged the door shut, turned the huge lock twice and with exasperating slams shot the two bolts home.

Pluto loved the keys so much that he placed them on the table in front of him in the guard-room. He had often been behind bars himself, and for the first time in his life he was in possession of the keys of a cell. A little later with great delight he started ringing up all the other NCOs on duty in the company billets. He wanted to know the numbers on their nominal rolls. That was a privilege the guard commander was entitled to avail himself of. Every time he got connected to a company he inquired:

'Your voice sounds sleepy. Have you been sleeping?' (Of course they all had.) 'I'll consider if it is my duty to report to the orderly officer about these slips of yours. What's that? "Who is talking?" The guard commander, of course. Who do you think?'

When he had talked to every one of the eight companies, he started at the beginning again. This time he asked the confused NCOs about the state of their sick-parades. Also for a list of the company's arms and ammunition stores; the list to be delivered at the guard-room by 8 a.m. That gave the poor NCOs more than enough work for the night.

Tremendously satisfied with himself Pluto leaned back in the big chair, threw his enormous feet on the table and grabbed the pornographic literature. He was just about to light an opium-cigarette when two recruits came crashing through the door. Between them was a very excited figure in a flowered cotton dress, a scarf on its head and infantry boots on its feet.

'Herr Guard Commander,' announced one of the recruits. 'Tank Gunner Niemeyer humbly reports that in the course of our patrol we arrested this person trying to scale the barracks wall by No. 3 Company billets. The person refuses to give any information and gave Tank Gunner Reichelt a killing punch in the face. His eyes and jaw have swollen dreadfully.'

Pluto blinked a little, but quickly pulled himself together. We had at once recognized Porta, Pluto pushed a chair forward and said with a smile:

'Madam, will you take a seat?'

'Shut your fat gob, or I'll shut it for you!' was Porta's disrespectful answer to the newly promoted guard commander.

Pluto waved the threat aside and shoved Porta into the chair.

'Excuse me, madam. Are you by any chance looking round for your husband? My name is Obergefreiter Gustav Eicken, guard commander, husband-collector, in whose sensitive hands the security of this barracks lies. Or perhaps, madam wishes something else?' With a sudden movement he flung up Porta's skirts so that his sharp knees were revealed in his long army underpants.

'Ah, the latest in Paris fashions no doubt? Very charming, madam. Not every lady possesses such dainty things.'

Porta hit out drunkenly at the big broad-grinning docker, and missed. Abruptly he gave up the struggle.

'God, I'm dry! Bring some beer.'

It all ended by us stowing Porta away in an empty cell. He was too tight to be transported to the company billet. He had been touring a series of shady pubs, from the 'Red Rose' to the 'Merry Cow'. According to him he had had enough girls to last him for two years. In his manoeuvres with the last girl he had had his uniform stolen. The only things left of his kit were his long underpants and infantry boots. These he swore he wore in bed. Somebody had written with oil paint 'Merry Cow' on his bare bottom.

Pluto put him in the guard-book as in by 11 p.m., one hour before the night passes ran out. That at that time he had not yet been promoted to guard commander he completely ignored.

The remainder of the night we played pontoon with our prisoner's money. As Pluto said, Reinhardt didn't need money now.

Guard inspection by the orderly officer came at 8 a.m. and

most of the twenty minutes were taken up by explaining what lay behind Pluto's report.

When at last Lieutenant Wagner got the facts into his head, he fell nearly weeping into his chair and signed his name helplessly under Pluto's long description in the guard-book of one of the most eventful nights in the depot's tedious history.

The dangerous point for Wagner was that he had not heard the shot. He must have been either asleep or absent without permission. His knowledge of Colonel von Weisshagen convinced him that the latter had been sitting patiently for hours waiting for the report that he as duty officer, should have given at once in such circumstances either to the commandant or his adjutant. And it was now six hours since the rifle had been fired. Lieutenant Wagner would be posted to a combat-unit now as sure as eggs were eggs.

As the tragedy dawned on him, he opened and shut his mouth without uttering a sound. But he let out a bellow like a bull's when Pluto smiling reported that the commandant had been well pleased with the patrol, and that this fact would have to be endorsed in the book by the orderly officer. Gnashing his dentures together, the broken Wagner staggered away to face what the day held in store for him.

4

One sunny morning we collected them from the prison. In a bumping lorry they took their last ride.

They helped by pushing the vehicle free when it stuck. They seemed to push their bodies forward to help the twelve bullets find their way.

It happened in the name of the German people.

State Murder

Porta was the last one to crawl into the big Krupp diesel lorry. The vehicle creaked and grated as the gears changed. We swung out from the company billet and made a short halt at the headquarters guard to collect the driving-permit.

On our way through the town we shouted and waved at girls. Porta started telling a dirty story. Möller asked him to shut up. A short but violent quarrel sprang up. It was interrupted as we drove into the infantry's barrack square. We halted in front of the Standort guard-room.

Sergeant-Major Paust, in charge of our party, jumped out of the driver's seat and rang the bell. Six of us jumped out and followed Paust into the prison's reception office. Here we found a couple of pale infantrymen who served as prison warders. Paust disappeared into an office to get the papers from the infantry sergeant-major. He was a huge bald fellow with nervous twitches around his eyes.

Interested, Porta asked:

'What do you fellows do in the can here to pass the time?'

'I shouldn't worry yourself, if I were you,' ventured an old fifty-year-old corporal. 'Your job in this profession lasts only for a moment. We work here day after day. We have known this lot for months. We've nattered with them for hours. They've sort of got to be friends. If only they were the last ones – but to-morrow there's another batch due. And so it goes on. It's just crazy.'

'Karl, you talk too much,' warned another middle-aged NCO. He pushed his friend aside and eyed us cagily.

Curiously, we looked round the small guard-room. Dirty cups and plates stood on the table. On one wall hung a blackboard with the names and numbers of the cells and the prisoners. Every name marked with green meant that its possessor was condemned to death. I counted twenty-three. Red marks denoted prisoners awaiting confirmation of their sentences by court-martial. There were plenty of them. Blue marks meant the prison-camps; there were only fourteen of these.

On the opposite wall hung two big photographs of Hitler and Keitel. They stared indifferently at the board with its record of the doom of human beings.

'What the hell's happened to them?' Schwartz wanted to know. 'It's yellow peas for dinner to-day; if we're late we'll be gypped out of our rations and get landed with the left-overs.'

'You're a fine lot,' said the elderly corporal. 'Thinking of food when you've this job to do. I've been to the pisshouse twenty times since yesterday because I'm so nervous. And all you can think of is yellow peas, God help you!'

'And why not, Grandad?' grinned Porta. 'Behave yourself. You foot-sloggers are too soft.'

'Shut up, Porta,' Möller said.

'Since when were you promoted to the class-conscious ranks of bastards with stars and cords and the right to order me about?' Porta wanted to know.

'You're a swine,' Möller said with finality.

'That's your opinion. Just wait till the musketry practices have finished, then I'll tell you something, you mongrel.' Porta smiled his evil smile and Möller carefully moved to the other side of the table.

The prison staff nervously made way for him. They seemed afraid to touch us.

The rattling of keys came from the office next door. A woman cried out.

Pluto lit an opium-cigarette and sucked voraciously. Stege kept looking down at his feet in their clumsy but unbelievably shiny ammunition boots. An infantryman sat at the table doodling nervously. The whole atmosphere was electric.

The 'phone rang. The senior NCO answered and stone-like he sat to attention in his chair:

'Standorts prison, infantry barracks, Obergefreiter Breit here. Yes, sir, yes, the detail is here. Everything is ready. Certainly, sir, the family will be informed as usual. Nothing else to report.'

He replaced the receiver.

'They are waiting for you at 'Senne', ' he said over his shoulder.

'By God, this is like a registry-office wedding, everyone is waiting,' said Pluto. 'I wish they'd hurry, then we'd get it over with before we get the jitters.'

No sooner had he spoken than the door opened. A girl from the army telephone service came in with a grey-haired NCO. They were both dressed in the denims used for barracks duty. They were condemned prisoners. Behind them came a cavalry sergeant-major and Paust with some papers under his arm. He tried to look unconcerned but his watery blue eyes blinked nervously.

The cavalryman looked up the register and asked:

'If you have any complaints, speak up now.'

The prisoners said nothing, but stared wildly at the five of us standing with our steel helmets and rifles.

Without apparently understanding what they did, they signed the register.

Paust and the cavalryman shook hands as they said good-bye. We almost expected them to say '*au revoir*' and thank you.

We filed out with the prisoners in the middle and got into the lorry.

The soldiers in the truck helped the girl politely inside although the old NCO was more in need of help.

'Ready,' cried Paust, and we started with a jerk. The guards at the gates stared frighteningly after the big diesel lorry as it swung with exploding exhaust out on the road towards Sennelager.

The first part of the journey we travelled in silence staring shyly and with curiosity at the two prisoners. Pluto broke the silence first. He offered them the packet of opium-cigarettes.

'Have a fag, it helps.'

Both grabbed their cigarettes and smoked greedily.

Porta leant forward.

'Why are you getting it?'

The girl let drop her cigarette and started sobbing.

'Never mind, I didn't mean to upset you,' consoled Porta. 'I only wanted to know how we stand.'

'You are a stupid swine,' shouted Möller and hit out at Porta. 'What's it got to do with you? You'll get to know soon enough at 'Senne'. '

He put his arm round the girl's shoulders.

'Take it easy, sister. He's a stupid lout who's always poking his nose into affairs that don't concern him.'

The girl wept silently. The engine droned. The lorry was climbing a steep hill. Paust looked at us from the cab window. We all sat smoking. The Old Un pointed to a heap of gravel at the roadside. Beside it stood a few prisoners-of-war and home-guards.

'At last they're mending the road. High time too. We always bump like hell on this stretch.'

Bauer wanted to know if Porta was coming to the 'Red Cat' that evening.

'Both Lieschen and Barbara are coming. There'll be fun and games all right.'

'Of course I'm coming,' said Porta. 'But only till ten. Then I'm off to take part in the opening of a new whore-house in Münchener Gasse.'

An ambulance streaked howling past our slow lorry.

'God's sake, what's happened now?' The Old Un said.

'There's always something sinister about the siren of an ambulance,' Bauer said uneasily.

'Maybe a birth with complications,' said Möller. 'My wife had a haemorrhage when she had the second one. They rushed her into hospital. It was touch and go for her and the baby.'

'Have you seen the new girl who's arrived in No. 2 Company's canteen?' asked Pluto. 'She's quite a girl.'

At that moment the lorry drove into a deep rut in the road and we were all thrown in a heap. Furiously Porta shouted at the driver:

'Can't you see where you are going, you dim clot?'

The driver's answer was drowned in the roar from the engine.

The sun had come out from behind threatening clouds.

'The weather is clearing,' said Stege. 'It'll be fine this afternoon. I'm off with a sweetie I met the other evening.'

Porta started laughing.

'Why the hell do you always take your tarts out rowing? You must get damp seats. All the boats the old bastard hires out are half-full of water. You'd do better coming with me to Münchener Gasse. Bring the girl.'

'Your heads are always full of girls,' snapped Möller irritated.

'Now listen here, your reverence,' Porta's voice sounded threatening. 'Lately you've been bellyaching too much. We don't interfere with your crossword puzzles or your cosy meetings with the chaplain behind closed doors. Have your fun and we'll have ours. Soon we'll be back at the front and then we'll see what's in you, you Schleswig bible-puncher.'

Möller shot up and furiously lashed out again at the tall, thin Porta. But Porta ducked and Möller's hefty fist just missed him. Neatly, the Berliner hit Möller in the throat with the edge of his hand and Möller fell in a heap.

Stege pushed him away to make room for our feet.

'It's his own fault,' said The Old Un. 'Even if we must allow for his age. He could easily be the father of most of us. I'll talk to him when we get back.'

'I'll grind his sour face one day,' said Porta with a ferocious grin.

Pluto said he had heard we were to be transferred to a big tank factory where we should try out the new Mark VI tanks called 'King Tigers'.

'Your friend 'Backside and Boots' no doubt told you that,' jeered Stege.

'What the hell are you needling for all the time?' Flaming with anger Pluto turned on Stege.

'And you ask that, you fat Hamburger slob!' exclaimed The Old Un. 'Is this an ordinary firing-practice? Have you no feelings, man?'

To our astonishment the old NCO interrupted The Old Un.

'Wouldn't it be nicer if you all were quiet.'

The lorry turned off along a secondary road rutted by heavy lorries and tanks.

Möller stood up and withdrew as far from the rest of us as possible. He looked more sour than ever.

It was the young girl who broke the silence.

'Has any of you a cigarette or an aspirin?'

We stared at her for a few seconds as she sat there in the old denim dress.

Stege handed her a cigarette. His hand shook as he lit it with the lighter he had bought in France three years ago.

Furiously we all searched our pockets.

Porta shouted forward to the driver:

'Any of you got an aspirin?'

Paust pushed the sliding window open and mockingly growled. We could see all his strong white teeth:

'The only tablet I have is in the magazine of my .38. That's a sure cure. Who's got a headache?'

'The girl.'

Long silence. Then an embarrassed:

'Oh.'

The windowpane was slammed. He chose to ignore Porta's 'Dirty dog!'

'It doesn't matter about the aspirin,' said the girl apathetically. 'It'll soon go away.'

'Will one of you do something for me?' asked the old NCO. Without waiting for an answer, he went on: 'I come from the 76th Artillery Regiment. Will you go and see Sergeant Brandt of No. 4 Battery? Tell him to make sure my wife gets my money. She lives with the wife of my eldest son in Dortmund. Will *you* do this for me?' He turned to Stege:

Stege stammered:

'Yes, yes, of course. What do you—?' Pluto interrupted:

'He'll only make a mess of it, old chum. I have a pal in the 76th, Paul Groth, staff-sergeant. Do you know him?'

'Yes, Staff-Sergeant Groth, I know him well. He's in No. 2 Battery. Lost a leg at Brest-Litovsk. Remember me to him – the 'gas-meter man'. That's what I was before the war,' he added.

The girl looked up with interest, life returned to her dead features.

'Will you do something for me, too?' she asked breathlessly of Pluto. 'Give me a piece of paper, please.'

At least ten pencils and notebooks were handed to her. The Old Un pushed his way to her and gave her an army letter-card.

She wrote quickly and nervously, read the card through, sealed it and gave it to Pluto.

'Will you send it for me?'

'I'll do that,' he said shortly and put the letter in the pocket of his greatcoat.

'You'll get a bottle of Sekt if you deliver it personally,' she said, nervously stammering, taking stock of the large docker in his oil-spotted tank battledress. He stood with his rifle in his hand, his steel helmet pushed back on his head, his legs splayed in their short shiny infantry boots. His black trouser-legs bulged like a pair of wide plus-fours. His short tunic, with the silver skull-badges on the lapels, was dragged down by the weight of his carelessly slung black leather bandolier heavy with the weight of the bullets peeping eagerly out of it.

'I don't want anything.' It came with a stammer from the usually quick-witted fellow. 'The letter is safe with me. I'm the best postman in the country.'

'Thank you, soldier, I'll never forget it.'

'It's nothing,' said Pluto.

We drove on in silence. The sun had come out really strongly now. There was warmth in it.

Someone started whistling.

'Frük morgens, wenn die hähne krähen'.'

Some of us began humming. Suddenly we all stopped, and

looked at each other confused. It was as if we had committed blasphemy in a cathedral full of praying people.

The lorry stopped. Paust shouted to the sentry:

'Special detail from the guard company. One Feldwebel, one Unteroffizier, twenty men and two prisoners.'

The sentry looked into the lorry. A sergeant-major hanging out of the window of the guard-house shouted:

'You are going to Area 9. Where the hell have you been? They've been waiting a long time for you there.'

'You're a joke, you are,' said Paust.

Without waiting for an answer, we drove on along a sandy road which led past the barracks. Soldiers lived in this large training camp during their service. Houses and barns, empty now, stared despondently at the uniformed men who day in and day out were being trained to kill.

'I hope they don't eat up all the peas before we get back!' complained Schwartz. 'It isn't every day we get something we like. Of course it had to be to-day we get detailed for this lot.'

Nobody answered.

'My God, there's a hare,' shouted Porta excitedly and pointed at something in the shabby-looking heather.

We all stretched to look at the hare leaping away.

'God help us! Real food under our eyes and we can't get at it.' Porta groaned.

'Last time we had hare was in Rumania, in the barracks by the Dubovila river,' said Pluto.

'Oh, yes, that was the time I took that Rumanian baron for everything he'd got,' grinned Porta.

The lorry stopped. Swearing, Paust jumped down:

'Where is Area 9? This dope here has lost his way. This is the sports ground.'

Nobody answered. He unfolded a map and turned it round and round before he got his bearing. The lorry backed and stuck in the soft grass verge. Everybody had to get out and push. Only the prisoners stayed in the truck.

Indifferently, we flung our rifles to them.

'You ought to get out to Russia, you,' said Pluto into thin

air. Nobody understood what he meant. 'Then you'd learn to know something else apart from this rotten training-camp.'

'We've had the peas,' said Schwartz angrily.

'I'll spit on your peas,' shouted Stege. 'Eat your own gristle if you're so hungry.'

'Nobody asked your opinion, you bastard!' Schwartz gave him back furiously.

It would have ended in a fight, but the lorry was now free and we had to jump in quickly.

Soon we stopped again. We were at Area 9. Paust shouted:

'Detail, fall in!'

Nervously we jumped out and fell in before Paust. We had forgotten the prisoners. They sat in the lorry, half-hidden in the corner by the driver's cab. A lieutenant from the military police had appeared and was swearing at them. Paust seemed in momentary confusion. Then he roared with a voice which echoed through the huge spruce trees in the background:

'Prisoners, fall in, get a move on!'

The two prisoners all but fell out of the lorry and took their places as if apologetically at the end of the file we had formed, the girl behind the old NCO. The lieutenant's face was red. He unnecessarily adjusted his broad officer's belt and his pistol-butt.

'Your word of command! What are you waiting for?'

Paust became more nervous, and with saliva at the corners of his mouth, he croaked:

'Attention, eyes right!'

He turned round, heels clicking and reported all correct to the fat and beery MP officer.

The lieutenant saluted with a flourish. Then he turned about and withdrew with the onlookers into the background.

A military prosecutor in colonel's uniform came across. He was followed by a staff-surgeon and others.

Paust leapt forward, clicked his heels and rattled off his report at the same time handing over some papers he had carried in a red cover.

'The prisoners in the middle, two men behind,' ordered the lieutenant.

With the minimum of movement the order was carried out.

Half-hidden by some bushes stood two long wooden boxes. We turned our eyes away from them.

The sun shone. Some of those with stars on their shoulders smoked. The rifles felt hot in sweaty hands. Stege played unconsciously with his sling.

The military prosecutor gave the papers to a major from the Panzer Grenadiers. He did not manage to get all the different coloured sheets in order at once. The wind teased him. In a falsetto voice he started reading out:

'In the name of the Führer and the German people the specially convened military court under the Commanding General of Defence, Sector 6, has sentenced Irmgard Bartels, born April 3rd, 1922, telephone operator in Defence Sector 6, serving in Bielefeldt, to death by shooting. The prisoner is convicted of communication with an illegal communist organization and the distribution of leaflets dangerous to the State, to her colleagues in the exchange as well as in the barracks where her section was billeted.

'Her confession in writing is witnessed by the prisoner. Court-Martial Counsellor Dr. Jahn, Major-General of the Police Schliermann and SA Gruppenführer Wittman acted as judges. The condemned prisoner is forever without honour and all her property falls to the State.

'In the name of the Führer and the German people the specially convened military court under the Commanding General in Defence Sector 6 has sentenced Unteroffizier Gerhard Paul Brandt, born June 17th, 1889, serving with Artillery Regiment 76, to death by shooting. The prisoner refused to obey orders during guard duty in Stalag 6. Three times his company commander warned him of the consequences of disobeying orders.

'His confession in writing is witnessed by the prisoner. SS Obersturmbannführer Dr. Rüttger, NSKK, Obergruppenführer Dr. Hirsch and Staff Court-martial Counsellor Professor Gortz acted as judges. The condemned prisoner is forever without honour and all his property falls to the State.

'The guard commander from the depot of the 27th (Penal)

Panzer Regiment has been detailed to carry out the execution. Clerical duty will be performed by Chaplain Curt Meyer. Staff-Surgeon Dr Mettgen will certify the execution completed. The military prosecutor Dr Weissmann, GE and Training Battalion 309, will see that the sentence is carried out according to regulations. The duty of notifying the prisoners' relatives lies with Standort Prison 6/6 Paderborn. The burial following the execution will be carried out by Sonderkommand from Pioneer Battalion 57.'

He beckoned condescendingly to the MP lieutenant who stepped over to Paust and gave him orders.

'Detail, right turn! Forward march!'

The sand was yielding under our feet. The girl stumbled, but Pluto grabbed her, and she recovered her balance. For a moment the firing-party broke step.

Round a bend in the road we came upon the posts we had expected to see: the posts the condemned prisoners were tied to. There were six of them: six ordinary thick fence posts, each hung with a piece of new rope in a ring.

'Detail, halt!' ordered Paust. 'Order arms! Open order march! Front rank with the prisoners forward mar-a-arch!'

The Old Un gasped loudly. Ours was the leading rank. For a moment we hesitated. Then the ingrained discipline took effect. We tramped forward silently to the posts which once had been swaying trees the wind had played with, but were now awaiting the clasp of the dying.

We stood detached from the rest. Behind us silently waiting, stood the fine gentlemen and the remainder of the detail. It seemed as if we had been thrust apart from them. We were twelve ordinary people with two in the middle about to die.

What if we ran away? Or if The Old Un's machine pistol barked backwards at those stars and cords? What then? There were only six posts here, but in other camps there were more, more than enough for twelve men.

The Old Un coughed. The old man in the denims coughed. It was dusty.

'Front rank halt!' The Old Un said quietly. He mumbled

something incomprehensible in which the word 'God' occurred. We knew they could not hear us behind.

The girl swayed, she nearly fainted. Pluto whispered between his teeth:

'Courage, lass, don't show the swine you're afraid. Shout what you like. They can't do anything more to you. Up the Red Front! Think of the 'Red Flag', if it helps.'

The Old Un pointed to me and Stege.

'You two go with Grandad, and you, Pluto and Porta go with the girl.'

'Why us?' protested Stege quietly. But we started without waiting for an answer. Somebody had to do it. The others were glad it wasn't them. They turned away.

The post was roughened at chest height. A reminder of the many times it had been used for this planned beastliness taking place in the name of the German people.

The nice new rope smelled of jute, but was a little too short. The old NCO pulled in his stomach to make himself thinner. It was a poor knot we made, and Stege wept.

'I'll shoot at the trees,' he whispered, 'listen pal, I can't shoot at you.'

The girl started crying. She did not cry as women normally do. Her cries were like an animal's bellows. Porta jumped back from the post, dropped his rifle, dried his hands on his trouser seat and picked up his rifle again. He doubled back to the main detail waiting some twenty paces in our rear.

We hurried away from the two bound figures at the posts.

An army padre with purple tabs and crosses on his collar instead of the usual eagle walked across to the tethered man and girl.

The girl was quiet now. The padre mumbled a prayer and raised both hands to the cloudless sky. He seemed to be trying to convince the invisible God that what was happening was just and proper in a world tormented by war.

The military prosecutor took a few steps forward and read out:

'We make these executions to defend the State against the serious crimes which these two criminals have committed.

The specially convened military court's judges have sentenced them in accordance with paragraph 32 in the State penal code.'

He stepped back quickly. Paust was pale and he looked desperately out across the sandy wastes.

'Detail, right dress! Eyes front! Load!'

The safety-catches clicked and the bolts rattled ominously.

'Detail! At your target – aim!'

The butt pressed against the shoulder. The eye went along the barrel. Something white appeared over the foresight – pinned to each breast. Behind it a heart thumped, as yet still pumping blood through a living body.

Stege sniffed and whispered:

'I'll hit a branch.'

'Detail . . . !'

The girl gave a pitiable whine. The squad swayed. The leather belts creaked. Behind us someone fainted.

'. . . Fire!'

A sharp rolling thunder from twelve rifles and a jerk in twelve tank-soldiers' shoulders. Two State-murders had been committed.

With wildly open eyes we stared hypnotized at our victims. They hung kicking in the ropes. The old NCO fell to the ground. The knot had broken. He kicked his feet and scratched with his nails in the sand on which a red patch was spreading.

The girl just managed to cry out: 'Mother!' A long rattling. 'Mother!'

Four pioneers from the 57th hurried across to the posts. The staff-surgeon cast an indifferent glance at the two in their patched denims, then he signed some documents.

Far away, as in a trance, we heard Paust's command:

'Into the lorry!'

Stumbling like drunkards we found our places. Round Stege's eyes and down his cheeks were tear stains. We were all white as milk.

We drove past the guard. None of them questioned us. None of us spoke. Only the engine roared unfeelingly as usual.

We reached the gravel heap where the prisoners-of-war worked.

'It's twenty past twelve, how time flies,' stated Möller quietly.

'We've had the peas,' burst out from Schwartz.

'You rotten animal,' howled Stege and went for the unsuspecting Schwartz.

'I'll knock your teeth in, then you won't manage to wolf peas again for bloody weeks!'

He sat on top of Schwartz who had gone down with a crash. He bashed him one in the face with one fist, while he tried to strangle him with the other. Schwartz was nearly dead when at last we got Stege away. He was frothing at the mouth and had to be held down by Pluto and Bauer.

Through the din we heard Paust shout:

'For God's sake cut out that row!'

Nobody took any notice of him. Everyone shouted. We reached the barracks and clambered out of the truck in a noisy heap.

'The firing-party has leave for the rest of the day, but remember rifles and belts clean first,' Paust told us.

We shambled past the staring recruits, just back from eating their dinners. As we reached our room Bauer shouted to Porta:

'See you in the "Red Cat"!'

Porta turned on his heel and threw his rifle at Bauer while he roared:

'What's it got to do with you? You stupid animal! Mind your own business!'

By quickly side-stepping, Bauer just dodged the rifle and ran for his own room.

'Somebody's got nerves,' a lance-corporal said, grinning.

He belonged to No. 2 Troop. Pluto swung his fist. It crashed into the NCO's face. Pluto said:

'And now somebody's got a black eye, eh?'

5

'Church parade's a big laugh,' said Porta.

'You've just got to drone along beautifully and make it all complicated enough so nobody can understand. At every fifth word you say "cum spiritu-tuo," then change to a happy, "Dominus vobiscum". That always makes a good impression. Then swing the monstrance hard enough and the whole congregation is satisfied.'

Porta as Pope

We sat in the armoury and played pontoon. A considerable sum lay in front of Porta. He was the only one who had any luck.

Quartermaster-Sergeant Hauser, fed up with playing, had lost nearly 200 marks.

'I've had enough. Bring the bottle,' he growled angrily.

Decorated with a petrol label, it contained a mixture of cognac and vodka.

Hauser passed it on to Porta and then round the table. Loud belches soon thundered out.

'That skinny one you were with last night,' said Bauer to Stege, 'where did you lassoo her? I thought she looked like Sergeant-Major Schröder's wife.' He added, convinced: 'It bloody well was her! That wiggle bum can be recognized a mile off. If he discovers it, I wouldn't like to be you!'

Stege threw himself back on to a heap of cleaning rags and roared with laughter.

'That fat swine is rattling along in a cattle-truck between Warsaw and Kiev right now, so he hasn't got much chance. And just because 'Backside and Boots' has punished him it doesn't mean she's got to be punished. It's her birthday on Thursday too. She's having a party. That means in good German I'm the star guest. At 9 p.m. the attack starts, and each of you must bring a girl as a pass. Mrs. Grass Widow

Sergeant-Major has promised us the old man's booze. The lady says he'll never need it, that he's so fat even a blind Russky can't miss if he only hears him breathe.'

Porta hooted with laughter.

'Yes, I was in the orderly-room when "Backside and Boots" gave him what for. Brandt and I nearly choked with laughter. He's transferred to the 104th Infantry, and if he doesn't get his block knocked off at the start, he'll loose his fat in fourteen days and look like a fence post.'

Pluto stood up copying von Weisshagen:

'Well, Hauptfeldwebel, things are not so well with you, what? We've been made fun of long enough by keeping you. On that broad chest of yours there's plenty of room for some decorations, don't you think? That stupid swine answered: "Yes sir," although he nearly dirtied his pants with terror at the thought of getting nearer the front than 300 miles. "Well, well," went on "Backside and Boots" as he stared at him through his shining monocle. "Then we agree. I like to think my men are satisfied. You'll soon be back with an Iron Cross. And maybe you'll honour your old formation by getting a Knight's Cross. And you want an opportunity to distinguish yourself in the field?" "Yes, sir," sobbed the poor beast. He looked sick. "Good Hauptfeldwebel," said the commander. "Then you'll wish to be where things happen. So I have arranged for your transfer to the 104th. That's the bravest regiment in the division. There you'll have rich opportunities to show your soldierly qualities; qualities which we here have appreciated – until the other day when we, to our great regret, found you unable to distinguish between duty and leave, canteen and guard-room!" You should have seen him crawl out. He looked like a sick hen.'

'Porta, come on, tell us a yarn,' asked The Old Un.

'Of course, my boy, but what? You can't just say: "tell us a story".'

'Tell us one with a bit of spice in,' answered The Old Un, easing himself comfortably against the armsracks.

'So that's what you want, you ungodly swine,' Porta said austerely. 'No, it's Sunday to-day so we'll have something decent. I'll tell you a really uplifting and edifying story from my eventful life, about the time I acted padre, or pope as the Russians say, to Ivan.

'It was when we were fighting in the Caucasus between Maikopf and Tuapse and Ivan was having fun with us and all those trees.'

'My God, what a mess he made for us,' grinned Stege. 'Remember how even the biggest bulldozer went to pieces trying to shift those mahogany trees?'

'Am I or you telling this story?' Porta wanted to know. 'After Tuapse we started on the dirt road made by the Georgian peasants in the Tsar's time. Drove on as fast as we could and reached a lousy village which Ivan had named according to his taste: Proletarkaja, beautiful. And here, my boys, the whole boiling stuck. The old one with red stripes down his trousers, His Excellency Kleist, was no match for Ivan's boys. We had to leave Proletarkaja, but before we left Ewald said to me—'

'Who's Ewald?' said The Old Un, astonished.

'You ask like the bloody fool you are, but that's why you're a sergeant. Ewald is our General, Field-Marshal Herr Kleist, you peasant. Now perhaps you'll not interrupt. As you have been training for some time, you know we always leave behind a small force when we evacuate our positions. That is so that Ivan will not discover at once that we have run away. When this lot starts feeling lonely after some hours they blow everything sky high before they run off. That's the sort of thing we did in the Caucasus before we said good-bye to our colleagues on the other side. Ewald knew very well I was a devil of a fine soldier. 'Listen, my own good Herr Obergefreiter Porta,' he said in confidence. 'You must have heard that Ivan has rapped us over the knuckles so severely lately that I can't spare many of my men when I go with Mister Hitler's vehicles. But you are worth half a foot-rag regiment and are indestructible, so I ask you, dear Joseph, if you'll give me a hand with evacuating the army corps' positions.'

'I saluted so that sparks flew round our ears and roared:

"Yes, Herr General Field-Marshal. I'll do that. I'm not afraid of anything".'

'Tell me, were you at headquarters that time?' said Stege as he winked at us.

'My God, I was,' answered Porta, angry at the interruption. 'You doll, maybe you imagine I ran round like an ordinary foot-rag candidate down there on the Ralmuk-Steppe? No, I served right among the dirty great generals and many a time I gave Ewald some smashing tips. He didn't pay any attention to his own staff officers. His whole Intelligence mob was nothing compared with me, Corporal by the grace of God, Joseph Porta.'

'It's very funny, you never became a general,' said The Old Un. 'I think General Field-Marshal Kleist must have been ungrateful considering what you did for him.'

Porta shook his head.

'You ask too many stupid questions. Think, you idiot, you know very well that the officer's uniform doesn't become me, and I can't for the life of me stand it. That red colour the generals carry on their collars just doesn't suit my complexion. But shut up till I've finished. Then we'll see about answering all your daft questions.

'I was left in the army corps' positions to have a little fun with Ivan. I thought about being caught. It wouldn't have done my health any good if they'd found out they had to deal with me. It might be a kind of insult to Stalin himself. My name being Joseph didn't mean he'd be any happier about it. By God, I thought, I must save my skin. I was very glad when I found a nice dead padre in a trench. I had heard that Ivan accepted all this nonsense about church and priests as in the Tsar's time. So I reckoned it would be a nice change to wear a uniform like that, especially should the devils across the line get hold of me. They wouldn't dare make too much fun with a padre. Most Ivans have a devilish respect for holy things. No sooner thought than done. I popped on the uniform and gave the padre mine, so he wouldn't offend anybody's modesty. But he looked indifferent and all my lice were sadly disappointed with his sour blood. When I gazed in the mirror I was very pleased with the handsome spectacle I saw. I looked so very good and godly with all that purple on the collar. The fine holy cross I had round my neck was just like a new decoration invented by fat Hermann. Yes, my dear children, you wouldn't have believed your eyes had you seen me as God's gospeller.'

'We don't doubt that,' said The Old Un quietly.

'To-day I owe the good God a great deal,' went on Porta. 'Because no doubt from him I got the holy inspiration to put on the dead padre's uniform.

'Shortly afterwards Ivan was on top of me and before I could wink an eyelid I was dragged in front of their commander, a wild devil of a colonel with shoulder tabs as broad as a dining-table for a big family. He rolled his eyes like a cannibal and opened his wet gob in a roar: "By Satan in hot hell, if it isn't a padre-devil you've brought me, my lads! By all the little pink devils, how dirt-holy you are across there. Just as we have hanged our own pope for rape and are racking our brains how to get a new one, another one bloody well drops into our arms. Padre, will you be our pope or will you rather hang?"

'I put on my most holy face and answered unctuously:

'"Sir, I'll be your pope!"

'At the same time I held the crucifix over his head and mumbled in the regulation fashion something like: "*Cum spritu tuo*, my little sucking-pig. I hope the smart boys at home are enjoying your wives, while you codfish are fighting for Uncle Joe." You should have seen his pious expression under my blessing. I changed the dead Nazi-padre's rags with his hanged Russian colleague's and looked mighty handsome. I got on famously with the whole mob; you see, lads, the most important thing for a padre is to drink well.'

Porta stopped for a moment and had a good swig of the new bottle we brought out to replace the empty petrol bottle. This one carried a 'rifle oil' label. He belched a few times and went on:

'Courageously steal, eat like a horse, love all pretty girls in the congregation and last but not least: play cards and cheat well according to rule. I was well up in all these essentials that make a good padre. You know that from experience.'

He patted the pocket where he kept the money he had won at pontoon and grinned engagingly.

'I got many friends, and was regarded as a particularly fine padre. In the evening I played cards with the colonel and the three majors and we all cheated so openly, even a babe-in-arms would have blushed. I remember one time particularly that makes me white with anger, and you know I'm not delicate. For a whole day we played gin-rummy without a single one of us managing to get an ace of spades home. We sweated like pigs as the pot for the ace of spades grew. It had grown into several thousand roubles; and then, just imagine, my lads, we discovered that the colonel, the swine, had been holding the ace of spades all the time. He now thought the pot big enough and was about to take the trick home. A terrible argument blew up, and if the creature hadn't called the guard we would have cut his liver out. But you'll admit it was a mean trick to cheat his subordinates, not to speak of me, a clergyman. And what do you think? The swine put us all in the nick. But after a quarter of an hour he joined us with the cards and some bottles of vodka. We forgave him and went on cheating each other, as is the habit when nice people enjoy themselves in the quiet of evening, when God's small stars wink and the moon shines like a drunk pig.

'Then one day the divisional general paid us a visit to inspect the regiment. I had to put on a pretty little church parade. I got hold of a beautiful field-altar with a whole lot of fine saints on the outside, and a fine selection of French pictures on the inside. I, too, had to have something nice to look at during our service. As it was impossible to get hold of any holy wine for mass I laid my hands on a barrel of vodka and blessed it. We diced half a loaf so we could use that as altar bread. You'll see that we had the right idea about what was appropriate at a church feast.

'As a drunken slob of a captain came to the altar and got a drink from the holy wine, the swine bawled blasphemously: "Joseph, this is bloody strong altar wine you're dishing out!"

and asked for another peg, so it won't surprise you I gave him one on the kisser and said: "Pjotr, you can go to hell!"

'After I had been singing and preaching prettily for the whole gang, it was time to bless them so I raised the crucifix and cried: "Go down on your knees before God!" But the heathen idiots just stood and stared like cows at a red-painted gate.

'Not one bent their knees. They seemed to think they were at the cinema so I took a deep breath and roared like our old Sergeant-Major Kraus in the depot used to on Monday morning parade when he discovered we had dirty boots: "To your knees, you damned donkey-stallions or I'll skin you alive, you drooling foot-rag acrobats!" The men knelt, but the officers and NCOs remained standing. I shouted even louder. My larynx worked overtime and gave off queer noises, I pressed it so hard. "To your knees and pray, you rotten Black Sea peasants, or I'll castrate the lot of you, and cut you up and make you eat yourselves, you dumb bog-animals!"

'The NCOs went down on their knees, but the officers still standing, played with their riding whips against their long boots. They stood there, by God, smoking as if each of the brutes was sending up smoke from a sacrificial fire.

'Well, I thought, it must be possible to get these officers to kneel. I breathed extra deeply and put all my strength in the roar I bellowed from the pulpit so that it echoed throughout Caucasia: "On your knees or I'll bash your skulls in with this crucifix and the splinters will reach your stomachs and poison your souls. I'll see to it that you'll land in the worst of Hell's torturechambers. As true as I am pope, you will be given the Evil One's most devilish jankers, and you'll stay for a thousand years!"

'At the same time I swung the chalice and the officers fell on their knees. Now the whole 630th Soviet Guard Gunner-Regiment were on their knees, their heads piously down in front of me, and their hands neatly folded around the top of the rifles. I guzzled a large swig of the holy vodka, and blessed them in the regulation manner, as laid down in the army Service Code on Blessing of Large Troop-Gatherings. Later, the divisional commander thanked me for the beautiful and gripping service, the best one he'd ever attended, he said.'

'I'd have given a good deal to have been there,' laughed The Old Un.

Porta got out his flute, took a large swig of pistol-oil and said:

'As we have now finished with the soulful moments, let's have a song. What about "It's lovely to be a pimp"?'

Rhythmically the vile song echoed round the armoury.

'You certainly can spin a yarn, you red-haired fake,' said The Old Un shaking with laughter. 'How do you think of it all?'

'Of all things,' bellowed Porta, 'the idiot asks how I think of it. My good sir, I don't make it up. I have a good memory, that's all. I remember exactly everything that has happened to me and see it's correctly re-told. You wouldn't say, would you, that I, Joseph Porta, by God's grace Corporal in the Nazi army, am a romancer? If you do, I'll personally skin off your sergeant's cords, thread them through you and clean you out like a rifle. Fall out, you unbeliever!'

We sat a while, chatted quietly and drank deeply.

'Just think, when the war is over,' said Stege a little later. 'I'll go out into a field of clover, lie down and talk to the birds. Oh boys, I look forward to that!'

For a moment there was silence, which Porta interrupted, grabbing a machine-pistol from the rack and swinging it in an arc.

'I have a few bills yet to settle with this little equalizer! There's at least a couple of dozen SS boys I'll make horizontal. And I've my eyes on Mister Himmler in particular. Believe me, or believe me not, that four-eyed bastard is going to get my combat knife so far in that he'll get piles in his throat!'

'Talk, talk,' interrupted The Old Un. 'And always of revenge and revolution. It wouldn't help us. It would only bring on a counter-revolution. No, my lads, it's better to forget the rotten beasts who've got us into this mess. Are they anything but lice, foul lice without souls? There's not a bit of difference between Ivan's red ones and our brown ones.'

I said:

'You were pleased enough when we shot Captain Meyer. Or would you rather forget him?'

'That was in self-defence,' said The Old Un. 'It won't apply to the others when Germany has lost. They'll all sit terror-stricken and listen for our steps. Let Germany's enemies deal with them if they can be bothered and are stupid enough. And I don't mean we should help them. Shut them out from our society, I say. Make it impossible for them to get work.'

'What if Germany doesn't lose the war,' I asked, 'what then? You talk as if it would be lost to-morrow and we'd go home on Wednesday.'

They all stared at me as if I was something peculiar from another planet.

'What the hell do you mean?' gasped The Old Un and Stege in one voice. 'Not lose the war? Are you daft? Have you got a bullet in the brain?'

Porta examined my head as if he was a monkey chasing lice on its young.

Irritated, I wrenched myself free.

'I mean what I say. Haven't you heard about the V-weapons? Who knows, maybe there's something worse in Adolf's pocket. God help us and Germany's enemies if Hitler's gang of chemists and technicians invent something devilish enough to end the war in a few hours.'

'If you mean gas,' said Bauer mockingly, 'we've had that all the time, but Adolf and his generals daren't use it. They all know they'll get a double helping back. No, Sven, you're full of complexes.'

'Complexes,' grinned Porta. 'They won't find much room in his bonce, he's such an idiot.'

'Oh, shut up,' I cut in, 'can't you be serious for a minute?'

'Serious,' answered Porta. 'No, my flower, I wouldn't dream of it. You see, when I get one in the tummy from the other side, I shall march gladly to hell with all the bands playing, while you cry for Mummy. That won't happen to me, Joseph Porta, Nazi Corporal by God's grace.'

'Do you really believe,' asked The Old Un distrustfully,

'That Hitler has any chance of winning his war? Or all this bloody nonsense about V-weapons?'

'Yes, I do,' I answered irritably. 'The nearer we get to the abyss, the more desperately they'll search for something to destroy their enemies. I'll tell you something which will make you think differently of this damned war. It's Hitler's war and of the greater part of the German people. If they don't win, they think everything will be lost because they haven't any imagination. They can never see beyond the last letter in the rules and regulations. Most of them are still in the grip of the military claw. Bloody few have got away! Last time I was in hospital I met a girl who took me home. I was asked to a party for her two brothers. They'd just got their pips. Speeches were made about these two heroes. Great importance was laid on the honour of serving as officers in the German Army; also on the proud fate that let them fight the barbarians who had attacked Germany, the old Holy Roman-German State. You should have heard their father blowing off: "I'm proud my two sons will carry the German National Socialist eagle on their chests!" The vicar who was invited to the party convinced everybody that these two Iron Cross apprentices were now God's tools, since they had got their pips.

'You don't imagine people like that ever dream about Hitler losing the war. They help him all they can. Should he lose, there'll be no more eagles and swastikas to sew on their child-heroes' chests. So they've got to win. Not one of them imagines we could start on a better foundation than the Nazi one. Not that I care a tinker's cuss, because I'm sure not one of us will survive to the happy end of this damned war, whether Hitler wins or loses. There are only fifteen left of us since we started three years ago, so why, for heaven's sake, should we get away with it? There's no end in sight yet.'

'I'm afraid you're right, Sven,' said The Old Un quietly. 'We talk about plans for when the war is over. It would be better if we all accepted our fate. We were created cannon-fodder to fight for a cause that isn't our own. We don't even protest when we are ordered to commit criminal acts. We trot nicely in front of the carriage we're harnessed to, Hitler's carriage, like a lot of donkeys with a carrot dangling in front. We don't use our heads. We fight only because we're too cowardly to break away.'

'Let's talk about something else,' said Stege with a deep sigh.

'Amen,' said Porta and belched.

'What about those trees at Tuapse?' asked Bauer curiously.

The Old Un took a long time to answer. Carefully he scraped out his old pipe with his bayonet and filled it calmly and thoughtfully from Porta's abundant tobacco-purse.

'You want to hear about the trees at Tuapse? We belonged then to Von Kleist's army, and had travelled for weeks in the Caucasus. We had come from Rostov and fought along the Black Sea coast. We were to get into Persia or Syria, or whatever they're called, but it proved a lie. Mr. Timoshenko, Stalin's sabre-swallower, saw to that. Our jäger troops had climbed the 17,000 feet high Elbruz mountains to plant the standard and enjoy the view, but Father Stalin's mountain-boys soon got it down again.

'As our whole circus reached Tuapse there was a lovely surprise in store for us. Ivan had covered the only road in existence with a sea of one and a half meter-thick mahogany and acacia trees. We were surrounded by bog and jungle. They had been cutting and sawing the whole lot down for weeks, and when we came round the corner they started, God help us, to burn them down too. Our pioneers from the 94th and 74th fought like tigers to clear the road. The biggest bulldozers were helpless. We had little petrol but we tried to burn a clearing, and very nearly roasted ourselves like Christmas turkeys. Ivan sat in the thick jungle and picked us off. Panic broke out. We started to run. Soon it was an avalanche. But, lucky for us, Ivan had cut so many trees they stopped him from chasing us. When the army corps after a few days got under control we dragged ourselves along to the Caspian. We were after oil. Do you remember how Goebbels bragged about all that oil we had in our tanks? At that time we were on the Georgian dirt road and hundreds of miles were between us and the nearest oil wells.'

'Oh, God, yes,' said Pluto, 'the Georgian "military road"! Nobody could forget it. A gutter of mud. All our carts stuck.'

Stege started to laugh.

'Do you remember how our "623" slid on its tracks, broke telephone posts like matchsticks and knocked a couple of our motor-cycles with sidecars in the mud so they were squashed flat like pancakes? The damned military road! The whole circus stuck like a bung in a barrel.'

Darkness fell over the armoury. We could hear the recruits singing as they returned from their latest field-exercise.

6

'Would you like a bath in beer?' Porta cried enthusiastically and poured the large jug of beer over the head of the blonde waitress. He did it slowly and carefully and then threw the jug in the air. It fell bang on the counter and the last of the beer splashed all over the place.

We jumped up and swore. Porta rubbed the beer off his hands and slapped the behind of the blonde, well-known under the title of 'The Cab Tart'.

Everything was wet. Tiny wanted to fight. The canteen had a great day.

Tiny and the Legionnaire

No. 2 Troop had been sent to the big tank and motor factory where we, with many other experienced front-line soldiers, were to try out new tanks and their guns. It was a lovely gentlemanly life, even if we often had to work fifteen or sixteen hours a day. Monotony in the depot was comfortably distant. Here we were able to hide among hundreds of civilian labourers of all nationalities.

Porta romped like an elk in heat. There were about two thousand female employees there, and he regarded them more or less as his private possessions. The foremen were nearly always willing to give us a pass to go outside the wired perimeter.

One day, though, Pluto went too far. He stole a lorry and drove from pub to pub, becoming more and more drunk. In the end he ran the truck into a wall three yards from the police station. It cost him fourteen days in the glasshouse. He could thank one of the foremen that it wasn't worse. The fellow swore he had given his permission for the vehicle to go out, and that Pluto was indispensable at the factory. But Colonel von Weisshagen gave him a full-scale dressing down in the presence of the whole depot and fourteen days. While the noble defenders of the Fatherland listened piously, he told the big, stiff-standing Pluto whose turn-out was made up of German uniformed splendour from four different decades:

'You are a stain on the military honours roll; a piece of stinking rottenness! God knows who smuggled you into your clean and disciplined training unit!'

As the military prison was over-filled, fate decreed that Pluto should share bread, bed and cell with ex-Sergeant Reinhardt, who had earlier fallen from grace and been forgotten by everyone, including God and the military judges. As it turned out, he stayed under arrest until the Americans liberated him in 1945. They made him a prison-inspector. Somebody had to be one, so why not Reinhardt? He knew the prison well. A good and conscientious warder, he followed the new régime well, so well that three years later he was in clink himself. A great shame, he confided to his cellmate: the uniform had become him so well!

In the beginning our platoon commander, Lieutenant Harder, often swore at us for un-military behaviour. At last he gave up, and in silent resignation sat in the employees' canteen drinking away his nineteen-year-old's idealism.

Unfortunately, during the war there were precious few people like that. They first appeared after the war. Then they had all been enemies of Adolf Hitler, even Himmler's closest colleague. Work that out, if you can!

Our lives were a noisy mixture of joy and misery. Live to-day, to-morrow you'll be dead. We lived wildly and violently. Not to think, only to forget. We were ruffians with the noose round our necks and it only needed the hangman to tighten it. Many would call us bullies and criminals. About seven million Germans did so. Don't forget we were C-class people. Our experience had taught us to take everybody for scoundrels till the opposite was proved. The proof we wanted was often a hard test for the ones we tried. Those not belonging to our little circle were looked upon as enemies. We tolerated them, but never lifted a finger to help them. We were quite indifferent whether they lived or died. We drank everything alcoholic we could lay hands on. We deadened our misery with opium-cigarettes. We went to bed with any female we got hold of. The bed was often a sentry box or a ditch. Even a lavatory was not scorned.

We had seen people die in their thousands; friends executed in front of our eyes. People dressed in the same uniform as ourselves had been shot, butchered and hanged. We had acted as military executioners, seen German men and women kick the sand, stain it red with blood. We had seen countless numbers fall on the Russian steppes, in the mountains of Caucasia or choke in the bogs of the Ukraine. Sometimes we wept, but only if we were drunk enough not to know what we did. We carried the stamp of the Man with the Scythe. We were already dead, but never talked about it.

Now, hanging about in the canteen, we ribbed the three waitresses.

'Here you,' Porta said to the blonde. 'What about taking some free exercises with me?'

No answer. Just a hurt toss of the plump neck.

'You try it with Daddy, then you'll want to run away from all this and come to the front with me.'

'Are you off to the front?' she asked curiously.

'Nobody said a word about that, but you never know what "Backside and Boots" will do,' grinned Porta. 'I am just inviting you to take a trip with me to the hammock. It won't cost you a dime. It'll be the experience of your life.'

'Doesn't interest me, smart guy,' she said to the shelves of bottles.

'Good God,' roared Porta, 'are you a Lesbian, my soiled lamb! That won't part us, my experiences are manyfold. Meet me outside "The Merry Cow" at seven. Give me a pint of Münchener Hofbrau – the light one – that's all I ask.'

She hit out for Porta and hissed, copper-red in the face:

'I'll report you!'

'Do that. I collect reports.'

Tiny elbowed his way between us and shouted:

'Here! Beer! Five glasses at once.'

He turned to a little scarred fellow who stood by the counter and drank alone.

'You'll pay for my beer, or I'll knock your block off!'

'By Thor and Odin, you don't mean me, sir?' the small chap asked, and pointed to himself with such a ridiculous expression on his badly cut face that we burst into laughter.

Tiny, who was the biggest fighting-cock and bandit in the whole of the command district, stared at the little one and answered, savouring each word:

'Just you, rabbit's scut.'

Carrying five large glasses he turned to the waitress and said casually:

'That piece of turd has promised to pay for this lot.'

Complete silence reigned while the small scarred man drank his pint, licked his mouth and dried it with the back of his hand.

'Are you Tiny?' he asked the seven-foot tall gorilla-like ruffian, who hadn't yet reached his table.

'Pay up and shut up,' answered Tiny.

'I'll pay for my own, but I'm no swineherd. I don't provide the swill for pigs. Fancy letting a pig like that come here,' went on the scarred little man. 'You belong in the pigsty, but you only get there to mate, I suppose. Funny, though, the last litter, looked like you.'

Tiny stopped dead. He let go of the five glasses. They crashed to the floor. In a couple of big smooth jumps he was at the counter, where the little chap stood quietly unconcerned, just reaching to Tiny's lower ribs.

With saliva foaming round his mouth, Tiny roared:

'What the hell did you say, you louse! Just say it again!'

The small man measured him from top to toe:

'Are you deaf? I didn't know pigs had poor ears.'

Tiny became white-faced and drew back his fist.

'Take it easy, great pig. Let's go outside and fight. We don't want to ruin the fine furniture.' The small man smiled disarmingly. 'That would be a great shame!'

He pushed his glass away and started for the door.

Tiny waved his gorilla-arms wildly and roared, almost inarticulate in his fury:

'I'll thrash you, you whelp, make mincemeat of you.'

The little chap laughed:

'Such a lot to do in your sty, little boar. Mind you don't tire yourself.'

Deathly silence fell on the crowded canteen. We could not believe our ears. The tyrant, the big killer of the factory, was being challenged and mocked by a shrimp of a man, barely five feet. The white armband with the word 'Sondersection', framed by two skull-bones indicating a penal regiment shone on his new grey uniform.

No sooner were the two outside, than the three hundred men in the canteen ran out to see the massacre of the small chap.

Tiny was shouting and roaring and swinging his arms. The other chuckled:

'Take it easy, pig. You'll exhaust yourself and be so useless in the sty, even the little ones will disown you!'

Then the impossible happened. The little fellow suddenly shot in the air, kicked Tiny in the face with his hobnailed boots, and the huge fellow fell down like a skittle.

The small man was on top of him quick as lightning, turned him face down, planted himself splay-legged on top and grabbed his red-blond mass of hair: then he ground his face in the sharp gravel and kicked him in the kidneys, spat contemptuously at him and went indifferently back to the canteen. The three hundred spectators stared open-mouthed at the fallen tyrant.

Ordering a pint of light beer, he drank it with great content. We went back to our places and stared curiously at the solitary drinker who had beaten the invincible bully. We were dumbfounded.

Pluto offered him a cigarette.

'Can you take an opium-cigarette?'

A short 'thanks' and he lit it. Another pint was put in front of him.

'With the compliments of Corporal Stern,' said the waitress.

He pushed the glass away and said:

'Return the compliments, but Corporal Alfred Kalb from

the 2nd Regiment of the Foreign Legion never accepts drinks from people he doesn't know.'

'Have you been in the French Foreign Legion?' asked Pluto.

'You heard, or have *you* poor hearing too, perhaps all big fellows have?'

Pluto turned his back and pretended he did not exist.

Tiny came back and sat in his corner by the window and muttered the most hair-raising threats. His face looked like mincemeat. He stood up and went across to the sink and put his face under the tap, rinsing off the blood and gravel. He was snorting like a seal.

Without drying his face he fetched himself three pints of beer and shut himself off in his corner.

Porta had jumped over the counter to be nearer the blonde Eve. In a manner worthy of a high-spot in a comical film he tried to kiss her.

'Has anybody told you, Eve, you have smart fetlocks? Are your thighs up to standard?'

He shot back over the counter, and turned like lightning to the former legionnaire:

'I overheard your remarks to my friend Pluto. You can perhaps get along with your Legion methods in the whore-shops of Morocco, but that doesn't mean to say you can stand up to Joseph Porta from Moabitt, Berlin. Or in good German: answer properly when asked or else shut up.'

The legionnaire slowly rose and bowed politely to Porta, at the same time swinging his service cap off in an old-fashioned aristocratic fashion, while his eyes widened comically.

'Thanks for the tip. Alfred Kalb from the 2nd Regiment of the Foreign Legion will remember Herr Joseph Porta from Moabitt, Berlin. My cradle also stood there. I don't want to fight, but if I have to, I can cope. That's not a warning, only an announcement.'

'What regiment do you belong to, chum?' asked The Old Un, peacefully.

'27th Tank, Ist Battalion, 3rd Company from 11 a.m. to-day.'

'What the hell, that's us!' burst out Porta. 'How many years did they give you?'

'Twenty,' said Kalb. 'Been locked up three for a "social attitude", that is, being politically unstable and having illegal service in a foreign army. Last resort Fagen Camp, Bremen.'

Tiny approached the counter, threw a mark down and ordered:

'One light Dortmunder.'

He remained at the bar and drained his glass in one swallow. He moved to the little legionnaire, put his hand out and said:

'Sorry, chum, all my fault.'

The legionnaire gave him his hand.

'Good, good, all right. Forget it.'

He had hardly finished when he was pulled like a comet against the big bully who smashed his knee into the face of the surprised legionnaire. At the same time killing blows rained at his neck. He was half unconscious. Tiny kicked him in the face, broke his nose, stood up and brushed his hands together and surveyed the crowd in the packed canteen.

Pluto took a swig of his beer and said calmly:

'They didn't know that trick in the 2nd Regiment of the Foreign Legion, but take care, Tiny, one day you'll be with the transport to the Eastern Front. I know three thousand men who'd want to put a filed bullet in your mug.'

'You're welcome to try!' snarled Tiny. 'But I'll return from hell to kill him.'

To the growl of our cursing he left the canteen.

'That character will meet a violent death,' observed The Old Un. 'And nobody will mourn him.'

A week later we were standing with the little legionnaire, who had had part of his nose cut out due to Tiny's kick, looking at a big metal drum being riveted. One end of the drum rested against the wall. Tiny happened to pass by and the legionnaire called cheekily to him:

'You're strong, come and hold on to the rivets, they keep jumping out. We haven't got the strength to hold them.'

Tiny like all bullies was stupid and full of brag. He proudly shot out his chest and jeered as he climbed into the drum:

'Weaklings! I'll show you how to rivet.'

No sooner had he entered the drum than we pushed a cement-loaded tip-wagon across the opening. We put wedges under the wheels to make it immovable. Tiny was caught like a rat in a trap.

Hell was let loose. Ten-fifteen pneumatic hammers and large mallets performed a hellish concert on the steel drum.

The little legionnaire pressed a steam-hose against a rivet hole and let the scalding, whistling steam off. It would have killed anybody except Tiny.

He spent three weeks in hospital, and when he turned up again, bandaged from head to foot, he at once got himself into more wild fights.

One day, Kalb powdered a glass and put it in Tiny's soup. We waited gleefully for his inside to burst, but he only seemed to have more *joie de vivre*.

A little later Porta saved the little legionnaire's life when he noticed Tiny pouring a dose of pure nicotine into his pint. Without a word Porta knocked the glass out of the legionnaire's hand. The little man had been accepted.

7

It started by chance with something as boring as coffee and sweet cakes – it ended with an air raid and marching orders.

War is war, morals disappear and love is short and unsure.

Fudge if you dare! It is only old women and men who have never known love who cannot understand those who seek, find it, and have to experience it.

Love Scene

High-heeled female shoes hit the wet pavement with firm taps.

In the sleepy light from the blue black-out bulb swinging on a rusty bracket from the wall where I stood hidden I was sure it was she: Ilse, my girl.

I remained in the dark so that she would not see me. I enjoyed seeing and not being seen. She stood, walked up and down, stood again and stared up the street leading to the poplar avenue. She looked at her watch, then tidied her green scarf.

An infantry soldier walked by, slowed down, stopped and asked:

'Come with me, I'll give you compensation.'

She turned down the street away from the love-hungry soldier. He laughed a little and went on his way.

She came back to the light. I started humming:

'Unsere beiden Schatten sahen wir einer aus,
dass wir so lieb uns hatten, dass sah man gleich daraus,
Und alle Leute sollen es sehen, wenn wir bei der
Lanterne stehen . . .'

She whirled round, stared into the darkness, and I went slowly forward. She was about to scold when she saw me but burst out into a ringing laugh.

Arm in arm, dead against military regulations, we turned and walked through the ruins. The war and the waiting were forgotten. We were together.

'Where to, Ilse?'

'I don't know, Sven. Where can we get away from soldiers and the smell of beer?'

'Let's go to your house, Ilse. I'd like to see it. We've known each other five weeks and spent them in pubs, grease-stinking coffee bars or in the dirty ruins.'

We walked on a bit before she answered:

'Yes, let's go to my house, but you must be quiet. Nobody must hear you.'

Our transport was a rumbling, shaking tram-car. Sad grey people were our fellow-travellers. We got off in a suburb. I kissed her and stroked her soft cheeks.

She pressed my arm and laughed quietly. We walked slowly on. There were no ruins here; only private houses and terraces where the wealthy lived. It didn't pay to drop bombs here; not enough would be killed.

The air-raid sirens sounded. We pretended not to hear them.

'Have you a night-pass, Sven?'

'Yes, till 8 to-morrow morning. Pluto organized it. The Old Un has gone to Berlin on three days' leave.'

'Has everybody got leave?'

'Yes.'

She stopped and pressed my arm. Her face was white. The eyes shone wetly in the light from the black-out lamp.

'Sven, oh Sven, does it mean you're going?'

I did not answer but nervously pulled her along and was silent. Soon she said in a whisper as if she had read the irrefutable fact in my silence:

'Sven, then it'll be all over. You are going. Even if my husband returns one day you have given me something he couldn't Sven, I can't do without you. Promise you'll come back.'

'How can I when I'm not my own master? The Ruskies and others decide. I'm not asked. I love you. It started as an adventure. You being married only added to the attraction. But it became more. Maybe it's just as well marching orders will part us.'

Silence again! She stopped by a garden gate and we tiptoed to the house. Away to the east we could see tracer-bullets from anti-aircraft guns soar into the sky.

Carefully she unlocked the door, and made sure the black-out curtains fitted before she put on the light. Just a small lamp with a yellow-shade, it seemed to radiate warmth.

I put my arms round her and kissed her violently, almost brutally. Passion started burning in her. She wildly answered my kisses and bored her slim body into mine. Heavily we fell on the sofa without our lips parting.

My hands followed the seam in her stocking, searching her lithe body. Her skin was cool, smooth, dry and smelling of woman. I forgot the depot, the gloomy armoury, reeking oil, beer and damp uniforms, sweating men, old socks – the ruined city with its barracks, hobnailed boots, bawdy songs, brothels, huge graves filled with corpses. I was with an expensively dressed woman, a woman fragrant with the perfume from the slopes of Southern France, with female legs, slim with one shoe on, the other off, black suede shoes with high heels, and round, dimpling knees in light grey silk stockings. The skirt was so narrow it had to be pushed up over firm thighs to make it comfortable. A fur coat on the floor, Persian lamb, beaver or calf? Women would have known it was Persian lamb, black as night, a symbol of wealth and luxury.

Buttons in the pink blouse have burst open under the soldier's battle-clumsy grip. A breast is made prisoner and examined, not roughly by the soldier but by the eternal lover's tender hand. The nipple smiles into love-hungered blue eyes which have wept and laughed, stared across the snowy wastes of Russian Steppes, searched for a mother, a woman, a lover like her.

She detached herself gently from my embrace.

'Shall I tell you what I think?' I asked.

She lit a cigarette and answered as she put another into my mouth:

'I know what you are thinking, my friend. You wish you were far away in a country behind the blue hills, a Shangri-La without barracks and shouts of command, away from a society of rubber-stamping civil servants, a place without the smell of leather and printing-ink, a land of wine, women and green trees.'

'That's what I'm thinking.'

I picked up a photograph from a table beside the sofa. A man in uniform. A handsome man with fine features. A man wearing the insignia of a staff-officer. In one corner he had written 'Your Horst, 1942.'

'Your husband?' I asked.

She took the photograph, put it carefully on the shelf behind the sofa and pressed her mouth against mine. I kissed her pulsating temples, let my lips brush over her firm breasts, bit her cleft chin, and pulled her head backwards by her dark hair.

She groaned with pain, passion and need.

'Oh, Sven, let us find our Shangri-La!'

From the wall a painting of a woman looked forbiddingly down on us. She was wearing a blouse with a high-necked lace collar. Her grey eyes had never dreamed of Shangri-La, but then she had never seen a city in ruins and women with their souls torn to shreds by screeching bombs.

To hell with morals. To-morrow you are dead.

Our half-open mouths were pressed together. Our tongues met like snakes in their mating-dance. We stiffened and relaxed in endless desire. Every frustration was sublimated. The cup of love overflowed. Our lips found themselves again and again in hungry longing. Her breasts were bare. Her turquoise coloured brassiere and slip lay on the floor. She was both an overwhelming need and a shining fulfilment as she lay naked, yet clothed. A completely naked woman disappoints a man. He always wishes for a tiny, fluffy fragment to remove.

A button became a frustration. She lifted her fevered hands to help. Her fingers played over my back, warm, soft, yet hard and wildly demanding.

The sirens hooted, but we were far away from war. We had crossed the last threshold. We gave ourselves to the age-old love's contest, the embrace which calls for eternity. We were insatiable. Heavy sleep overcame us. The sofa seemed too small. We slept on the thick carpet.

When we woke, we were tired but content. We had had a night which would have to last a long time. She dressed and kissed me as only a woman in love can kiss.

'Stay, Sven, stay. Nobody will look for you here. Oh, stay.'

She burst into tears.

'The war will soon be over, it's madness to go back!'

I freed myself from her clinging embrace.

'No, that sort of thing is done only once. Don't forget him in France. He too will be back. And then where do I go? Torgau – Fagen – Buchenwald – Gross Rosen – Lengries? No, call me a coward, I dare not.'

'Sven, if you stay, I'll divorce him. I'll get you false papers!'

I shook my head and wrote my field postal number on a piece of paper: 23645. She pressed the scrap of paper against her breast. Dumbly her stare followed me as I left. Quickly, without turning, I disappeared from her eyes into the morning mist.

8

We stopped at many stations. We stood for many hours queueing to get a little thin soup, made of nettles.

Many times we sat crouched by the railway trucks in rain and snow to ease our bowels.

The journey was slow. For twenty-six days we trundled along, and were far into Russia when we left our cattle-trucks.

Return to the Eastern Front

For fourteen days we limped along in a troop-transport train of thirty or so cattle-trucks for the troops and two old-fashioned third-class passenger carriages for the officers. In front of the engine we pushed an open goods-truck filled with sand in case the partisans had laid mines on the track.

Our troops could easily have been trailed by the excrement we left between the rails at the stations where we stopped.

On the long journey between Poland and the Ukraine many peculiar events befell us before we were unloaded on the dilapidated station at Roslavl.

We were marched along dusty, sandy roads rutted by thousands of heavy vehicles to reach the 27th (Penal) Panzer Regiment's positions at Branovaskaja. Here we were received like long-lost friends by Captain von Barring. He looked deathly pale and exhausted. Rumours had it he suffered from an incurable stomach disease. He had spent a short time in hospital, but they had quickly bundled him off to the front again cured, at any rate on paper. Then followed jaundice and that did not improve matters.

It cut us to the quick to see our beloved company commander in such a state.

If it hadn't been for Porta and Pluto and the former Foreign Legionnaire who had joined us, we would still have been sitting safely back at the depot. As it was, these three had made life impossible for one and all in a mile's radius.

It had started really with the fight between Tiny and the legionnaire in the canteen. The former landed in our mixed marching company, a fact which did not please him. But it was Porta who tipped the balance by going to town illegally in civilian clothes. He, of course, became drunk, and all but raped a girl he had stumbled on in the back-room of the 'Red Cat'. We could hear him bawl:

'Now, my fine miss, you'll see who has arrived here!'

The girl cried with fear and drink. When we hurried in, Porta had peeled off most of her clothes and she lay in a most inviting position. Porta had only his shirt on.

Pluto christened them by pouring a bottle of beer over them:

'I tell thee, thou art created to increase!'

Then we withdrew satisfied, but next day when the girl had sobered up she wondered what had happened. It seemed to her that some private soldiers had been present at the love-making. So it was rape and everything belonging to it. She told her story to her father, a reservist and, to make matters worse, a quartermaster in the auxiliary battalion. He hurried to Colonel von Weisshagen, and, even if Von Weisshagen did not exactly love reservist quartermasters, the mill started to grind. Pluto was recognized, Porta, too, when the girl innocently marched past the paraded company. So the glasshouse again opened its hospitable gates.

But Pluto almost surpassed Porta. One day he invited us for a trip in a training tank, which is a tank with the turret hatches removed. It resembled a bathtub on tracks. He whizzed about the garage area at a speed of 40 kilometres per hour, even though the speed-limit was 15 km.p.h. for all vehicles.

When we had completed four or five circuits with roaring engine and rattling chains, Pluto let go of the steering rods and turning to us in our bathtub said:

'I'll bloody well show you that the old jalopy can do more than forty.'

Covered in a huge cloud of dust, with a roar we jumped out on the road. Then like a jack-in-the-box a little Opel appeared. What followed happened in a flash. We hit the car with a bang and it flew across the ditch and landed on the parade ground. There it turned over three or four times. Two wheels were torn off and careered desperately along to be stopped by the wall of the dining-hall.

'Thank you very much, Pluto,' said Porta with admiration. 'Blimey, what a kiss you gave that pram. You don't do anything by halves, do you!'

'Now we'll see who'll win the slanging match, the master-driver Pluto or that chump in the Opel,' said Pluto calmly.

To our horror our adjutant crawled out of the smashed car with his uniform in shreds. When he reached our training-tank he swore furiously at the dumbstruck Pluto.

That joy-ride cost Pluto fourteen days in a dark cell and the rest of us our trip to Russia. Maybe it was cheap at the price.

In anger Porta threw down his equipment on the floor of the cottage we were billeted in. He shouted at the old Russian who sat in the corner by the stove scratching his lousy back against the wall:

'Joseph Porta has arrived. You've got plenty lice, dear Soviet citizen?'

The Russian grinned without understanding a word so Porta went on in Russian:

'You see, comrade, Joseph Porta and his followers have arrived on the Eastern Front again. Even if I'm a damned good soldier the whole Germanski war apparatus will soon turn west to the good city of Berlin. Your very red brothers will soon be here to set you free, and make you happy and content with lots of dialectics before they hang you.'

The Russian stared and stuttered:

'Germanski go? Bolshevik soldiers come?'

'That's it, comrade,' Porta grinned.

Porta's prophecies took immediate effect and the nine civilian Russians in the cottage held a whispered conference in the stinking room. One made off, presumably to spread the rumour in the sad, grey village. Some of them secretly packed their belongings into bundles. Porta made them start by shouting:

'Don't forget your victory flags!'

Pluto was on his knees fixing his bedding on the floor but Porta's commentaries made him collapse with laughter.

When he recovered he picked up his machine-pistol, patted it significantly and announced in broken Russian:

'When tovarich commissar come, you dead quick because you not partisans. Hurry up and be partisans!'

The old Russian went across to him and said with an odd dignity:

'You not funny, Herr soldier.'

With our gas-mask containers serving as pillows and wrapped in our greatcoats we tried to snatch some sleep before moving into our battle positions. Rumour had it we were to serve as infantry. We had heard that the 19th Panzer had been wiped out by our Russian colleagues. All our own tanks were lost too.

'We've landed in a real muck-pot,' said Stege. 'But, of course, we're the whipping-boy for all Hitler's army!'

'You've said it,' said Möller, 'a chap from the regimental staff told me that the whole of the 52nd Army Corps had run for it with Ivan at their heels.'

'God help us,' Pluto burst out. 'If that's right we're going to get it bloody hot. But those beauties in the 52nd were always ready enough to run.'

'They've mostly got mountain-monkeys,' said Stege, 'I never could stand those hill-billies with their imbecile Edelweiss on their caps and sleeves. Looked like a bunch of wreaths when they were on the march.'

Slowly peace fell over the room. The last speech we heard was the Little Legionnaire swearing in German, French and Arabic at the biting lice. Soon an orchestra of snores was the only sound.

It was still dark when a foot kicked us awake and a voice whispered: 'Alert!'

Porta, half-asleep, muttered angrily:

'What are you whispering for? Do you think Ivan's out there with his ear stuck to the keyhole? Get out of it, you sod, or I'll bash your skull in!'

Slowly we got up and collected our equipment. We crossed to the assembly area swearing and stumbling in the night. There we joined the rest of No. 5 Company. We were all dirty and frowsty with sleep.

Flash-lamps blinked as papers and maps were studied. Low-voiced commands, the clicking of steel against steel filled the wet night. Tiny gave off abuse, threatening to fight anyone who came near.

Von Barring who came along in his long coat with a hood attached – the kind privates wear on guard-duty – was without shoulder-tabs or badges. He quickly interrupted the talk between Sergeant-Major Edel and the section-leaders:

'Good morning, Company! Ready to march?'

Without waiting for an answer he ordered:

'Company, attention! Rifles will be slung. Automatic weapons will be carried as most comfortable. No. 5 Company right turn. Follow me. March!'

Both Porta and the Legionnaire were cheekily smoking. Several more followed their example. We marched in a lumpy confusion. Friends sought friends as a protection against fright and darkness. Porta put an egg-grenade in my hand and said:

'I've no room for this muck, you take it!'

Without a word I put it in my pocket.

The equipment rattled and jingled. Everyone was jittery. The rain ran off the steel-helmet down the back of the neck. We went through a spinney and then across a trampled field of sun-flowers.

Tiny, all the time quarrelling with the others, was getting very loud. A fight was imminent.

Von Barring stopped and let the company pass by. Lieutenant Harder was alone in front swinging his machine-pistol by the leather strap.

When Tiny came past von Barring we heard the captain say in his gentle but firm manner:

'You, I've seen your papers and heard about you. I warn you. We don't stand any form of provocation. You're in a decent company. We treat everybody properly. But don't forget we have our methods with scoundrels and rascals and we're not afraid to use them!'

Von Barring marched up to his position beside Lieutenant Harder again. He wore an officer's cap. From his right shoulder dangled his machine-pistol. On his way up he hit Porta on the shoulder and said:

'Hey, you red-haired monkey!'

'Same to you, sir,' responded Porta familiarly. He turned to The Old Un and me and announced loudly: 'Barring is one of the few officers I know who isn't a complete swine.'

'Shut up, Porta,' von Barring's voice came through the darkness. 'Or else there'll be extra parades when we get back.'

'I report, sir, that Corporal Joseph Porta has corns and is flat-footed. The doc has exempted him from extra parades.'

A quiet laugh came from von Barring.

The artillery-fire was not heavy. Rather dispersed and desultory shooting came from both flanks. Now and again machine-guns barked. It was easy to tell the Russian ones from ours. Da-da-da said the Russian, our MG 38 sounded more like tik-tik, and the new fast-firing MG 42 was one long evil snarl.

Round about tracer-bullets opened up and sank to the ground in a blinding white light. Stege started to laugh hysterically:

'I once read a book about a soldier: "He was a solider and feared nothing. He was big and brave. Death was his friend and helper. He behaved with sureness and confidence as only the brave do"! The writer-sod who wrote that should see us now as we march the steppes, shaking with fear.'

'Shut up, Stege,' said The Old Un.

He was walking slightly bent smoking his ancient pipe. He had put the hand-grenades in his long boots, and his fists were buried deep in the pockets of his greatcoat.

A short distance in front of us a whining shell fell in a field and exploded with a bang.

'15.5,' said The Old Un, and pulled his head even lower between his shoulders.

Some of our new men threw themselves into shelter. Porta started jeering.

'The depot-stallions like the smell of the Russian earth!'

'Do you mean me?' snarled Tiny behind us. He too had thrown himself down.

'Does the cap fit?' asked Pluto.

Tiny shovelled his way through the ranks and grabbed Pluto. Porta jerked his sniper's rifle forward and hit Tiny a colossal smack in the face with the butt.

'Be off, you fat pig,' he hissed threateningly.

Half-stunned, Tiny whirled round, waltzed out of the ranks and fell to his knees with blood spurting from his nose.

Quietly The Old Un stepped out of the column and with the barrel of his pistol pointing at the kneeling giant said calmly:

'Get up and join the ranks where you belong, or we'll kill you. If you're not in place in ten seconds, I shoot!'

Tiny stood shakily up and growled, but a well-timed thrust from the muzzle of The Old Un's pistol silenced him.

'Split up,' von Barring's voice came out of the darkness. 'Put the fags out.'

Whee! Crump! exploded a new 15.5. Da-da-da stuttered a heavy machine-gun.

Porta laughed a little.

'Just like coming home again. Good morning, pisspots,' he greeted a couple of panzer grenadiers crouched under a tree. 'Corporal Joseph Porta, graduated State-murderer, humbly reports back to the Eastern Front "slaughter-house".'

'Look out, when you get to the ruin in front there,' said one of the grenadiers mechanically and without rancour. 'Ivan can spot you there. When you walk through the trench you'll come to a place where there's a dead Russian lying. Get down flat there. Ivan is using him as an aiming-mark for his machine-guns. We lost nine men there yesterday, so you're likely to have a few crosses among you, too!'

'God, you're cheerful,' said Porta coolly.

Pluto and the Little Legionnaire looked at each other.

'Do you smell corpses, chum?' asked the Legionnaire. 'Like Morocco, in the old days, only the pong was stronger there.'

'Ho, ho,' cackled Pluto. 'Just you wait till an east front

partisan explodes. Then you'll see what your own innards'll look like, you Arab. You'll drool for sweet smells of sunny Morocco!'

'A couple of Ivans won't scare me. I've got the cross with four palms and three stars for fighting in the Riff mountains and Indo-China,' said Kalb.

'Ha,' jeered Porta, 'even if you've a cross with a whole forest of palms from your desert trips you'll be desperate here when Ivan is in form. Just wait for the Siberians to come and cut your Adam's apple out to play ping-pong with!'

'We'll see, we'll see,' said the Little Legionnaire. 'Allah is wise. I'm a damned good shot, and can use my knife. My cradle stood in Moabitt!'

'Be careful you don't win the war single-handed,' The Old Un said ironically.

The company slid and slipped on the slimy, muddy path which led past the ruin of a farmhouse.

A little in front where the trench was shot to pieces the whole company sought shelter like a fan suddenly folding. We had to crawl past the dead Russian who lay on a small mound and gave us a little cover.

Whispering, von Barring announced.

'Quickly, get to the other side. One at a time. Press yourselves flat, use the Russian as shelter. We have a heavy Russian machine-gun to the left just in front. If you are seen you've had it!'

The rattle of equipment had ceased. We were like wild animals ready to pounce, silent as the night.

Porta crouched at the edge of the trench with his sniper's rifle at the ready. In a corner of his mouth hung a dead cigarette butt. At his side stood the Little Legionnaire who had developed a dog-like devotion to the red-haired street urchin. He had his light machine-gun on his hip, prepared to fire.

The first of us were already past the danger-point. Then a star-shell burst over our heads, its blinding white glow lighting up the whole area.

The next few desperately pressed themselves down by the fallen Russian.

The Old Un swore:

'The whole fireworks is coming now. Ivan must have smelt us here.'

He had scarcely finished when it started. Tra-tra-tra the heavy machine-gun yammered. The corpse jumped as if life had returned to it.

Rusch-ram-rusch-ram boomed the mortar-bombs and splashed us with mud. These small devil-bombs could be heard only when they exploded near us. More machine-guns joined in the concert.

'Quiet, quiet, don't shoot,' von Barring's voice came soothingly through the darkness. He was pulling himself along on his stomach past the whole company.

Perhaps it lasted an hour, perhaps three minutes. Then it was all over and we again started to slide past the Russian in his brown uniform.

The Old Un gave me a light tap on the shoulder to indicate it was my turn.

I nearly vomited as I lay beside the corpse. It was swollen and gruesome with green liquid pouring out of nostrils and mouth. The stink was terrible. After me came Porta and the Little Legionnaire. They were the last. A mortar made us all fall flat. Behind us someone started to yell. Another few mortar-bombs landed in the mud, soaking us.

'Blimey, what a spa we've landed in,' Stege moaned.

The Little Legionnaire took a deep breath.

'This must be what is called a Russian bath.'

'No. 2 Platoon take up their positions here,' ordered Lieutenant Harder. His voice shook a little. He was not yet front-trained.

Pluto had difficulty with his huge machine-gun and swore grimly as he arranged sandbags in the right places.

A bullet hit one of them with a smack just by his head.

'You Russian muck-heaps!' bawled the big docker.

'Good thing we know where to find you, you bloody eunuchs. I'll smash you into pulp!'

Furiously, he threw a hand-grenade across just to underline his threats.

'Take care, lads,' warned The Old Un. 'He's a sharp-shooter across there, and uses real bullets!'

Another bullet whined and landed in the middle of the forehead of one of the tank-gunners. Bits of skull and brains spattered the Little Legionnaire who scraped them off with his bayonet, grimacing.

The gunners from the 104th Artillery whom we were relieving, confessed we had landed in fairly thick soup.

'Take good care about seven o'clock in the morning and five in the afternoon, that's when Ivan really lets go. Apart from then you've only got to cope with machine-gun fire and mortars and a little sniping.'

We lit our Hindenburg-candles in the dug-outs, and No. 2 Platoon settled down to some recreation.

Porta got out the greasy old cards. The top-hat he had found somewhere he placed on his head, elegantly askew. It had a few dents in it and the silk was a little worn, so Porta had painted one blue and one red ring round it. It looked like the funnel of a steamer. He screwed the monocle he had got in Roumania into his eye. It had had a few knocks and a deep crack made his eye look completely idiotic. Its black-horn frame was fastened to his shoulder-tab with a black cord, part of some girl's underclothes.

As if he were a croupier in Monte Carlo he superciliously shuffled the cards and cried:

'Stake your money, but no credit, mind. I've lost dough before because some silly sod got bumped off by Ivan before paying out. Smallest stake 10 Hitler-marks or 100 Stalin-roubles.'

He dealt out twelve cards and turned the thirteenth up: it was the ace of spades. Without a word, he scooped the stakes into his empty gas-mark container which hung round his neck. He won eight times running. Then we started staking more carefully. Nobody said what was in their minds: Porta was cheating. For on each side of him lay a machine-pistol and behind sat the Little Legionnaire caressing a P.38 with the safety-catch off.

The Old Un was reading a book his wife had given him.

From time to time he took out his old, worn wallet in which he carried some snaps of her and the children. He suffered unbelievably hard from home-sickness. We had often seen him shed tears over the family snaps.

Captain von Barring and Lieutenant Harder came into the dug-out, sat down beside The Old Un and chatted quietly.

'We can expect Ivan about 3 p.m., so Intelligence tell me,' confided Barring to The Old Un. 'You'll see that everything is OK here. The commander of the gunner-company we have replaced said we've landed in a hellish corner. Battalion orders are that in no circumstance must we evacuate map reference Height 268.9.

'As long as we can stay here we dominate this area. Let Ivan through and the whole division will have to retreat, or capitulate, and Ivan knows that only too well.'

'That means,' said The Old Un thoughtfully, 'that we can be pretty sure Ivan will throw in his whole machinery against us. Do you think he'll use tanks?'

'Not while the ground isn't frozen, but as soon as frost comes he'll be over us. Hope we've got our own armour here by then,' said von Barring tiredly. He glanced round the dim-lit dug-out and spotted Porta in his tall, colourful silk-hat.

'God help us,' he burst out. 'What have you got that mad hat on for again? Get your cap, and stop fooling around with that thing!'

'Yes, sir,' answered Porta, as he shovelled another lot of winnings into his bursting gas-mask container. Then he placed his uniform cap on top of his silk-hat.

Von Barring shook his head and said with a laugh to The Old Un and Lieutenant Harder:

'That scoundrel is impossible! If he runs into our battalion commander with that thing on his head he's for it!'

Just at that moment a terrible din came from the players. Tiny had discovered that Porta had used two aces of spades. He roared and was just about to thrash Porta when he was stopped effectively by the muzzles of a P.38 and a machine-pistol with the safety-catches off.

'Do you want a few more holes in your body apart from your mouth and your backside?' asked the Little Legionnaire as he rose and kicked Tiny in the stomach. The big man fell back with a grunt.

Captain von Barring and Lieutenant Harder ignored the incident and cleared off. Shortly afterwards play went on. We pretended we had no evidence of cheating. Tiny took part and was allowed to win a couple of times. This put him in a very good temper. He hit Porta enthusiastically on the back and humbly begged his pardon for having entertained the idea that Porta had cheated. He had forgotten he had ever seen two aces of spades. Soon, however, he was losing again and imploring credit, but Porta was unmoved.

Tiny groaned with frustrated gambling passion. Quickly he tore off his wrist-watch and pushed it across the table. He asked 300 marks for it.

Lazily the Little Legionnaire bent forward and examined it closely; then he announced:

'We'll give you 200 marks, and that's plenty!'

Porta polished his cracked monocle, tilted his hat and examined the watch like a professional watch-maker. Then he pushed it back to Tiny with disgust:

'Stolen goods, 150 marks and not a fraction more, but hurry up, or you can go!'

Tiny wanted to make trouble as usual, but instead he just opened and shut his mouth a few times, then nodded agreement dumbly.

Two minutes afterwards the watch lay snugly in the gas-mask container with all the other winnings.

Paralysed Tiny stared at Porta, who went on dealing as if nothing unusual had happened.

When everybody but the banker was broke play stopped for sheer lack of momentum. Porta shut his bulging gas-mask container with a snap, sank down on the straw-covered ground and pillowed his head on his winnings. He grinned knowingly at Pluto and the Little Legionnaire. Then he pulled out his recorder and started to play the number about the girl who was made love to electrically in a factory. The other two joined raucously in the unbelievably filthy song.

Tiny tried, unsuccessfully, to make trouble. Nobody could be bothered to fight.

9

The divisional commander was famous for being a complete nitwit: a typical German soldier of the Third Reich. Oddly enough he was deeply religious. He was in possession of that peculiar Prussian ability to mix Christianity with Chauvinism.

Every morning Lieutenant-General von Trauss prayed at his mobile field-altar with the divisional padre von Leitha. They prayed for a complete victory for the German forces.

He made long nonsensical speeches about a coming German hegemony when all sub-humans were to be exterminated. Everybody who did not carry small swastikas in their brains were sub-humans. Porta of course suggested a more suitable placing for the swastikas.

At 11.30 a.m. The Germans will be Blown Sky High

It was The Old Un who woke me up.

'You and Porta are going out on a listening-post job. Take one more man along, but not Pluto or Stege. I can't do without either if Ivan should attack.'

'I can see why you've been made a sergeant,' snapped Porta. 'You're good at dishing out rotten messages at breakfast time.'

'Shut up, Porta. Who will you take with you? Time's short, Ivan's got something on, and I can't send any half-wits across there.'

'Oh, thank you! Fancy you saying I'm intelligent after being declared a complete imbecile by a trick-cyclist over that burglary in Dahlem.'

'Shut up, Porta, who will you take?'

'Easy, Grandpa. Don't let it go to your head because the Prussians have given you a little silver on your shoulders, a cheap carpenter like you! We'll take the Frenchman.'

He started shaking the sleeping Legionnaire who lay curled up like a dog.

'What the hell's the matter with you, you red-haired bastard!'

'What do y'think, brother? We're off on an excursion to meet the giant of the steppes, and he'll just love you.'

'Bloody nonsense, where are we off to?' The sleepy Legionnaire did not respond kindly; he sat up in the straw scratching his lice-bitten chest.

'Wait and see, brother,' Porta answered shortly. 'Maybe we're off to count the spots on Ivan's face.'

We strapped on our equipment and packed our extra rations. Then we followed The Old Un up to the heavy machine-gun post.

He explained the territory.

'You can stay hidden about three fingers' breadth left of that bush. From there you can see the white of Ivan's eyes without being seen yourselves, but mind – no movement. Return only after dark. Colonel Hinka is sure Ivan is up to some dirty tricks. That's why you're going out to listen in.'

'Blimey, you're sending your best pals across there! You bloody jumped-up sergeant! Haven't we got enough Iron Cross candidates who were born for the job?' Porta demanded indignantly.

Captain von Barring and Lieutenant Harder materialized out of the darkness. In whispers von Barring explained a few things The Old Un hadn't known.

'See too, boys, that you don't stir up any trouble out there. Safety-catches on the rifles. No shooting if you can help it, only in extreme danger.'

We placed our combat-knives in our boots, put the egg-grenades in our pockets and the machine-pistols in our belts.

Von Barring pointed speechless at Porta's tall silk-hat, and managed to get out:

'Do you intend to keep that thing on going across to Ivan?'

'It's my lucky charm, sir,' said Porta simply and crawled out after the Little Legionnaire.

We snaked along on our stomachs. The ground was muddy

and rough. We crawled under the barbed-wire defences. Not a sound disturbed the silence. We were surrounded by a treacherous darkness, varied only momentarily when the moon peeped out between the rushing clouds.

I was the last to reach the bush. The Little Legionnaire put a finger to his mouth to remind me to keep quiet. I got a shock when I saw how near we were to Ivan's positions. Ten yards away two Russians were manning a huge machine-gun. With great care we placed our machine-pistols on the ground beside us. Then we covered ourselves with a camouflaged tent.

A few of the Russians were quarrelling and swearing so much you would have thought Tiny was among them. Soon they were having a real scrap.

For two hours we were as quiet as corpses. Then Porta soundlessly took out his field-flask. The vodka gave us warmth. We smiled at each other. The Little Legionnaire pointed to a spot in the Russian positions where a staff-colonel and two other staff-officers were apparently on a tour of inspection. They stopped almost beneath us to talk to a couple of infantry officers. We took a firmer hold on our weapons.

The colonel moved across to the heavy machine-gun and ordered a couple of bursts to be fired at the German line. The Germans immediately retaliated. The colonel grinned and said something about paying out those Nazi dogs.

When darkness fell and we were about to return we heard a voice from the enemy lines:

'We can't make contact with the battalion. The communication-trench is flooded. The river has broken its banks. Fritz up there is dry enough while we're likely to drown in this dump, but then . . .'

The voice faded in the darkness which was heavy and ominous. We could only dimly see the Russian positions. Soundlessly we returned.

We went back to the same spot for four days running without hearing anything of worth and von Barring decided we should bring back a prisoner. Then we heard that a patrol had found a Russian telephone-wire. Two minutes later we had made a connection and were tapping the conversations. Two days passed before our patience was rewarded. Porta suddenly woke up and threw the receiver at me. A rough voice came gratingly:

'How are you getting on, George?'

'The same old grind. Wish the whole outfit to hell.'

Then followed a few Russian curses.

The first voice laughed hoarsely.

'Got any vodka?'

'Yes, a large ration arrived to-day. If only we had a few tarts too, everything would be all right. Shall I send you some vodka, Alex?'

'No, thanks. We're joining you to-night.'

Surprised George asked:

'What's going on?'

'To-morrow morning at 11.30 we're blowing the Germans to hell. The whole hill will fly up. It's going to be beautiful fireworks. The green lice will be blown to hell!'

The Little Legionnaire hurried back to Captain von Barring, who immediately reported to headquarters.

We got as much help as could be scraped together. One company from the 104th gunners, one 8.8-cm. anti-aircraft gun, two poor 7.5-cm. guns on gun-carriages, along with a useless company of 50-year-old reservists. The whole lot became a storm battalion under the leadership of Captain von Barring. While the morning mist still covered everything in a protective veil, he ordered the trenches to be evacuated to avoid the risk of being blown in the air with the hill. We prepared a warm welcome for Ivan when he advanced after the explosion.

To our immense joy a company of engineers with flame-throwers arrived too. We knew them and could depend on them. They were experienced front-line soldiers like ourselves. None had cleaned his nails since 1939.

We were waiting in the reserve trenches, our hearts thumping with anxiety. The hands on the watch-face scarcely moved. Tiny was lying beside Pluto. He did not say anything, but it was obvious he preferred the company of the big docker in an emergency.

Stege and I lay beside Porta and on his other side the Little Legionnaire hung on like a limpet. To our left lay Möller, Bauer and the others.

The hand-grenades felt sweaty in our hands. Cigarette after cigarette was smoked in one long endless chain during this nerve-racking waiting period.

Somewhere deep in the earth the Russian sappers were working with the explosives under the hill which was meant to be our grave. Instead we were lying waiting for the fireworks to begin, all because an alert patrol had discovered a thin telephone wire.

The watch said 11.15. In fifteen minutes hell would be let loose. Tensed, we stared across the foggy swamp-landscape. Nothing yet. Another fifteen minutes. Still nothing happened.

Suddenly it dawned on us that the Russians' time of course was one hour behind ours.

'This is worse than waiting for the Berlin tube,' said Porta.

'By God, it's like waiting outside an African whore-house with a crew of only ten tarts,' whispered the Little Legionnaire. 'And a hundred fellows in front before you get your helping . . .'

'What of it? How can you be interested in a whore-house?' said Tiny. 'They fixed you, made you useless in Fagen, didn't they?'

'Repeat that,' whispered the Little Legionnaire, 'and I'll empty my pistol in your skull.'

'Quiet!' Von Barring's voice sounded angry.

Waiting, waiting, insufferable waiting. One hour passed. The time was 1 p.m. Still nothing happened.

The tightly packed force in the trench was beginning to get restive. With oaths and damnations they changed places. At the bottom of the trench the old reservists sat apathetically; they already carried the death-mask. The engineers stood smoking among us, the tank-gunners. We knew what to expect. Ivan was sure to throw in a heavy concentration of troops.

Pluto arranged the strap round his shoulder to be able to run with his sub-machine-gun at hip-level when shooting began.

To our surprise Tiny too had got hold of a sub-machine-gun although he was supposed to pull the gun-carriage. Nobody asked what had become of it or about the sub-machine-gun. Several hundred rounds in bandoliers hung in long ribbons round his neck and shoulders. In his belt was tucked a sharpened intrenching-tool ready for close combat.

Porta lay with a flame-thrower beside him and the Little Legionnaire carried the petrol supply on his back. Porta looked completely insane as he lay there with his flame-thrower and his top-hat on his head.

The artillery crews had sited their guns behind our positions, but because of the long-waiting period, some wanted to remove their guns, maintaining it was a false alarm.

Von Barring had an angry argument with the lieutenant in command. It ended with von Barring forbidding the guns to be removed and threatening with the death sentence anybody who tried to take any away.

Grinning, we nudged the engineers. Von Barring was an old fox. He smelt rottenness. He knew what he was doing. We could depend on him.

Another half-hour passed. Several men suggested we should knock off for a meal. Von Barring forbade it. The old reservists noisily started to make trouble.

Precisely at 14.05 it let loose. The whole hill disintegrated. It flew skywards in one black rushing storm cloud. Within a second completely and deathly silence reigned. Then tons of earth, stone and tree-stumps poured down over us.

Simultaneously the Russian artillery let off. Mortar-bombs of every calibre dropped on what had previously been our positions. Although the artillery attack lasted only a short time, all our telephone wires were in shreds, and every aerial was useless, but only a few of the troops were killed or wounded.

Our whole position was enveloped in a heavy, corrosive and nauseating smoke. Through it we could see Russian infantry soldiers storming our former positions, intent on capturing Height 268.9 before the Germans on the flanks discovered the position was blown skyhigh.

'Storm-battalion, follow me!' roared von Barring and jumped out of the trench, shooting furiously with his machine-pistol. Our legs moved of their own volition. Like savages we stormed the colossal crater. We reached the edge of it ten yards in front of the Russian storm-troops. To their amazement they were met with heavy firing.

Close combat with sub-machine-guns at the hip and twenty to thirty flame-throwers would make even Satan blanch. The Russian soldiers became like burning catharine-wheels. Panic broke loose in the tightly knit infantry ranks. They threw down their weapons and rushed back to their positions with our artillery chasing them wildly with red-hot guns. Some managed, even so, to hang on to the other side of the crater-edge only twenty-five yards from our dug-outs. Now the Russian artillery let loose in earnest. For twenty-four hours it plastered the tiny area known to us just as a map-reference, with a hell of fire.

We learned from the few prisoners we had captured that we had the 21st Guards Engineers, an *élite* unit, against us. The fighting was wild and furious while the artillery pounded our rear positions.

Tiny swung his machine-gun with one hand like a truncheon; in the other he used his sharp spade. He was covered with blood from head to foot.

Porta fought like a berserk. After his petrol-supply had run out he used his flame-thrower like a flail. With his top-hat on he stood in the small trench shouting wildly and murdering merrily left, right and centre.

By his side the Little Legionnaire fought on with a captured machine-pistol.

Hour after hour the close-combat fighting rolled up and down the narrow trench, but at last we had to give way.

Leaving our dead and wounded behind, we leapt back to our own positions. The Russians immediately followed, but had to withdraw when our supports laid on a killing cross-fire.

Breathing heavily we lay in our mud-filled positions. Bauer had got half his cheek chopped off. Möller's nose was smashed. Tiny's middle finger had disappeared. Funnily, he did not want to go back to the dressing-station. He was bandaged. Groaning and swearing he turned down the invitation.

'Be off, you lousy pill-merchants! I'll stay with these bandits. Tiny will die here, not in your muck-hospitals.' He hit out at the orderly, jumped up on the edge of the trench and sent a wild shower of bullets at Ivan's positions. Roaring like a bull he shouted:

'Here you red Stalin-ponces! This is medicine from Tiny in the 27th Killer and Arson Regiment. I'll castrate you, you bog-boars, just wait!'

At once the Russians answered with a wild and aimless fire. Tiny stood completely without cover. With his machine-gun at hip-level and roaring insanely with laughter, he sprayed the Russians with fire.

Bauer made an unsuccessful attempt to pull the obviously mad fighting-cock to cover. He stood splaylegged and like a rock.

The madness spread. Pluto leaped up and started firing. Porta with his top-hat and flame-thrower followed, along with the Little Legionnaire. They stood beside Tiny, roaring like lunatics with laughter.

'You bloody depot-animals, you can't take us,' shouted Porta. 'Here, you carrion, let them have it!' And his flame-thrower spurted death.

The Little Legionnaire started yelling:

'En avant, vive la legion!' He stormed forward flinging his hand-grenades ahead.

Porta flipped his hat in the air, grabbed it, smacked it back on his head and bellowed:

'Follow the desert rat!'

He hurried after the Little Legionnaire, as did Tiny and Pluto who were firing like madmen. The rest of the battalion became possessed by the same lunacy and ran, howling like hungry animals, after the others.

This attack was irresistible. It shovelled Ivan out of his positions. We bit, growled, cut and hit during the insane hand-to-hand fighting, and we recaptured our positions. For three weeks these became home. During them we suffered under heavy artillery fire.

Slowly our mixed storm-company disintegrated. Many got shell-shock and bashed their heads against the walls of the trench. Some ran out into the concentrated artillery fire to be turned into bloody bundles.

For long periods Porta sat in a corner playing his recorder, and the Little Legionnaire played his mouth-organ.

Lieutenant Harder twice got shell-shock. Tiny had made himself a punch-bag out of a sand-bag. Once when it swung back and hit him hard in the face he went mad with fury and ripped it to pieces with his combat-knife. He swore at the silent sand-bag like a lunatic.

We had hardly any food while we stayed on Height 268.9, although Porta discovered an old depot with a few tins and we ran, jumped and crawled to momentary safety and back to our lines through heavy artillery fire with our prize.

At last we got help from the division. They threw in two grenadier regiments and lots of heavy artillery. For two more days we battled for the damned hill, then were relieved by the 104th gunner-regiment.

We buried our many casualties by the side of those who had fallen during the advance in 1941. Both sides fell for a large lump of unknown earth. It is only marked on the general staff's special maps. Even to-day anyone passing by on their way to Orel would never even notice it. Yet here lie ten thousand German and Russian soldiers.

The only tomb-stones a few rusty steel-helmets and mouldy leather belts.

10

It was just like a cinema. We had to pay before entering. There were three different kinds of tickets: Red secured one girl for one quarter of an hour. Yellow two girls for two hours. Green – the colour of speed ahead – gave you a whole night's love with five girls.

The Field Brothel

We were billeted in Moschny a little north of Cherkassy. It was a Russian village with dilapidated, clay-covered huts lining an enormously wide straight road.

Little by little we relaxed after the wearing battles we had been in. New troops had arrived from the training batallion and we had regained our regulation strength of two hundred men. But the troops we got were very poor. They needed vigorous training before they could be used in the vicious fighting which had spread south of Cherkassy. That is a place few of us will ever forget. But at this time we were in happy innocence of what lay in store – the Second World War's Verdun.

It was cold and as we had very little fuel, Porta suggested we should play 'arse-slap', a brutal game suitable only for roughnecks. As the name suggests, one man bent over so that his trouser seat was taut. One of the players standing in a half-circle round him had to give him an almighty slap behind, and then he had to guess who had hit him. If he was right that man was in.

Even if you used all your strength it was impossible to hit Tiny so that he noticed it. He pretended he did not even feel it.

'Blimey, you'd think it was butterflies bumping against me,' he grinned. 'Why the hell can't you white-livered rabbits put some strength into it!'

When Tiny wasn't the target, he always wanted to slap,

with the result that the unlucky man who was 'in' was sent flying several yards forward.

Tiny's turn coming round again, the Little Legionnaire found a plank with a nail at the end. He winked as we stood round the expectant Tiny who laughed mockingly at us.

Aiming with the care of a baseball player, the Little Legionnaire swung the plank and hit Tiny's behind with a bang like a gun-shot.

With a roar of pain Tiny leapt in the air, with the plank stuck to his seat. The nail had gone in full length. He beat the air with his gorilla-like arms and roared with pain and fury. His eyes rolled wildly about in search of the culprit as he tore off the plank with a growl and sent it flying to crash against the side of a house.

'You lousy swine, is this the way to treat a pal?'

Then he changed his tactics and asked gently but with a murderous smile on his lips:

'Who was it? I know, but let's see if he's man enough to own up!'

Accusingly he pointed at no one in particular.

'If you volunteer I'll let it pass, but if you don't own up I'll tear your guts out and strangle your bastard neck with them!'

The only answer was a mighty belly-laugh from us all. Then he gave up acting the diplomat and growled:

'You bloody Nazi rat! Own up or I'll kill you!'

'It was no party-member who hit you,' gurgled Pluto.

'Was it you, you bugger?' bawled Tiny and stepped threateningly across to Pluto. He was curled up with laughter.

'No, by God, it wasn't. If only I could have thought of it,' he hiccupped between roars of laughter.

'If you know who it is, why ask?' The Old Un said.

'Cretins and curs, I don't know, but the rotten swine who treats his faithful and affectionate pals with low-down tricks like this will get his desserts!'

'"Faithful and affectionate"! Do you mean yourself?' cried Stege.

'Well, what of it, you student-codfish. Don't get uppish because you can say backside in Latin!'

'I'll willingly teach you Latin,' offered Stege.

'Go to hell,' said Tiny.

He went from man to man quizzing each. Spit formed round his mouth.

'Did you hit Tiny with a plank?'

For answer he got grinning and head-shaking.

'I'll give that lousy son of a whore *this* if he doesn't own up in ten minutes!' He punched his fist into the grass but unfortunately a stone lay under it. Roaring with pain he kicked out at an imaginary enemy and swearing terribly went off followed by Porta's neighing voice:

'Does it hurt, Tiny? Did you graze yourself?'

Bellowing, Tiny ran along the road to the village. The last we heard of him was:

'Rotten lot I've landed with. Not one honest pal. But just you wait, I'll get him later!'

We were lying in one of the huts drinking vodka and smoking machorka.

'I hear they've got a field-brothel in Bjel Zerkov,' announced Bauer thoughtfully.

Porta shot up, swallowed the machorka he was chewing the wrong way down and started to cough violently.

'And you tell us only now! To keep back such information is high treason. That's the place for me. I'm the boy for tarts – from fourteen to seventy!'

Pluto wanted to know how Bauer had got his information.

'A medical orderly I know. He serves at the field hospital at Bjel Zerkov. He says it's a first-class stable full of French and German mares.'

'Oh, my God,' interrupted Porta, 'how sweetly that rings. At last something to hear and feel. I'm fed up with that wireless whoring every night at ten when some stupid cow bays out 'Lilli Marlene'. Old Un, get cracking for a bunch of passes.'

The Old Un laughed quietly.

'Don't count on my company. Love on conveyor belts is not my idea of fun.'

'Nobody is forcing you,' said Porta amiably. 'They'll earn enough without your contribution. I'll have one for at least twelve hours.'

'You'll come along,' he said to the Little Legionnaire. Then he suddenly became visibly embarrassed and added: 'Sorry, chum.'

The Little Legionnaire merely laughed.

'I'll come to study. My dream has always been to open a whore-box in Morocco. War experience will count. I've never seen a German brothel. It's bound to be instructive. You don't mind me watching while you work?'

'Not a bit,' answered Porta. 'But you'll have to pay ten per cent of the cost.'

'Any objection if I come?' asked Tiny.

'All right,' Porta and the Little Legionnaire answered grandly.

The Old Un went across to the office to see what he could do.

One hour later we were on our way in a truck. Porta had brought twenty to thirty pornographic magazines which he studied in order to be well prepared.

A field-gendarme with the head-hunter crescent on a chain round his neck stood outside the brothel to show the way. Just inside the entrance sat another field-gendarme to inspect our pay-books. Then we were turned over to a medical sergeant who checked us for venereal disease.

Porta went wild with joy when he was let through.

'Oh, Daddy's going to work. Who knows when we'll get another chance.'

Tiny was radiant. He announced what he was going to try before he was dragged away.

'A mattress-polka and a bullet in the skull, then you'd die a happy man,' he sang.

Porta had two quarts of vodka with him.

'That's for disinfectant,' he said. 'You never know what's been going on before you!'

A soldier was thrown out by the chain-dog who shouted with a schoolmaster's voice after him:

'Disappear, you baby, before I put you in the can. We don't allow children under eighteen in here.'

Comically enough, soldiers under eighteen were not allowed to have anything to do with women, smoke or drink: infringements were heavily punished. But they were allowed to kill or be killed. Mark you, only when it happened in battle against so-called enemies. The Fatherland is often peculiarly fastidious.

Pluto and Tiny stormed in. They brushed away the other soldiers in the waiting-rooms and passages. One artillery sergeant started to grumble. Tiny landed him one on the skull, and the fellow fell to the floor with a grunt.

'Make way for the 27th Murder and Arson Regiment,' shouted Porta. 'Hand over the girls. Let us see the goods!'

A chain-dog bawled:

'Quiet, or you'll be out!'

Tiny gave him a threatening glance. The gendarme wisely drew back from the seven-foot giant.

With a bang the doors to the living-room, or as the chaperones called it the reception-salon, flew open. Here sat a dozen females between twenty and fifty, dressed in the most provoking clothes, from deeply decollette party dresses to transparent pants and brassieres. They were ready to receive the love-starved invasion in its noisy infantry boots.

Porta literally fell into the lap of a black-haired beauty in pale-blue underwear. He forced the vodka bottle between her lips and asked beguilingly:

'Hey, my treasure, shall we shake ourselves warm?'

Two minutes afterwards they had disappeared.

Pluto threw himself enthusiastically at a heavy-weight – she was his ideal, he said.

Tiny was left standing in the middle of the room staring from one girl to another. He could not choose! The result was that there were no girls left. Then he bellowed:

'Thieves, robbers, bastards! Get me one. By Satan I want a bed-artist!'

A chaperone tried to calm the huge bandit. He grabbed the impressive lady and cried:

'Are you a whore? Get a move on, then, Tiny has arrived. This is a pleasure-house, not a mission-house!'

The chaperone shouted for help as Tiny started to tear off her party dress. Another chaperone arrived, but Tiny had gone mad. After half-tearing the dress off the first one, he grabbed one under each arm and made for the door where the others had disappeared. With kicks and cries the two women tried to get away, but they were caught like two harpooned whales.

'Don't try cheating Tiny for what he came for. Have I bought you or not? I only ask!'

He banged up the stairs with the two shouting women.

'Shut up, girls! I only want my rights!'

He kicked open the door of the first room he saw, but Porta was lying there with his black-haired beauty. In the next room Pluto and Stege were acting out an insane play with two loud-voiced girls.

Tiny swore and tried his luck farther down the passage. Every room was engaged! He charged up to the second floor. The first room he burst into was used by a flak-gunner.

'Out of my way, stupid swine,' ordered Tiny. 'A drawing-room soldier like you had better be off when decent people come to town.'

The flak-gunner protested, but Tiny made short work of him. He flung the two kicking girls on to the broad bed, grabbed the gunner and sent him flying out of the door. His girl sat up in bed stark naked, staring at the two chaperones and Tiny who stood menacingly in the middle of the room. Then she curled over backwards with howls of laughter. That a customer had been torn away from her in the middle of love's act was funny enough, but even funnier was the plight of the two chaperones.

'Off with the rags,' neighed Tiny gleefully and peeled off his trousers. He kept on his cap, tunic and boots.

'What are you thinking of?' one of the women began shouting. 'I'll—'

The rest of the sentence disappeared in an angry terror-stricken cry. Tiny had peeled off her dress and slip and grabbed her by the ankle. Her mauve pants flew in an arc over his head. He threw himself at her and held on to the other two with his petrol-reeking iron fists. But love's pleasures relaxed. Tiny's attention and the flak-gunner's girl managed to get away, but not very far before she was caught by a half-naked soldier and borne off in triumph to his room.

On the floor underneath Porta and Pluto enthusiastically changed girls. When they were fed up with that they started playing dice for the girls.

An infernal noise came from the reception-room where the waiting customers were making difficulties because there were only twelve girls for over a hundred soldiers.

Hell was let loose that night. The worst off were the two chaperones subjected to the pleasure-drunk Tiny. He grunted and roared with satisfaction. At length, when he found them a little monotonous, he burst into another room which was being used by an infantry soldier and his two girls. Without explanations he ordered them to change partners. They protested but everything turned out to Tiny's satisfaction.

In between his wild excesses he drank vodka. Porta and Pluto who had heard the noise came to his room with their girls. They competed in insane perversions. Porta's pornographic magazines were left sadly behind.

Porta dressed himself back to front in a black brassiere. Apart from that all he had on were his boots and top-hat.

Tiny, more modest had removed only his trousers. He was dressed in his cap, tunic, belt with pistol and clumsy boots.

Pluto tore around as he was born, apart from the black regimental sweat-rag round his neck.

All the girls were stark naked. A few tried in terror to get away, but Tiny, roaring with laughter, caught them deftly and flung them on the sofa.

Porta found a louse on his red-haired chicken breast. Proudly he displayed it before he generously let it drop on the stomach of a shrieking girl.

Tramping boots thundered up and down the stairs and passages. Steel-helmeted field-gendarmes trooped into the room and, bellowing, ordered us to leave the establishment.

'Do you mean us?' Porta asked good-humouredly.

The head-hunter sergeant who led the other two chain-dogs became red in the face and answered in a voice choking with fury.

'Out! At once, or you'll be charged with indecent behaviour in public buildings!'

Pluto opened the window and relieved himself in a big arch. His big naked bottom smiled at the stiff Prussian field-gendarmes. They took themselves and their duties very seriously.

The sergeant groped for his revolver-holster. As usual it was hung much too far back for him to reach without curling himself round like an acrobat.

The Little Legionnaire popped up behind them and at once grasped the situation. He started intoning:

'Allah-akbar! Vive la legion!'

The next minute he was hanging like a panther round the neck of the field-gendarme, who fell heavily forward, taken completely by surprise.

The other two were overcome, disarmed and sent flying down the stairs.

Porta suggested it would be a good thing to get away. The girls immediately rallied round and helped to bundle the uniforms together.

Porta, Pluto and the Little Legionnaire quickly made their getaway out of the window, and with the help of the girls got across the roofs to disappear among the neighbouring houses. Only Tiny refused to leave the battlefield. He preened himself like Napoleon after a big victory.

'Let the whole Nazi army come,' he cried and spat on the floor. 'I'll deal with the lot! I'm here to have tarts, all I can manage, and I'm having them in a quiet and decent manner!'

Growling happily, he flung himself at one of the girls.

The field-gendarme returned with reinforcements. Five men strong they clattered into the room and tackled Tiny in the broad bed. A fierce fight started and even the girls did not escape unmolested. One got such a big black eye she quite forgot she was a chaperone in the establishment. Getting hold of a chair she swung it into the face of one of the field-gendarmes. He immediately gave up the fight.

With the girls on his side Tiny fought like a grizzly bear. The chain-dogs were flung down the stairs and greeted with jeering bravos from the spectators downstairs.

Tiny now had what was in effect an attack of rabies which came out in a form of persecution-mania. He was convinced that even the naked girls were against him, so he bundled them down the stairs after the field-gendarmes.

Then he started to barricade the door, using the smashed furniture.

An officer from the chain-dogs asked what was going on. One of the naked chaperones sobbed:

'Herr Wachtmeister, this is a disgrace to the establishment. We are respectable ladies, doing our duty for the ultimate victory, and now we are exposed to such treatment!'

The other one, crouching in a coma at the bottom of the stairs, sniffled:

'What will all the others think when this gets around? This immoral evening has shocked me deeply. But my friend who is Stabszahlmeister knows the Führer. I'll see that he complains to him. My membership card is in good order too. I must ask you to deal properly with these fellows, Herr Wachtmeister.'

'Who is up there?' asked the Wachtmeister impatiently and adjusted the chin-strap on his steel-helmet.

'The wild animal from St John's Revelation,' stuttered a very upset girl who sat rocking on the bottom step of the staircase with the remains of a pair of military underpants covering her knees.

'Fetch the brute down,' the Wachtmeister ordered his head-hunters. He stepped aside to get out of their way as they attacked Tiny's fortress.

A sergeant took courage and ordered the door to be broken down. He motioned with his pistol as if prepared to shoot his three colleagues. They heaved at the closed door, but it withstood their first assault.

A savage growling came from Tiny behind the door. One of the field-gendarmes asked:

'Is a human being in there?'

'I don't know,' answered his colleague, 'but I curse the day I joined the police!'

The three strong men then put their shoulders to the door and it collapsed into Tiny's boudoir.

He was over them like a lion. 'What the hell d'you mean by this?' he roared. 'Breaking in without knocking. Attack me when my trousers are down? I'll see you get your desserts, you lousy mongrels!'

There followed horrible bangs and crashes. Animal roars sounded through the whole brothel.

One of the chaperones in despair cried:

'Throw him out of the window! Shoot him. Our reputation! Our reputation!'

In the end Tiny had to give in to superior force, but even when he was unconscious the head-hunters furiously beat him with their truncheons. They chucked him down the stairs. The Wachtmeister gave him an expert kick.

Three weeks passed before we saw Tiny again. Despite numerous beatings he had not given away the names of his companions. They only knew the men came from the 27th (Penal) Panzer Regiment. So the whole regiment was forbidden to visit any field-brothel for six months.

Tiny's sentence was three months mine-detection in no-man's-land. He took part in what we called the 'ascension party' for five days. After that nobody remembered to send him out again. Our battalion commander Colonel Hinka knew better than any court-martial how to tame a wild fellow like Tiny. He also understood the art of evading the clumsy, man-destroying edicts of the higher command.

No. 5 Company taciturnly agreed to make a human being out of the monster that was Tiny. He really was a great big naïve child to whom fickle fate had given great strength in a too large body but had forgotten to add the brain.

11

The soldier in war is like a grain of sand on the beach. The waves wash over it – suck it out – throw it back to suck it out again – it disappears without anyone noticing it or caring about it.

Close Combat in Tanks

It started snowing, a porridgy ice-cold snow. Everything was turned into a bottomless mess.

It was shortly before midnight. We were sitting half-asleep in our tanks. We had not had one moment's peace for five days. Many of the regiment's vehicles lay scattered – burnt out wrecks – across the enormous area where the fighting had taken place. But we kept getting new reserves of men and material in a steady stream so somewhere behind the lines we knew there must be a great concentration of supplies . . .

We are getting unbelievably dirty with gun-powder, mud, oil and slime. Our eyes are red with lack of sleep. We have not seen any water apart from what we collect in muddy ditches. Food supplies have broken down and that bombastic nonsense – the iron-ration – is long since eaten. Porta is famished. The Little Legionnaire several times goes out in search of something to eat, but where we advance seems to be vacuum-cleaned of edibles. The only supplies behind the lines are ammunition, tanks and crews. As The Old Un says:

'They seem to have found out they can earn money by trading the rations of the coolies.'

Now somewhere in the town some distance from where we sit we hear the rattling of tank chains.

'Hope it isn't Ivan,' says Pluto and stretches his neck to look into the rumbling darkness which surrounds us.

Many of the tank crews are getting nervous. All ears strain to identify the goose-flesh pregnant chain-rattling coming from behind the silent buildings.

The engines are revved. The gears growl. The dynamos sing.

Nervousness is spreading. We cannot make out whose tanks they are. Porta who is a specialist in detecting tank noises is hanging half-way out of his driver's hatch in the front of the tank. He listens tensely. Suddenly he pops back and categorically says:

'It's healthier to withdraw with clean noses. They're Ivan's tanks in there, T34s.'

'Not on your nelly,' comes from Pluto. 'It's our Mark VI tank. Sounds like an army of Dutchmen in clogs. Anybody can hear that. You need to gargle those cardboard ears!'

'Why the hell are you so careful then?' snaps Porta with a jeer. 'But we'll soon see, lads.'

He bends back and looks up at me:

'See that you have your pop gun ready!'

'If that's Ivan,' says Tiny, 'call me Adolf. It's either the Mark IV or heavy artillery.'

Colonel Hinka is coming down the long columns of tanks, talking quietly to the company commander.

A little later von Barring reaches our tank and says to The Old Un who is sitting in the turret:

'Unteroffizier Beier, make ready for a reconnaissance patrol. We have to find out who's in front of us. If it's Ivan, hell's breaking loose. He's liable to get behind us, the way we're sitting.'

'Yes, sir, No. 2 Section is ready to patrol.' The Old Un took out his map and went on: 'The section will move—'

Then a few shells come whistling down and burst into a house.

'Ivan – Ivan . . .' the cry goes up.

Everybody is rushing about. Machine-pistol and rifle-shots split the air. Panic spreads. Some jump out of their tanks. The fear of burning to death in a tank is deep-seated in all tank-crews.

A pack of the dreaded T34 tanks is coming down the street rumbling menacingly, spreading fire from all guns. A couple of flame-throwers stick out their blood-red tongues at a flock of panzer grenadiers squeezed up against the walls of a house. At once they are changed into living torches.

Several of our tanks are burning and illuminate the streets with their deep-red blaze. Explosions come from petrol-tanks and ammunition going up. Everywhere is chaos.

Tanks collide in their attempt to escape. Nobody knows who is friend or enemy.

Two Russian tanks smash together with a rain of sparks. They fire simultaneously and in a second are swallowed by flames. The crew of one appears from the turret, but a burst from a machine-gun mows them down. They grill there, hanging half-out of the red-hot hull.

Four 10.5-cm. field-guns start ragged firing directly at the T34s. Red and white balls of fire fly skywards. The Russian tank-guns blaze incessantly. The whole battle is completely without plan or direction. All leadership has ceased.

Several of our tanks firing furiously with all guns swing out and seek desperately for shelter.

Tiny, our loader, is standing with a couple of tank-shells under each arm and bellows:

'Fire, you fool, fire!'

I bid him shut up and take care of his own job.

'Muck-heap,' says Tiny.

Porta sitting at the steering-rods grins.

'You're trembling round the gob, what, lads? Well, that's how it is when you don't believe Porta. Lovely tanks, T34s, eh?'

He backs the tank into a wall which collapses on top of us in a cloud of dust. Quickly he gets the huge tank free, makes full speed ahead and crashes thunderously into a T34.

I just manage to see part of its turret in my periscope before I fire. The fire from the muzzle and the shell-explosion merge at this short distance. The breech shoots back. A hot shell-casing rattles down to the bottom of the tank. Tiny flings high-explosive S-shells into the gun.

The Old Un roars.

'Back! Hell! Porta, you idiot, back! Another one is coming down the street. Turret at eleven. Got it? Fire, for God's sake!'

. . . I stared wildly through the periscope, but could see nothing but a river of tracers rushing through the street.

'You imbecile cow, the turret's at 9, not 11. Turn to 7 minus 36. Got it? Fire, man!'

A shell whistled past the turret. And another. The next moment our 60-ton Tiger tank nearly overturned as Porta backed. Scarcely five inches from our bows a T34 trundled past. It swung round flinging water and mud sky-high, then slid a dozen yards, but Porta was just as quick as the Russian driver. His tank spun two or three times round on its axis with Porta sitting at the huge steering-rods grinning genially.

I pressed the pedal. The turret swung round. The triangles met in the sighting mechanism. A shell sped out, and another. Then it seemed as if the tank capsized. Our ears were ringing and clanging with the din of steel meeting steel.

Pluto was half-way out of his hatch, when it dawned on him that we'd been hit by a T34 at full speed. For a moment the Russian tank rocked in its tracks. Then the engine roared as the driver speeded it up to its full stretch. Like a ram running wild it bashed into our left flank. Our tank rose in a forty-five degree lurch.

Porta was flung on top of Pluto, tearing out all the radio-wires in the fall. I was sent flying and landed in Porta's seat. Luckily I had my steel-helmet on. My head crashed with terrific force against the steering-rods. Only Tiny remained standing as if welded to the tank-floor.

The Old Un hit his head on a steel edge and fell unconscious with blood spurting from a deep wound in the head.

'Bastards, swine, bloody Stalin-droppings!' shouted Tiny out of the hatch which in his fury he had opened.

A couple of stray shells hissed past the turret and he hurriedly banged the hatch to. He shovelled shells out of the lockers till they lay in wild confusion on the deck of the turret. It did not seem to disturb him that the heavy 8-cm. shells time and time again landed on his feet. He slapped oil-saturated rags on The Old Un's head, tore a piece off his shirt to bandage him, and then pushed him into an empty ammunition locker.

'I'm the biggest and strongest here,' roared Tiny. 'I'll take over command!'

He pointed at me:

'And you, you miserable pimp, all you have to do is fire. That's why we were sent to Russia.'

He stumbled over The Old Un's protruding legs. It was a miracle that his head was not shattered as the gun-breech banged back. Speechless he glared at me, then full of rage burst out:

'You little devil, you'll kill your commander! What in flaming hell is the good of firing that pop-gun? I refuse to take command. I won't be shot at!'

Porta and Pluto collapsed with laughter at Tiny's ranting. For a moment we forgot the deadly danger we were in. We were surrounded by confused masses of guns, tanks and infantry. The whole scene was lit by the furious waves of machine-gun bullets. Two 8.8-cm. flak-guns were in position a little way from us. They sent off shell after shell into the darkness. But the muzzle-flashes betrayed them and they were soon ground down by a T34.

. . . This night is an apocalypse when everything is cleansed by the annihilating fire. The cry for medical orderlies from hundreds of wounded German and Russian soldiers is the accompaniment of the death-dance in the inferno of darkness.

The only helpful thing is to press your nose to the dirt and flatten yourself to escape the whistling bullets.

Our tank is hit, and in a second becomes a roaring ocean of fire. Tiny looks like a satyr standing bathed in flames as he throws The Old Un out of the side-hatch before he jumps away himself in a shower of sparks. He rolls on the ground in his oil-saturated uniform to extinguish the leaping flames.

Exhausted we lie, gasping for air, coughing painfully with smoke-filled lungs. Only Porta is indifferent. He lifts up the mangy cat he had adopted and now carries in the breast of his tunic and shouts:

'We got away by the skin of our teeth again, old pussy-lad. Only a few hairs on your backside singed!'

Panic everywhere. Grenadiers, pioneers, tank-gunners, home-guards, infantrymen, artillerymen, officers, NCOs and privates, all in a disorderly mob. Sharp pings from the snipers sound round us. Porta clutches a magnetic fuse. We get hold of some T-mines. Like snakes we crawl towards the huge T34s.

I see Porta jump at one. The fuse is placed where it ought to be. An explosion. Sharp flames lick out of the turret.

Tiny crawls up to another tank. Carefully he places the big T-mine beneath the turret, pulls out the stick and lets himself drop from the bucking tank. A thundering boom, and another T34 is finished. Tiny is going mad.

'I've finished one. Blimey, I've sent a whole tank to the gods.'

That such a clumsy oaf as he is not hit is a miracle, but evidently he is bullet-proof.

I unlock a T-mine, but I can't get it up on the tank crashing by. It explodes a little behind it, and the air pressure sends me several yards along the gutted street.

The roaring steel monsters turn and twist like sledges when they brake. Shell after shell thunders from their guns.

Slowly it dawns on us that these are not just a few stray tanks which have broken through our defences. Fortunately it is only a fraction of their left flank we have contact with. We flatten ourselves against the ground, pretend we are dead. The soil tastes sweet. Our friend affording us shelter! Lovely, dirty churned-up earth! Never have you tasted so delicious, although your porridgy mud and slush penetrate our ears, mouths, noses and eyes.

You blood-saturated lovely earth, you hold us in your embrace and hide us in your bottomless mire. The water running in at our collars feels like a caress from a gentle woman's hand.

The dirt on our equipment and uniforms makes us look like animated clods of mud.

At eight o'clock in the morning all is over. But near the eastern part of Cherkassy town we can still hear heavy firing and the rattling of tank-tracks.

Nobody suggests they might be Mark IVs. Never again will we make that mistake when we listen to that rattling, banging sound.

. . . Many years after the war. I have woken up, wet with sweat, because in my dream I had heard that rattling death's herald of the terrible Russian T34.

Slowly we emerge from the mud. Porta, thank God you're alive! The Old Un? Where's The Old Un? We breathe relief. There he is, still alive. Stege, Bauer, the Little Legionnaire, Möller although always sour, full of pessimism and religious killjoy – all embrace because they are alive. Tiny shouts with joy:

'A few rotten T34s don't blow Tiny's breath away!'

He is kicking at the peeled off tracks of the burned-out wreck of a T34, the one he destroyed with his T-mine.

'Come on, you red devils, and I'll deal with you!' he bellows in the direction of the clanging tracks.

Pluto is sitting in the mud with his legs outstretched. He stares down the shattered street where tanks, guns, cars and trucks have been ground into one charred mass of wreckage by the Russian tank attack.

Colonel Hinka and Captain von Barring are tottering down the street. They sway like two drunkards. Von Barring is bareheaded. Hinka wears a Russian fur-hat. His greatcoat is black with perspiration and charred. He throws a handful of cigarettes at us.

'So, you're still alive,' he says in a tired voice.

Blood drips from a cut in his forehead, and runs down his cheek. He wipes it off with the back of his hand, only to smear his whole face with it. The red blood and the mud give him a grotesque, almost diabolical appearance.

A quarter of an hour later we march away. The regiment has suffered terrible losses. Seven hundred killed, eight hundred and sixty-three wounded. Every tank lost. Other regiments have fared no better.

The fallen lie everywhere. Despite the dirt and mud we can make out different units by the shoulder-tabs. There lie a dozen panzer-jägers, ground to a porridge. The barrel of one gun points straight at heaven like an accusing finger. Shells lie widely scattered.

Across there, by a burnt-out row of houses, stands a whole

battery of 8.8-cm. guns, crushed and flattened by the Russian juggernauts. We stare and stare. It is unbelievable that so many can die in such a short time.

The winter had come in all its horror, with frost and gales that killed many more than the Russian guns.

It made men hard and brutal. Terror started, and terror breeds terror.

We became rabid, blood-thirsty animals. We mocked the dead and shouted jests at the crushed men.

12

Knives, Bayonets and Spades

We are surrounded. We have no tanks. We are again fighting on foot. It snows and snows. The gale races howling over the steppes. Whistles through the thin forests. Puffs the snow into a huge cloud of powder. It puts an icy layer on cannons, machine-guns and small arms. Brings its grim greetings from Siberia.

A man can do sentry-duty for only one quarter of an hour, then he must be relieved or become a corpse. We weep with frost-pain. In our beards hang icicles. Our nostrils freeze up. Every breath is like a stab of a knife. Take a fur glove off, touch a piece of metal without thinking, and the fingers stick making it impossible to withdraw them without tearing off the skin.

Gangrene becomes uncomfortably commonplace. Stinking, rotting limbs are a daily sight. Amputation after amputation takes place in the dirty huts which serve as dressing stations: a little bit of leg, a hand, a large piece of leg, another arm, sometimes all at once, other times piece-meal.

Newsprint has become an expensive black-market commodity. One newspaper fetches fifty cigarettes. It will save you, soldier, from gangrene.

In the corner is stacked a heap of blue-black gangrened amputated limbs. Even when they are deep-frozen and your nostrils are frozen up, you can detect a faint odour.

The field-surgeons operate as best they can. A few Hindenburg-candles are often the only light available at operations.

When one of the wounded dies he is quickly thrown outside. The door opens and shuts quickly to prevent the frost getting in to those who still live.

The regiment lies in reserve at Petrushki. The completely destroyed regiments have been reinforced with new troops. There is a rumour about new forces being parachuted to us; yes, even about troops from special training colleges in Germany. But not one of us old sweats believes it.

It looked so nice and cosy on paper. In the Goebbelsrun UFA magazines we were a fine, big army, well equipped with modern arms and trained troops. The truth was sadly different. Our reserves were poorly trained and had poor weapons. The recruits we received had been taught parade-marching and a fine salute according to the army regulations. Many hours had been wasted teaching them the ranks of officers and NCOs. That was of great importance. After all, what would a Prussian depot be without recruits stiffly saluting the brilliantined chair-borne officers who swaggered at home right up to the bitter defeat of the Third Reich?

Some of these heroes popped up in the prison-camps where they went on playing officers and NCOs. As I write several are strutting about in uniform, crying bombastically about the defence of the Fatherland. It is very comical that we never once saw any of that race at the front, I mean in the front-line where we were able to count the buttons on our enemies' tunics. All our officers belonged to the reserve and were hatched on hurried courses lasting a few weeks.

We were now lying near the little village of Petrushki waiting for new arms and cannon-fodder. The period was shortened by playing pontoon, catching lice, and quarrelling with everybody.

The Old Un was filling his pipe with the ill-smelling machorka. He had a peculiarly soothing way of doing this. It was almost possible to dream yourself back to a fishing-village by the sea on a moonlit night when the light-house flirted with the calm sea.

We started to chat as only men who have gone through serious events together can. We chose our words with care.

Thick volumes might have been written on the thoughts which lay behind The Old Un's slow words:

'Children, children.'

Even the fool Porta with his incessant obscene vocabulary shut up.

After a moment's silence. The Old Un said:

'You'll see, Ivan will throw in the whole of the 42nd Corps here at Cherkassy.' He puffed out a thick cloud of smoke into the room, put his feet in their clumsy boots on the table littered with greasy pots, sketches of the terrain, hand-grenades, a couple of machine-pistols and a half-eaten loaf.

'In my opinion Ivan is very keen on getting his reinforcements together here. His generals are already rubbing their hands together and hoping for another Stalingrad. Mark my words, the whole 4th Army will go to hell in this lousy hole!'

Porta laughed loudly:

'Well, why not? Sooner or later we'll all go to hell and salute the devil in proper army fashion: "Heil Hitler! Red Front!".'

'True, and if a T34 gives you a push in the arse you'll land right in the devil's arms.'

He and Tiny slapped their thighs and laughed.

'Well, maybe we'll have to dig lead and Kolyma before we reach what you call hell,' interrupted Möller.

'Yes,' said Bauer thoughtfully. 'Maybe we'll welcome the padre's hell after Stalin's. Personally I've no wish to be introduced to the country round Kap Deshnev.'

'Nobody's going to ask what you want,' grinned Porta. 'Our colleagues on the other side will serve you with the padre's hell with the help of a shot from a Nagan, then you can start looking round for the other half of your head. Plenty of blood, brains and boneshavings. That's what'll be left. Only your ragged black uniform will show you're a German tank-soldier. Or maybe they'll do it a little slower. Maybe they'll send you to a dirty, cold place behind the Urals, for instance Voenna Plenny, and then after a few years they'll bash your bones to bits with a rifle-butt or a Nagajka. For you it will be all the same. If you're lucky you'll get a bloody great big rock on your head down there in the lead mines. Then it will be curtains, quick and painless.'

The Old Un sucked heavily at his pipe.

'If we get out of this cauldron, a new one will come soon after. And at last, when the whole rotten lot is finished we'll be sent east. It's rotten luck to have been born in filthy Germany just when that paperhanger Adolf decided to imitate Napoleon. If only you could be sure of the people at home.'

Stege laughed in his own inimitable gurgling and infectious way:

'Well, well, one thing is sure enough. Adolf has lost his war. If we could only destroy the red Nazis along with our brown ones it would be the first time a war had ended in a sensible way.'

An orderly interrupted our chattering. The Old Un was to go at once to Captain von Barring.

'I smell a rat, dear friends,' shouted Porta. 'I, Corporal by God's grace in the freezing Nazi army, humbly report that The Old Un is going to Barring to have whispered in his ear that our short rest has come to an end. We're at it again. The 27th Murder and Arson Regiment will again be the lever for the chair-borne strategists. To hell with them!'

Freezing in his thin grey coat. The Old Un stamped through the snow to von Barring's quarters, at the other end of the mile-long village. The gale had increased. It raced whining across the blood-soaked Russian soil. With forty degrees of frost it was sheer hell when the snow whipped into our faces. The cold was worse than anything else, except perhaps the lack of sleep.

Porta was right. After an hour The Old Un returned and announced that our company with the 3rd and 8th were to form a fighting-group and to make a wedge for the regiment in an attempt to break out of the cauldron. Our task was to push towards Terascha and there force an opening. The enemy had dug themselves in in strong-built snow positions. As soon as we reached the village the reinforced No. 5 Company were to clear the enemy forces out quickly. We were to have no help from the artillery. Our only chance lay in a surprise attack by night. Lastly, there was a great shortage of small arms ammunition. The element of surprise was to compensate for our weakness against an enemy with far more troops.

Colonel Hinka came across and took farewell of us. He shook hands with the three young company commanders. They were not ordinary 'gold-pheasants' but officers who had risen from the ranks.

We had no illusions. We knew our job. It was the only thing they had taught us, but they had taught us that well.

'You know what it's all about,' Hinka addressed us. 'I rely on you and on Captain von Barring, your leader. To make the surprise complete attack will be with fixed bayonets without a single shot fired! Good luck!'

We went off filled with apprehension. We did not know that the action was to last for days. Neither did we know that only a few from the three companies would get away alive.

At dusk von Barring attacked the southern end of the village Terascha. The night was moonless and icy cold, and the snow glistened whitely. Yet because of its very severity the weather was our ally.

All day we had had a camouflaged reconnaissance patrol lying just in front of the Russian positions. Its leader had reported only a weak concentration in front of us.

Our task was to act as a storming party on the right flank of the fighting-group. Just before we crawled out, Stege whispered:

'One consolation is that we're on our way to liberty.'

Nobody answered. Where was liberty really to be found? On both sides the barbed wire and the oppression was the same.

Every man clung to his weapons and stared into the threatening night. Behind and on both flanks we saw the tracer ammunition. It told us clearly the cauldron was getting smaller all the time. Soon Ivan would have us. The attack was only a last desperate attempt to break out of the trap.

The orders were whispered carefully from man to man.

'Fixed bayonets! Advance!'

The companies moved slowly. They were almost invisible in their long snow-shirts.

The enemy discovered us when we were a few yards in front of their positions, but it was too late. We stormed forward and after a short, furious scrap the position was rolled up. The other sections from the regiment coming in at our heels finished off the last Russians.

We went forward despite a hefty curtain of fire from the woods west of Selische. We ran forward completely hypnotized by our luck. Porta sprayed the next positions at point-blank range with his hissing flame-thrower. This time too our luck held and we had hardly any casualties.

When, breathless and exhausted, we reached the Sukhiny-Shenderovka road in the middle of the night, we could clearly hear engines in the direction of Sukhiny. Whispered commands ordered us to shelter by the road-side.

Every man dug feverishly to make a hole in the snow. We lay behind a couple of anti-tank guns and listened as the engine-noises grew even louder.

We had not long to wait. An enormous column of huge lorries appeared on the snow-packed road. They trundled past in bottom gear with roaring engines.

We crouched in silence waiting, savage animals poised to kill coldly and pitilessly what travelled on the road. They were men whose mothers and fathers would be crushed by grief when the message reached them: 'Your son has fallen in the fight against the Nazi bandits, defending our beloved proletarian country . . .'

Was it much different on our side? Did we not have fathers and mothers at home dreading what was in effect the same message: 'Fallen for the Führer and the Fatherland . . .' As if a ridiculous phrase could ever console a mother who still looked on her son as a boy whatever uniform he wore. How many mothers were to receive this message before we had finished fighting at Cherkassy? Yet the blood-bath there was mentioned in the newspapers and army reports only as 'a local defensive action in the area near Cherkassy.'

We judged the trucks to be a unit on its way to the point

where we had broken through. Evidently the Russians were ignorant of what had happened.

The surprise was complete when we opened up with all our automatic weapons at ten yards distance. The first few trucks heeled over and burst into flames. Some of the crews managed to get off a few bursts from their machine-pistols before they were wiped out by the concentrated fire from our weapons.

Three trucks loaded with mortars were destroyed in a few seconds. One single crew managed to let off all their rounds but the shells exploded far behind us without doing any damage. A couple of survivors who tried to run off were mowed down by our machine-guns.

At three o'clock in the morning our fighting group again attacked, this time at Novo-Buda. We had not yet heard a single shot from the village.

Captain von Barring decided we should attack in a scissor-like formation from the north and south, again with the hellish fixed bayonets only.

We advanced like ghosts on the first sentries at the entrance to the village. I saw Porta and the Little Legionnaire cut the throat of one of the sentries. Tiny and Bauer saw to another. The sentries did not even sigh as their throats were cut from ear to ear. One of them kicked a little in the snow and the blood spurted out of him like a fountain.

We crawled forward like snakes, as soundless and just as dangerous. In one of the first houses we broke into, led by Porta, we found some sleeping Russians lying on the clay-trampled floor, rolled in their long coats. We were at them like lightning. Breathing heavily, we stabbed furiously with our long combat-knives. My knife sank deeply into the chest of one. He gave a short cry. In desperation I stamped on his white upturned face with its panic-stricken eyes. Time and time again I kicked with my hob-nailed boots what had once been a face.

The others were equally busy destroying lives. Porta ran his knife into the crutch of a giant of a sergeant who had almost managed to get up.

The smell from hot blood and steaming intestines was fearful. I vomited violently and helplessly. One of our men started to weep and was on the point of screaming when Porta's fist knocked him cold. A mad-man's cry at this point would have been fatal.

We stormed out and went down the long street. From several huts we heard muted sounds of combat and groans from the men fighting their evil battle. It became one of the biggest mass murders we committed.

Tiny had got hold of a Cossack sabre. I saw him behead a Russian lieutenant in one swipe. I jumped as the head rolled over the floor and hit the Little Legionnaire who kicked it.

We ran from cottage to cottage, and when we came out no living thing remained inside.

At six o'clock the village was in our hands. With feverish haste we started to dig ourselves into the snow. As soon as the Russians realized what had happened they would try to recapture the village. Not one would escape with his life if he fell into Russian hands. One rule only reigned here. The same old high-falutin one which Hitler and Goebbels had repeatedly shouted: 'Fight to the last man and bullet!'

The only difference was that we cared nothing for the Fatherland or Hitler's war-aims. We fought only for our lives. Maybe we had fought only a local defensive battle.

The whole of our group had settled down in a big communal hollow in the snow. The Old Un lay on his back, his head supported by his gas-mask container and his body wrapped in a Russian greatcoat. Porta squatted like a Muslim on his haunches on top of a couple of packs of loot. He held a half-full bottle of vodka, licked his lips and belched loudly.

'Blimey, what a war we're in. First our enemies run away and now the devil's after us. And to think the doctor has forbidden me to run. I'll confide in you, my friends. I've got a weak heart and have to avoid any kind of exertion. The doctor who told me this was not, worse luck, a party-member, that's why I was sent to prison and put into this stinking Nazi army. Of course now nobody asks about my heart or if I can stand this round trip of Russia. If you don't run Ivan'll prick your bottom with his bayonet, and judging from reports that hurts. If only we could come to terms with the beasts over there, we could slow up a bit, I believe Stalin must have promised them mashed potatoes with diced pork and lumps of butter when they get to Kurfürstendamm: Something must be dangling in front of their conks to make them run so fast.'

He swallowed a mighty draught from his bottle and his excessively developed Adam's apple jumped wildly up and down. It always looked as if the apple got drunk before he did.

He handed the bottle to the Little Legionnaire and said to The Old Un:

'As you're a "silver-pheasant" sergeant you'll have to wait till other decent people have had a draught of the ripe grape from the gentleman's vineyard – so light your pipe!'

He tore the bottle from the Little Legionnaire:

'You bloody desert-rat,' he screamed with feigned fury. 'Is that how you drink? By God, you must have been born a camel!'

He had another drink himself before he passed the bottle to the next man. This was repeated each time, and when the bottle reached The Old Un it was almost empty. He swore!

Porta lifted one eybrow, pressed his monocle in and adjusted his top-hat:

'Dear Old Un, don't forget, you "silver-pheasant", that here you're with noble men of good education. Watch your tongue. Stand to attention, you lousy sergeant! Can't you see by God's grace a Corporal? Mind your behaviour, you bloody cow. But we'll learn you, you poor old sod.'

He eased up his seat and emitted one of his usual rude noises.

'It's a wonder all your patter doesn't choke you, you red-haired ape!' said The Old Un. 'But you'll forget your talk when Ivan comes. Something tells me our colleagues are mad to get at us.'

'You're remarkably sharp,' said Porta with a contemptuous grin. 'I thought Ivan was going to build a triumphant arch to let us parade through with nice goose-steps. Then may-be when we get out of the cauldron a couple of comrade commissars from the Red Army Guards'll be waiting with ice-cream and strawberries. Is that what you imagine, you dope? Don't you know yet that we're at war to make Lebensraum? That means hordes on both sides killed to make a little elbow-room, and on the last day of the scrapping all you gold-and-silver-pheasants will cop it, so that you won't take up all the nice new Lebensraum. That's nice, eh, you Iron Cross hunter?'

He pulled open one of the packs, searched for another bottle of vodka, and cracked the bottle-neck.

'Let's stoke up a little. It's very draughty in this modern block. It's a good thing the stove's portable, so that we're not dependant on the landlord's stoking.'

The vodka warmed us wonderfully. We laughed and shouted loudly enough for the Russians to hear us.

Colonel Köhler jumped down into our hollow followed by Lieutenant Harder. Köhler shook off some loose snow and started to roll a cigarette from machorka and newspaper.

'Grrr, but it's cold . . .'

He handed the finished cigarette to Porta and started another.

Porta grinned straight at him.

'I don't normally accept anything from officers.'

Köhler went on rolling and said calmly;

'Put a sock in it, you red-haired ape.'

'They've no manners all these big shots,' Porta continued, adding a rude gesture for the officer-class. 'I think I'll send in my resignation and go home. Since my recruit course acquaintances have become sabre-swallowers, it's impossible here. There are no educated men left.'

Paying no attention to the clowning Porta, who was becoming drunk, Köhler said:

'The Russians are gathering their forces to attack at the northern outskirts of the forest. I think you'll be bang in the middle when our colleagues arrive, so keep watch!'

Porta, who had got hold of a portable radio, found a German station broadcasting light music. A man with a caressing syrupy voice bleated a pop hit.

For a second we looked at each other, then burst out laughing.

'That's good,' shouted Köhler between the gusts. 'Here we are waiting to be slaughtered in a snow-hollow at forty degrees of frost and at home they are singing about the great love, girls in enticing dresses and golden moons. Throw that damned thing away!'

Someone turned the wireless off. Porta brought out his flute and began to play something we all understood:

'Es geht alles vorüber
Es geht alles vorbei.
Den Schnapps vom Dezember
Kriegen wir im Mai.
Zuerst fällt der Führer
Und dann die Partei.'

They joined in the singing from the other hollows, and the last two lines were shouted out across the snow-desert with such fervour that it would have warmed the hearts of the gentlemen mentioned.

13

They were wounded. You need imagination to get the meaning of that. To go through hospital to understand it.

Head-wounds, lunacy, spine-casualties, paralysis, double amputations, four-limb amputations with only a trunk and head left – eyes shot out – blindness – lung wounds – kidney cases – stomach wounds – bone fractures where splinters worked out every day – nose and mouth wounds – joint wounds that would cause a man to drag his body round all his life and to let his feet fall down the stairs: bump-bump-bump, tempting children to cat-call after him: 'hoppity-hop!'

Cherkassy

The moon is cold. It hangs slantingly in the sky and drips frost on trees and bushes. The frost crackles. Even we who have been drinking vodka are freezing. We have been watching for twelve hours in our snow-hollow dugouts of the frozen soil. You cannot resign yourself to the coldness of Russia. It makes fur-hats stiff. The flaps slap you in the face. It is already swollen with chilblains and sores. Your lips too are swollen and bursting with purple scabs. When in addition you suffer hunger in its most brutal form, life becomes intolerable.

The omnipotent German military leadership in its bombastic manner has forgotten to make provision against the worst of our enemies – nature.

More soldiers died of frost and illness than by enemy fire. The Russians' best ally was nature, the Russian winter. Only the Siberian troops could withstand it. It seemed as if the winter made these small soldiers with their high cheek-bones more content and full of fight.

Porta first spotted a movement in the landscape in front of us. He nudged me and pointed silently. We peered anxiously into the darkness.

Then they were over us. The snow-shirted forms sprang out of the void and landed like wolves in our positions. I fired furiously with my machine-pistol hugged to my hip at everything that moved. The hollow teemed with fur-hatted, slant-eyed Siberian riflemen. In close combat they used the dreaded 'kandra', the Siberian knife which is sharpened on both sides and looks like a long butchers' knife, only it is stronger. A single stroke from a kandra will part the head from the body of a winter-clad soldier.

Back to back we use our guns as truncheons. Ivan is so near that we have no time to re-load.

After a few minutes we jump out of the hollow and run back to the huts. We throw ourselves into cover behind the walls. Manage to re-load our guns. Gunfire rattles. Tracer ammunition scores the air which is full of yelling and screaming.

It is difficult to distinguish friend from foe in the snow-filled night. You fire by instinct. We hit our own men. This also happens to the Russians.

Our fighting-group is completely scattered. Any communication between the units has ceased.

Captain von Barring and Lieutenant Harder get some of the men from our company together. Using the huts and the snowdrifts as cover we run back through the village. On the way one of the seventeen-year-old recruits is hit by an explosive shell. He screams loudly and accusingly, spins like a top and then doubles up.

A heavy machine-gun starts hammering us from the left. The bullets land by the dead recruit, whirling up the snow.

We reach a hut, tear inside and fling ourselves breathlessly on the floor. But we have hardly entered before the door is flung open and a couple of small fur-hatted men from far-off Siberia stand silhouetted in the doorway. A burst of fire sweeps through the hut and reverberates painfully in our ear-drums.

We are eighteen men lying like dead, we almost believe ourselves dead. Then it is all over. The two Russians run for it hounded by the hollow detonations of the hand-grenades.

They speed into the night. We try to catch them, but we stumble and sink in the deep snow. We feel as if we are choking.

A moment afterwards we lie breathing hard and, with a sickening pressure behind our eyeballs, we disappear in a huge snowdrift where we lie in our white snow-shirts indistinguishable from the landscape. The whole thing is a ghastly nightmare.

Then two human forms spring up right in front of us. Quick as lightning. The Old Un and the Little Legionnaire bring their storm-rifles to the shoulder and the shots rain at the two shapeless forms. Hell breaks loose. Tracer ammunition rains from everywhere.

I see Tiny throwing hand-grenades like a man bewitched. I lose my senses and press myself desperately down. I scream. My nails come off as I scratch at the hard-frozen snow. The Old Un pulls me along when we run back.

Everywhere is confusion. I have been running alongside a Russian; he is as scared as we are. Fortunately I spot him first. I swing my machine-pistol into his face with a killing blow. Heavily he falls to the ground.

The Old Un shouts and points forward. Paralysed we stop and stare at the grey sky; then we see some screaming things each belching a hundred-yard tongue of flame. They are coming fast at the village we have regained.

As if obeying orders both the Russians and ourselves run for cover. What are coming through the air cannot distinguish between friend and foe: they are 'Stalin organs'. And to make matters really hot the Germans start firing rockets at the doomed village.

It is like an earthquake every time a salvo lands. It all lasts only a few minutes. Houses are scattered like antheaps. Nothing is left of the village.

The flames are sucking out both us and the few surviving villagers. The cold no longer tortures us; now it is the searing-hot ocean of fire. The animals go crazy with pain and terror. Children with bare feet run lost among wildly sobbing women. The firing from the automatic weapons barks and yammers in this inferno. People fall cursing in their death-agony.

God, Devil, Dictator, Fatherland – anybody or anything they blame for their torment.

How this heap of rubble called Novo-Buda came into our possession nobody in the fighting-group could have said.

The report sent to headquarters was short and laconic:

'Nova-Buda cleared of enemy forces. We hold the position. Waiting for orders.

Fighting-group Barring'

From the Russian side we heard engine noises from heavy vehicles all day long. Porta was sure Ivan was preparing to liquidate us. If that was so we had no chance. We were going to be flattened.

Porta and a radio man called Rudi Schutz, another corporal, had managed to contact the Russians' wave-length.

Now we were listening to their conversations. On the other side they seemed to have the same trouble with their staff-officers as we with ours. Threats and more threats underlined every order going out to the men in the front-line.

We were lying in our snow-hollows, having seen to it that our automatic weapons had a wide field of fire. There were forty-seven degrees of frost and snow had started to fall again.

Oddly, Ivan tried only a few aimless attacks that day which we easily countered. But we did not doubt that something was in store for us.

Hour after hour we listened to Schutz's radio until early in the morning we heard an enemy commander ask:

'Can we take N?'

'Certainly, colonel, but it's going to be difficult. We think there are strong enemy forces in N.'

After a few minutes' silence we again heard the voice of the enemy commander:

'The battalions have re-established contact. You attack at 13.45.'

'Yes, understood. We attack at 13.45.'

This conversation was the beginning of a battle which was to be unbelievably tough and bitter.

It started dead on time. The Russians attacked with stop-watch precision. They arrived with T34 and T60 tanks. Slowly they ploughed their way through the yards-deep snow. They provided good hunting for us.

For some reason the Russian infantry held back to see what result the tank-attack would have, but during the night they managed to work their way to the middle of the village. We withdrew with heavy losses, leaving our wounded be-hind.

Again we dug ourselves into the snow and defended our-selves against the furiously attacking Russians.

For hours the battle raged. Then the Russians withdrew. During the morning we had received some so-called support-units as replacements. But they were of little use. They could never be grouped together on their own without stiffening. As soon as they saw a Russian they fled.

In the evening we again listened to the Russians on the radio. One desperate battalion commander was reporting back:

'The infantry can't move. Our tanks are stuck. The crews are killed or taken prisoner. The trucks are in snow-drifts which are getting bigger and bigger. We are being strongly attacked from Sukhiny with mortar shells and artillery. Despite strong engine noise from north-west we have not observed tanks or storm-artillery. Believe Fritz will attack from south to east at Sukhiny. They have great forces concentrated there. Four officers have been executed for cowardice.'

After a few minutes' silence the enemy commander burst out in oaths and curses and threatened his listener with degradation, court-martial and rehabilitation-camps. Then he came to the point:

'You must take N. At any price. Try from two sides. Attack in an hour, at precisely 15.00 hours. Don't dare to be beaten. You'll get no artillery support. That'll help you to surprise the German dogs. Finished.'

At once we reported, and von Barring made the fighting-group's automatic weapons ready to give our colleagues a warm welcome.

The minutes dragged by. It seemed as if each minute lasted an hour. Only Porta was calm. He lay on his back chewing dry bread he had found in a Russian pack. The flame-thrower lay across his belly ready to use.

He had a peculiar love for this deadly weapon. He really was a sharp-shooter. Who had made him a flame-thrower nobody knew. We, the older ones, had a faint recollection that it was just after the 27th Regiment had fraternized with the Russians at Stalino. It was so long ago that everybody had given up asking the red-haired Berliner where he got his flame-thrower from, or how he still managed to retain his sniper's rifle with its telescopic sights.

When the Russians attacked it was with such verve and fury that they nearly took our breath away. Still, we managed to hang on to that damned village. How, nobody knows. But hold on we did and avoided court-martial just as our colleagues on the other side did too as we heard some hours later over their radio:

'How did you get on at N?'

'We were forced back after the last attack. Our riflemen are exhausted. Colonel Bleze has shot himself.'

'Good! That was his duty. We have no use for inefficient infantry commanders. Major Krashennikov from the 3rd Battalion will take over the regiment.'

After a short silence the enemy commander asked:

'How did the Germans behave?'

'They are very rude. Some of them shout cat-calls at us. They must have some Frenchmen there, and perhaps Mohammedans.'

'What are they shouting?'

'*"Je m'enfous"* and *"Allah-akbar"*.'

'We'll see to them, but get a few prisoners so that we can find out if they have any French volunteers. If they have they'll all be liquidated. We are going to bash them with artillery for two hours and then you'll follow – N's got to be liquidated!'

The Russians hammered loose at us all day. The bombardment shrieked, banged and thundered. All through the night 'The Lame Duck' (the old Russian one-engined bomber U^2) discharged its deadly cargo over us. One night they threw eight hundred bombs on an area of five hundred square yards.

The only place we could dig in was where a house had burned down and thawed out the deep frozen snow. There we sat and watched the ever-increasing fire from mortars, cannon and big rocket-batteries (Stalin organs). They went on hammering at us for days and all the while gathering reinforcements. You would have thought we were an army corps and not a paltry infantry fighting-group consisting of a few exhausted companies at times insane with fright at the countless enemy attacks.

We have placed our wounded in a bunker we dug under a burnt-out peasant's hut. Here they lie with stiff-frozen bloody bandages round their wounded limbs.

To enter one of these dug-outs is like visiting an inferno.

Round about, behind the inadequate cover available, the machine-gunners are ready to load their guns. The lightly wounded serve as helpers.

We chew frozen potatoes to ward off the nagging hunger. We are all dressed in thin greatcoats with dirty snow-shirts on top. Like Porta and Tiny, some have been lucky enough to get hold of a few Russian furhats and felt-boots, but others, who have only the idiotic jack-boots and a scarf wound round their heads, have no protection against the icy frost.

On January 26th communications with the rear, including the telephone-link, are broken. We are wholly on our own now.

Lieutenant Köhler who is sitting in our dug-out with Captain von Barring and Lieutenant Harder makes an indifferent gesture with his hand to express his resignation when the news is brought to us.

'Well, the division has written us off. Funny thought. There's only one way out left now, lads. That's forward, and there sits Ivan.'

Porta, the Little Legionnaire and Pluto are lying in a dug-out right out in front. They have made themselves a veritable fort. Despite lack of ammunition they have got hold of a box of Russian hand grenades. Porta and the Little Legionnaire have each got a sniper's rifle, and Pluto has a Russian light machine-gun which he has adjusted to fire single shots. All three are extremely good marksmen. From time to time they laugh loudly, and we hear Pluto applaud.

'Fine, Old Porta. There goes another bastard!'

'Allah is wise. He leads my hand and eye,' says the Little Legionnaire in all seriousness as he presses the trigger and hits a Russian who rolls over immediately.

'It's a bloody shame we can't get some party-lads from our own rat's nest,' says Pluto and raises the rifle quickly. A shot cracks out. 'Ha, you Stalin-pig, got a headache now, eh?' He lowers the rifle and goes on: 'If we only send Reds to hell the Devil's going to be wild with our threesome's monotonous deliveries.'

'How many have you got?' asks Porta. 'I've got thirty-seven marked up.'

Pluto looks at a piece of paper kept under a hand-grenade which acts as a paperweight. He makes a cross every time he is certain of a kill, and a dash when he is unsure.

'Twenty-seven hell-travellers, nine hospital-cases.'

'You'll be reported to the RSPCA if you keep on wounding those Red beasts,' suggested the Little Legionnaire. 'All mine are guaranteed to hell. I have forty-two and seven were officers. The red enamelled star they carry in their fur-hats are wonderful bloody targets. When they get to that big pine there we've got just a quarter of a yard to pick them off.'

'Good work, boys,' beamed Porta. 'We've beaten our own record to-day with nineteen corpses. That's grand. Hey, you foot-rag acrobat!' he shouted and pressed the trigger. 'We've got twenty now. Did you see how his whole head jumped off? I bet he was never so well shaved!'

The Little Legionnaire cupped his hands round his mouth and cried to the Russians:

'*Monte la-dessus, tu verra Montmarte!*' He pressed the trigger.

The answer came in the form of a shower of bullets from a heavy machine-gun. All three of them jumped down into the dug-out. There they lay laughing.

'Let's sing to them,' suggested Pluto.

They sang loudly:

'Wir haben noch nicht
Wir haben noch nicht
Wir haben noch nicht
Die schnauze voll!'

Lieutenant Harder and The Old Un swore at them for this wanton firing which would only irritate the Russians and tempt them to desperate actions. But as Porta had been a soldier while Lieutenant Harder was still at school, he did not take any notice of Harder. The Old Un he did not even acknowledge as a superior. Without taking his eyes off the Russian positions he answered with a sneer:

'Listen you two Iron Cross apprentices, Pluto, the desert-rat and I are fully occupied with our own total war. Since we saw that crucifixion Ivan had fixed up for two gunners from the 104ths the other day, we've decided to cut the nails of those Red bastards across there. And because we love shooting, you'd better take care we don't bang a filed bullet into your gob to stop your nagging. Heil Hitler, kiss my bottom, my dove! You might as well beat it: the three of us'll see to Ivan!'

He raised his rifle with its telescopic sights, pressed the trigger and announced with a grin to his two chums:

'Another disciple from the Siberian transport-company has bought his ticket to hell!'

We had placed a machine-gun post in a particularly well-built bunker on the southern flank of the ruined village. It had successfully warded off several attacks, but early one morning the Russians broke in and took everybody manning the post prisoner except the section-leader an old NCO. They killed him. We saw them make him kneel in the snow and then hold a pistol to his neck. He twisted as he was shot, then rolled like a rubber ball down the hill, the snow in a cloud round him.

The eight prisoners were marched off escorted by two Reds who walked behind with their machine-pistols. They had to pass an open stretch where we, from Porta's dug-out, had a good field of fire.

Porta and his two confreres lay with their weapons ready. Three shots rang out like one and found their targets, namely the heads of the two Russians walking behind the prisoners.

Our eight captured comrades understood immediately that their chance had come. As if at a word of command they all sought cover near our positions.

Pluto jumped up and stormed across to the bunker with his machine-gun at hip-level. He kicked the door open and stood splay-legged in the opening while he sprayed the tightly-packed Russians with bullets. His giant's body swayed with the recoil of his weapon. He screamed with laughter as he poured bullets into the shouting Russians. They went down like grain before a well-oiled harvester.

Two Russians staggered out with their hands up. Pluto took one step back, kicked them down in the snow and emptied his magazine into their trembling bodies.

'Come out, any of you that's alive,' he shouted. 'Then I'll show you how to treat prisoners in your own style!'

We heard a faint whimpering from the bunker, but no one appeared. He grabbed two hand-grenades from his belt and threw them into the bunker. They exploded with hollow thunder in the corpse-heap.

During one of the last attacks Köhler got an eye poked out. He was half-crazy with pain but despite von Barring's attempts to persuade him to go to the sick-bunker, he insisted on staying with his company. He was afraid, no doubt, of being held with the wounded in the bunker.

We all had a terror of falling into Russian hands. We had seen too many of the atrocities committed on the prisoners taken by the Russians to have any illusions about getting off lightly.

Neck-shots, crucifixions, crushed arms and legs, decapitated limbs, castrations, poked-out eyes, empty cartridge-cases hammered into the forehead. These were common, unless you were destined to travel to Siberia where an even worse fate awaited you.

On the morning of February 27th Ivan started a peculiarly dispersed shooting. First it was directed at us, next at No. 8 Company with Lieutenant Wenck, then at No. 3 Company, Lieutenant Köhler's company.

It lasted about an hour. Then there was silence, an uncomfortable silence which you normally experience only in mountains and large forests. It seemed to want to crush us.

Nervously we kept an eye on the Russians, but everything stayed threateningly quiet.

Three or four hours of this deadly silence passed.

Von Barring scanned the landscape through his field-glasses, then whispered to The Old Un who lay beside him:

'Something bad's going to happen. This silence is almost sucking the marrow out of my spine.'

Suddenly he screamed some orders. Then we saw. On No. 3 Company's position the Russians were teeming.

'Köhler, fire, for God's sake, Köhler, fire, fire,' von Barring shouted.

Lost, we started at them. They were everywhere in that sector.

Some hand-grenades exploded and broke the deep silence. We groaned with frustration at having to witness this debacle without being able to assist.

The Russians had fallen silently on the rear of No. 3 Company from the left. A couple of men defended themselves desperately with spades and rifle-butts until they were knifed down.

Pluto and Tiny wanted to rush across, but von Barring held them back while he sobbed:

'It's too late. We can't help them.'

We saw two Russians hang on to Köhler while a third bashed his head with his machine-pistol.

It lasted no more than ten minutes. Then No. 3 Company did not exist.

The Russians whirled round at us, but thanks to Porta and the Little Legionnaire, we succeeded in warding them off.

Without waiting for von Barring's orders they raced for the bunkers on the outskirts of the village. Von Barring quickly gathered his group and with The Old Un at his side stormed along to the bunkers at the top of the hill. Our only chance was to get there before Ivan's infantry.

'Shout for all you're worth,' roared von Barring. 'Shout like hell, shout like savages!'

Screaming and shouting we raced forward. For a moment the Russians stopped in astonishment.

Tiny and Möller blazed away furiously during the race to the bunkers.

Then Porta's flame-thrower started belching fire. The Little Legionnaire stood crouched, firing furiously at the wave of Russians.

A giant of a captain who towered over his men roared inspiring words from the works of Ilya Ehrenburg. We could hear him plainly as he swung his machine-pistol like a truncheon above his head.

Pluto kneeled and aimed carefully. The captain, brought to a standstill, let go of his machine-gun, felt his head with both hands, twisted half-round, and fell slowly to his knees.

'Now that brute can carry on his Ehrenburg shit in hell,' said Pluto with a deadly smile.

Lieutenant Harder had an attack of fanaticism. He tore forward gripping his storm-carbine and shrieking crazily.

Bauer howled like a dog. He carried his light machine-gun over his shoulder and in each fist a hand-grenade. He flung one at a group of Russians storming the hill. As it exploded an arm was hurled through the air. Next moment Bauer's second grenade burst among the wounded Russians.

Gasping for breath we reached the top of the hill just in front of the Reds. Three machine-guns spat noisily at them.

The attack faltered. The Russians started to retreat, but lunacy had taken possession of us. We jumped up and followed von Barring's command:

'Fighting-group, fixed bayonets, follow me!'

We charged shrieking at the Russians who were now panic-stricken. They threw their weapons away and ran.

A couple of officers stood, shouted, and tried to stop them. I reached one and thrust my bayonet into his back. I just managed to get my bayonet out before he went down with a single scream. I fired at his head and stormed on, yelling.

The Russian positions were quickly rolled up with hand-grenade and bayonet. Von Barring ordered us to withdraw. We brought away some mortars and boxes of shells.

Porta managed to get hold of some American tinned goods from an officer's bunker. Then he exploded it with a Russian mine.

When we arrived back at our own positions two sections were formed from the men from different units of the fighting group. These two now replaced the butchered No. 3 Company, Lieutenant Harder took command.

Silence surrounded us. Darkness fell. Softly the snow drifted down. The Old Un wrapped his coat tighter around him, but the cold still penetrated. Porta lay on his back caressing his cat and talking nonsense to it.

'What do you think, old boy? Should we give in our membership-cards to this society for the maintenance of the war we've landed in? That's the only right thing to do, isn't it?'

Möller laughed mirthlessly.

'It would be nice if we could!'

'Only one reason for giving up membership will be accepted: a bullet in the head,' said von Barring.

'Maybe that applies to Möller,' interrupted Tiny. 'But not to me. I don't dream about being shot by these snotty-nosed steppe-bandits across there!' He half stood up and shouted at Ivan: 'Hey, Tovarich! Hey Russki, Russki!'

A voice from the Russian positions answered:

'What d'you want, you German swine? Come here and we'll castrate you, Fascist-dog!'

'Come here, you scabby gipsy, and I'll boil you in your own grease!' Tiny roared back.

For half an hour the most obscene swear words were exchanged, then Captain von Barring stopped it.

Silence fell over the white wastes. Then all at once to the right of our position: Roosh-roosh-roosh!

Astonished we ducked down into our holes.

'What on earth was that?' asked Bauer staring at the wood where the shells had fallen with ear-splitting explosions.

'Mine-throwers or nebelwerfers,' grinned Porta. 'And they are ours.'

Another explosion was heard and the fire-radiant projectiles flew through the night.

'I'm willing to bet Ivan's getting what he asked for now,' laughed Stege. 'If only we had a couple of "stovepipes" like that here we'd be able to stop their bragging.'

They went on firing the big stuff all night long and kept us awake. To fall asleep was deadly dangerous.

At dawn Porta and the Little Legionnaire started to throw hand-grenades at something we could not see. A couple of machine-guns sited in front of the big bunker barked in prolonged bursts.

We peeped nervously at them.

'Is Ivan breaking through again?' asked The Old Un without getting an answer.

We took a firmer grip on our weapons. We were ready to receive Ivan again, but in the next quarter of an hour the shooting died away.

The Old Un cupped his hands and roared across to Porta:

'What's going on across on your side?'

Porta answered:

'Will you promise not to tell anyone?'

'Yes,' replied the astonished Old Un.

'We're having a war, my pet,' was Porta's answer.

The regiment again got in touch with us. They ordered us to hold our positions. They promised to help us soon, but three days passed before the promised help came. Then it arrived with a vengeance.

On March 8th in the morning we heard the Russians for the last time on our radio.

'How's N getting on?' the enemy commander asked his regimental commander.

'We can't raise our heads. We're under heavy machine-gun fire. They have also got heavy mortars and this morning they've got support from the air.'

'Where have you got to?'

'The regiment is lying just west of N. Our last tanks were stuck in the snow and the crews were liquidated by Fritz.'

'That's impossible. A ruined village with a few hundred Germans still holding out! Attack at once with all you've got, and I mean all. Take care that N is occupied. When you've taken N, bring the enemy commander to me. You're responsible with your life for the fall of N with this attack. Finished.'

It was the fifty-third attack staged by the Russians during our stay in Novo-Buda. When it started, to our great joy we got support from a whole squadron of fighter-planes. They came roaring along very low with the guns spraying the Russians, who were panic-stricken at the flying death which screamed over them.

The fighting-group attacked at once. With hoarse cries we stormed into the enemy. Deep in their positions we fought like lunatics. We were drunk with blood-lust. We stabbed and cut on all sides while the planes rained bombs on the enemy artillery in the rear.

Porta let his huge flame-thrower spray into the bunkers to burn every living soul lurking there.

The hand-grenades burst with their hollow detonations. The crisp rattling of the storm-carbines mingled with the harsh barking of the machine-guns.

A party of Russians began to charge us from the left only suddenly to wheel round and disappear.

We could hear the voice of a commissar whipping up the men with slogans from the inevitable Ilya Ehrenburg. A little later they came out, but the attack was half-hearted. We had no difficulty in warding it off with concentrated machine-gun fire.

Stege jumped with a roar at a Russian commissar. Evidently he wanted him alive. But the Red was a small quick fellow and dodged deftly in order to avoid capture. The chase went on a little longer, then Stege stopped running, raised his machine-pistol and shot off the commissar's head: he fell instantly as if his legs had been shot off as well. Stege hurried to him and tore off the gold-encircled red star on the commissar's arm. Like a Red Indian who has taken a scalp, he gaily brought the emblem to von Barring.

Lieutenant Harder's machine-pistol had jammed while he was fighting a whole pack of Russians. One shot him in the neck and a thick gush of blood pumped out of his throat. With difficulty we got him bandaged and transported to the bunker where our many wounded lay.

During the night we were withdrawn and put in a quieter sector to rest.

14

Such were their conversations. Such their big and small sorrows. Such their comradeship. The bushman's fright. The Stone Age man's brutality.

They were not like that in the beginning, but time, tyrants and war made them what they were.

Rest Camp

'You see, lads,' announced Porta, 'once again our guild has escaped from the Russian riflemen. D'you know what it proves?'

Tiny looked at him and blinked his eyes.

'It proves we are lucky.'

'God help you, you tart-expert, what else would we expect from you!'

'Are you being fresh?' said Tiny belligerently.

'Yes,' said Porta, 'which is more than you are.' He pointed at him with an accusing finger and said: 'Lie down, big mongrel, or Ivan'll come and bite you. No, it proves I'm a smart and courageous warrior. You lousy Prussian dogs! Can you honestly believe you could cope with Ivan without my help? No, you stinking skunks, this war is finished when I, Joseph Porta, Corporal by God's grace, am pensioned off – or is it post-war credits they call it?'

'If it's post-war credits,' laughed The Old Un, 'I've waited nearly ten years, but don't be scared, Porta, you'll get neither pension nor post-war credits when this war is over. At best you'll get a kick out of the army or into that concentration camp they fetched you out of to fight nicely and properly for Herr Hitler.'

'God knows what'll happen when the war is over,' said Bauer dreamily. 'I wonder if it'll be possible to be normal again?'

'Not for you,' screamed Porta. 'You've never been normal

since you were an infant at the breast and drank all that Nazi science from your National-Socialist mother. It's different for me. I'm Red, and I've got papers to prove it. Got 'em before you were able to pick your nose. Not one of you dim-wits has ever been normal. You are and will remain cattle. Your horizon stops at becoming section-leaders in this path-finder society. Do yourselves and the world the service of falling for our beloved Adolf-Führer and the Third Reich in a nice regulation manner. Then the victors will be free of the duty of punishing you.'

'Oh, put a sock in it, you clown,' stuttered Pluto. 'I'm an honest, dutiful thief from Hamburg, and that's just as good as a Red from Berlin. But I'm only asking—'

'You heard!' shouted Tiny, 'I'm also a nice and polite thief who'll be sorely needed when the war is over.'

Pluto leant forward on his straw bed, which stank of damp and mildew, while he bobbed his coal-black naked toes up and down in front of Porta's nose.

'You see, Porta, you don't understand what community-spirit is. But I'll give you a little instruction, you red-haired bull. When this thirty years' war has ended in a nice and decent way with the whole caboose in ruins to the satisfaction of the generals, the community will have to be rebuilt. That means they'll throw out the gang now sitting in the chair and biting his nails, for a new gang just like the one we have now. They'll take their seats on the big sofa, put up new wall-paper to suit their tastes and make a few new laws. New laws – that's all poppy-cock. It'll be all the old paragraphs, and it'll stay just the same. Keeping inside the law, they'll keep on stealing from those who are fools enough to let it happen. So they'll need the help of smart chaps like Tiny and me while Red dogs like you'll be in the back-seat.'

'Shut up, you big bastard,' cried Porta and threw an empty shell-case at Pluto who quickly ducked.

Tiny asked naïvely:

'Is it true that you've done some crooked business, Porta?'

'No, by God, I haven't.'

'Oh, yes, you have,' chuckled Pluto, 'you stole from the

goods you brought from the shops when you were an errand-boy in Bornholmerstrasse.'

'Put your vodka-stinking snout away,' threatened Porta, 'or else the Children's Society will come and fetch you away! What is this peculiar stink in here?'

Stege was completely convulsed with laughter at Porta's wonderful appearance. He sat there with his monocle and top-hat sniffing the air.

Porta grabbed his cat by the neck-fur and dipping its nose in a saucerful of vodka said menacingly:

'Drink, you red cat-pig!'

Pluto bobbed his black toes a little nearer and whispered sweetly:

'Put your conk a little nearer to the ground and you'll soon discover the source of this wonderful fragrance!'

Porta stared down and discovered Pluto's toes.

'Shame, filthy fellow! Aren't you going to wash your toes? They're still full of muck from Caucasia and of old dry goat's shit into the bargain.'

Tiny leaned forward the better to study Pluto's feet.

'Well, they're a bit dusty. You can't visit your tart like that.'

'Well, what's the matter with that? Maybe I keep my boots on, like you,' said Pluto.

The Old Un sucked furiously at his pipe.

'Well, well, children. You always talk about the end of the war, and who can blame you? To-day I'll bet the whole world talks of nothing else. The children say they'll have new clothes. Where they haven't felt the hammering of war people say: "When the war's over we'll see all the places where battles raged and air-raids happened!" Others say: "When the war's over rationing will end!" The front-soldier just says: "When the war's over we're going home to eat ourselves silly and sleep!"'

'Yes, and make revolution,' said Porta, grinning and pushing his top-hat a little forward.

'By God, yes, and first and foremost whoring,' burst out Tiny radiantly.

'Didn't you get enough the last time you embraced a tart?' asked the Little Legionnaire.

'Enough? Why ask? Tiny never gets enough. I could keep twenty well-stocked harems fully occupied!'

'Well, if you fancy you're so good at it,' said the Little Legionnaire, 'I'll give you a life-membership card for all the Moroccan brothels I intend to open once the war's over.'

Porta screwed his monocle into his eye and leaning forward to the Little Legionnaire said:

'Tell me, desert-wanderer, is a Moroccan bird all that good?'

Before the Little Legionnaire was able to answer The Old Un broke in:

'I wish you'd shut up for a few minutes, Porta!'

Porta put his hand to his lips and shushed at The Old Un.

'One question at a time, dear friend. Well, desert-wanderer, are those Moroccan parcels good?'

The Little Legionnaire laughed quietly.

'Yes, you can lose all reason when they wiggle their bottoms.'

'That sounds good,' said Porta. 'Get me the timetable for the trains leaving for Morocco.'

Tiny started howling with laughter.

'Me too. Those Morocco tarts'll make me sign on for seven years with the Legion.'

'Oh shut up, can't you!' The Old Un said with real determination.

'Is that an order, dear Old Un?' asked Porta. 'Since you're a sergeant why can't you say in a nice and military fashion: 'I order Obergefreiter Joseph Porta to shut his mouth!'

'By God then, it's an order! Shut up, will you!'

'Now, don't get fresh, you Unteroffizier-crap. When you speak to me you're kindly asked to do so in the regulation army manner addressing me in third person. Full stop.'

'All right. I, Unteroffizier Willy Beier, 27th (Penal) Panzer Regiment order Obergefreiter Joseph Porta to shut up!'

'And I, Obergefreiter by God's grace in the Nazi army, Joseph Porta, who's beaten the world record in obstacle-racing, am completely indifferent to the Herr Unteroffizier's orders. Amen.'

'What did you want to tell us, Old Un?' asked Stege.

'Oh, about our eternal natterings about the end of the war. First, it'll be a long time yet. Second, I doubt very much if any of us'll live to see it. Shouldn't we try to live together without always speaking of the future? It's only got horrible things in store for us. We'll have to learn to understand that the only thing which matters to us is the present and that all we possess is a noisy loneliness where important and less important things have no value. We curse the Nazis and we curse the Communists: the snow, the frost, the gales; the summer with its intolerable dust and heat and mosquitoes. We swear at the mud in the spring and autumn; we are furious when Christmas comes because we're here. We damn the "lame ducks" when they drop their bombs over us. How many oaths and damnations haven't we blown off at the Russians? Children, children, we're once and for all at war and we'll have to put up with it. I don't think one of us'll get home now. The 27th Regiment was grey and unknown when the war started. It'll burn to grey ash before it's over. Just think of all those in the 27th who've disappeared. At Stalingrad 5,000 went to hell. At Kubaner bridge-head another 3,500. At Kertsch 2,800. Here in Cherkassy we've already lost at least 2,500. In '41 in the Mediterranean 4,000 were lost. Then add every small battle and scrap we've taken part in. What's the cost in dead? Do you really believe we'll get away with it? We've got to live, live all the time, every minute. To have taken part in the swine-war to surpass all swine-wars is also living. To sit in the doctor's surgery after a spell in hospital and to be declared fit for war is also living; to curl up in a heap of straw after having eaten your fill of stolen grub is also living. Yes, even cleaning your rifle is an enjoyable life. It should be done with slow movements without thinking of why you do it or of how many hours you've wasted doing it. Everything has beauty in nature, and as we are nature's beings we have to search unceasingly to find what is beautiful in it or else we'll crack up.'

A violent sobbing shook him. He fell forward on the table shaken by an almost paralysing weeping.

We were completely taken aback at his reaction to his own, and to us his extraordinary, speech.

'What the hell's the matter with you?' burst out Porta.

Stege stood up and went across to the sobbing Old Un and patted his back.

'Take it easy, Old Un. It had to come, even to you. Pull yourself together, old friend. It'll sort itself out.'

The Old Un straightened himself slowly, stroked both his hands over his face and said quietly:

'Sorry, it's my nerves. I try to forget there's something called Berlin where the bombs fall every night and where a woman lives who's the mother of my children. But it didn't come off.'

He banged both his fists down with such violence that the old table creaked, and cried out, completely uncontrolled:

'To hell with it all. I'll run away. I'll spit at their court-martial and damned head hunters. I'll manage. I don't want to die here in Russia for the lies of Hitler and Goebbels!'

He cried wildly and violently, but later calmed down.

We sat quietly, each absorbed in his own thoughts. This at least we had learned: to sit quietly with our thoughts and each other without filling the empty space with obscenities at the wrong moment.

It is cold. We freeze, despite the heat from the big stove in the hut, but not bodily; only in our souls. We can kill and kill willingly. What have they made of us?

Now even the calmest of us has broken down weeping because he thinks too deeply about his wife and children in bomb-ridden Berlin.

We drink noisily. Not that we shout and clown. We drink deeply of the vodka and the grain-liquor. The bottle is passed round. We drink as long as we can without taking the bottle from our mouths and we are masters at it.

Then we are quiet again while watching another man who is carefully binding his dirty feet in foot-rags; or we catch lice which we throw in the Hindenburg candle where they explode.

We talk with slow, low voices as if we are afraid someone is listening. We quarrel too. We rage at each other, shout the most terrible things, swear and threaten while hugging our combat-knives or machine-pistols as if we were about to murder our best friends.

But just as fast and violently as it starts it dies down.

Outside in the darkness a flaming, roaring explosion sounds. Instinctively Stege ducks his head. Pluto laughs loudly:

'Can't you learn not to put your skull down when you hear a few bangs?'

'Some people never can and I belong to them,' says Stege. 'Perhaps you're used to the idea of getting a bullet in your skull one fine day?'

'They'll miss, my treasure!' replied Pluto with conviction. Pulling out a bullet from his pocket, he held it between two fingers above his head for us to see. 'This funny thing was fired at your father by a fellow in France. If I had stayed put where I was lying and I was lying bloody comfortably, this would have hit me smack between the eyes; but I stood up and bang the thing got me in the hind-leg. That was my death bullet, but it gave me a miss. So you see I'm going to get away with it.'

Outside, the impact of the huge shells shook the ground again.

'It's starting again,' said The Old Un.

'Well, we haven't got to wait long now before we're playing fire-brigade for the division again,' Möller observed.

'This waiting drives me mad!' burst out Bauer. 'You wait and wait and wait!'

It is really quite comical how much time a soldier wastes just waiting. In the depot you wait to be sent to the front. At the front you wait for the softening-up firing to stop so that you can attack, or you wait to get into battle.

When you are wounded you wait to be operated on. You wait for the healing of the body's wounds, for the health of your soul is passed forever. We await death with patience. We await the peace with time to watch the birds migrate and the children at play without thinking that we have no time.

Even if we are a noisy community in a big war, we ourselves remain a small and sometimes gay community: we are only eleven friends or you might say: eleven brothers with different parents, our bond of union being that we are each condemned to death. We are really moody. One minute we are up in the clouds, the next down in the dumps. Our wishes for the future are peculiar. As Stege once said:

'I long for the day when I can scratch a pig's ear without my mouth watering at the thought of how such a noble animal tastes when cooked with windfall apples.'

Many of our conversations were about women, not only those we met in brothels, or the too-willing Russian girls or the nurses and telephone girls who served us behind the lines, but the unobtainable ideal girls who to us were incomprehensible but fragrant, reminding us of living spring flowers. Women who gave us a friendly smile and nothing more, or comforted us with words and perhaps a single caress which meant so much – these were the girls we dreamt of marrying.

The Old Un was quite different from us. As just now when he had wept. It often happened when he got letters from home. It was really The Old Un who led the company even if Captain von Barring was the company commander. The Old Un decided most things for us. His word was law. What The Old Un said was sense. The Old Un was our father. When something serious happened we sought comfort and advice from him. He brooded with his half-shut blue eyes, and sucked heavily on his antique pipe before he answered. If it was especially difficult, he would take the pipe out of his mouth, dry it carefully and then answer. If we were on exhausting route marches The Old Un always decided when it was time for a rest. Von Barring always asked his advice. The Old Un saw to it that our newly-appointed section-leaders and tank-commanders were experienced NCOs. It didn't matter if someone from the officer colleges wanted front-line experience. The inexperienced meant death and mutilation to our tight-knit body of friends. They did no regulation training with us. The war and the front-line saw to that. When The Old Un said a man was good then he was good.

When The Old Un and Porta took a man to the medical sergeant you could bank on it that someone next day would get orders to see the doctor and that man would go to hospital with a temperature. How it was managed nobody asked. The whole regiment knew that Porta was a law unto himself. Nobody believed he was honour personified or even a street boy with a newcleansed soul, but no bishop could have found any basic fault in him if he had analysed the particular soul that was Porta's.

As he sits, grossly dirty, with his top-hat and monocle, drinking and belching, he radiates the exact opposite of reliability. He is a soldier, a vagabond, a perfectly trained killer who without winking pushes his long combat-knife into the guts of his enemy, afterwards drying off the blood on his sleeve with a grin. With deliberation he files his bullets down to dum-dum shape, hoping they are destined for a hated officer such as Captain Meier. He coolly kills for a piece of bread. In addition, he would, without a single qualm, send a whole bunkerful of people sky-high if he had orders to do so.

Who has made him into this human savage? His mother? His friends? His school? No. Totalitarian government, the barracks mixing-machine, the military fanatics with their bloated ideas of fighting and Fatherland. Porta has learned the slogan that was dinned into his head as well as ours. 'You may do as you like, but never be caught. If you are you've had it. You must be tough and cynical, or else you will be trampled to death. There are thousands behind you ready to crush you if you become soft. There is only one way to get through: Be tough and brutal. If you give in to humanitarian ideas you are finished.'

Thus was Porta moulded. It is not the Nazi Prussian military creed only. It exists everywhere where totalitarianism reigns.

Get in behind the barrack-gates, use your eyes and you will grow pale with shame. Try for once to study the military disciples objectively. Imagine them with their unnatural broom-stick bodies, their comical chest-swellings, their staccato speech, lipless faces with a couple of stupid reptilian eyes. Imagine this bunch dressed in striped prison-uniforms being inspected by a psychiatrist. What label would the unwilling scientist have to hang on most of these sinister apprentices to the military trade? I know because I have spent many years among men who passed their apprenticeship.

15

They had crushed all that was human in us. We knew only retaliation with the murderous weapons they had pressed into our hands.

Our knowledge of anatomy was worthy of a doctor. Blinded, we knew where a shot or a knife would cause the maximum pain.

Satan sat behind a stone and laughed.

The Sneaking Death

Our wounded had been flown out. Lieutenant Harder and all the others were now lying in hospital miles away from the white Russian hell.

Again we were made a fighting-group. Lieutenant Harder was replaced by a Lieutenant Weber. He led No. 5 Company and Captain von Barring commanded the fighting-group.

It was self-evident that the fighting-group led in any attack. Weighed down by weapons and ammunition we were now edging along to the attacking point.

'Ascension – to – heaven – detail as usual,' Pluto growled.

'You mean hell-travel-detail,' mocked Porta. 'Not one of you clots will go to heaven!'

The Little Legionnaire asked:

'Will you, then?'

'Yes, any objections, you unhappy desert nomad?' Porta said, and crossing himself he merged into the darkness: 'Amen, in my name!'

Tiny guffawed.

Lieutenant Weber came running along the column and whispered exasperatedly:

'Shut up laughing. You'd think you wanted the Russians on top of you.'

'Oh dear, no, we're afraid of them,' came from the darkness.

Lieutenant Weber cried hoarsely:

'Who was that?'

'Saint Peter and the Holy Trinity,' came the answer.

Several of the men started laughing, everybody except Lieutenant Weber who had not recognized Porta's voice.

The Lieutenant became angry and forgot to be quiet:

'Step forward, you smart Alec,' he cried. His voice shook with rage.

'No, I daren't, I'll be spanked,' Porta's voice came from the dark.

'Stop!' raged Lieutenant Weber.

'Yes, I agree with you too,' conceded Porta.

The lieutenant rushed into the column and grabbed the first man he could lay his hands on as he hissed:

'Who dares to make fun of an officer? I order you to give me his name or the whole company will suffer. I know how to tame you, you swine!'

A growl was the only answer. From the darkness threats were issued:

'Have you heard, lads, that somebody here wants a grenade on his head?'

'You'll have to use another tone here, sabre-swallower. We're not used to your kind!' (that was Tiny's voice).

'Swinish slum-droppings!' Weber shouted and ran forward to Captain von Barring. We heard him complaining and shouting about mutiny and courts-martial.

Von Barring received him coldly.

'Stop this nonsense. We've other things to consider here than depot "bull".'

Snow crunched under our boots. Frost was the herald of the dark velvet night. When one brushed against a tree-branch the disturbed snow fell like a shower of needles.

Our orders were to penetrate the Russian positions in a silent attack. No firing except in extreme emergency for self-defence.

Porta pulled out his combat-knife, kissed it, and grinning said:

'You'll soon be back at work, my pet. You'll be licking Russian stomachs and picking out Adam's apples just as the girls at the factory meant you to do when they made you.'

The Little Legionnaire and Tiny preferred spades, which they weighed testingly in their fists. In such ways each one prepared for what he was picked to do.

'Allah-Akbar,' whispered the Little Legionnaire and disappeared.

We slid forward without a sound, just as the Finns had taught us at the training course. We were masters at employing our close combat weapons. But so were our colleagues on the other side, particularly the Siberian skirmishers. And they loved this form of warfare.

We reached Komarovka without firing a shot. Several of us were smothered in blood and, as the blood quickly froze, our clothes were soon as hard as boards.

Porta had his combat-knife broken in a fight with a Russian. Stuck between two ribs it was not to be prised loose, so he acquired a Siberian knife which he used with marvellous dexterity. He had tied on his top-hat with a cord under the chin. It was spattered with blood.

Just outside Komarovka we had to destroy a 15-cm. field battery, but here they were fully awake. Before we reached it the shells rained over us and exploded in fire and thunder in the middle of No. 7 Company which had been detailed to help us.

Limbs and bodies whirled through the air. Screaming ferociously, we stormed forward at the brave but desperate artillerymen. Some tried to run away when most of the battery was destroyed but well-aimed bursts from our machine-guns and machine-pistols dealt expertly with them.

The few who gave themselves up we shot. It was impossible to look after prisoners. Both sides shot prisoners. Who started it nobody knows . . .

The first time I saw it happen was in 1941 when I myself was taken prisoner. A few miles behind the front-line I witnessed how NKVD riflemen got rid of a whole heap of German officers and SS men. Later I saw it happen on our side several times.

There were many different reasons why prisoners were shot. For instance if we fought behind the enemy lines it was impossible to take along prisoners. Worse was when we found our friends tortured to death. That gave rise to revenge murders. I have seen rows of Russian prisoners mown down by machine-guns – not to mention the countless times men were shot 'trying to escape'.

The fighting-group stayed in position to let the regiment catch up. We immediately dug ourselves into the snow. Porta announced in his own kind of broadcast what he would eat when he got out of the battle area:

'First I'm going to steal some potatoes and a lorry-load of pork from some idiot who's been stupid enough to hide it until my grand progress brings me to his house. Of these heavenly articles I'm going to make mashed potatoes with small pork-dice.'

'Do you use dripping in your potato-mash or do you chop parsley into it?' Tiny wanted to know.

'Dripping is best. Greenery is very nice, but it slides down quicker with dripping. That means you can fill yourself quickly, shit it out, and start all over again.'

'I never thought of that,' Tiny said quite seriously. 'Thanks for the tip!'

'My God, eating!' groaned the Little Legionnaire. 'Wish we had something to stuff ourselves with right up to the gullet.'

'Well, we haven't got much time to talk about grub. We must think seriously about what we're up to here,' Porta went on. 'This war is no picnic. We've got to starve and at the same time keep shitting our guts out. You get tired of a war like this. It reminds me of an obstacle race at the training battalion where you take turns at pricking each bastard's neck with a bayonet when he won't run fast enough – all designed to give everyone a complete understanding of how serious war is. Hell, if it wasn't serious they'd never have mentioned war in the Bible.'

'God in heaven, help us,' said Tiny and peeped across at the Russians. 'If only we had a baton like that Israelite field-marshal had at the Red Sea crossing. That would have been a miracle weapon to make Stalin's eyes pop!'

'Did he really get across with the whole division?' asked Pluto doubtingly.

'He did,' answered Porta, 'and when that Egyptian Stalin came running behind, the old field-marshal flipped his stick out and all Pharaoh's horse-drawn T34s landed at the bottom of the Red Sea.'

'By God, how Ivan would gape if Porta had a stick like that next time we get to the sea!'

'The next time you see the sea it'll be the Atlantic,' laughed The Old Un, 'and with the speed we're going it won't be too long.'

'Look out,' cried Möller and raised his stormcarbine.

Porta sent a burst from his machine-gun at a body of Russians who had hidden just in front of our position and were now trying to get back to their own line. They did not succeed. They were literally chopped to bits by Porta's precision-firing.

Lieutenant Weber came running, swearing at us. He lectured The Old Un who was No. 2 Platoon commander.

'What are you thinking of, Sergeant? Why don't you stop your men firing? Ivan's all around us and is just waiting for a chance to lay us flat. How can you, a senior NCO let things like this happen when you've got the strictest orders not to fire. If it happens again you'll lose your stripes, Sergeant. I tell you when we're out of this you'll have me to deal with!'

'Yes, Herr Oberleutnant,' was The Old Un's short answer.

A short giggle from Porta and Pluto made Weber whip round.

'Who's got the cheek to laugh at me – a German officer!' he shouted hysterically.

'Ivan!' It came from the dark night.

'Step forward that man! Nobody dares play with me,' bleated the agitated Oberleutnant Weber.

The Ordnance Officer, Lieutenant Bender, came silently up and cut Weber short by saying:

'The orders are complete silence.'

Weber turned round and glared at the little ordnance officer.

'Are you teaching me orders, Lieutenant?'

'Out here the officers usually address each other in the second person,' announced Bender quietly.

'We'll see about that, "Herr Leutnant"! There are still a few decent officers in the Germany army and we wish to maintain proper discipline and respect for all superior ranks.'

'Let's forget it till we're out of this battle,' said Bender with a smile.

Porta's voice rang out loudly and clearly in the darkness:

'Discussion in the officers' mess at Cherkassy. Temporary picnic spot for the Nazi army. Heil! Kiss me on my bare . . .'

Weber nearly had a fit. He screamed again about a court-martial for all of us when we got out.

Porta cackled mockingly in the dark.

'Oh, my pink one, fancy educated people believing in miracles. Do you hear, lads? "When we get out"!'

'Why not a quick little duel with flick-knives, Herr Oberleutnant,' guffawed Tiny who lay in the same hollow as Porta and the Little Legionnaire. 'We'll cut your matrimonial prospects out of you!'

Weber lost all vestige of sanity.

'This is mutiny! Mutiny, you swine! You threaten my life!' He waved his machine-pistol in the air and had difficulty in breathing. 'This company is not worthy of the German Führer's uniform. I'll see to it that all this gets straight to Adolf Hitler, our godly German Führer.'

The whole of No. 5 Company laughed uproariously and Porta bawled:

'We'll throw away Adolf's rags with pleasure here and now, but they're a bit threadbare!'

'Half of mine aren't Adolf's, they're Ivan's,' cried Tiny.

'You are my witness,' shouted Oberleutnant Weber to Lieutenant Bender.

'Of what?' Bender asked astonished.

'You heard what this man said, and the threats and insults this rabble have uttered against a National Socialist German officer.'

'I don't know what you're talking about, Herr Oberleutnant. You must be shell-shocked. Captain von Barring will be very surprised to hear your judgment, not to speak of Herr Oberstleutnant Hinka. He always reckons No. 5 Company to be the best of all the eight companies in the regiment.'

Indifferently Bender slung his machine-pistol over his shoulder and left Oberleutnant Weber raging and frothing.

The advance to Podapinsky during the next few days was a real nightmare. Again and again a man would throw himself down in the snow and refuse to go on. Only rifle butts and brutal kicks managed to drive exhausted soldiers forward.

The Russian troops we encountered were fanatics. They fought as we had never seen them fight before, wildly and bravely. Even small isolated groups went on to the last man. At night they attacked in small groups and we suffered constant losses among our sentries. From our prisoners we learned that our opponents were the 32nd Siberian Rifle Division from Vladivostock, supported by units from the 82nd Soviet Infantry Division and reinforced by two panzer brigades.

We received help against these two *élite* units from our 72nd Infantry Division, but felt the whole time that the Russians were about to snap the pincers behind us.

They caught two NCOs from No. 3 Company and the next morning we heard them screaming. It gave us gooseflesh. Drawn-out and gurgling, their cries echoed across the snow-hell.

We could hardly believe our eyes when our colleagues on the other side put up two crosses on which the two NCOs were crucified. Each had a piece of barbed wire wrapped round his head like a crown of thorns. When they fainted the Russians stabbed their feet with bayonets till they started to scream again.

In the end when we were unable to stand their screaming any longer Porta and the Little Legionnaire crawled out to a shell-hole and shot the two crucified men dead.

The Russians on discovering what had happened roared

with rage and battered us with mortar-shells. It cost us eight fallen.

At Podapinsky our foes succeeded in taking an entire section from No. 7 Company. The captured men roared and screamed during the treatment our colleagues gave them. A commissar shouted at us through his megaphone:

'Soldiers of the 27th Panzer Regiment, we're going to show you what we do to people who don't volunteer to put down their arms and come across to us, the Soviet-Russian workers and peasant army.'

An inarticulate roar from a human being in intolerable pain and need swelled across to us. Then it died down slowly.

The commissar continued:

'Did you hear it? Don't you think Gefreiter Holger cried nicely? Now you'll hear Gefreiter Paul Buncke cry just as nicely as we take away some of his body adornments. Listen, soldiers, of the 27th!'

Again we heard those terrible screams and choked roars. This time they lasted a quarter of an hour.

'My God, what on earth can they be doing to them?' whispered The Old Un with tears in his eyes.

'Just wait, you Communist swine,' hissed Tiny. 'I'll make you scream. You poisoned bastards, you'll soon discover Tiny from Bremen is on a visit to your bloody country!'

The voice of the commissar started again. He was laughing as he shouted:

'He was a tough fellow that Paul Buncke, but even he couldn't stand having an empty cartridge case knocked into his kneecap. More amusements are on the way! We'll now see if Feldwebel Kurt Meincke is equally tough as he's a unit leader and has got close-combat gongs plus an iron cross of the first-class. He's bound to be a very fine Hitler soldier. We thought we might cut his navel out, but first soften him up by cutting his toes off with the barbed-wire cutters. Listen now, lads!'

Again came the inarticulate roars, but this time they were a little easier to bear, only eight minutes according to Pluto's stop watch.

Porta was white as a sheet.

'I'm going across. Who's coming?'

The whole of No. 5 Company wanted to go with him but he shook his head and without a word pointed out twenty-five men for his use. They consisted of the whole of our group and the larger part of No. 2 Platoon, all old experienced patrol and close-combat men.

In a fever we made ourselves ready. We got hold of some T- and S-mines and made several satanic explosives. In addition we had Porta's flame-thrower and three more.

As Porta prepared his flame-thrower he said icily:

'Remember now, we want some officers and the commissar, all unharmed. We'll butcher the rest of the gang.'

Lieutenant Weber opened his mouth to say something, but a glance at the killer-party made him stop. His face was chalk-white and he shook like an aspen.

Our path lay through a peaceful-looking wood, behind the Russian positions. We sneaked along through bushes and undergrowth.

Tiny and the Little Legionnaire kept close to Porta. The Old Un never said a word. His face had turned to stone. We all had one thought: revenge at all costs. We were far from normal. We were people sunk to the level of savage animals in primeval times and we could sniff our prey.

'Quickly, take cover,' ordered Porta suddenly.

We pressed ourselves into the snow and followed Porta's actions. He lay still behind a tree and stared through his binoculars.

Scarcely 200 yards in front of us sat two Soviet soldiers on a fallen tree-trunk. They were sentries judging by the rifles which lay supported by the tree.

Porta and Tiny crawled up to the two unsuspecting men from the side.

Breathless, we watched them as they crept nearer their quarry. One of the Russians suddenly straightened up and stared into the wood.

Without a sound Porta and Tiny sank into the snow. The Little Legionnaire gripped his LMG tighter and his eye travelled along its sighting-line. Both the Russians would have been shot the minute they spotted us. But to our relief the one put down his rifle again, took out a piece of bread from his pocket, and started to eat it.

The other filled his pipe and said something to his friend. Both laughed softly and contentedly.

Porta and Tiny crawled nearer, yard by yard. With an enormous leap they fell on the Russians. The one with the pipe fell forward, his head split by Porta's entrenching-tool. The other had his throat cut while Tiny held him in his bear-like grip.

Indifferently they threw the corpses aside. One still clutched his uneaten bread.

Tiny collected the fallen pipe and put it in the pocket of his snow-shirt.

The Old Un consulted the compass and the map.

'We must go farther south or else we'll get too far behind the main front-line.'

Porta hurried on. He had the flame-thrower on his back again. He waved us on impatiently.

'Now remember, we must get a couple of their bosses alive,' he grinned and patted his long combat-knife.

'Allah is good,' whispered the Little Legionnaire. 'To-night many will leave this vale of sorrow helped on their way by my little knife. I'll get an honoured place in Allah's garden when I go!' He put his combat-knife lovingly to his lips.

Then the silence was broken by a couple of drawn-out explosions. A carpet of fire rolled over the sky. It looked like a glowing blind being pulled up.

Startled and frightened we pressed ourselves flat to the snow. Four more explosions, then silence.

'Katjuscha,' whispered The Old Un, 'they must be quite near.'

Soundlessly and carefully we crawled on. Through a gap in the trees we saw a battery of the feared Russian 30-cm. rocket-thrower M13, called 'Katjuscha'.

Without a word our party fanned out ready to destroy the battery.

Four huge Otto-Diesel trucks stood unmanned 200 yards away on the forest road. Bauer quickly went ahead and placed a sticky-bomb in each engine so that the vehicles would blow up when the fuses detonated.

'They must feel bloody safe here without a single sentry to guard the trucks,' said Stege.

'Quiet,' The Old Un whispered sharply.

The Russian artillery men were busy loading the twelve barrels of each gun. It takes fifteen minutes to load a rocket-thrower like that even when you are well trained.

The Old Un pointed out each rocket-thrower crew to the separate parties detailed to eliminate them. It was essential for each of our four parties to attack at once and to reach its target at the same time.

Just as we were about to rush at them a light shone from a bunker between the trees where someone opened a door, and a voice gave some orders. Then the door was shut again.

'Porta and Tiny take care of that bunker,' ordered The Old Un. 'But no shooting, or else we're sold.'

We pulled out our knives and entrenching-tools and went forward as one man. Only one of the rocket-crews had time to defend itself.

The whole thing took only a few minutes and not a single shot was fired. The Russians lay in their blood-stained snow.

We sat down sweating after the short but violent battle. Möller, visibly shaken, sat rocking while he mumbled a prayer.

Porta looked at him:

'What are you mumbling about, brother?'

Möller started and looked around nervously before he whispered in a stutter: 'I prayed to Him who reigns over us all.'

'Hm, I'm sure that'll help. Why not ask Him to stop the war?'

'Stop blaspheming the only beauty that remains,' said the fanatical Möller. The anger in the glance he gave Porta was clear for all to read.

'And if I don't stop, what'll happen?' said Porta, silkily threatening.

'You're too damned sure of yourself,' raged Möller, 'but there's a limit to what you can get away with, and if you blaspheme God you'll have me to reckon with.'

Porta half stood up and threatened Möller.

'Now listen, holy-man, take care we don't have an extra casualty on this picnic.'

The Old Un interfered in his calm way which always brought us to our senses.

'Porta, leave the holy-man alone. He's not doing any harm.'

Porta nodded haughtily and spat over the head of Möller.

'All right, holy-man, what The Old Un says goes. But for your own sake, don't come too near Joseph Porta. And tell your God to keep his distance too.'

Just before we reached the first of the Russian positions we found the body of a German NCO with his hands cut off and a piece of barbed wire stuck up his rectum. Both his eyes had been cut out.

'The bloody swine!' burst out the Little Legionnaire. 'They're even surpassing the Riffs and that's saying plenty. Let me get my hands on the bastards.'

Our skins crept at the thought of falling into Ivan's hands and giving him a chance at us . . .

We were lying in some undergrowth waiting for Porta and Little Legionnaire who had crept forward to find out where we had best attack.

Half an hour went before they came back. They had done their work well. Porta maintained it would be child's play to roll up the positions.

With a cigarette dangling in his mouth he whispered his plan of attack. He made a sketch in the snow of the whole sector and explained where all the sentries were posted.

'Here on the left, when we go down in the trench, is a company bunker or some such thing. At least four officers are inside. Let's try and get 'em alive. A few hundred yards further down is a sharp bend and here's a telephone bunker. I wouldn't be surprised if the commissar isn't sitting there.'

'It would have been nice if you knew for sure,' interrupted The Old Un.

Porta completely forgot to be quiet and cried out:

'You're a smart fellow. Should I have gone down, knocked on the door and asked: "Pardon me, Ivan, are you a commissar? If so we're going to take you prisoner!" '

'Shut up, Porta, I didn't mean it literally.'

A little later we were on our way. We all wore Russian fur-hats which we had taken from the dead rocket-crews.

A faint death-rattle broke the silence. Tiny had strangled a sentry with a piece of thin wire.

Then it broke loose. A machine-pistol flamed up before us. Three of our chaps fell, killed on the spot.

The Old Un flung a mine at the first visible forms and hand-grenades flew through the air. Between the explosions we heard surprised Russians shouting: 'Germanski, Germanski!'

Porta ran laughing through the trench spraying fire at the dark figures running about completely confused. The Little Legionnaire and Tiny were immediately behind him with barking light machine-guns.

The Old Un and I kicked in a door of a bunker and some Red colleagues fell out of their beds, but before they realized what was happening they were killed by our machine-pistol fire.

A huge officer came tearing down the trench. His coat was open and flapping. As we leaped at him he lost his cap with the green cross in the crown. I bored my knife into his groin and cut swiftly upwards. His blood spurted out.

The Old Un stormed after Porta and the others. By now, they had almost finished their macabre mopping-up.

I had lost my machine-pistol in the fight, but with a spade in one hand and my 7.65 pistol in the other I raged on. A chop at a mounted soldier who tried to sit up. A burst from the pistol. On and on. The legs moved automatically. Then it was all over.

Mines were flung down in the bunkers as a last farewell. They burst like a thin crust of earth during a volcanic eruption. The Old Un sent up red and green lights as a signal to our own people that we were on our way back.

Pushing five prisoners in front of us we arrived breathless at our starting-point.

Lieutenant Weber bombastically ordered us to send the prisoners back to regimental headquarters so that information might be extracted from them.

Porta laughed in his face:

'No, Herr Oberleutnant, those Russians stay here. They are our own private loot. But information you'll have, Herr Leutnant – as much as you want.'

Weber started to shout about mutiny and special courts-martial, but nobody took any notice of him. We were far too interested in our prisoners.

Porta grabbed the nearest and dug his thumbnails into his nostrils tearing them apart with a quick movement. The prisoner howled.

Porta put his mouth to his ear and roared:

'Who gave orders for the performance of that little play we saw this evening?'

The prisoner, a captain with the gold insignia of a commissar on his arm, kicked desperately to get away from the satanic hold.

'Answer, you bastard! Who crucified our pals? And what did you do with the others?'

With an oath he let go of the terrified man and flung him to the floor of the bunker, while Tiny kicked him.

'Bring the next one,' roared Porta.

Tiny and the Little Legionnaire pushed a major forward to Porta who, pointing to the screaming commissar, said:

'Look at him, you swine, and hurry with your answer before I have your eyes out.'

The prisoner jumped back and started screaming.

'No, no, I'll tell you everything!'

Porta guffawed mockingly.

'Ah, you know the method, comrade! I used to think our SS men were the only culprits. Who crucified our friends?'

'First platoon, Sergeant Branikov.'

'H'm. Lucky, a dead man. Who gave the orders? But no dead man's name this time, you swine!'

'Comm . . . ommissar Topolzniza.'

'Who's that, you bastard?'

Without answering the major pointed to a prisoner who stood with the others who were being looked after by the Little Legionnaire.

Porta went slowly across to the man indicated and stared for a moment at the little officer, who squeezed himself against the wall of the bunker.

Porta spat in his face and knocked off his cap with its green cross.

'So it's you who likes playing Satan? I'm going to skin you alive, you animal, but first you're going to talk, you pig.'

'I'm innocent,' shouted the commissar in fluent German.

'Sure,' grinned Porta, 'but only of the Düsseldorf murders.'

He turned round and walked across to the pale major who was standing in the middle of the bunker, just where Porta had left him.

'Hurry up now, talk, or you'll be shot, you Soviet turd. Who put the barbed wire up our pal and cut his paws off? You'd better talk, brother, or shall we have your ears off?'

'I don't know what you mean, Herr Obergefrieter.'

'It's funny how polite you dogs suddenly are. It must be the first time you've addressed a paltry Obergefrieter properly. Does your memory require a little prodding?'

He smacked his pistol-butt into the major's face and his nose broke.

Tiny slid across and whispered, leering devilishly:

'Let Tiny fix him up. I remember all the fifty-five tricks they used in Fagen on us Zebra-men. Hell, Porta, let Tiny fix that SS Soviet man. I swear that in less than a minute he'll have confessed to everything.'

'Do you hear, you snivelling wreck?' grinned Porta. 'Tiny wants to train on you. What about our pal? Who put that barbed wire in him? Who cut his paws off? Talk, you skunk!'

He nodded almost imperceptibly at Tiny. Tiny rushed at the major with a joyful cry, grabbed him by the seat of his pants and swung him like a doll over his head: then threw him right across the bunker where he landed with a crash against the wall.

Tiny was on him like a tiger. We heard brittle snapping sounds like dry sticks breaking.

The major gave a cry which made the hairs on our heads rise.

The Old Un groaned:

'No, no, let me out. I don't care what they've done. I can't look at this.'

He went out with some others among whom was Lieutenant Weber, who was white as a sheet.

Tiny did his work thoroughly and effectively. Many years of accumulated revenge and hatred were vented on a disciple of the system which did not differ much from the brown regime.

Maybe we felt some justification and reminded ourselves that the major had himself taken part in the sort of thing that had now befallen him.

When Porta stopped Tiny, the major was unrecognizable. His uniform was in rags. He looked as if he had been trampled by a furious gorilla.

One of the prisoners fell forward in a collapse at the sight of him.

The Little Legionnaire gave him a kick. It did no good; the man was half-dead with terror.

Stutteringly, the information came from the major's broken and now toothless mouth. The prisoner who had fainted was pointed out as the instigator of the torture on our pals. It had been he who had given the orders about the barbed wire.

When the man came to, the Little Legionnaire questioned him:

'What's your name?'

'Captain in the Red Army, Bruno Tsarstein.'

'It sounds German, doesn't it?' asked the Little Legionnaire thoughtfully.

No answer.

'Are you German, you gallows-bird?'

Silence, frightened silence.

'What the hell,' roared Tiny, 'can't you hear the desert-rat's question? Do you want Tiny to make jam of you?'

'Do you hear?' said the Little Legionnaire, laughing evilly. 'Are you German, you commissar-pig?'

'No, I'm a Soviet citizen.'

'That's a good one. The lads here aren't satisfied with that,' grinned the Little Legionnaire. 'I'm a French citizen, but German all the same. I became French because I knew how to kill France's enemies and you've become a Soviet citizen to kill the Soviet's enemies.' He put his hand gently into the breast-pocket of the pale captain and jerked out his pay-book which he threw across to Porta who thumbed it without understanding a word in it.

The Russian major was more than willing to oblige with a translation into German. It seemed that Captain Bruno Tsarstein had been born in Germany on April 7th, 1901, and had lived in the Soviet Union since 1931. He had been through the prescribed political college courses for commissars, and had been appointed as battalion commissar to the 32nd Siberian Rifle Division.

'Ho, ho, you bastard,' the Little Legionnaire grinned again. 'I've got to punish you extra severely according to paragraph 986, part 2, in the penal code. It says that everyone is punished who leaves the country and takes up foreign citizenship without informing the National-Socialist attorney general's office. And you haven't have you, louse?'

'That's a good point,' Porta joined in. 'You will pronounce his sentence my desert-wanderer. Just do what the hell you think's right.'

'Tell me,' said the Little Legionnaire pleasantly. 'Do you know what they did to me when I came home from the Legion Etrangère? Make a guess comrade commissar. They hit me over the kidneys with iron chains. Have you tried passing blood?'

Porta interrupted the Little Legionnaire to roar into the German-Russian commissar's ear:

'Answer, by Christ, or we'll cut your eye-balls out and make you eat them.'

Tiny pricked Tsarstein with his bayonet. He leaped forward but Bauer's rifle-butt made him jump back.

'Answer, you dog. Didn't you hear what the gentleman said?' Porta exhorted him. 'I ask you again. Have you tried?'

'No, no,' whispered the commissar hoarsely and stared as if hypnotized at the Little Legionnaire who in turn looked back with an almost fatherly smile.

'Do you want to try?'

'No, Herr Soldat.'

'I didn't want to either, brother. But your colleagues in Fagen forced me. Have you heard about Fagen?'

'No, Herr Soldat.'

'Do you think you ever will now?'

'Answer, you snotty cow,' roared Porta.

Tsarstein swallowed his saliva with great difficulty. Every word hurt him when he spoke:

'No, I don't think so.'

'I don't either. They gave me a hit across the kidneys with the chains for each quarter of a year I'd been in Le Legion Etrangère. They might have chosen each month, week, or even day. But then I'd have been dead and imagine my sorrow if we hadn't met – you and I? SS Unterscharführer Willy Weinbrand thought it great fun to see me licking spit. Ever tried it, Herr Commissar? No? But you've tried crucifying people. Don't you think it hurts to be crucified?'

Tsarstein squeezed himself desperately against the wall, trying to get away from the staring fanatical eyes of the Little Legionnaire.

'You don't answer. Have you tried?'

'No, Herr Soldat.'

Tiny spat on the floor.

'Lick it up.'

Bruno Tsarstein's head spun. He looked as if he was about to collapse. Hypnotized, he stared at the slimy blob on the bunker-floor. We had all tried spit-licking. We knew what stirred in Tsarstein's body.

Tiny grabbed him and flung him down.

'Eat it up, comrade-commissar-murderer!'

The Little Legionnaire pricked his neck with his bayonet.

'Seek and you'll find,' he said thickly. 'Allah is great. *Inshallah!*'

Tsarstein started to vomit. It seemed as if his stomach turned itself inside out.

'Good gracious me,' said the Little Legionnaire quietly. 'That sort of thing was severely punished in Fagen!'

He kicked him in the side and the NKVD man rolled over the floor.

The Little Legionnaire bent confidentially over him:

'Your SS colleagues castrated me with a kitchen-knife in the bog. Ever seen anything like that?'

'No, Herr Soldat.'

'God help us, what an innocent you are!' His voice cut like a knife. The sound of it remains to this day in my brain. 'How many have you castrated in your concentration camps?'

'No Germans, Herr Soldat, only anti-social elements.'

An ominous almost satanic silence reigned. It enabled the commissar to crawl, back to the other prisoners, but they, his own comrades, drew back in terror.

'So, only anti-social elements,' the Little Legionnaire said, as if thinking aloud. He savoured the word 'anti-social'. His voice rose in a shriek of rage: 'Get up, whore's spawn, or I'll skin you alive!'

He kicked the commissar, who tried to shield himself with outstretched hands.

'You say anti-social, you bloody bastard. Here we're all anti-social in the eyes of your SS chums. You think that gives you the right to make us all half-men? Get his pants off!' he roared.

Tiny and Pluto literally tore the clothes off the commissar who screamed hollowly like a frightened animal.

The Little Legionnaire opened his combat-knife and tried the edge with his thumb.

Just then a sharp command rang through the room.

'Section, attention!'

We started and obeyed.

There stood Captain von Barring, the ordnance officer and The Old Un. Slowly brushing the snow off his greatcoat, von Barring advanced into the bunker. He glanced indifferently at the prisoners, and, at the half-naked commissar creeping into hiding.

'Lay off it, boys.' Von Barring turned to us. 'Prisoners are to be sent to regimental HQ. Didn't you remember?'

Porta started to explain, but von Barring cut him short.

'All right, Porta. I know what you're going to say.' He pointed to the prisoners. 'These fellows will be dealt with, you can be sure, but we're not torturers here. Remember that, and never let me catch you at it again. This time we'll pass it over.'

'Can't we punish them?' Porta insisted.

'No, leave that to HQ.' Von Barring nodded at The Old Un who called in some men, infantrymen from the 67th Regiment. 'Escort the prisoners to the rear,' von Barring ordered a sergeant. 'You'll vouch with your life for their safety.'

As they went Tiny prodded his bayonet into the commissar's thigh.

The ill-treated man gave off a bellow.

'What's this?' Von Barring sounded threatening.

'One of the prisoners stood on a nail,' answered Porta innocently.

Without another word, von Barring and the ordnance officer left the bunker.

'Oh, bloody hell,' swore the Little Legionnaire, 'we were just getting going. Why must von Barring always interfere in our bits of fun?'

'It's unfair competition,' Porta declared and scowled at The Old Un. 'It's your work, isn't it? You told von Barring, eh?'

'Yes, I did,' answered The Old Un firmly. 'You'd all have done the same if you hadn't lost your reason.'

'The next commissar I lay hands on will get a bullet in the back at once,' Tiny announced, swinging his pistol.

'Maybe we'll be allowed to deal with those dirty dogs once Hinka's had his private chat with 'em,' said the Little Legionnaire speculatively . . .

With great difficulty the fighting-group fought its way through the impassable terrain. We moved, groaning, stumbling and tottering, through snow which seemed to suck us down with every step.

We did not have to walk far before the weaker types threw themselves down weeping, and refused to go another step. The rifle-butts thundered down on them until they again stumbled along. We resembled a flock of small, black ants in the vast white snow-landscape.

We had to fight for every *kolhoz* and village. When we thought we had cleaned the enemy out they were again over us like wolves.

No. 5 Company went into quarters in a *kolhoz* just south-east of Dzhurzhenzy. We were completely exhausted. We had taken off our greatcoats and equipment and snuggled down in the straw. Then shots rang out. Furious bursts from Russian machine-pistols. We heard shouts and screams.

'Ivan, Ivan, alert, alert!' our sentries warned us and we jumped into hiding firing at the Siberian rifle-men who were pouring in from all sides.

'Out!' cries The Old Un and snatches his machine-pistol and some hand-grenades. He charges without his cap and great-coat.

We stumble about in confusion, but in a few seconds are out in the dark.

Pluto who has been lice-hunting rushes out dressed in pants and boots only. He races round the house with his machine-pistol and runs smack into three Russians. They hang on to him like limpets, trying to get their combat-knives into him. Roaring like a bull he kicks and bites as he fires with his machine-pistol. One of the Russians slides across the yard on his stomach like a sledge. The other two he grabs by the throat and flings them away. One gets his chest nearly carved in two by my machine-pistol and the other sinks to the ground with Pluto's flick-knife deep in his chest.

Porta and the Little Legionnaire are using their automatic weapons like truncheons and raging and swearing.

'Here you are, you Red bitch!' shouts Porta and a whistling blow hits a Siberian fur-clad head.

'*Allah-akbar!*' cries the Little Legionnaire.

Tiny dashes about among the small Siberians, swinging a Cossack sabre like a scythe. It bites both ways, for Tiny has sharpened both edges.

More than a third of the company are dead when two hours later we fight the Siberian troops back.

Again we stumble through the white hell. The fighting-group is slowly but surely being exterminated. The greater part of the troops, frost-curled corpses, lie spread over the snowy wastes.

Round each the snow slowly grows in a drift like a grave.

The village of Dzhurzhenzy is a lonely God-forsaken place with one *kolhoz* and a railway line on its northern fringe.

Here we have to blow up each little mound and fight for hours for each house. Not one of these Siberian rifle-men from the 32nd Regiment gives himself up. Every one is killed in close combat. They do not yield an inch during the battles.

In Dzhurzhenzy, Möller, our holy man, falls. He dies in the arms of Tiny and Porta behind a stack of railway sleepers. It is ironic that Porta is the one to say the last *Paternoster* over him.

We shovel snow on him before going on with our death march.

We are so worn out that we let our friends lie in the snow if they cannot resist the temptation to sink into it and sleep to death.

Almost snow-blinded, sobbing with fatigue and frost pain, we reach something resembling a road indicated by a long row of telegraph poles.

Then suddenly we see in front of us one, two, three, four, oh my God, five, no, many more tanks looking out of the snow-blizzard. The commander of each vehicle sits in the open turret straining to see through the whipping snow.

Dead-beat and silent, we sink down and stare in panic at the huge white-painted monsters. They growl their way along with the long cannons pointing like accusing fingers from the turrets.

Sergeant Kraus from the 104th gunner-regiment stands up and wants to run at them.

The Old Un has to tug him down in the snow.

'Careful, I think it's Ivan. Those fellows are certainly neither Tigers nor Panthers. I wouldn't be far wrong in saying they're KW2s!'

The snow incessantly blinds us as we stare at the growling tanks.

'Oh, my hernia-bandage!' bursts out Porta. 'They're Uncle Joe's lads on a picnic. They've got stars on all their vehicles and Adolf doesn't care for that. So you see, it must be Stalin's transport-business rolling forward.'

As soon as we are sure, we start feverishly digging ourselves in. We use even our fingers to get hidden from the tank-commanders.

We count fifteen T34s and two of the larger KW2s. There may have been more made invisible by the blizzard.

We glare nervously as they disappear like ghosts.

Then suddenly it dawns on us in all its horror that they are advancing at Lysenka. There, our whole Ist Panzer Division is preparing to advance and break us out of the net we are in.

Captain von Barring quickly makes up his mind: we must hurry to Lysenka to warn the Ist Panzer Division of its deadly danger.

Again we move westward in the ever-increasing snow storm which blows straight at us. To walk eight miles through it weighed down by ammunition and heavy infantry arms is not easy. Even if the enemy tanks are bothered by it they stand a better chance to reach their objective first.

The storm makes visibility sink to about two yards. Suddenly machine-gun fire rattles at us. Tank-engines get into lower gear and whine like frightened babies.

Through the blizzard the outlines of tanks show themselves. Our artillerymen and infantrymen run about screaming. They throw away their arms, fall down and are crushed by the heavy caterpillar tracks. Some stop and put their hands up to signal their surrender, but the next moment they are mown down by the whipping machine-gun fire.

The red star shines coldly and mercilessly at us.

Stege and I throw ourselves in cover behind some bushes and press ourselves desperately against them. A few yards away the howling T34s race by, churning up the snow in a dense cloud. The hot exhaust from the pipe hits us like a glowing kiss. Our bodies are goose-flesh.

The rest of the fighting-group run about like scared rabbits. With uncanny precision they are picked off one by one.

A quarter of an hour later we can hear only a few shots being fired in the distance. Tottering on westward again we run into more tanks. They are chasing some infantrymen from the 72nd Regiment.

It is a horrible race. The only thought anyone has is: get away from the fire-spraying steel-killers!

In one place we have to throw ourselves down and let the tanks roll over us, as they told us to do in the training manual.

Panic-stricken, we press ourselves down. Rumbling, rattling and whirring, the vast tonnage of a T34 thunders over us. Its belly strokes us caressingly as it were, over our backs, while the screaming, clanging chains toll past us on both sides.

You are no longer normal when an event like this hits you. You shake and tremble. Your speech is confused and slurred. You cannot believe you are still alive.

Several miles in a south-westerly direction we again make contact with the remnants of the von Barring fighting-group. Only a hundred troops of the five hundred are left. Among the survivors are, to our immense relief, most of our best pals.

Pluto has got one ear torn off. A small shell did that.

Porta bandaged him with something closely resembling a mother's touch.

'What a good thing the pea-shell didn't hit your behind, my pet. This ear was no use to you, my little bird. You never listened to anything sensible people said. Didn't your old father tell you war's disagreeable? But of course you stupid dopes had to go out to get some "Lebensraum". You see what comes of it, you miserable peasant!'

Von Barring had re-established contact with HQ and told them that all the companies had had severe casualties. To our astonishment he received the following laconic orders:

> 'The von Barring fighting-group will join with the remnants of the 72nd Infantry Regiment. The group will go back to Point 108, position Dzhurzhenzy. If the Russians are again in occupation, win it back.'

'God, what idiots,' shouted Porta. 'This is just a game of musical chairs. Why the hell don't they start a regular tram-service?'

Without any proper Intelligence information or flank-support laid on, we turned apathetically back.

Porta swore that if he had to run away again he would not stop till he reached Berlin.

Morning came with thirty degrees below freezing. Seven men froze to death during the night. They were pushed over our snow-parapet and rolled down towards the other side.

First we examined them to see if it was worthwhile taking their boots off. One of the dead had a pair of almost new felt-boots. They fitted the Little Legionnaire beautifully. He put them on, his face beaming.

'One man's death, the other man's boots,' he grins and stamps radiantly and enthusiastically off.

We try to dig deeper into the ground, but both spades and picks are useless in the iron-hard earth.

In the afternoon the Russian infantry again attacks. Huge numbers storm forward with wild hurrahs.

We open a concentrated fire from our automatic weapons and mortars. Surprisingly the Russians give up soon and withdraw to their own positions.

We ward off eight attacks in forty-eight hours.

But worse than the attacks, the cold, hunger, bombs and

shells, is the feeling that has taken a grip on us: the fighting-group has been put in a spot which is lost – given up.

Our call for help to Regimental HQ meets with no response.

After the fourteenth attack von Barring lets our radio-operator send off a desperate S O S:

> 'The von Barring fighting-group almost exterminated. Only two officers, six NCOs and 219 troops alive. Send ammunition, bandages and rations. Given up. Waiting orders.'

The answer from HQ is short:

> 'Cannot help. Stay to the last man.'
>
> Army Corps Commander.

The Russians now try to bomb us out. They hit the village with twelve Martin bombers in low-level attack. The bombers unload their deadly cargo over us.

The following night despite orders, to die where we stand, Captain von Barring, risking a court-martial and a sentence of death, orders the fighting-group to leave the village, abandoning the mortars and heavy infantry weapons.

The numerous casualties we place in an even row on the ramparts of our abandoned positions.

With glazed eyes the dead gunners from the 104th Regiment, the panzer-gunners from the 27th and the old grey infantrymen from the 72nd stare at the Russian positions where the Siberian riflemen sit.

Man after man falls like a ripe apple from trees in autumn storms. But we are no longer interested in who receives the kiss of death from the frost.

What's that coming? Tanks? Hysterical with fatigue, completely worn out, we sink into the icy snow-drifts. The tears stream down our cheeks in desperation. We have only hand-grenades to fight steel juggernauts.

The engines jeer and whine at us. They sing our elegy. The elegy of the 27th (Penal) Panzer Regiment.

Without a word we bunch our hand-grenades together. If we are going to die let it be as costly as possible.

It is lunacy to fight on and equally insane to stop. The sum total is the same. Death under the tracks or by machine-gun bullets.

'Here we come to the end of our war,' snarls Porta. 'Just two thousand miles from Berlin. Well, nothing can be done about that. Porta is waiting for you in hell. I'm fed up with this running about.'

'You shan't wait long,' Tiny says hoarsely. 'I'm coming soon, too, but first I'll fetch one of the Red bastards along with me.'

'Allah is great, but these are greater,' pronounces the Little Legionnaire and points at the great pack of white-painted tanks which rolls towards us.

'Take care,' shouts von Barring. 'Here they come!'

Stege is about to stand up and run away, but The Old Un and I grab him.

The machine-guns open up. The men begin to die. A corporal from the 104th sits up and puts his hands to his head, then he folds like a pen-knife.

The small ordnance officer runs forward and slings a whole bunch of hand-grenades at the nearest tank; he falls and is crushed beneath the tracks. His grenades landed just short.

Several start to run. Von Barring shouts desperately:

'Lie still, let them roll over. We'll take 'em from the back. They've got no infantry protection!'

But more and more of our troops are stricken by the tank panic. They run clumsily about until they are mown down by the Russian machine guns.

Porta prepares his special, home-made bomb, gives it a kiss and throws it. It lands underneath the tracks of the nearest tank. The tank jerks and then stops.

At the same time Tiny throws his own bomb which also hits its target. He pats Porta's shoulder in his delight.

'Let's be quietly crushed now. We must have earned the devil's warmest greetings!'

The Old Un shouts:

'Stop, stop, they're German tanks! Look, there's the swastika!'

We stare open-mouthed at them. The Old Un is right. Wild delight. We wave our snow-shirts and steel helmets. The tanks swing round. The hatches in the turrets open. Our tank-comrades wave to us.

Weeping, we fall into each other's arms.

Of the whole fighting-group, thirty-four 'other ranks' and only one officer, Captain von Barring, have survived.

Major-General Bäke jumps out and comes across to us, small and sturdy. He squeezes the hand of everyone of us, then waves his arms and the Ist Panzer Division is on its way to Cherkassy to widen the hole we have made in the net. Inside that net nine divisions are still fighting desperately.

Oberleutnant Weber has fallen. A German Tiger tank has crushed his body. Never again will he threaten anybody with court-martial.

Now, like clockwork dolls, we trudge along the road to a village where we will be reinforced – we hope.

'I'll give you the recipe you down-trodden peasants,' Porta said loftily. 'This is the ambrosia of Olympus.'

And then, of course, our Russian colleagues had to interrupt our lovely gastronomic fantasy.

Mashed Potatoes with Diced Pork

On the fringes of a forest some miles north of Popeljna the 27th Regiment was put into peaceful positions with only a little local artillery-fire not worth mentioning.

Our party was sent on a reconnaissance trip into the forest. With our guns slung carelessly over our shoulders and cigarettes dangling from our mouths we set off.

Porta ordered a little rest.

'The bloody war won't run away if we stop a little here.'

He was gleefully supported by Tiny and the Little Legionnaire.

The Old Un shrugged his shoulders.

'It's all the same to me. There can't be any Russians or we'd have seen them ages ago.'

We sat, twelve men, on a fallen tree-trunk like swallows on a telephone-wire.

Porta started to explain how his favourite dish of mashed potatoes and diced pork ought to be prepared.

'The most important thing is that this dish, which is fit for the gods, should be prepared with feeling.' He gesticulated. 'Without feeling it is no use.'

Tiny interrupted him:

'Half a tick, Porta, I want to write down the recipe.'

He asked Stege to give him pencil and paper, and Stege obliged grinning.

Tiny rolled over on his stomach, wetted the pencil and told Porta that he might go on.

'First you pick out some beautiful potatoes. You might steal them in the field or find them in a cellar. Anyway, when you've got them you sit on a good chair. If your backside is sore get a cushion. Then you peel 'em. The bad parts, if any, are neatly and lovingly cut off.'

'What badness can you find on a potato?' Tiny asked.

'Haven't you ever seen a potato with syphillis?'

'No, I didn't know potatoes whored.'

'Well, there are many things you don't know,' replied Porta with irritated condescension. 'But do as I tell you. Cut the syphillis out. Drop the peeled potato in a bucket with lovely cold spring water with a saucy little splash like a virgin weeing in a stream on a spring evening while the mosquitoes play in the bushes.'

'My God, Porta, you're quite a poet,' laughed The Old Un.

Porta squeezed up his eyes.

'What's poet? Anything to do with whoring-boys?'

'It is possible that among them you'll find a poet,' grinned The Old Un. 'But never mind, go on with your cook's course.'

'When all the spuds are peeled, boil 'em. Then mash them nicely and according to the rules into a porridge. Now take care and listen carefully. It's most important. Go into a field or a village where the fragrance tells you there's cattle. Find a female cow. I take it you know the difference between a he and a she. If not just lift the rudder at the back end, but keep your nose away. You see, the exhaust sits just beneath it.

'When you've found the proper animal, draw off a pint of juice from the milk-container. It is an apparatus under the stomach and looks like an electrical fitting. Pour the milk into the mashed potatoes but, for the sake of the holy Elizabeth, be careful you've not found a goat or a donkey. It would be a tragedy to pour the milk of a she-donkey on the lovely spuds because donkey's milk is used for bathing in.'

'Oh, hell,' Tiny burst out, 'it's bad enough bathing in ordinary water, but in milk it must be horrible. I'd rather carry my dirt around until the funeral-fellow scrapes it off. It's a lie. Porta. Where did you get that from?'

'Read it, my lad. Once upon a time there was a tart named Poppaea Sabina. A beauty from Italy. She snitched that emperor-fellow Nero away from an old witch called Octavia. This Poppaea was fished out of a brothel by the emperor. Of course she got an aggrandisement complex and started washing in donkey's milk. So, you see: no donkey's milk in the spuds. They are not a sewer-cleaning station.

'When the pure cow-milk has been poured on the spuds, stir round elegantly and well. Then take a pinch of salt and gently drop it in the spuds, but for heaven's sake with feeling and for the sake of Saint Gertrude stir with a wooden spoon all the time. If you haven't got one, use your bayonet. Remember to wipe off any blood or oil.

'Then, break ten eggs and in your most charming manner stir them up with sugar. Pinch the sugar from the quartermaster, but for the sake of Holy Moses' blue eyes, stir slowly, dear friends, slowly!'

'Why slowly?' Tiny wanted to know.

'What the hell's it got to do with you, you stupid flat-footed vulture? Just pour it slowly as I told you and stop interrupting. You're always such a nosy parker. Boil the whole thing on a slow fire. Never use manure for fuel. It stinks!'

Porta stopped and glared at Tiny who had put up his hand like a schoolboy.

'What do you want now!' Porta asked angrily.

'I only humbly ask, Herr Super-Cook Porta, if I may use birch-wood soaked in petrol stolen from Hitler's vehicle park?'

'By God, you may! Any more questions? If so, ask now.'

Tiny shook his head.

We who lay near him saw that he wrote in large childish letters: 'Birch-wood and stolen petrol may be used.'

'The pork is browned over a glowing fire made of birch-wood,' Porta added quickly and looked at Tiny whose tongue-tip was sticking out of the corner of his mouth in an effort of concentration over this difficult office work.

'You cut the pork conscientiously into cubes and let the pieces slide into the mash. It must be done with loving care and feeling. The most important thing is to put one's whole Catholic soul into the job.'

Tiny roared:

'Have you got to be a Catholic to make potatomash?'

'Of course,' answered Porta, 'ever since the Thirty Years War it's been an established fact.'

'All right,' said Tiny, 'I'll find a Catholic to make my mash under my direction.'

'While singing a Russian autumn-song,' went on Porta, 'you cut up a few chives and with a winning smile you spread it over the mash. A pinch of paprika is also very good. And not to be despised is a half-full cartridge-case of pepper. But for the sake of the Holy Jordan don't leave it on the fire too long. You see, lads, this is called "Burning Love".' He looked warningly at Tiny: 'Don't you dare say anything obscene about this holiness!

'Before you sit down to eat this manna, rinse your spoon well in boiling water. It would be a truly deadly sin to eat the mash with a dirty spoon.

'Remember to use the meat of a white pig for the cubes; at a pinch use a black one, but never a red one. That would be blasphemy.'

He lifted his behind and put an effective full stop to the lecture. The quietness of the wood heightened the effect.

A little later The Old Un throws away his cigarette-end and we trudge on.

The lane has become a narrow path, winding between huge dense firs and spruces.

We reach a sharp bend in the path. Suddenly we are faced with a Russian patrol. Like ourselves they are evidently surprised.

For a few seconds we stand and stare, our cigarettes hanging from our mouths and our weapons over our shoulders.

Not one of us thinks of firing. The surprise is too complete. Both parties turn and run, the Russians one way, we the other.

Porta is far in front of us.

Tiny shrieks with fright, his legs moving like a cyclist's in the 'Tour de France'. In his terror he has lost his machine-pistol.

We would have run ourselves to death if Porta had not stumbled over a root and fallen down a fifteen yards steep incline. He screamed like a horse with wolves at his heels.

After much trouble we got him up. A wild discussion started about how many Russians we had met.

The Old Un and Stege maintained it was a company.

'A company,' screamed Porta. 'You must have been hit in the eye by a wood pigeon. It was a battalion at least.'

'At least,' Tiny said. 'It swarmed with Russians.'

'*Ma Foi*, they stood there in hundreds between the trees rolling their eyes,' said the Little Legionnaire. 'You may stay on here, but for my part I'm off.'

At company headquarters we cheekily reported we had met an enemy battalion. At once the report was relayed to the regimental HQ.

Field-telephones were blocked. The division was alerted. Three storm-battalions were sent to the frontline. Firing orders went out to the 76th Artillery Regiment and the 109th Mortar Regiment. Two storm battalions of light artillery advanced.

Shells and rockets rained down on the spot where we had reported meeting the enemy 'battalion'.

The Russians too were busily shooting. Our colleagues must also have reported a similar exaggerated number of their foes. Meanwhile they sat in their trenches as we sat in ours and admired the energetic work of the artillery.

Porta said dreamily, while his eyes followed the screaming track of a large shell in the black night:

'It makes me quite proud to think this festive firework display is all our own work.'

17

She was slim and lovely. Dark and passionate. The most experienced lover a woman-hungry man could desire.

What I did not know about women she taught me.

We loved, clung as if for the very last time. When it dawned on me that I might be punished for race-outrage, I laughed as I had not for a long time, and my friends laughed with me.

Leave in Berlin

I had to wait seven hours in Lemberg. The waiting room was cold. Invisible frost sneaked in under my great-coat. It rained and blew from the east.

Russia gave me a cool welcome after four day's leave – four lovely, unforgettable days. All leave has only one drawback. Half of it is ruined by the thought of the return to the front.

You must remember what you did. Not forget anything. They are expecting to hear everything, those out there who drew blanks when the only leave-pass in the company was distributed. Von Barring had placed two hundred paper-slips in a steel-helment, but one hundred and ninety-nine were blanks. Number 38 was a pass and I drew thirty-eight. They congratulated me with a lump in their throats. The disappointment and envy were hard to hide. I was about to give The Old Un my pass, when he said as if he had read my thoughts:

'Good thing it wasn't me. Then I'd have had to forget all over again how nice it is at home.'

He did not mean it and he knew I knew. He wanted the pass very much.

Tiny was honest and unostentatious. He threatened me first with a beating if I did not give him my pass. When the others took my part he offered to pay for it. Porta overbid him; but I would not sell. They knew I wouldn't. But it was worth trying if the man with the pass had gone mad with joy about winning the jack-pot.

Porta, Pluto and Tiny tried to make me drunk, still hoping to buy the pass, and, just before I stepped into the truck to take me to the station, Tiny tried again. He offered me his next ten leave-passes if he could have mine now.

I shook my head and drove off as they sang:

'In der Heimat, in der Heimat,
da gibt's ein Wiedersehen!'

The journey to Berlin went quickly. I stepped into a hospital-train at Jitomir and at Brest-Litovsk got a straight-through leave-train. In this way I gained an extra day.

It was dark when the train for Minsk steamed into the station. All the carriages were filled with soldiers. They lay everywhere. On the luggage-racks, under the seats, along the corridors, in the toilet.

At daybreak we passed by the border-town of Brest-Litovsk and rolled towards Minsk. Late in the evening we arrived.

I was so tired and sore I could hardly walk. In Minsk I had to report to the MTO. My papers, which I had got from Berlin, stated: Berlin-Minsk over Lemberg-Brest-Litovsk.

In the station office I was received by a sergeant. He consulted some lists, stamped my papers and said:

'You are going to Vjasma. There you must report to the MTO and get a new route, but hurry up – your train is on track 47.'

I arrived at Vjasma the following day about three in the afternoon. Hungry, tired and wet through, I fumbled my way to the MTO office.

An NCO disappeared into an office with my papers. A little later he re-appeared with a stout, elderly captain. Placing himself in front of me with splayed legs and gloved hands on hips, he glared nastily at me and asked:

'What the hell are you thinking of?' He croaked like a hoarse raven. 'What are you doing here, travelling half round Russia. You've had leave and now you're playing truant?'

I stood stiffly to attention and stared blindly into the room. A stick in the stove crackled. It smelt of fire-wood, birch-logs.

'Is he dumb?' coughed the captain. 'Answer, spit it out!'

('Choose the right answer Sven. What you say now will decide your fate. How that captain reeks of sweat and grease.')

'Yes, Herr Hauptmann?'

'And what the hell does that mean?' he raged.

The flames in the fire played warmly. It looked cosy and lovely. (Your leave is over, quite finished.)

'I humbly report, Herr Hauptmann that I travel round half Russia.'

'Ah, you rat, you confess. Wise of you. Take that chair, jump ten times at the double and then another ten. Quickly now, front animal!'

Stiffly I bent my knees, gripped the heavy office chair and held it with straight arms while jumping with bent legs.

The captain grinned contentedly.

'Faster, faster!' He beat the rhythm with a ruler.

'One, two, one, two, big jump – one, two, big jump!'

He was not content with two times ten, but three times ten satisfied him.

With the station staff loudly applauding him, he ordered:

'Other way round, now, lazy animal!'

A respirator container hit me hard on the neck as I raced across the desk and crawled underneath a row of chairs placed to resemble a tunnel.

It blackened in front of my eyes. The blood pumped. Far away I heard the raven's croak:

'Faster, faster, idle dog!'

Who shouted 'Room to attention?' I stopped automatically and stretched my dirty fingers along my trouser seams and stared stiffly at a photograph of Hitler. Did the picture move? Or did I?

My head ached. Red spots danced in front of my eyes. The picture came and went.

A razor-sharp voice cut the silence:

'What's going on here?'

Silence. The fire was full of joy. It smoked birch-sticks. It smelt beautifully of forest and freedom (birch-trees are friends. Friends are birch-trees. Oh, nonsense!).

'Now then, are all you gentlemen struck dumb?' It was the cold voice again.

'Herr Oberst, Hauptmann von Weissgeibel, detailed for station duty humbly reports the punishment of a gunner who has been dawdling behind the lines. The punishment is completed.'

'Where's the gunner, Herr Hauptmann von Weissgeibel?'

The voice was rough but polite.

The captain, small, fat, glistening with grease, pointed a sausage-finger at me. A cold, smooth face beneath a white fur hat stared at me.

'Easy!'

Automatically my left foot slid out to the side. The hands relaxed a little. Every muscle is ready to spring to attention again if the small mouth commands. A colonel's mouth. A colonel with many crosses, white, black, red and blue.

'Gunner? Come here, Herr Hauptmann. Where are you?'

The captain rolled across, glared at me and shifted his short legs in the far too large boots.

'I humbly report, Herr Oberst, this man is a tank-gunner.'

'You think so?' The colonel smiled thinly and dangerously. 'Forgotten the German army's rank badges?'

A long finger encased in black leather touched my belt buckle.

'Report, soldier!'

'Report, Herr Oberst, Fahnenjunker Hassel, 27th (Penal) Panzer Regiment, No. 5 Company, travelling from Berlin to Minsk via Brest-Litovsk after completion of leave. From Berlin MTO office orders of new route in Minsk. Ordered from Minsk to Vjasma. Humbly report arrival at 15.07 hours with train No. 874.'

'Easy, Fahnenjunker!'

A hand is stretched imperiously out.

'Your papers.'

Boots bang across the wooden floor. Heels click together. Voices report humbly. The colonel says nothing. He reads the papers with the green and red markings, thumbs the tickets, screws in a monocle, studies the rubber-stamps. The monocle disappears in the pocket between the third and fourth button. He considers the situation.

Like arrows the orders shoot out. The captain trembles. The NCOs shake. The clerks at attention beside their desks swallow hard.

Only the front-line soldier wishing his pals were here does not listen very carefully to what happens. The amusements have been interrupted by a fighting officer on his way to front-line headquarters. A small colonel with only one arm and a merciless, smooth and handsome face. A colonel who is dead inside. A colonel who hates everybody because everybody hates him.

A clerk takes his seat behind his typewriter. Springily the colonel walks up and down before him dictating, the empty sleeve hanging loosely.

He looks at the typewritten sheet. With two fingers he hands it to the captain.

'Sign it; it is to your liking, isn't it?'

'Yes, Herr Oberst,' stammers the Captain nearly weeping.

The colonel nods.

'Read it out, Herr Hauptmann!'

It is a short and concise military application for a transfer. When the captain reads the thanks to Colonel von Tolksdorf for his concern in so quickly sending off Captain von Weissgeibel and his station staff's transfer request to an infantry battalion, his eyes bulge.

Indifferently, quite impersonally, the colonel puts away the three folded applications in his pocket. The station staff's fate is sealed.

A few minutes later I am in a train on my way to Mogilev.

In front of the engine we push an open truck filled with sand. A precaution against mines. How it works only God and the German railway-security service know.

The ice-roses on the window change into faces. The faces come and go. Berlin – House Vaterland – Zigeunerkeller – and all the other places where we had been, she and I.

She approached me as I stood on the Schlesischer Station in Berlin.

'On leave?' she asked. Her eyes measured me, coolly and firmly.

Deep grey eyes, heavily framed by mascara, with a little grey-blue. She was *the* woman, the woman every soldier on leave must have. It was my duty to get a woman.

In my imagination. I undressed her. Maybe she had got a girdle like that girl in Porta's picture, a red one. I nearly trembled. Perhaps black underwear?

'Hell and death,' Porta would have shouted if he had been me.

'Yes, I'm on a four days' leave.'

'Come with me, and I'll show you Berlin. Our lovely Berlin of the eternal war. Party member?'

Without answering I showed her my armlet: SPECIAL SECTION framed by two death's skulls.

She laughed quietly and we walked quickly down the street. My footsteps drowned the elegant tapping of her high heels.

Kurfürstendamm – Lovely! Friedrichstrasse – dark, but lovely – Fasanenstrasse – a wonder. Leipziger Platz and last but not least Unter den Linden. Lovely, eternally young Berlin!

Her face was calm, beautiful, a little hard but picturesque. Her chin was lifted high and haughtily above her elegant fur collar.

Her long fingers stroked my hand.

'Where to, my kind sir?'

Stammering a little I got out that I did not know. Where does a front-line soldier take an elegant lady? A front-line soldier with pistol, gas-mask, steel-helmet and heavy crashing infantry-boots.

She threw me an inquiring glance. I suspected a smile in the cold eyes.

'An officer doesn't know where to take a lady?'

'Sorry, I'm no officer, only a Fahnenjunker.'

She laughed a little.

'Not an officer? Much happens in this war. Officers become privates, privates officers. Officers become dead bodies dangling from ropes. We are a great and well-disciplined nation which does as ordered.'

What was the matter with her?

The train gave a violent jerk. It nearly stopped. A long whistle and it was on its way again. Rat-tat-tat-tat. The ice-roses again became a picture-book of a leave which now seemed far, far away . . .

Zigeunerkeller with soft music. Sighing violins which wept for the gypsy prairies. She knew many people. A nod, an understanding smile, a whispered conversation and many bottles with scarce labels appeared on our table . . .

Her girdle was red, her underwear sheer. She was insatiable in her erotic wildness. She collected men. She was a drunkard, an erotic drunkard. Men were her drug.

I had much to tell the lads in the bunker out there. Much can be experienced during four days' leave. A new world can transpire. An old world disappear.

The last night she wanted my Iron Cross. She got it. It fell into a drawer among several other decorations and rank-badges from men who had visited her.

She called herself Helene Strasser. She laughed as she told me. She showed me a yellow-star carefully wrapped in silk. She threw her head back, shook her hair and laughed.

'That is *my* decoration.'

She looked at me expecting a violent reaction. But I was indifferent. Once there was an SS man who tried to forbid Porta to sit on a bench with the notice: 'Only for Jews'. The SS man died.

'Don't you understand? I've got the Jew's star.'

'Yes, but what of it?'

'You'll be sent to prison,' she laughed, 'because you've been in bed with me. Was I worth it?'

'Yes, but how is it you are free? And living here?'

'Connections, connections.' She showed me a party membership card with her photograph.

*

The train rumbled across the steppe past forgotten villages. Sleepy Hungarian guards looked after its many unbelievably dirty trucks and ages-old passenger carriages.

One of my friends, a colonel's son, at a military college had to leave Germany because his wife's great-grand-father was a Jew. They were divorced on paper. Further the discipline could not reach. We drove him and his wife to the Swiss border in a Mercedes staff-car, with a three-cornered flag on the mud-guard and SS number plates right up to the frontier. He went across with his wife whose ancestors had been Jews, and in a wood at Donaueschingen the SS plates were changed with WH plates.

They arrested his mother and her father, for the sake of symmetry presumably. Her mother and his father they let go, but they never received any ration-cards. In 1941 his father was shot. They said it was suicide. There was a nice wreath from the army. Officers followed behind the colonel's coffin. Nice speeches were made.

In Nogilev I changed trains. On the platform I ran into the MT officer who stopped me and asked after my well-being. He offered me a cigarette and addressed me: 'Herr Fahnenjunker.'

My astonishment was great. I was almost frightened by this unexpected politeness. He was dressed in the uniform of the cavalry with finger-thick yellow cords, high glossy boots with huge silver-spurs which jingled like sleigh-bells.

He regarded me benevolently through his monocle.

'And where are you off to, my dear Herr Fahnenjunker.'

I crashed my heels together and answered in the fully regulated manner:

'Herr Rittmeister, Fahnenjunker Hassel humbly reports that he is proceeding to the regiment via Mogily and Brobrusk.'

'Do you know when the train starts for Brobrusk, dear friend?'

'No, Herr Rittmeister.'

'I don't know either. Let's guess.'

He stared up at the grey racing clouds as if he expected a timetable to drop down from heaven. He gave up.

'Well, well, let's see. How was it? You want to go to Brobrusk, my dear Fahnenjunker? Have you got the standard you bear with you?'

My eyes rolled with sheer confusion. Was he making fun of me? Was he insane?

I glanced round. There were only two people, two station-staff men far down the platform.

He smiled wildly, took his monocle out and polished it.

'Where's your standard, dear friend. The regiment's beloved standard?'

He started quoting Rilke:

'Meine gute mutter,
Seid stolz: Ich trage die Fahne,
Seid ohne Sorge: Ich trage die Fahne,
Habt mich lieb: Ich trage die Fahne—'

He put his hand on my shoulder:

'Dear Rainer Maria Rilke. You are a hero, the pride of the cavalry. The Great King will reward you.'

He walked up and down, spat at the sleepers and went on in his falsetto voice as he pointed to the rails:

'What you see there is the railway. It's so named because it consists of two parallel steel-rods. These are called rails in the handbook for railway employees. The bed you see under the rails is made of gravel, shingle and broken stones. By scientific tests it has been established that the best method is to put sleepers across with a distance of 0.7 metres between them. On these wonderful, precisely-cut sleepers the steel-rails are bedded and screwed, each single unit secured by bolts and buttjoints. The distance between the rails is, according to the text-book for the railways, termed gauge. The Russians have a special gauge because they've got no culture. But the National-Socialist German army-state is changing the whole Russian railway net to our cultured gauge as our liberation army marches into Russia to bring light into the darkness.'

He bent towards me, blinked his eyes solemnly, adjusted his belt, and rocked comfortably on his heels.

'On September 27th, 1825, the English had the unheard of cheek to open the first railway. According to accurate information obtained by our intelligence, the train consisted of thirty-four carriages weighing ninety tons. The distance was covered in sixty-five minutes.

I dared to ask the distance.

He tapped his teeth with a silver tooth-pick, sucking a little at a tooth. When his private dentistry was complete, he whispered confidentially:

'Twelve and a half kilometres. But I take it for granted that Herr Luftmarschal Hermann Göring's bombers now have annihilated this danger to our Holy German-Roman State.' He took a few deep breaths and went on: 'You can with the help of special explosives from the army's arsenal at Bamberg break up any existing railway line. But according to the laws of nature it must be done only by German troops in time of war, and only then if our culture is threatened. Do you understand all this, Herr Fahnenjunker Rilke?'

I nodded dumbly. 'Now you know what a railway line is made of,' was my only thought.

'You are going to Brobrusk. To collect the standard, I presume.'

Suddenly he became angry and swore at me for losing it at Brobrusk, but changed back almost immediately to the polite nobleman.

'So you want to go to Brobrusk. Then you'll have to get the times right. I presume you want to take advantage of our excellent National-Socialist trains. Let me see, you want to go to Brobrusk.'

Again he became quite mad and shrieked with a breaking voice:

'What the hell do you want there?'

He looked at me oddly.

'Ha, I thought so! You're off to send the whole railway line into the air? Shut up, Herr Fahnenjunker, your job is to carry the standard, the old blood-soaked standard. Keep away from Brobrusk. Stay here with me.'

He started whistling 'Horst Wessel', but it didn't suit him, so he started humming something like this:

> *'Muss i denn, muss i denn zum Städeke naus*
> *Und du, mein Schatz, bleibst hier?'*

He danced up and down, then suddenly stopped and neighed with delight: 'Well, here is the black hussar. Fahnenjunker Rainer Maria Rilke without his standard, bloody swine. You're off to the glasshouse, but we'll wait till this lovely war is over and victory-drunk cavalry troops thunder through the Brandenburger Tor greeted by spontaneous ovations from our wonderful women.'

After a short pause he added heartily and with conviction:

'And our lousy people. Well now, off you go to Brobrusk, Fahnenjunker. The train leaves at 14.21 on platform 37. It's train No. 156 but God help you if you don't bring back the standard. A regiment without its standard is like a railway without trains.'

I peeped nervously at the elegant officer who was either drunk or mad, or perhaps both.

I clicked my heels together and shouted:

'Herr Rittmeister, Fahnenjunker Hassel reports: The time is now 19.14 hours. I humbly ask confirmation that the train stops at platform 37?'

He rocked on his heels, his boots creaked, he lit a cigarette and blew the smoke in a cloud.

'So that's your question? You see I carry this cross. Don't you believe me? Does it mean you're insinuating that an officer from the horse-guards is full of lies?'

'No, Herr Rittmeister.'

'Shut up and listen, Fahnenjunker without standard.' He spat with disgust. 'You, you, you're a bastard. It doesn't concern me what time it is. You understand?'

'Yes, Herr Rittmeister.'

'Herr Fahnenjunker, all the watches are going to hell. Train No. 156, platform 37 leaves for Brobrusk at 14.21 hours. Enough! And by the Holy Moses it'll go at 14.21 hours. But if it'll be to-day or in a year, ah – that's where the corpse is buried! But we must have discipline. Don't touch the military regulations.'

He danced up the platform while he counted:

'One, two, three, four, five, six.'

Then he stopped, looked at the many tracks and shouted:

'*Alles einsteigen. Zug fahrt ab!* Berlin – Warsaw – Brest-Litovsk – Mogilev – Hell!' He clicked his tongue and chuckled. 'There, I cheated his excellency the field-marshal. That was the train for Paradise. Well, well, Herr Fahnenjunker, as you see you've got to be smart here with these Imperial Russian railways. Only last week I managed to send another general to Paradise: now I suppose he's with St Peter playing with his pigeons. When you get to Brobrusk remember me to Her Majesty the Empress Catherine. She sells Stalinchocolate in the market at Brobrusk. But don't tell her, she doesn't know herself.'

Curiously enough the train did stop at platform 37, an ammunition train going to Brobrusk.

Without further difficulties I reached my destination: the 27th (Penal) Panzer Regiment.

Again I stood in a Russian hut. A small, dirty stinking room. What a change from Helene's light, friendly flat with its fragrance.

Tired out I threw myself on the musty straw on the clay-floor and fell into a deep sleep.

Next morning the company returned from its job of building positions. Tiny greeted me with delight and shouted:

'Brought any fancy pants for me? I'm dying for a pair. Light-blue pants would make me rear like a horse!'

The Old Un had got the parcel from his wife. He retired to a corner, lost to the world.

For hours I talked about experiences. Not a button, not a strap was overlooked.

'Did she have fringed pants?' Porta wanted to know.

'What, fringed?'

'Yes, I mean these thingamebobs beautiful girls edge their pants with.' His hands described what he meant.

'Oh, I see,' I lit up. 'She had lace.'

'Do you call it lace?' Porta thumbed through his pictures and showed me an especially daring example. Grinning slyly, he asked:

'Did you do it like that?'

'No you dirty swine, I didn't go to a brothel. I visited a real girl, a Jewish girl.'

'A what?' They all shouted with one voice.

Even The Old Un woke from his dream of wife and children.

'Does frippet like that still exist?'

They got the story of Helene.

In the middle of the night Porta and Tiny woke me up.

'Tell us,' whispered Porta. 'That girl, did she have a bright red girdle, and real thigh-long stockings? With only a little bit bare?'

'Yes, bright red, and very long stockings,' was my sleepy reply.

'Hell! A bright red girdle,' groaned Porta.

'And very long stockings,' went on Tiny.

They fell heavily back in the straw.

'Didn't she have even one tiny louse?' Porta asked from the darkness.

'No lice, you must be mad.' I answered with dignity.

'And didn't she smell even a little bit of dirt?' asked Stege from his corner by the stove.

'Smell . . .'

A sigh. Snoring.

18

A clerk sat in the office. A slip of paper was on his desk. His brain was nearly paralysed by the regulations. He let the case take its course. A man was hanged. A girl lost her father. The war went on.

The Partisan

It was the day after the head-hunters took away a Russian farmer. He had been sitting in the cells outside the orderly-room. Really he was meant to be left to sit there only until he became sober, but the orderly-room sergeant, Heide, party-member and home-guard, saw his great chance. The farmer had fallen into his hands like a ripe plum. He reported at once to his superiors and the papers were signed with the CO's rubber-stamp. So the avalanche broke loose. Nothing could save the farmer. Soon the train would go off to a safe spot in the rear, carrying Sergeant Heide decorated with an Iron Cross of the Ist class.

Two bottles of vodka had been emptied. The farmer and a sergeant from No. 2 Company had come to blows. The sergeant was locked up in No. 2 Company's lines and appeared when he was sober. Everything happened according to regulations. A report on a slip of paper became the fuse to set off a chain-explosion of events.

At Jitomir they were very keen on courts-martial and special charges. They loved them dearly. And this case was blown up as always happens in the army.

The prison commandant, Major-General Hase, was an old man. Over seventy. He always kept a lock of hair from the executed neatly arranged in a box lined with velvet. He collected executed prisoners as others collect butterflies. What could the mighty gentlemen at Jitomir do if they did not execute people? Once the war was over the general would again become the nice headmaster in a small town where for the sake of the *bourgeoisie* he would have to give up his hobby of collecting locks of hair.

The farmer was a worn, poor man, who had had one over the eight of strong vodka. On paper he became a nasty partisan who wanted to harm the Third Reich.

The head-hunters fetched the farmer Vladimir Ivanovitch Vjatschslav away. They flung him into the truck, grinning as they did so, and waved good-bye to us as they trundled off to Jitomir.

One of the head-hunters hit the farmer on the head with his rifle-butt. He was only a Russian farmer, the lowest of the low in the eyes of a Prussian head-hunter. He would have been forgotten quickly enough if it had not been for the girl in the green head-scarf.

One becomes accustomed to everything, even the hanging of many 'partisans'. After their death they became Soviet heroes. Had they survived they would have become Soviet-strafnjik in the Ukhta-Petjora camp because they had *not* been hanged as 'partisans', but had tilled the earth while Hitler's soldiers stayed in their village.

The girl with the green scarf came into the canteen which was a converted hut. It was the quartermaster's idea to have a canteen. He was a business man. One of the 'sixty per cent profiteers'!

She hesitated before she approached the table where Porta and Tiny sat with the rest of us.

'Where's my father? He's been here for three days. Anastasia and I have no food.'

'Who is your father, you little thick-head?' The Old Un asked quite affectionately; and Porta clicked his tongue lecherously.

The girl responded with another click. We all roared with laughter.

'My father is the farmer Vladimir Ivanovitch Vjatschslav who lives in the yellow cottage by the river.'

For a moment there was silence.

The Old Un scratched his neck and looked desperately around for help, but we all edged away from him. What were we to say? A trial in Jitomir was a nasty affair. They liked to see the rope dangle from the rafters, and it was better if a man was hanged by the rope.

'Little girl, the army police took him away. Something silly happened. A clerk wrote a few words too many on a piece of paper.'

'Where did they take Father?'

The Old Un pushed his hand through his hair. Porta cleaned his ears with the stick from the roll-mops.

'Well, I don't really know. They drove westwards to the main road.'

The girl, who was barely fourteen years old, stared round with frightened eyes which took in the bearded dirty faces with drops of vodka in the corners of their mouths and bits of machorka-cigarettes hanging in their beards. They were foreign soldiers in strange uniforms who arrested poor farmers, hanged them, or sent them far away to the west from where nobody ever returned.

'Are you alone by the river?' Stege asked, for the sake of saying something.

'No, Anastasia is there, she's ill.'

'Who's Anastasia?'

'She's my sister. She only three years old.'

The soldiers coughed and blew their noses. Tiny spat.

'To hell with the whole world and first of all the head-hunters!'

'Who does the cooking?' The Old Un asked.

The girl looked at us. 'I do, who else?'

'No, that's right. But you've got no food. Where's your mother?'

'She was taken away by the Russian NKVD when they fetched grandfather a long time ago. Long before they started shooting.'

Tiny had crossed to the quartermaster. After a short but violent argument he returned with a loaf and a bag of salt.

'Here, take it from Tiny.' He kicked irritably at the table-leg. 'Take it before I throw it away.'

The girl nodded and put it away in a pocket under her skirt.

'Sit down here, sister,' Porta commanded.

The soldiers shuffled together to make room.

She sat down.

Porta spooned Tiny's, Stege's and his own food together in an empty dixie-lid and pushed it across to the girl.

'Eat it. You must be hungry.'

'Perhaps Father's come home. I think I'll run home.'

She looked questioningly at us.

Nobody returned her glance. We smoked silently, filled our pipes or drank long draughts from the vodka bottle.

The Old Un pulled at his nose.

'No, sit down and eat. Your father hasn't come home.' After a short pause he added, subdued: 'Not yet, anyway.'

Carefully, a little shy, she sat on the edge of the rough seat. She pushed the green scarf back and greedily filled her mouth full, chewed, swallowed, drank, shovelling more in and swallowed again. Ignoring the spoon The Old Un offered she used her fingers.

'Got a lassie just about her age,' explained The Old Un as he rubbed away a treacherous tear from his bearded cheek. 'She's going to be all alone now.'

The quartermaster came across with a saucepan full of warm milk. Without a word he put it down in front of the girl.

Tiny raised a bushy eyebrow and whistled expressively through his teeth.

'What's that?' shouted the quartermaster, furious at having betrayed any common human emotions. '*You're* going to pay, you great big swine!' He waved threateningly with his pencil. 'I'm going to write with this pencil on a piece of official paper, and I'll put Tiny's name down so there'll be no mistake if I die. Tiny from No. 5 Company. Don't think you'll get any credit without interest. No, no, you've got to pay the sixty per cent overcharge. Ha, ha, you vulture! You didn't expect that!'

Tiny went on whistling and winked confidentially at Porta.

'Did you hear what the dealer said?' Then he jumped up and threw his flick-knife after the retreating quartermaster.

It nearly caught him in the shoulder, but the long blade thumped in the wooden wall and laughed murder at him.

'Bring back my knife, swine,' roared Tiny. 'Bring it back! Bring it *back*!'

The quartermaster loosened the knife and placed it respectfully in front of Tiny. He was just turning away when Tiny grabbed him by the breast of his tunic, lifted him up and shook him violently.

'You're a bloody pig and a bloody thief. Aren't you? Repeat, you . . .'

'Striped swine,' Porta helped him out.

'Yes,' shouted Tiny. 'A striped swine, a blue striped swine. Bloody hell, you'll repeat it now!'

Half-choked the quartermaster repeated the abuse.

Tiny wanted it three times over.

Nodding frantic agreement, the quartermaster repeated it, almost purple in the face. Tiny flung him away and he rolled like a ball towards his counter. The last stretch he crawled on all fours.

Tiny bent down to the girl who had shrunk against the wall.

'Don't be afraid, my pet. Tiny is a God-fearing man who protects the weak. Amen!' He made the sign of the cross as he thought was proper when he became God-fearing.

Stege took a bundle of roubles out of his pocket and threw them to the girl. Several others followed his example. Even Porta, who loved money, took out a sheaf which he counted carefully before putting a rubber-band round it and handing it to the girl.

Tiny snapped his fingers at the quartermaster, who came running at once.

'A parcel of food for the girl and some roubles,' ordered Tiny.

Without a word of protest, the quartermaster made up a parcel and put a bundle of roubles in.

The girl wanted to go home. She knotted the green scarf firmly under her chin and tied up tightly with a piece of string the old army coat she was wearing.

Stege and the Little Legionnaire elected themselves to see her home. They took their pistols, put on their snow-coats and went out into the dark with the girl between them.

The Hindenburg-candle fluttered. Someone threw tallow into the container. The flames danced.

'Do you think they'll shoot him?' Bauer asked of the omniscient Old Un.

'Well, it's become a habit to kill people. Many youngsters have to experience what that lassie with the green scarf is just going through.'

'Good thing we don't know every time someone dies,' said Pluto. 'Do you think that fellow they guillotined the other day in Karali had any children?'

'You never know. But you should never ask; it only hurts. And it becomes too difficult to live,' replied The Old Un.

Porta suddenly brightened up and straightened his bent back.

'What about swiping the girl's father?'

'And how are you going to do that?' sneered The Old Un. 'Do you think he's there without a guard?'

'Why the hell can't we do it?' Porta cried angrily. 'If we can dish it out to Ivan in the trenches do you think we'd find it hard to lay a flock of pale head-hunters horizontal?'

Pluto nodded.

'You're right, Porta. Four or five of us could easily pick the adam's apples out of the gullets of those stiffs, and, hey presto, we've disappeared in the night with the farmer.'

'It's possible, but what's going to happen afterwards?' asked The Old Un.

'Afterwards?' Porta glared at him.

'Yes, afterwards. Do you think the rest of them would go back to bed and forget that someone had cut the throats of a flock of head-hunters?'

'Bah,' said Porta haughtily. 'By that time we'd be miles away. They'd never know who did it.'

'No, you're dead right. They'd never find you, and they'd never believe you if you told them. You see, sonny, they'd do something far worse. They'd raise hell about partisans. They don't believe they've caught a partisan now. They know very well he's an innocent farmer. But if we get him out by shooting they'll have a whole SS unit in this district within five hours and several villages will be annihilated. Thousands of women and children will be shoved into concentration-camps as a reprisal for the missing farmer who'll then become a dangerous and long-wanted partisan leader. If we and others keep our paws off only the farmer Vladimir Ivanovitch Vjatschslav will be hanged. The general will enjoy his day. The commander of the head-hunters will receive his decoration. And it'll be quiet until the general gets bored again. If Vladimir kicks and makes it difficult for them so much the better. The district will have peace for a bit because it was such a fine execution and it'll provide the flatfeet with small-talk for a long time. The farmer Vladimir Ivanovitch Vjatschslav is the price of peace in this district.'

'Let me get my hands on these dirty bastards when the war's over,' hissed Porta. 'I'll pour molten lead down their throats.'

Stege and the Little Legionnaire had returned. They swore angrily, especially at the military police and the station in Jitomir.

Then the Little Legionnaire suggested in all seriousness that we should get a few officers from the station and export them to Ivan.

'You must be raving mad,' The Old Un burst out angrily.

'Don't you think we'll manage?' shouted the Little Legionnaire.

'Easy,' said Porta before The Old Un could answer. 'The desert-nomad, Tiny and I can kidnap the whole pack of officers at the station, including Lord High Executioner Hase.'

'I don't doubt it at all,' answered The Old Un, 'but you'd have to be idiots to try. Or perhaps you want hell to descend over all the farmers in this district? Even you madmen must see what would happen here if you pulled this job off?'

'Well, then we'll—' Porta stopped as the door opened and stared at the man who stood there shaking the snow off his coat.

Tiny blinked his eyes, nodded a few times and whistled between his teeth.

The quartermaster stood at his counter and played with an empty bottle. He gave a nod with his bald bull's head towards the door as a knife whistled through the air and embedded itself in the floor at the feet of the NCO in the doorway.

The Little Legionnaire rose and slid like a panther across to the door. He jerked the knife away, kissed it and hummed a tune.

'Allah is great and wise.'

The silence was evil. It pressed against the walls and roof.

Sergeant Heide, the clerk, smiled.

'Somebody's being cheeky here. You think you can have fun with Heide?' A large Nagan machine-pistol was in his hand. With a click, he cocked his Nagan. 'I'll make mincemeat of your mongrel-brains. Just tell me when and where.'

Silence. Threatening silence. Murder lurked in the shadows.

'Cod-fish!' decided Heide and ordered a pint of beer.

'Nothing doing,' came thickly out of the quartermaster's fat gob.

'A small vodka.'

'Nothing left,' smiled the quartermaster with thin lips and eyes full of poison.

'What have you got?' Heide demanded, pushing his head forward like a butting ram. He rested his right hand in his coat pocket which held the Nagan.

'Nothing, you bastard!' bawled the quartermaster and crashed the bottle to smithereens.

'You refuse to serve me, Unteroffizier Julius Heide, you greasy grocer?'

'This is all I've got,' growled the quartermaster and held the broken bottle in front of Heide's face.

Tiny guffawed.

'Come here, sucking-pig, we've got plenty.'

Heide whirled round, stared confusedly at Tiny and took a few steps across to the table.

Tiny stabbed his long knife into the table and roared:

'This is what we've got, you louse, if you're not out of this nice room in two seconds.'

'What the hell's wrong with you all?' stammered Heide astonished and confused.

'What's wrong?' sneered Bauer. 'What do you think, you bloody coward? Maybe we've got constipation.'

Heide stepped back like a tiger ready to pounce. The Little Legionnaire barred his way. The Nagan pointed coldly at him as he slowly advanced on the nattily turned-out NCO clerk.

'If you take another step, you Moroccan ponce, you'll sneeze blood,' hissed Heide, staring desperately at the little fellow with the deadly green eyes.

We waited for the Nagan to fire, but nobody moved.

Quicker than a flash the Little Legionnaire's foot flew up and kicked the Nagan out of Heide's hand. Heide backed with a shriek of pain.

Tiny collected the pistol, tore out the magazine and flung it in a corner.

The Little Legionnaire jerked forward and hit Heide in the stomach. He went down with a crash. Smiling evilly, the Little Legionnaire kicked Heide's teeth in and broke his nose with a ferocious stamp.

'So you meant to shoot, you rat? You'll have to learn how first. You're better at writing, eh?'

Heide collected himself, sat upon the floor and dazedly wiped the blood off his face.

'What do you mean?' he babbled. 'Are you mad? I come to get a pint of beer and for a peaceful natter, and you ambush me without the slightest reason.'

The Little Legionnaire came across and sat down with us.

'A sweet lad. All holy innocence. Get up, you snotty mongrel, or you'll get a knife in your gullet!'

With difficulty Heide got up and collapsed on the bench. Porta handed him a mug of beer. Heide looked thankfully into the inscrutable face of the red-head beneath the top-hat where only the blue, pig-like eyes betrayed any life.

Heide is bringing the mug to his mouth and is just about to

take a sip when Porta with a savage grin knocks it out of his hand and the glass describes an arc through the air.

Tiny shouts, full of delight:

'The silly has lost his beer, the silly has lost his beer!'

Heide springs up and glares furiously at Tiny. He scrambles over the table to get at him. Tiny starts to run round the room howling like a small child after a spanking.

'It wasn't me, it was Porta! It wasn't me, it was Porta!'

Suddenly he stops and kicks out backwards. Heide collapses and is thrown against the wall.

With a dreadful roar Tiny is over him, swinging his arms like a windmill.

A few half-choked cries, and Heide resembles a butchered pig.

The Little Legionnaire throws a couple of buckets of water over him. Shaking and sniffing he gets to his legs, but stumbles and falls insensible across the table.

Pluto flings him into a corner.

The quartermaster appears from his cage behind the counter and offers us all beer laced with vodka.

Pluto, spitting at the unconscious Heide says:

'Informer!'

19

It was easier for a camel to get through the eye of a needle than for Tiny to enter into Allah's garden.

He tried everything after they had told him his life-line was short.

He threatened, implored, wept, and prayed, but he had to confess to his sins.

He had much to thank Ivan for when the Russians interrupted the Little Legionnaire's confessional.

Tiny Receives Absolution

'Twenty-one,' bawled Porta and smacked the cards down on the ammunition box we used as a table.

Suspiciously we stared at the greasy cards. Tiny started to count on his fingers, but it was undisputedly twenty-one.

With a smooth gesture Porta brushed his winnings into his steel-helmet.

'Want to go on, lads?'

Porta had won for the thirty-seventh time. Tiny who had lost everything did not want to go on although Porta generously offered him and the rest of us credit against a hundred per cent interest.

'We'd have to be imbeciles,' said Stege. 'We can go to the sixty per cent men and pick up a hundred marks. But whatever we do we'd lose.'

Tiny sat staring thoughtfully in front of him, then he leaned confidentially across to Porta.

'You wouldn't cheat Tiny, would you?'

Porta blinked his colourless eyelashes, polished his monocle and pressing it into his left pig's-eye said:

'No. Joseph Porta would not cheat Tiny.'

'I didn't think so,' answered Tiny relieved. A terrible doubt had been dispelled.

The Old Un came down into the bunker.

'Now we're sold. No. 2 Platoon is going to be rearguard for the 104th gunner-regiment when they go out of the line. They're getting ready now. Not one of us'll get away alive.'

Porta laughed and pointed to himself.

'You're wrong, Old Un. The old man here'll get away with all his whiskers intact.'

'How do you know?' asked Tiny with interest.

'A fortune-teller whispered it into my ear. First she saw it in my palm. Half an hour later she spread two pounds of coffee-grounds on the table and read the very same thing.'

Tiny moved nervously and inched along the seat to Porta.

'What did she read, Porta?'

'Well, that French madame told me I'd get away with my life in this war, marry a rich wench and live many happy years as principal shareholder of several prosperous whore-houses.'

'Blimey,' said Tiny. 'You don't think she played you up?'

Porta shook his head.

'Certainly not.'

Tiny took an interest in his own hand.

'What's this line here?' he asked Porta.

'That's the life-line, my friend. And it's damned short.'

The Little Legionnaire looked up and pointed warningly at Tiny.

'Get your face towards Mecca. Allah is great and wise.'

Tiny swallowed nervously.

'Who in hell would want to make Tiny cold?'

'Ivan,' said Porta laconically.

We had received many new men in No. 2 Platoon. Among them a former SS Unterscharführer who had been two years in Torgau camp. Von Barring had warned The Old Un against him.

'Keep your eye on that fellow. I don't trust him.'

Now Stege told us that the SS fellow who had been attached to us, Heide and some others had made a pact to liquidate our gang when the chance came.

One of the new ones, Corporal Peters, sat down beside us. In his taciturn way he said without any introduction:

'There are twenty-five men who've decided to fix you lot up.'

Tiny was about to react, but a warning glance from Porta made him pause, although he mumbled something about short and long life-lines.

'Where do you get your information?' asked the Little Legionnaire, his cigarette hanging from his lips.

'Oh, I just know,' Peters said without expression. 'And now you know too.'

The Old Un held him back.

'Where are they going to do it?'

Peters shrugged his shoulders and pointed to the Russian positions.

'Kraus, the SS fellow, thinks Ivan's behind us and that the platoon's completely cut off. When your little mob has been made horizontal they'll be off.'

The Little Legionnaire spat out his cigarette.

'Aren't you going with them? Or are you fed up with life?'

Peters looked at him through slit eyes. He said inscrutably:

'I don't care about life much, but I don't like murder.'

'Then you ought to have kept away from here and gone into a monastery,' said Porta. 'In the Eastern Front winter-sport society we deal only with murder. Like this!' he shouted and emptied the magazine of his machine-pistol with a thunder on the ground in front of other members of our platoon farther down the long bunker.

They jumped up, swearing. The SS man grabbed his machine-pistol but let go of it as if it was glowing hot. He was looking into the muzzles of four machine-pistols and one 'stove-pipe'.

'Did it scare you amateurs?' grinned Porta as he flung an empty shell-case in the face of the SS man. He fell backwards with only a grunt.

Porta pointed to some of the others.

'Fetch the swine here.'

Smiling satanically he tore a piece of white cloth from his

bread bag and ordered them to sew the patch on the back of the unconscious man.

When the SS man came to, he sat up dazedly and glared at Porta who announced cheerfully:

'You've got a white patch on your back. That's my target. If you get too far away from me your heart'll leave your body with the help of this comforter.'

He patted his machine-pistol expressively.

'If by any chance you lose the patch, you'll be a dead man!'

'Great gun, isn't it?' the Little Legionnaire inquired gently.

Tiny had again been studying the lines of his hand. He jumped up, grabbed Corporal Krosnika, one of the Kraus group of newcomers, by the throat and bashed him against one of the wooden roof supports.

'You bloody goat, did you want to shoot Tiny? You've cut away half my life-line!' Bellowing like a wounded bear, he fumbled for his knife. 'My life, my life, my short life!'

Krosnika kicked and hit out to get free. His face turned slowly purple and his kicks and punches became weaker. If The Old Un had not taken a hand he would have been choked.

With a terrible oath Tiny let go of his prey who fell down half-suffocated between Heide and a former sergeant from the military concentration camp at Torgau.

Porta laughed.

'A small warning, otherwise, bound over to be of good behaviour, as they say in educated circles. You others,' he shouted and swung his machine-pistol menacingly, 'will get your knobs shaved off when we find it suitable. So no monkey-business, see!'

Peters sat with his back to the bunker-wall. In his lap lay a Russian machine-pistol. He sat smoking indifferently.

In a short time the routine relief of sentries fell due. A violent quarrel was started by the SS fellow and Krosnika. They did not want to do sentry-duty, and tried to change with a couple of other men.

The Old Un suddenly threw down his cards, rose slowly and pointed at the SS fellow with his pipe.

'You and Krosnika are not going. Heide and Francke will take over.'

Triumph shone in the eyes of the SS man, but it disappeared quickly enough when The Old Un went on:

'You and Krosnika will go across to Ivan's positions and come back with an accurate report of what's going on.'

Calmly he sat down and resumed the interrupted game.

The SS man and Krosnika started muttering.

The Old Un played an ace of spades, gathered in a jack-pot and looked calmly at the pair of them:

'Didn't you hear my orders?'

'It's personal persecution,' shouted the SS man. 'We can't go across to the enemy line without being covered. We object to your order.'

The Old Un leaned against the wall and fingered his P38.

'So you object. Better use your head a little. You who are a volunteer and a party-member. What do you think your Führer would say?'

The SS man leaned threateningly across to The Old Un.

'What do you mean? My Führer. He's yours also, isn't he?'

'You're a little bit slow, my friend.'

Tiny was about to say something, but The Old Un went on:

'You've chosen the Führer voluntarily and are his man, and he's been forced on me. Anyhow, perhaps you've never heard about the special courts?'

'Don't try to threaten me with that,' jeered the SS man. 'You need to be at least a company commander to convene one.'

'You seem very sure. Don't you know we're cut off from the others, and that a leader of a detail like this can convene a special court when he suspects danger to the detail in the form of a meeting, treason or objections to orders. I can mount a special court for you any time and place I like.' The Old Un banged his fist on the ammunition-box. 'Get out, or Tiny and Porta will see you out!'

Without another syllable they swung their weapons over their shoulders and left the bunker.

Tiny passed a bottle of vodka round. When it reached Porta, Tiny said hopefully:

'Doesn't this life-line ever cheat you?'

'Never, it's dead certain,' was Porta's sad answer. He looked pityingly at Tiny's deeply concerned face. His delight was great when he discovered that the Little Legionnaire's hand too had a short life-line and became quite dotty when he found that the Little Legionnaire's line was even shorter than his.

'You'll march to the muck-heap before Tiny!' he bawled.

The Little Legionnaire looked long and searchingly into Tiny's face. Tiny had become quite exalted and drank greedily from the vodka bottle.

'Allah's ways are inscrutable but true,' mumbled the Little Legionnaire loud enough for Tiny to hear. 'I'll get into Allah's garden. You who are an infidel will go to hell's terrible suffering and corruption.' With a motherly hand he patted Tiny's head. 'We'll pray for you, poor infidel, who'll have to suffer untold horrors when somebody in Allah's good time sticks a knife into your back.'

Tiny had the bottle half-way to his mouth and stared at the sinisterly friendly Little Legionnaire.

'Oh, shut up with all this spooky talk. Do you really believe in all this this cock about heaven and hell?'

The Little Legionnaire nodded seriously.

'There is only one God, the true one, Allah, and he knows how to sort the ewes from the rams.'

Tiny looked frightenedly round him, and leaned over to the Little Legionnaire while he nervously picked his nose.

'Tell me, pal, how'll I get into Allah's garden?'

The Little Legionnaire smiled a tired and hopeless smile.

'It'll be very difficult for you, my friend. Much will be demanded before you'll be let in. Oh, Allah is great!'

With hearty conviction Tiny said: 'Oh, to hell with that! Just tell Tiny what he'll have to do to wing it to Paradise. Of two evils you pick the lesser, don't you?' he asked Porta.

Porta nodded in his serious agreement.

Tiny stared at him a moment.

'Are you holy? Will you land in Allah's garden?'

'Of course,' answered Porta. 'I've seen to that a long time ago. I'm no idiot. For God Almighty's sake, what if one were shot this minute and had to endure the eternal tortures of hell.'

Tiny asked every one of us if we were holy.

Everyone convincingly averred his holiness.

Almost weeping he addressed the Little Legionnaire.

'My God! Tiny'll go all alone to this bloody hell you talk so much about. If only one of you would come along it wouldn't be so bad. But all alone I'll never stand it. There's no justice. You'll have to help me, pal. Tiny'll do anything you wish to make his peace with Allah.'

The Little Legionnaire looked sternly at him.

'Are you sure you'll do everything?'

'Yes, yes,' Tiny said, nodding furiously. Hope shone in his desperate face.

'Good. You'll have to forgive your enemies. Can you do that?'

'Easy,' cried Tiny and grabbed the Little Legionnaire. 'I'll forgive you all the evil things you've done to me.'

'Me?' groaned the surprised Little Legionnaire, when he was released.

'Yes, you,' beamed Tiny. 'Up to two minutes ago you were my arch-enemy.' He searched his pockets and gave the Little Legionnaire a small bag of white powder. 'That's rat poison. I was going to put it in your beer on Victory Day because you were my enemy – you kicked me on the head and broke my nose.'

'Bloody hell,' burst out the Little Legionnaire and stared at the happy Tiny.

'Do you know?' Tiny had it all worked out. 'You were first just to have a peep at the Tommies when they marched through the Brandenburger Tor.'

'The Tommies?' asked Stege, astonished.

'Yes, who else? They'll win the war.'

Tiny turned to the Little Legionnaire again.

'When you were going to the pub with us to celebrate the

Tommies' victory and were sitting dreaming about your life among the tarts in the Moroccan whore-boxes, you were to jump off your chair like a mad cat that's sat on a red-hot stove. This mecidine would have taken you ten minutes to conk out. But you needn't worry now. Tiny's forgiven you!'

The Little Legionnaire nodded in a friendly way.

'Good. I've accepted your confession. But, as you haven't a lot of time, you'll have to pay a fine.'

'What the hell's that?' asked Tiny suspiciously.

'All your booze and tobacco must be handed over to me to convince Allah you've repented your evil plans against a faithful and loyal comrade-in-arms.'

Tiny was about to protest but was warned: 'Remember hell's terrible torture and hand over the prescribed fine.'

'Have you any other evil tricks up your sleeve? You'll have to confess now to get complete absolution.'

Tiny shook his head.

'What? Haven't you committed any atrocities?' shouted Porta.

'No, never,' said Tiny. 'I've always lived a peaceful and quiet life and faithfully performed my daily job.'

'Well, I'm damned! If that's so I must be super-good and as pious as the holy Anthony himself!'

'Now think well,' the Little Legionnaire admonished. 'It would be very sad if within half-an-hour you were playing "Rocking-horse" on the lap of the Evil One and sneezing in the sulphur-steam.'

Tiny shook his head, glared, rose and kicked a steel-helmet over the head of Corporal Freytag who jumped up furiously while Tiny screamed in a frenzy:

'Sit down, or I'll cut your throat and take you with me to hell. I won't be lonely . . .' He stopped frightened, and looked imploringly at the Little Legionnaire.

'What do you want to know, pal?'

'I don't want to know anything. It's Allah.' He salaamed piously and mumbled: *'Allah-akbar!'*

'Now tell us calmly what you've been up to in your thirty years of wicked life,' Bauer said severly.

Tiny drew a deep breath. He wanted to fight somebody and played thoughtfully with his combat-knife.

Porta was ready to crown him with a hand-grenade.

Tiny perspired.

'Blimey, it's hard to become holy. Well, well! Let me get going. I kicked a stupid clot in the stomach and he died. But that's a long time ago. And he was a real cretin, a piece of muck, a dirty swine.'

'Why did you kick him?' the Little Legionnaire asked curiously. 'You're usually so calm.'

'I can't rightly remember.'

Tiny tried hard to get away from the awkward question, but the Little Legionnaire was merciless.

'Did he die shortly after your kick or suffer for a long time?'

Tiny dried his forehead with his rifle-rag and so covered his face with dirty oil.

'That Franz was a scoundrel. He would have been hanged in any case.'

Tiny was becoming solemn. 'By God, I did society a service by kicking the stupid swine. He was No. 1 enemy of the world. He cheated the tarts of their money.' Delighted with this idea, he went on: 'Yes, that's why I kicked him. By God, that's why! Fancy cheating a hard-working whore. It was my duty to do something.'

Tiny brushed his hands together and looked happily around.

'Tiny, you're lying,' interrupted the Little Legionnaire sternly. 'Do you want to go to hell all alone? Thirst always among the greedy flames? Load the Devil's heavy mortars all day long?'

Tiny licked his dry lips and was about to take a swing from his bottle when he remembered he had given the Little Legionnaire the contents. He wrung his hands and groaned loudly.

'To think that swine's got me into this situation! But it was his own fault things went as they did. He cheated me. He'd promised me all the beer I could drink, and when I politely asked him to honour his word he became cheeky and hit me here.' Tiny pointed to his left ear. 'And it hurt, so you see it was a sort of self-defence. I had to go on parade with a dirty belt and that rotten animal, Sergeant Paust, had me in the book for it. And there were other things that bloody Franz had promised to do, too. But I don't bear him any grudge any longer.'

'You mean he didn't want to pay for your beer when you tried to force him. And he wouldn't be your slave?' said the Little Legionnaire brutally.

'Now, it's not necessary to say it like that. It sounds so bad.'

'Was it like that or not? Allah sees everything. Allah hears everything.'

'All right, if that's the way you want it, he was a rotten animal, a paralysed ox, a castrated ram who did no good.'

The Little Legionnaire raised his hand.

'What you said just now, I take as a personal insult, Tiny, my former arch-enemy, my present friend. Will you give me a bottle of vodka in fines?'

Tiny nodded silently.

'You'll have to give two. Go on with your explanation.'

Tiny swallowed painfully, roughed up his wild hair and pulled at his collar.

'Franz would certainly have been hanged if he had survived. I couldn't help it that he fell out of the window and hit a stake in the flower-bed.'

The Little Legionnaire shook his head.

'This is a grim tale.'

Tiny looked nervously at him. 'You don't think Allah will throw me to hell for that little episode? I give you my word of honour . . .'

Porta hooted at Tiny's solemn mouthing of the word honour.

Tiny looked reproachfully at him.

'You needn't laugh, Porta. I'll tell you that my word of honour is something holy for me, and I give you my word of honour that Franz was a scoundrel Allah would have turned away from in disgust.'

The Little Legionnaire pointed accusingly at Tiny.

'You'll get your absolution, but it'll cost nine litres of vodka or good German liquor.'

'And where the hell will I get it?' shouted Tiny.

'You'll find it, and in a hurry. Remember your short life-line,' the Little Legionnaire answered implacably.

'As you wish. You'll have it.' He spat in his palms and looked at the rest of the section. 'You bloody insects will all soon be heavily taxed by Tiny, you life-line thieves!'

This interesting development in Tiny's spiritual odyssey was interrupted by the SS man and Krosnika who came running into the bunker.

'Ivan's gone! There's not a soul left in the trenches. We heard engine noises and trucks rattling on the road. It's T34s and they're behind us!'

The SS man stopped to catch his breath.

The Old Un looked calmly at him.

'Did you expect them to ask us when they were going to chase our units?'

'Oh, shut up, I'm not an idiot,' hissed the SS man furiously. 'We've got to run for it or we're trapped.'

'Run? That's the second time you've given us talk of that sort,' jeered The Old Un. 'You fellows are heroes of another sort when you shout "Heil!" back home. I hope it's clear to you that I give the orders here. Maybe I've decided to follow the advice of your crazy Führer and fight to the last man and bullet.'

The SS man nearly exploded with indignation.

'You call our Führer crazy? I'll take a note of that!'

'I hope you will,' sneered The Old Un. 'But answer me this: Do you want us to fight to the last man and bullet? *You* can decide whether we follow the Führer's orders or not: die in battle or save our lives!'

The SS man shifted his weight from one foot to the other. He opened and shut his mouth but not a syllable was heard.

'I take it your silence means we're going to fight. Follow your Führer. Well, get out on the road with that "stove-pipe" Pluto's got there. Krosnika and Heide will carry the ammunition. You'll fight the T34s at once, and ruin as many as you can before you're crushed by the tracks.'

'This is nonsense,' burst out the SS man.

'*You* say that – a former member of Adolf's SS? Well then, you agree that Adolf's crazy – a blood-thirsty maniac!'

Tiny's voice cut through the conversation.

'Let me see your hand, you dope!'

Before the SS man could answer, Tiny grabbed it.

'Hm, you've a short life-line, you mongrel. Get out on the road or it'll be even shorter!'

The Old Un chuckled.

'All right, we agree to save our lives despite the Führer's orders? It's always easier to fight to the last breath when you can't see Ivan or hear his T34s.' He turned to Pluto and me: 'You two and Heide will go up the road and see if we can get across. That's our only chance.'

He unfolded the map on the ammunition-box. With interest we followed his dirty finger as it traced the way he thought we could escape.

'It looks a bit large, all that green,' said Stege. 'Is it all jungle?'

'Yes,' answered The Old Un, 'and most of it is swampy.'

Swearing, the three of us started through the forest. Heide dragged the 'stove-pipe'.

The rain streamed from the steel-helmets down our backs. The belts rubbed. We shivered in the wet uniforms. Our feet sank knee-deep in the mud and the water seeped into our boots. Every step was torture.

Pluto swore loudly and volubly.

'You bloody well shut up,' hissed Heide. 'You'll have Ivan here with all that shouting.'

Pluto raised his machine-pistol threateningly.

'Shut up yourself, you rat. Don't forget we've got accounts to settle. If Ivan comes, we'll tell him all about your bloody acts.'

'To think a dirty Black Sea farmer can get you all so het up. How thin-skinned you are! Anyway, it was all a mistake on my part.'

Pluto stopped.

'A mistake!' he shouted. It boomed through the wet forest. 'You bloody cow, you stinking muck-heap, just wait and I'll cut your loud-speaker for you. Then you can talk about mistakes with the blood pumping up your throat.'

'Put a sock in it, Pluto,' I tried to mediate. 'Leave that idiot alone. Shoot him or let him go to hell.'

'It's got nothing to do with you, you Fahnenjunker-boy. Don't get on your high horse with Pluto. Do you think I'm afraid?' He swung his machine-pistol over his head and roared into the darkness: 'Hey, Ivan, bloody curs, Stalin-craps, come and get an informer-swine, Unteroffizier Heide! Hey, Iva-a-a-n-n!'

Heide let go the 'stove-pipe' and ran as fast as his legs would carry him.

'Take care you don't fall and hurt your head,' Pluto shouted after him.

I collected the 'stove-pipe' and we went on silently through the forest. The branches whipped us wetly in the face.

'What a muck-war,' hissed Pluto. 'Panzer soldiers running round like "foot-rag acrobats". God, what a monkey forest, not a damn thing to be seen.'

'I wish you'd shut up. Write to Stalin or Adolf and complain!'

'Oh, bloody funny!' Pluto snarled.

Then suddenly the road appeared in front of us. Tightly packed columns of Russian infantry wrapped in capes marched past. Huge trucks and gun-carriages thundered westwards. Here and there Aldis lights winked short signals.

'We'll never get across this,' whispered Pluto. 'Let's get away before the swine see us.'

Noiselessly we disappeared.

Astonishment was great when we stepped into the bunker. Heide tried to get away, but a kick from Pluto sent him across to Tiny and Porta.

'We thought you were on your way to Berlin,' growled Pluto. 'You're a good runner. This little mistake is called cowardice in the face of the enemy according to military law. Just you wait.'

Heide was white as a sheet. He shook with fright as he sat between Tiny and Porta. They were eagerly engaged discussing how best to dismember a pig.

The Old Un rose quietly when he had listened to our report. He pointed to Heide.

'We'll deal with you later. Let's get cracking. We've to get across that road – and before daybreak.'

I threw the 'stove-pipe' at Heide.

'Here, and don't lose it!'

In single file we started off. Thorns and climbing plants laced themselves round us as if to keep us back. The rain became a veritable cloud-burst.

The Old Un and Stege got down near the road. The rest of the platoon sought cover a little way behind in the dense undergrowth.

Porta was lying there unconcernedly with his top-hat covering his face. The cat sheltered under his coat. It looked extremely sorry for itself with its drenched fur.

'It's no bloody fun being a soldier,' he mumbled to the cat, 'is it?'

Tiny sat tailor-wise on the wet ground beside the Little Legionnaire exploring the possibilities of his advent to heaven.

Pluto had hung up his groundsheet and was playing patience.

Two men quarrelled over a cigarette-end. They sounded like Bauer and Krosnika.

Stege came silently across to us.

'Ready lads? We're off. We're going up on the road to march along nicely with Ivan until we can see our way to escape to the other side. The Old Un's hoping they won't discover what kind of army we are!'

'It'll never come off,' said Bauer. 'Marching along hand in hand with Ivan! For heaven's sake, let's get away from here.'

The Old Un stood up calmly and signalled us to move.

The gravel crunched under our boots as we marched up on the road.

Barely a yard away from us a Russian infantry company marched past. We hardly dared to look at them. They might read the fright in our faces.

Porta cheekily started whistling a Russian soldier's song, and invisible forms in the darkness fell in.

Slowly The Old Un edged over to the middle of the road. We were nearly across when a voice shouted:

'Keep right, keep right!'

We jumped like grasshoppers to the right as a panzer column went racing by.

A figure leaned out of a car and swore at us for marching in the middle of the road.

It spat a puddle of mud at us in farewell.

The Old Un again started to pull us towards the left side and soon we were standing in the undergrowth.

Porta slapped his thighs in delight.

'That's a good one! Told off by a Russky colonel for not marching nicely on the side. He'd wet his pants if someone told him who he'd sworn at.'

'Don't laugh too soon,' warned Bauer. 'We aren't through yet.'

'How far is it to Orcha?' asked Stege.

'Seventy-five miles,' answered The Old Un. 'Through swamps and forests. More like 200 miles of ordinary road.'

At dawn we reached the swamp. Exhausted we threw ourselves down in the mud. We were only half aware of Pluto's quarrelling with the SS man.

'You're a louse!' shouted Pluto. 'Fancy volunteering – do you enjoy murder? Nazi-bug, clean my boots.' He put a dirty boot under his enemy's nose. 'Lick the muck off or I'll choke you!'

'You dirty vermin,' cried the SS man and went for Pluto.

He kicked and bit desperately. The great red scar left by Pluto's amputated ear was opened and the blood welled down his neck and shoulder.

Tiny made short work of the fight by hammering the butt of his machine-pistol on the head of the SS man. Gurgling he fell down with a large wound in his head.

Pluto fought for breath. Tiny kicked the SS man in the groin. With every kick he swore long and sulphurously.

We all looked on with complete indifference.

The Old Un ordered us to march on. Someone asked what to do about the unconscious SS man.

'Kick his face in,' Porta said. 'Or leave him to rot.'

The whole day we waded in water sometimes up to our shoulders or jumped from tuft to tuft in the sagging swamp.

An eighteen-year-old recruit misjudged his jump and landed with a cry in the sticky substance. Only bubbles showed where he had disappeared.

By late afternoon we reached fairly firm ground.

Porta stumbled, and the flame-thrower shot away from him.

A little later The Old Un ordered a rest.

Cross and angry, we threw ourselves down and fell at once into a trance-like sleep. Slowly the rest of the platoon reached us, dragging their feet.

We had been resting for about a couple of hours when Pluto jumped up with his machine-pistol at the ready.

At once we were all alert. Without a sound the 'stove-pipe' was brought into position and a shell rammed into the breech.

Two figures appeared from among the trees.

To our astonishment we saw the SS man and Krosnika. We dropped our arms and lay down again.

Stege's voice broke the silent forest darkness.

'Didn't you have the mortar with you?'

We half sat up, instantly on guard. There was a threat in the air.

Krosnika breathed heavily.

'Didn't you hear the question?' hissed Porta. 'Where's the mortar?'

'What's it got to do with you?' said the Torgau corporal. 'You aren't the platoon commander.'

'Where the hell did you spring from?' shouted Pluto.

'Balls to you!' answered the corporal.

Throaty animal-noises came from the darkness.

'Stay where you are, Pluto,' shouted The Old Un sharply. 'I'm not having any more scrapping. Krosnika, go for the mortar at once and don't come back without it.'

Krosnika disappeared among the tree-trunks. We lay quietly and listened to his footsteps.

'We'll never see him again,' whispered Bauer.

Nobody bothered to answer.

Three hours later The Old Un ordered us to move on.

The boots hurt. The belts and straps rubbed. Steel-helmets were thrown away, followed by gas-masks and their containers.

From a steep hill we could see an enormous green landscape stretching before us. It looked as if we were in the middle of a huge green ocean.

The Old Un permitted only half-an-hour's rest. Then we chopped our way through the dense undergrowth with entrenching tools and axes. Our small quantity of rations was soon finished.

Hungry and thirsty we fought our way forward. Wild quarrels took place continually. The smallest remark was regarded as a dirty insult. The Old Un alone was calmly collected. He walked along smoking his antique pipe. His machine-pistol bounced from his shoulder. From time to time he consulted map and compass.

Porta managed to shoot a fox and a big hare. Both were eaten raw. We did not dare to make a fire. The smoke might betray us. The fox-meat was rubbed in onion to take away the nauseating smell. But, smell or no smell, everything was eaten to the last sinew.

Several of the men dropped behind. We tried only cursorily to get them moving, and then went on without looking back at the sobbing friend who implored us for a minute's rest.

Some caught up with us at our brief resting-places. The Torgau corporal ran beserk when we stopped at a water-hole. He suddenly threw himself at Porta and gave him a long cut in one cheek and a deep wound in the arm.

Tiny and Pluto parted them. Tiny knocked the corporal

out. Porta drew his knife and was about to gash the corporal when The Old Un stopped him.

'Let him be. We're going.'

Pluto nodded silently, bent over the unconscious man, took his weapons, spat at him and then plunged on.

Stege marked the trees every five hundred yards so that those who were left behind could follow.

On the fourth day we reached a narrow forest road clearly marked by horse-and-cart tracks.

. . . They stood leaning against a tree. Two small men dressed in brown with machine-pistols hanging by their sides. The wind carried a faint odour of machorka to us.

At once we became killers, twentieth-century cave-men.

Silently we crouched in the grass and snaked along. A small watercourse afforded us much wanted cover.

Nearer, sure of our prey, we crept. Porta winked at Pluto who settled himself in readiness behind a tuft. He bent the grass aside to make a clear field of fire.

The sun broke from behind clouds and lit up the two men. One pushed his cap with the green cross back on his head. A whip – the nagajka – dangled from his wrist.

With a shock we realized the significance of nagajka and green cross. These were NKVD.

The rolling thunder from three machine-pistols rapes the silence. The tearing rat-tat-tat lasts only a few seconds.

Two brown men with green crosses in their caps and Siberian prison-nagajkas at their wrist fold at hip-level and pitch forward. Bloody foam oozes out of mouths and ears. Steel rattles against steel as new magazines are loaded in three German machine-pistols.

The silence of the forest again descends.

Porta whistles like a bird, a long calling note. The birds answer, at first a little timidly but soon in a great chorus.

We lie waiting tense as steel-springs.

The Old Un orders us to fan out silently. The four light machine-guns are sited to cover a wide field of fire.

The Little Legionnaire creeps forward and slinks down in some thick bushes with Heide. They have the 'stove-pipe'.

'Ji fob tvoi matj,' someone whispered in the thicket.

We were able to see only the upper parts of their bodies. The rest was well hidden in the bushes. Silently they moved forward, about thirty soldiers led by a lieutenant.

A loud cry. They stopped and gathered round a sergeant. They had found their comrades.

'Mjortyvj,' one said. They looked about. *'Ubjivat,'* another said.

The Old Un who had raised one hand let it fall with a chopping motion.

Muscles were flexed. The green cross decorated men with the long nagajkas were about to receive their extreme unction.

A long, sharp and terrible cry of revenge rent the air:

'Allah . . . ! Allah Akbar . . . !'

A knife glinted, whined through the air and then buried itself in the lieutenant's chest.

Machine-guns and machine-pistols spat at the closely grouped Russians who were all but paralysed by the frightful shriek.

Suddenly the firing was stilled. We stormed forward, cut, thrust, and hacked.

Breathlessly we sank down, dipping our faces in the stream and drinking voraciously.

Heide and two others began to collect the pay-books from the fallen Russians.

One feigned death, but a bayonet in his thigh soon got him to his feet.

Stammering, he told us they were a prison-transport detail. The prisoners farther back were guarded by twelve men under a sergeant.

Porta knotted a piece of steel-wire round our prisoner's neck and made him understand that he would be choked at once if he played us false or failed to lead us to the other party.

Pluto first found the enemy position. Three men were sitting in a tree. Pluto's machine-pistol rattled, and they dropped like ripe apples. One was still alive but a P.38 did for him.

The Old Un made the platoon spread out. The machine-guns took up their positions as our section advanced.

Porta, who was in front, suddenly cried out sharply:

'*Stoj kto kidatj gjearp*!'

He beckoned us forward. We joined him behind a tree. He pointed at ten men in brown uniforms in the open with their hands in the air.

Stege and I remained behind the tree with our machine-guns covering our friends as they went forward.

Porta lifted a knife to the throat of a big sergeant.

'Where are the prisoners?'

The sergeant answered in a language we did not understand. One of the Russians translated.

'The prisoners are behind the trucks back in the forest.'

Tiny and the Little Legionnaire went off and a little later returned with a dozen German soldiers and some civilian Russian men and women.

Bauer fetched The Old Un who at once ordered the Russian soldiers to be searched. Then he shrugged his shoulders and nodded to Porta:

'You know what we've got to do. We can't bring them along and we can't leave them here to warn the whole battalion.'

Porta smiled wolfishly.

'I'll willingly shoot the NKVD lice.' He waved to Bauer and Tiny. 'Let's get them into the forest.'

Pointing with the machine-pistols they made the prisoners march along in front of them.

A German corporal who had been with the prison transport shouted:

'Give me a machine-pistol. I'll shoot the swine. Last night they shot a hundred and five of our company. Across there.' He pointed in a northerly direction. 'Our company commander Lieutenant Hube had a cartridge-case knocked into his forehead after they had tied him to a tree. And we had an awful lot more civilian Russians when we started off on this trip five days ago.'

Pluto threw him a machine-pistol.

'Let 'em have it.'

Some whipping volleys echoed through the forest. There were a few cries, then the sounds died away.

Porta dressed himself in a Russian uniform. The Little Legionnaire had to hold up a pocket-mirror in order to let him admire himself.

'Why don't you put on the lieutenant's uniform?' asked Tiny.

'By the Holy Peter, you're right! That's my only chance of becoming an officer in this war.'

He ran off and a little later came strutting out of the bushes dressed in the NKVD lieutenant's uniform. The long nagajka swung from his wrist. He hit out after us and shouted:

'Off with you, filthy bastards. Here comes Super-Comrade Commissar Lieutenant Josephski Portaska!'

'Stop that nonsense,' ordered The Old Un.

The civilian Russians humbly made way for the shouting and thrusting Porta.

He tried to mirror himself in the stream.

'It's a bloody shame we haven't a camera,' he raged. 'It would make'em sit up in old Weddingen if they got a post-card with Herr J. Porta as a Stalin-SS-Stormführer.'

Tiny also wanted to put on a Russian uniform, but could not find one big enough. He made do with a cap with a green cross.

Trying to do a cossack-dance with a nagajka in each hand, he got himself tangled up in the long whips and rolled into the stream.

In single file we went on with our interrupted march. A mile farther on we found the bodies of the hundred and five troops killed by the NKVD men. They had all been shot in the back of the neck by Nagan-pistols.

Flies and ants now crawled on the twisted bodies.

One sobbing woman among the rescued collapsed and refused to get up. She exhibited her worn, holed felt-boots which barely covered her bloody feet.

With an indifferent shrug we moved on. For a while we

heard her crying like a wounded animal. The forest folded round her. The shadows lengthened. The night hid the living and the dead, the forgotten and the deserted.

Deep in the darkness one Russian with a fractured skull crawled about. He stumbled, cried upon God, cursed his country and shouted brokenly for his friends. Another, sobbing, endlessly searched his pockets. Another, dying, clutched a tuft of soft moss and wept quietly for his mother behind the great mountains of Georgia. A Ukrainian peasant-girl ran panic-stricken in circles trying to escape the darkness which threatened her reason. Twenty-eight German infantry-men and panzer soldiers, with fourteen Russian men and women, fought wearily through the dark forest.

It was early morning when we reached the new frontline area. We stayed the whole day. Tired and worn-out we lay under the bushes half-asleep on top of our weapons. Every sinew and muscle ached.

Some civilians had not been able to keep up with the tough-trained troops who were now lying on the edge of the forest waiting for darkness.

Porta removed his boots. His feet were bloody. Carefully he cut the lacerated skin away with his combat-knife. He sniffed it with interest, nodded with satisfaction and went on cutting.

'Doesn't it hurt?' asked Tiny, who was sitting with his legs outstretched chewing a piece of wood.

The Little Legionnaire lay on his back with his hands folded under his head, sleeping heavily.

Stege and the SS man sat in a tree. They were camouflaged with branches. You saw only the machine-gun peeping menacingly through the leaves.

As darkness fell we broke camp and followed a narrow path. Porta walked in front dressed in the Russian uniform. The long Russian coat fell in folds about his thin body. He had changed his top-hat for a tall Russian fur-cap. His machine-pistol at the ready was under his arm.

Behind and flanking him, the Little Legionnaire and Pluto marched.

A hollow cough made us halt as if hit by lightning. Porta found his wits first. He pushed Stege in front and shouted:

'Isiso dar?'

A large Russian appeared. He swore at Porta's shouting, but his voice changed amiably when Porta brayed in Russian:

'I've caught a German!'

The sentry suggested they ought to shoot Stege at once. He cocked his machine-pistol and with the barrel pushed Stege to his knees. He had a little difficulty to get Stege to bow his head properly.

Suddenly the Russian's arms fanned the air. He dropped his machine-pistol and fell over backwards gurgling hoarsely. Porta lifted him and got his wire-noose free. He had tip-toed up behind the sentry flinging the wire round his neck. In less than two seconds the man had been strangled.

Stege gave a strained laugh.

'Don't try tricks like that again, you daft swine!'

Porta only chuckled.

Silently the Very-lights travelled up over the frontline. Machine-gun fire rattled from both sides. In the sky we heard bombers growling westwards. Tracer-ammunition rose at them and faded again.

Porta lifted his hand. Noiselessly we stopped and stood like tree-trunks among the trees. Just in front stretched a Russian trench. We could clearly see the dug-outs. A figure passed and disappeared up a traverse.

Porta waved us forward. A quiet whisper and we raced over the parapet, across the trench, over some earth-mounds, fell, rose, fell again, slipped on the greasy soil and rolled down a slope. A machine-gun started to stutter. Bullets whined. Automatic weapons emptied their magazines at us. A couple of mortars barked hollowly. The bomb-splinters hissed past us like angry wasps. We lay flat at the bottom of a shell-hole.

A German machine-gun started to send long bursts over the hole. One of the Russian women began shrieking and before we could stop her she was over the edge. She swayed backwards and folded up with a dying inarticulate scream. The whole of her abdomen was perforated with machine-gun bullets.

The Old Un swore.

'Now they'll know something's going on. I wouldn't wonder if they started bombarding us with heavy guns.'

He had hardly finished when the air shook with mortar-bombs and 7.5-cm. shells. Star-shells burst, and then the Russians started.

One of the prisoners got his face ripped off by a shell-splinter. Three others were killed trying to scramble out of the hole.

At daybreak the firing ceased, but to get away we had to wait for darkness to fall.

Tiny stared at the dead. A wounded man whimpered loudly. Tiny pointed to the man's torn face.

'What a lot of muck one's got in the face when it's opened up. What's that grey stuff?'

Stege bent forward.

'Brains, and that other stuff's crushed bones. Look, that eye hangs down to what used to be his mouth. How large the teeth look when all the jaw-bone's gone. Blimey, what a sight.' He turned to Tiny. 'What the hell are you staring at it for, you nosy bastard.'

'Shut up, Stege,' interrupted Porta. 'Leave Tiny alone. You're always getting at him.'

Tiny was quite moved.

'That's true. The whole lot of you are always ill-treating Tiny. I never bother anyone.'

The Little Legionnaire patted his shoulder.

'Don't cry, Tiny, you're making me weep too. We'll be nice to you and chase away the bogey-man.'

A sergeant-major among the freed German prisoners burst out irritatedly:

'Is it necessary to make fun of everything? You're not all there, you gangsters.'

Porta half rose.

'Tone down a little. You're our guest. If you don't like it, push off. Two steps up and straight ahead. If we hadn't come you'd have been on your way to Kolymna, and I don't mind betting you'd have been buried at Dalstroj within two years.'

'What the hell are you thinking of?' stormed the sergeant-major. 'Since when does a corporal speak to a sergeant-major this way?'

Porta shook his head wonderingly.

'God Almighty, man, have you lost your reason? Do you still believe it's the old days when you opened your gobs and us poor bastards licked your boots?'

'I'll talk to you when we get back,' snapped the sergeant.

'By Christ,' said Bauer, 'It sounds like a threat. Court-martial, jail, twelve men on special detail. A courageous fellow, this infantry-boy. Great hero. What's his name?'

'I'll talk to you when we get back,' snapped the sergeant-major.

Pluto bent towards him and examined his shoulder-tabs.

'Judging from your white cords you're an infantry-man all right.'

'Silence!' raged the sergeant-major. 'I'll see to you yet.'

'We'll see to everything ourselves meantime. I'm giving the orders here,' The Old Un said quietly.

The sergeant-major turned and stared at The Old Un. He was lying at the bottom of the hole with his eyes shut.

'Forty yards to Ivan, seventy to our blokes and the ground between not too much chewed up. A very courageous fellow, this infantry-boy,' sneered Bauer.

A couple of hours after darkness the Little Legionnaire crawled noiselessly out and stomached his way to the German lines to warn the gunners not to fire at us.

Three hours passed before the expected signal of two Very-lights came.

One by one we snaked across the ground until we jumped into our own trenches.

Porta was the last one to arrive. The sergeant-major was missing. Nobody knew what had happened to him.

20

For dinner we had our most fantastic wishes granted. We became insane with grandeur. Porta even ordered Stege to polish his boots.

Half-smoked cigars were grandly thrown away. Tiny insisted he always did that.

The Old Un ordered a napkin with his coffee. We were all very grand. Pluto was the grandest of all – but not for long.

What do you want to eat?

The position was sited in a wood. Lovely and quiet. A couple of shells exploded every five minutes but nicely distant. The sun shone spring-like and warmed us to the marrow.

Pluto was on the parapet sitting on a tree-trunk darning his socks. He had thrown off his shirt and tunic. From time to time he shouted down to us in order to play his part in our chatter.

Our rations were brought out to us, double portions of everything – even pipe-tobacco and a packet of ten Juno's for each.

Porta held his in the air and shouted happily:

'*Berliner raucht Juno!* I can almost smell Weddingen and good old Friedrichstrasse with the 10-mark whores.'

'Ah yes, tarts,' sighed Tiny. 'I wonder if we'll get a little heavy action again soon?'

'That would be nasty,' said Pluto. 'Fancy buying it before you'd had your go at the whore-shop!'

Tiny stared at his palm.

'Boy, you make me frightened. Let me see your life-line.'

Pluto held out his hand.

'Yours is shorter than mine. That's nice. As long as you're allowed to run about clowning, I'll know I've got time left. Funny, those lines in your paw.'

The quartermaster, breathing hard, asked importantly what we wished to have for dinner next day.

'You mean we can have whatever we want?' Porta asked suspiciously.

'Yes, just order anything and you'll get it. I'm easy. What you want you'll have.'

'A duck roasted with chicory, prunes, claret and the whole Turkish orchestra,' ordered Porta and let off a thundering fart. 'Sniff it in, you bastards! The whole alphabet of vitamins dance in the air!'

The quartermaster wrote it down conscientiously as he repeated the order to himself.

We gaped. Stege stuck out his neck.

'Pork-brawn with mustard for me.'

'Certainly,' said the quartermaster calmly.

'Holy Saints! Are you mad?' said The Old Un. 'Or have you swiped a whole lord's manor?'

The quartermaster looked hurt.

'I'll pretend I didn't hear that. What do you want to stuff yourself with to-morrow?'

'Anything I like?' The Old Un asked narrowly.

'What do you want for dinner to-morrow?'

'Whole roasted sucking-pig with sweet potatoes.' The Old Un announced triumphantly, dead certain that would rock the quartermaster.

He wrote, completely indifferent: 'Whole roast sucking-pig with sweet potatoes.'

'Are you willing to swear I'll get it?' shouted The Old Un.

'It's what you want, isn't it?'

The Old Un managed to nod weakly. His face bore an imbecile expression.

'Well then, you'll get it.'

Pluto fell from his high perch. Lying on the ground he stared at the quartermaster.

'Partridge, two, with everything a king could wish for.'

'Certainly,' was the quartermaster's answer as he wrote in his book.

'Heavens,' whispered Tiny. 'Nobody's asked me yet. What's going on? Are you blokes going to be shot to-morrow?'

'Shut up and sing out your order for dinner to-morrow,' the quartermaster interrupted impatiently.

'Pig's liver with creamed potatoes and warm milk with egg-dumplings. That's supposed to be very nice, and I'll have a go. Perhaps it's my last chance.'

'*Poussin* with haricots verts and *pommes frites* for me,' ordered the Little Legionnaire.

The quartermaster stared uncomprehendingly at him.

'That's a dish I bloody well don't know. Talk German, scum.'

The Little Legionnaire handed him a note with his wishes written down.

'Look it up in the dictionary, but God help you if you get it wrong.'

'Oxtail-soup and ten leeks with spaghetti. Fifteen fried eggs with onion, fried on both sides,' beamed Bauer.

'All right,' the quartermaster answered. 'I'll see that even the onions are fried both sides, you stupid swine.'

When we had all given our orders the quartermaster shut his book and placed it under his cap.

'You'll get your wishes granted, you stupid animals. It's von Barring's orders that you'll all have what you want. The battalion have come across some extra rations. He wants to make a splash.'

'What are you going to have yourself?' Porta asked.

'Pig's trotters with sauerkraut, chopped vegetables, small birds with cloves – I think, roast pigeon and roast chicken. If I can eat any more I'll have a filled pudding.'

We stared speechless at him as he moved off.

Pluto crawled back to his tree-trunk and went on darning his socks.

The Old Un turned to Peters who as usual was by himself smoking his pipe.

'What have you been doing to land up in the 27th Regiment?'

Peters looked at The Old Un in silence, knocked his pipe out and filled it with calm thoughtful movements.

'You want to know why I'm here?' He scanned the

expectant faces. 'Well, I'll tell you. In 1933 my wife's family were prominent. My father-in-law became an Ortsgruppenleiter. I was not wanted as a son-in-law. They asked me to pack up. They had witnesses to prove I was a criminal. Unfortunately, I was so naïve I said no. The next move was underlined with a mild threat, and, ass that I was, I kept saying no and told them to go to hell. They kept quiet for a couple of years. Then the last warning came. It happened one morning, and in the evening the police arrived. I got eight weeks in the cells. Then they put me in front of a small devil of a magistrate. Very correct, perfectly correct. Tie, handkerchief, socks and shoes all carefully blended. His face was correctness itself. So well shaven, and such a neat haircut. Every word I said was carefully taken down in shorthand by a woman who sat grinning at me.

'When they took me to the cellar I still had not heard why I was suspected. The SS man who took me down entertained his mate with what they were going to do with me:

'"He's off to the large mincing-machine in Moabitt. Hey presto, head off!" Instead of keeping my big mouth shut I protested that I was innocent.

'They hit me with rubber-truncheons and shouted: "Yes, you're innocent of the Reichstag fire!"

'They fetched me out three or four times nightly and after the usual introductory kicks and ear-cuffings I had to jump up and down the corridors along with a few others. We had to howl like wolves or caw like crows according to the whim of our warders.

'One old man of seventy they forced to do hand-stands. Every time he was half-way up they hit him in the groin.'

'How long could he take that?' asked Stege.

'Not very long,' answered Peters. 'Every hit was short and sharp, precisely in the same spot. Three hits, and the old man fainted. But you can revive a person five or six times with sulphuric acid and other refined methods. At two o'clock in the morning I was called for re-examination in court. First they called my wife as a witness. She pointed to me and cried: "Take that scoundrel away, that child-ravisher!" She spat at me. Two policemen had to hold her down to stop her from tearing my eyes out. I was speechless, as you can imagine.

'My father-in-law looked me straight in the eyes and said: "How could you violate your own daughter! We pray for your soul!" The rest of the witnesses were the usual bunch, right down to the parson with the Iron Cross from 1914–18.'

'Isn't it funny,' interrupted The Old Un, 'how so many unemployed officers chose to become parsons. How was that?'

'That's obvious,' answered Porta. 'To be an officer in peace-time is just child's play for people who can't be bothered to work. When these boys become unemployed they look for something that compares favourably with the lazy officer-life. And what does? A parson's life, dear friends. Nowhere else can a man nurse his laziness so well and also camouflage his stupidity. Another thing too: remember how simple souls look up to the cloth. On top of that the devil-dodgers are able to tell people off from the pulpit without anybody answering back – it reminds them of barracks tyranny.'

Peters went on with his tragic tale:

'Little by little the cat was let out of the bag. They charged me with indecently assaulting my daughter. She had died three months earlier of diphtheria. Well, you know the form. Four days in the cellar and I confessed. Signed on the dotted line that I had not been a victim of pressure and that my treatment had been correct. The court proceedings lasted ten minutes. They were busy. Seven were condemned to death that morning. I got five years. "Small sentence, almost laughable," said a habitual criminal, who got twenty. Do you know Moabitt? No? Boye, the head warder, was a genius when it came to keeping us in form. He could scare your pants off when he came tripping on his rubber-soles to look through the glass panel in the cell door. He could open cell doors like a world champion. The large keys were fitted in the lock like a flash. You heard a click and the door jerked open with a bang. You saw a row of shiny buttons on a navy-blue uniform. Beneath a large cap you saw a small, evil face. God help you if you didn't spring to attention the second he appeared. He loved to stamp on people's toes.

'Unfortunately for me, one day he found a piece of pencil-lead outside my window. God only knows how. I had thrown it out. Luckily they didn't find the illegal letter I had written. We called him X-ray eyes. It suited him. That lot cost me twenty whip-lashes with the cowtail. And yet Moabitt was a holiday-camp compared with Schernberg.'

Peters looked at us, lit his pipe and shrugged his shoulders:

'It's not necessary to go into details. You know about Torgau, Lengries, Dachau, Gross Rosen and all the other concentration camps. In Schernberg they tied us to the radiators until our backs were roasted. Then we were turned about. Seventy-five strokes with the cow-tail wasn't unusual.

'They were past-masters in varying the executions. We often heard the knife of the guillotine whistle down. And once the hangman's rope broke so many times that in the end they forced a prisoner to poleaxe the condemned man in the forehead like a butcher slaughtering a calf. We even had a warder who executed people with an old knight's sword. That was forbidden by the commandant. But he put a "traitor" in an acid-bath with only his head showing over the acid.'

Porta glanced at our SS man.

'What do you have to say to that, brother?'

'They ought to be put on the rack,' whispered the SS man. 'It's unbelievable, but don't misunderstand me. I believe every word. And I swear I don't believe in Adolf and his gang any longer. Show me one of his chums and I'll bring you his head.'

Porta grinned and nodded vigorously.

'I'll come back to that. Maybe you'll be allowed to hunt with Joseph Porta one fine day. Keep your ears cocked for the hunting-horn.'

'One day I was fetched to the doctor,' Peters went on. 'He sterilized me. I came under Paragraph 175, you see. Some months later I was in the penal training-battalion. What happened there you all know, and now I'm one of you. I feel at home here. For the first time for ages I am relaxed. And I don't wish to return home!' Tears ran down his cheeks. 'If my courage fails me, you'll have to put up with me. It isn't death I fear, but another go of prison, either in Germany or with the colleagues on the other side.'

'You're not going to die in Russia. You're coming home with us to make the revolution,' decided Porta and patted Peters's shoulder.

'Well, well,' said The Old Un. 'There's many an account to settle. The only desperate thing is, nobody will believe a word we tell 'em. I'd like to meet anybody who'll believe the truth about our nice well-oiled Kriegswehrmacht-Haft and Untersuchung institutions. They'd only shake their heads and tell you the stuff you've just been telling us didn't happen; that you've been beaten up, yes, but that you didn't die of that. You really expect to be allowed to take revenge? Then you're unbelievably naïve!'

'You mean we'll never be allowed to speak out when the war's over?' asked Porta.

'No, by God. I'm sure of that,' said The Old Un with conviction.

'Well then, from now on I know my damned duty,' said Porta. 'Every party-member or SS madman will be laid horizontal if he crosses my path.'

He lifted up his sniper's rifle and opened and shut the bolt with threatening bangs.

'Nonsense,' sneered The Old Un. 'You'll be easy. You don't want to go to Torgau?'

'You evidently don't know Joseph Porta, Corporal by the grace of God. But you'll eat your words when the hunter's call sounds.' He started whistling:

'Ein Jäger aus Kurpfalz, der reitet durch den grünen Wald.'

The Old Un shook his head.

'You're crazy. If you don't want to listen to me at least keep quiet!'

'I don't want to do either, old wet-pants,' grinned Porta.

From time to time several of us had jumped up on the parapet. We were sitting with our backs to the enemy. They were behaving in the same unconcerned manner.

Not a shot was fired. Only a few shells banged high over our heads every five minutes.

Porta played his flute. The cat lay purring in his lap.

Tiny shouted up to Pluto on his high perch.

'If you see a shell coming this way warn us.'

'I'll do that,' Pluto roared back at him so loudly that the Russians looked in astonishment at us.

When they saw that no attack was in the offing they waved and laughed. One of them shouted to Pluto:

'Careful, it's draughty up there!' as he pointed to an exploding shell.

'Thanks for the warning,' Pluto shouted back. 'I'll take care.'

'Have you any vodka?' Ivan called.

'No,' screamed Pluto. 'Have you?'

'We've not seen a drop for a week. This is a lousy war. We don't even get vodka issued now. Is your bunker dry? We've got a good stove. It's not too bad here.'

Pluto put his hands to his mouth and trumpeted:

'It's dry here too. What we want is some girls. Have you got any?'

'No, the stupid swine haven't seen to that either. We haven't had a bit of crumpet for five months.'

The Russian waved and disappeared.

Pluto turned to us and said conversationally:

'Did you hear that the fellow who wrote: "*Es ist so schön, soldat zu sein*" has committed suicide?'

'Why?' asked Porta.

'Well, you see,' smiled Pluto. 'When he was called up he realized what a lunatic he'd been when he wrote that song. He got depressed and hanged himself with a pair of braces in front of the colonel's door.'

Pluto guffawed loudly. A shell exploded near him.

Quickly we slipped down to the bottom of the trench with shrapnel whistling round our ears and thumping into the trench wall.

I felt a hefty thump in the back. When I put my hand to it, it got covered in blood. Sticky and hot, it clung to my fingers.

Astonished, I sat up. Then my mouth opened and I felt the blood draining from my face. Straight in front of me lay Pluto's decapitated head, the eyes staring glassily at me. The lips were drawn back from the teeth as if in laughter. Long fleshy tendrils hung from the open neck and blood soaked into the dry earth.

For a moment I was paralysed. Then panic seized me. With a drawn-out scream I jumped up. If The Old Un had not hung on to my leg I would have run out into the open to death.

Beneath a fir tree in the forest we buried Pluto. Porta cut a cross in the trunk with our dead comrade's name beneath it.

'Another of the old ones from 1939,' said The Old Un heavily. 'There are precious few left.'

Tiny was deeply shaken.

'My turn next,' he groaned. 'Pluto's life-line was only a little bit shorter than mine.'

Nobody answered.

Stege went through Pluto's possessions. An old purse with a few marks and roubles. A small faded photo of a girl with a bicycle. A pocket-knife, three keys, one ring artistically fashioned from a bone, and two light-blue field postage stamps. A half-finished letter to a girl in Hamburg. These were Corporal Gustav Eicken's only worldly possessions.

A good friend was no more. For him there would be no great feast, and we would never be able to sit with him on the quay by the Elbe and spit in the water.

We were silent for a long time.

21

I sincerely regret to inform you that your son has fallen, but I am happy to be able to write that he fell like a brave soldier in the field of honour fighting for Adolf Hitler and Great Germany.

He died like a man, faithful to his oath of enlistment. Heil Hitler! The Führer greets you and thanks you for your sacrifice. God will reward you!

Twenty thousand times that was repeated to this one regiment.

Childbirth

Porta was madly excited. He kept running round the big new Tiger tanks the regiment had received. He kicked the tracks in delight.

Tiny filled the tanks with petrol. The lockers were packed with shells and machine-gun ammunition.

The Little Legionnaire was kissing a large S-shell.

'Just you stuff Ivan up the back,' he said to the steel and threw it up to The Old Un and me.

The large 8.8-cm. tank-gun was pulled-through for the twentieth time. The two machine-guns were over-hauled. The sighting-mechanism was tested. Porta tried the engines till the ground shook.

It was dark when we started, the engines growling. Huge steel tracks ate crushingly through the mud and undergrowth. The small huts shook as the great battle-ships of the land trundled past with the cooling-turbines whining.

'What are we really up to?' shouted Porta from among his steering-rods. 'They order: "Drive!" and we drive, but where the hell are we going? It would be nice to know a little more.'

'You drive because there's war,' interrupted Tiny. 'When you see some Russians running round this sledge, you nice and politely say: "Dear Tiny, will you be good enough to let those bandits have it?" I bend my finger, and the old comforter spreads a little confetti over Ivan.'

'Shut up,' said Porta. 'You've no idea what war is, you stupid clot.'

North-east of Olovsk we halted. The company commanders were called to a conference to be given the plans for each company.

Grey forms popped out of the darkness. They were our grenadiers and gunners.

We sat on top of our tanks and talked to them. A sergeant from the 104th maintained there was something important going on.

'It's swarming with troops from every imaginable unit. Look, here come the flame-thrower pioneers!'

We bent forward to see the unique sight. He was right. There they came, small, tough men, loaded with the easily recognizable containers on their backs. They were silent, taciturn people who answered in short syllables when we asked them about their ominous job.

A sergeant, irritated by Tiny's question whether he thought it a difficult job being a flame-thrower pioneer snapped:

'No, we enjoy ourselves, you dope.'

He threw a dull container at Tiny. 'Try racing and jumping with that thing on your back when our colleagues point all barrels at you!'

Tiny gave the sergeant a nasty look, but the sergeant went on sourly preparing his men's kit.

'Sorry I asked.'

'What the hell!' screamed the sergeant. 'That big animal wants a clout on the snout!'

Tiny slapped his thighs with glee.

'Oh Jesus-Maria, that baby's bum from the "Blacks" has delusions of grandeur!'

Like lightning the sergeant hit out at Tiny and bashed him on the chin with a hollow smack. But Tiny stood like a rock.

Then the sergeant ran at him and hit him in the stomach with the same negative result. A third smack landed with the precision of a sledge hammer under Tiny's ribs, but before the sergeant could get away Tiny grabbed him and held him up. He threatened him:

'Be good now or Tiny'll be angry and smack you.'

He pushed the sergeant away and he rolled over on the ground. Without further notice Tiny crawled upon the tank turret and spat at the pioneers. He turned to Porta who was hanging out of his driver's hatch.

Tiny and Porta became involved in a long discussion with the Little Legionnaire about the mixing of schnapps. When this subject was exhausted they threw themselves into a debate about how girls ought to look in order to afford the utmost satisfaction.

'Enemy tanks!' The cry suddenly goes up. The shout makes everyone instantly alert.

The engines roar. Lights flicker. The tanks swing out. The tracks rattle.

The companies growl through the village. Pass over a hill. Four miles east we cross over a broad road. The Jitomir-Lemberg Road most likely. Then another hill.

The whole 27th Regiment attacks in a broad wedge with No. 5 and No. 7 Companies out in front.

Tiny is standing ready with an S-shell in his hands. The read lamp shows a black F. A sign that all fire-arms are unshipped. Death's apparatus is ready for the big kill.

Porta whistles unconcernedly down by his steering-rods. His eyes are glued to the small look-out slits.

The Little Legionnaire blows in his telephone to test the radio. A couple of swift, instinctive motions load his machine-gun and he is ready.

We hear Stege over the transmitter. He is commander of No. 2 tank. He grins at the Little Legionnaire.

I look at the images in the sighting mechanism.

From the hill the landscape lies like an enormous panorama beneath us. The roads are jammed with Russian vehicles and artillery. On one flank, five or six miles away, we see T34s and SU85s. Lugini lies under heavy Russian artillery-fire.

About noon we discover, about a thousand yards away, a

collection of tanks parked in parade-ground formation. Tank behind tank. In the binoculars we see the crews having a chat while they smoke. All the tanks are painted white like ours, with black numbers on the turrets.

Nervous questions fly through the transmitters.

We hear von Barring asking Hinka:

'What are these tanks?'

He answers hesitatingly:

'I don't know. Drive slowly forward. We've got to identify them. Maybe they're from the 17th Panzer Division. They're going to support us on the left flank.'

The hatches are opened. Carefully we stick our heads out to see better.

'They're ours,' whispers the Little Legionnaire.

'You see that long gun and short bonnet? It's a Panther.'

'I think you're right,' The Old Un says slowly. 'They've got no turret-dome. It can't be T34s. Why the hell did they make the Panther so like the T34? Slowly Porta, slowly! If we get too near and it's Ivan he'll crush us before we can say Amen.'

Tiny is hanging half-way out of the turret.

'Damn it, it can't be Ivan. You can't mistake those wheels. It's a Panther. They're already sitting there grinning at us because we're so scared.'

We are now within 600 yards without anything happening. Our nerves are almost snapping with anxiety.

Sweat is pouring into my eyes and my legs are shaking. Every second sixty huge barrels might open fire at us.

Slowly, rocking, we advance. It seems as if the tanks too are sweating with fright.

Suddenly there is life in the men across there. They jump into their tanks. Four swing round and drive straight at us. Simultaneously an infernal row comes from the radio. Some of the words we make out:

'Open fire, Russians! Attack straight ahead, fire!'

Before a single shot is fired by us the rounds thunder from the Russian panzers. Despite the short range they miss.

Then seconds later the four Russian tanks rolling towards us are blown to atoms. Uncountable shells hit them from every tank of ours which have had them in the sighting mechanism and triggered off simultaneously.

All eight companies in the 27th Regiment hurl a broadside at the Russian tanks. At that range even our 7.5-cm. guns are deadly to the T34s.

We trundle forward furiously, earth and mud flying round the tracks. Shell after shell wings to its target. The whole area is very soon filled with a coal-black, nauseating smoke from the many burning enemy tanks.

The crews try to escape, but are mown down by machine-guns and flame-throwers. Others are crushed by the great caterpillar tracks.

A dozen tanks try to get away, but our 10.5-cm. guns smash them. A support squadron tries to draw our fire from them, but they are herded together like pigs escaped from the sty.

We chase them down into a depression and they get hopelessly trapped. We sit in wonderful cover and pick them off as if at the shooting-range at the depot.

After a wild moment of firing, the 'cease-fire' signal goes up.

When the battle is over, eighty-five T34s are standing like burned-out wrecks. It all happens in a short half-hour.

'My goodness,' laughs The Old Un. 'This goes one better than Goebbels's wildest fantasy. What on earth was Ivan thinking of sitting there like a target? I wouldn't like to be the commander of that lot after this. He'll lose his head for sure.'

Intoxicated with success the regiment rolls forward, almost recklessly. At Norinsk we surprise a whole cavalry-unit and after a short but violent fight they are scythed down.

Wild with panic the riderless horses race round the tanks. Possessed with killer-fever we point our machine-guns at them, and shoot them down one by one.

Horse after horse rolls over, and they cry like children. A Panther IV trundled over one at full speed and blood and guts spray up both sides of the tank.

The river is filled with corpses. The soldiers who have tried to save themselves have been caught by the whispering machine-gun bullets.

Before the last tanks leave the village every house, every shed is in roaring flames and a terrible reek of burned flesh is spreading across the plain.

No. 2 Platoon is chosen for a reccy. With four tanks we roll past Veledniki in the direction of Ubort.

The third tank tips over backwards when we go up a steep slope. Two are killed and Peters is fatally wounded. Both legs are crushed. He whimpers when we put him into a motor-cycle combination to send him to the casualty-clearing station. We try to stop the blood by tying a couple of belts round his thighs, but it's like a spring-tide.

The Old Un shakes his head.

'It's hopeless. What in hell's name can we do to stop the blood?'

Peters smiles with difficulty at Tiny.

'You can take it easy now, big pig. My life-line was much longer than yours. So it doesn't always count.'

'You'll get over this, old man. Pecker up. You're going to get a pair of bloody fine leather legs with silver hinges. They never use wooden-legs now.' He grins encouragingly at the groaning Peters who has already turned yellow, death's mark. 'You'll have a lot of fun with legs like that. At the depot in Paderborn we had a lad like that. He used to run his knife into his thighs and the girls shrieked with fright and collapsed. We called him "thigh-cutter". It's much more fun with legs like that. Wish it was me.'

Tiny pushes a handful of narcotic cigarettes into Peter's breast-pocket.

The Old Un signals to the driver of the motor-cycle and shakes Peter's hand.

'My love to Germany and be prepared for the revolution.'

Peters died three hours later on the stone steps of a village school. They buried him in the kitchen garden. They had placed a steel-helmet to mark the spot but someone had played football with it so we could not even put a cross on his grave when we returned.

The reccy party went on with the job minus one tank.

We travelled across ravine-country. We had the greatest difficulty in getting through.

At last we were again out on the big steppe. There we came upon fifty or sixty T34s rolling west.

After reporting to the regiment we received orders to keep them under observation and to go on with our reccy job.

The enemy tanks soon discovered us and showed an uncomfortable amount of curiosity.

Porta crawled half-way out of the tank and waved at the Red colleagues who waved back, believing us to be theirs. They turned away and went on their jerky way.

Tiny let off a yelp:

'Holy Virgin! Do you see what's coming here!'

We looked. From Olovsk came an enemy unit even larger than the first. Apart from T34s, it counted KW 1s and KW 2s.

Porta asked The Old Un:

'Don't you think we ought to run away?'

'No, I'm staying here until orders for withdrawal come.'

'What a nice Iron Cross candidate you are!' Porta shouted, red-faced with fury. 'Just you wait till the colleagues across there start banging with their 12.5 cms. That'll bring you to your senses.'

'12.5s!' asked The Old Un and stared through his binoculars.

'Yes, 12.5s! You nit-wit!' raged Porta. 'Don't you realize what sort of sledges these are? KW 1s and KW 2s, my flower! We'll be blown to the roof of the Chancellory in Berlin. Then we'll be hanged for scaring the pants off Hitler.'

The Old Un thought for a moment.

'Well, let's go.'

'Good,' beamed Porta and tore the tank round. 'If you're wise you'll fasten your safety-belts, as the pilots say. You're off on a trip you'll never forget.'

The tank leaped forward as he put on full speed. The Old Un hit his head against the turret-casing.

'Mind how you go, you daft clown!' he shouted at Porta as he wiped the blood off his forehead.

'Joseph Porta, Corporal by the Grace of God, drives this

tank in a manner in which, he humbly submits, it ought to be driven with or without your permission. If you don't fancy riding along, get off.'

The radio started to speak. The Little Legionnaire answered:

'Golden Rain here. Over.'

The regiment answered:

'Flower Garden here. Golden Rain return. Over.'

'Golden Rain understands. Which way. Over.'

'Hinka and Löve engaged with superior forces. Large losses. Seventeen of ours torn up. Golden Rain's starting-point stopped. Finished.' The radio became abruptly silent.

This meant the regiment was engaged in hard fighting with large Russian panzer forces and had suffered heavy losses. We, the recce-party were to try to escape, but we had to look after ourselves. Our escape route was blocked by Russians. And it was forbidden to use the radio.

The three large tanks thundered through the hilly terrain. Mud splashed sky-high. We tore through a village without either people or animals living. A few houses were burning and some dead civilians lay on the road.

Porta tried to steer clear of them but the tank drove over one. We fancied we could feel it.

A short way out of the village we spotted some trucks escaping to the north. When we travelled through a ravine we were received with hefty machine-gun fire. Our own machine-gun answered and the enemy were quickly silenced.

They turned out to be wounded Russians sheltering in the ravine. When we disarmed them we found a woman in a first lieutenant's uniform. She was wounded in the chest, and said she had been the commander of a T34 which had crashed at Veledniki.

We left the Russians and went on westwards. Near a small spinney a pack of T34s discovered us and followed. The rearmost of our tanks was hit by several shells and within seconds became a sea of flames. Not one of the crew of five escaped. We saw the tank commander stand up in his turret and then fall into the blood-red flames.

Stege's tank was hit next. Four men got away. We turned

our tank to cover them and they climbed on at the back of our hull. A corporal got entangled in the tracks and was crushed as we drove off. His screams echoed across the open country. Stege put his fingers in his ears and his face twisted in pain.

We did not get very far before five Russian tanks loomed up in front of us and started firing. We shot one neatly and set it on fire. The other four turned furiously for another attack.

The Old Un ordered us to get out. Short of breath, we ran across the soft-churned earth, beautiful targets in our black panzer uniforms. There was no shelter. We had once chance: to pretend we were dead.

One by one we fell down, very quiet but with hammering hearts.

A hundred yards away the tanks halted. We did not dare look at them. Lie still.

Some minutes passed. It seemed like an evil eternity. One engine revved up. The exhaust exploded. Very slowly one rolled past us only three or four yards away. The second and third followed. At last the fourth, so near that we feared it would roll over us. We could have touched the tracks by putting out a hand.

It had barely passed when Porta jumped up and sheltered behind it. We remained where we were, panic-stricken.

He waved us on, but we were paralysed. A shell whined above our heads and exploded a few yards away.

The Russian tank turned at once to answer the fire. It came from some German Panthers which were speeding towards us.

The ground trembled as they rocked by. The T34s hurried off, pursued by the Panthers.

We jumped on the last Panther and presently rejoined the regiment – shaken but alive.

Next day we had new tanks and went east where large forces of the 3rd Panzer Army were said to be surrounded. Our task was to open the noose the Russians were pulling tighter and tighter. We were three experienced panzer divisions with over 400 tanks rolling forward.

Our opponents were supposed to be the 6th Russian Cavalry Corps under Lieutenant-General Meschkin, the 149th Guard Panzer Division and the 18th Cavalry Division.

For me this march seemed to go on for ever. The moon shone brightly over the steppe and made the night ghostly. When a cloud hid the moon everything was wrapped in a velvet darkness and we had the greatest difficulty in maintaining contact.

Time and time again we got lost and the tanks had to turn and twist in impossible places. Several slid into rivers and stayed their with their bottoms up. The crews drowned like rats in a trap.

The order was that firing was strictly prohibited. Nobody was to open up, whatever happened.

In one place we saw five T34s barely fifty yards in front rolling north. They disappeared without taking any notice of us. We also saw fortifications on both sides of the road. The Old Un swore they were manned by Ivan.

In the middle of the night the column stopped. Nobody knew why. Silence reigned everywhere. Ominous silence. We stood there in a mile-long row, tank behind tank.

The Old Un was half-way out of the turret, but dropped back with a cry.

Tiny stared at him:

'What the hell's wrong?'

'Well, you have a look,' answered The Old Un.

Tiny put his head and half his body out of the sidehatch, but was back again quickly.

'God help us, it's Ivan!'

'Ivan?' asked Porta. 'Where?'

'There,' whispered Tiny and pointed.

At the same time there came a light knock on the tank's steel side and a voice in Russian asked for a cigarette.

Porta pulled himself together first. He opened his hatch and without a word he handed out a cigarette to a dark form. A match flared and lit up a bony face with a Russian cap. The Red drew deeply and breathed happily:

'*Sspassibo!*'

The Russians teemed round the tanks. More and more appeared out of the darkness. They evidently thought we were Russians.

Every second we expected firing, but the Reds leaned on the tanks and chatted. They tried to joke with us, but we remained silent, but for a word here and there.

One cried:

'You petrol rabbits are a dreary lot! Not a decent word from any of you!'

The others agreed. The Old Un had to hold Tiny down when someone promised to box his ears because he did not answer.

Sotto voce he hissed:

'Nobody's yet invited Tiny to fight and got away with it. Do you think I'm shy of a bunch of lousy Ivans?'

'It'll be your funeral,' grinned The Old Un, 'if you jump out and fight. It seems to me there are millions of Ivans here.'

Tiny glared out. We were stiff with fright in case he started to shout.

'Damn it, they must see we've got swastikas on the sledges and not stars,' whispered the Little Legionnaire.

Porta started to chat in Russian to the Little Legionnaire who succeeded in answering with one-syllable words.

Very quietly we collected our pistols and handgrenades to be ready in case something happened.

'What the hell are we going to do?' whispered The Old Un. 'This can't go on.' Carefully he looked out of the turret. 'Ivan's everywhere. Blimey, we must have stopped in the middle of a whole infantry division!'

Only one explanation was possible. The Russians did not dream that we could be enemy tanks. We had come sixty to seventy miles into their positions behind the main front-line without a single shot, and had travelled in route-formation.

We could easily have shot them all as they stood round the tanks. But firstly, firing was forbidden, and secondly I don't think one of us had the heart to fire at these nosy colleagues standing there joking and teasing us.

Over an hour passed. Then a terrible swearing started up in

front of the column. Shots were fired. Some machine-guns coughed hoarsely. We disappeared into our tanks and made the hatches fast.

Our colleagues looked astonished at the firing.

A tank came racing down the column. A figure dressed in leather and an impressive helmet stood in the turret. A Russian officer. He shouted at the men. They flew to all sides. All at once they realized who we were.

Banging and thundering started from all sides. The tanks swung out to the flanks and soon the whole position was overrun. The shells from the cannon exploded like volcanoes over the whole area.

We did not get much further before large Russian tank units were thrown against us. A murderous battle started. After six hours we had to give way.

Planes from both sides swept low and brushed away every exposed living thing with their machine-guns. In great shoals the Russian Yaks, Migs and Laggs came howling through the air and mowed our grenadiers down like grass.

All our tanks ran westwards. The Russians nearly managed to get us in a scissor-like manoeuvre but small groups fought independently with desperate courage. Neither the Russians nor our leaders knew quite what went on until it was too late to take advantage of the situation.

We drove on west over the churned up roads, filled by thousands of refugees. We could hardly get through. Russian peasants, city-dwellers, young and old, women and children, Germans lacking weapons and Russian prisoners who dare not stay behind because they feared the consequences of having been captured.

Everywhere the shout went up:

'Take us along, take us along!'

Imploring hands were stretched at us. Money, food and jewels were offered in exchange for a seat in the tank. Mothers held up small children and prayed us to take them along. But we went on regardless. We turned our faces away, not to see the accusing eyes.

Russian fighter planes, called 'butchers' by us, came tearing low along the road and stirred the horde of refugees to one single cry to heaven. They fired mercilessly at everything they saw.

Chaos everywhere. The west was a big magnet pulling this desperate horde of people along in ever-increasing panic. Parents threw their children up to the foreign soldiers who rolled by. Some threw the children off again. Others tried to make room.

Tiny and the Little Legionnaire sat on our tank. A child was thrown at them. A little girl of two or three. The Little Legionnaire missed her and she fell under the tracks and was crushed by the huge rollers. The mother became crazy and threw herself at the next tank. She was ground under the caterpillars.

Tiny let out a long-drawn howl. We thought he had become insane. The Old Un shouted:

'What's the matter, you big peasant?'

'By Satan! By Satan!' He stood up to his full height and leaned forward. It looked as if he was going to jump off. 'Listen you jokers, Nazi-dogs, Tiny's mad. Tiny's got a screw loose!' A long, terrible wolf-howl came from him.

Nobody knows what would have happened had his cry not been interrupted by a swarm of Jabos. They came shrieking at us and literally ploughed up the road with their guns.

Instinctively Porta flung the tank off the road and drove at full speed into a narrow ravine completely hidden by bushes.

We had hardly stopped in this heaven-sent shelter before the Jabos returned and let loose at the great mass of people on the road.

From this shelter the five of us witnessed the most terrible scenes yet.

Low over a group of trees fifty Jabos came racing. The flames from the guns spewed at the road. Hollow splashing explosions rent the air. The next minute most of the tanks were in flames, covered with a tarry phosphorous substance.

The Jabos treated the people on the road the same way. They ran around like living torches. Many tried to shelter in nearby cottages. The ground shook. Licking flames shot from the noses of the howling devils with the red stars on their wings. In a second the houses changed into roaring gales of yellow-blue flames. People smeared with the incendiary liquid from the exploding shells came out screaming and were changed to mummies.

This was our first acquaintance with the latest military invention.

Tiny had apparently become calm. He was sitting under the tank's nose playing dice with Porta and the Little Legionnaire. He grinned broadly when he threw six ones and when, at his next throw he threw three sixes, he became unmanageable. He rolled about roaring with laughter.

Porta glared enviously at him and said to the Little Legionnaire:

'What do you think, desert wanderer? Have you ever seen such a jackal? What's he laughing at, the stupid animal?'

'That,' gulped Tiny and pointed at the six dice. Each one was lying there challenging them with a six. 'You try it, you two Iron Cross candidates. It's easier for you to get a Knight's Cross than beat Tiny's master-touch.'

'Hell, I'd rather have six ones or six sixes than the Knight's Cross,' said Porta angrily.

Tiny swept up the dice and kissed them. He swung his arm and hit his left hand with his right fist while spitting over his right shoulder.

'God help us, what a superstitious hill-billy,' said Porta, spitting at a headless body which was lying a few yards away.

'That's what you think,' laughed Tiny, and flung the dice down.

'It won't help you a bit,' Porta jeered.

Tiny did not listen. He did head-over-heels and banged his head on an empty ammunition-box, but took no notice of it in his beaming delight.

The other two could hardly believe their eyes, but the dice spoke the truth. They lay there smiling a 'possible' at the two doubters.

A whimper, breaking into a scream, made us sit up and hold on to our weapons. Frightened, we looked into the undergrowth. A jerking, weeping, whimpering came to us as from a wounded animal.

'What the hell's that?' asked Porta and cocked his machine-pistol. 'Come out, you filthy devils,' he hissed, 'or we'll lay you horizontal!'

The Old Un pushed away his machine-pistol.

'Stop it, you red-haired daft bugger. That sort of whimpering is past being dangerous.'

He crawled through the bushes. Nervously we lagged behind. Tiny had his machine-pistol ready. The Little Legionnaire and I both carried hand-grenades in our sweaty hands.

The Old Un called us. Carefully we crept forward.

On the ground lay a young woman, her body arched like a bow. From her pale face blood-shot eyes stared at us.

'Is she shot in the stomach?' Porta asked The Old Un who knelt beside the woman.

'Of course not, stupid.'

'Where's she hit?'

'Has a bullet got her?' Tiny wanted to know, and bent over Porta's shoulder.

The Little Legionnaire whistled meaningly.

'Well, well, it looks as if we are going to be midwives.'

'This is no labour-ward,' growled Tiny. 'I've heard no man ought to see this kind of thing.'

'To hell with what you've heard.' The Old Un brushed him off. 'You're in this with us, and we've got to see it through.'

Tiny stared at The Old Un in astonishment.

'Old Un, can't we just finish this game. I've got—'

The woman started to whimper again and twisted in agony as her labour-pains increased.

Rapidly The Old Un gave his orders:

'Desert-nomad, you stay with me. Porta, get hold of some soap and a bucket of water. Sven, start a fire, a big one. Tiny, a tent-sheet and some wool. Cut the wool in two lengths, 30-cm. each.'

'My God, it's never happened to me before that a real winner of a game is ruined because he's a midwife. What a bloody war this is, and it's all Adolf's fault, to hell with him!'

'Shut up, Tiny, and hurry up,' The Old Un shouted impatiently and dried the sweat off the groaning woman's brow.

Tiny turned.

'Will you—' A drawn-out cry from the woman interrupted him. 'God help us,' he shouted and tore off through the bushes to carry out his instructions.

The woman was placed on a tent-sheet. We boiled water on the fire. To Tiny's horror The Old Un ordered us to wash our hands.

The labour-pains became more frequent. Pale and excited we watched the human drama.

Tiny cursed the absent father.

'What a bastard! Fancy leaving the girl alone. What an immoral bastard.' He cried angrily and stroked the woman's hair. He promised the unborn child's father terrible punishment if they met. 'What a traitor. What a piece of rotten skin!' Tiny gesticulated wildly in the direction of the road where we heard heavy trucks rolling past.

We camouflaged the fire as much as possible.

The Old Un threw the two pieces of wool and a combat-knife into the water.

'Why the hell are you boiling the knife?' Tiny asked curiously.

'Don't you know?' The Old Un was nervous and trembling. He spoke soothingly to the woman. She groaned and twisted in pain.

'It'll be soon now,' The Old Un said as he started to wash the woman with clumsy, untrained hands.

The birth started. The head appeared and made us groan as if we ourselves were giving birth.

'Do something,' shouted Tiny and Porta to The Old Un.

The Little Legionnaire bent forward and stretched his hands entreatingly to the woman. Sobbing, he repeated what the other two had said:

'Do something. Maybe she'll die, and then what about the infant? We can't breast feed it.'

'Stupid swine, filthy, stupid swine,' The Old Un raged. 'You can whore, but you can't be bothered to help a child into the world, you lousy dogs!'

Shaking, he placed both his hands round the infant's head and helped with the birth.

The Little Legionnaire sat by the woman's head. She pressed both his hands until her nails cut deeply into his fingers, and arched her body to the climax of emission.

'Skin my fists if you like,' sobbed the Little Legionnaire, 'if it helps. Let me get hold of the swine who's responsible for this. Fancy exposing a woman to this sort of thing!'

During much shaking and swearing the child was born.

The Old Un rose pale and sweaty, put his finger into the child's mouth and removed some slime. He held the child by its feet and gave it a brisk slap on the bottom.

The next second. The Old Un flew backwards after being hit by Tiny's enormous fist.

'You pious swine,' roared Tiny to The Old Un who lay on the ground half-conscious. 'What the hell do you mean by smacking such a tiny thing? It hasn't hurt you. It's the worst thing Tiny has ever seen and I'm not over-sensitive.'

'Oh, my holy God,' groaned The Old Un. 'Don't you see it was to make the child cry?'

'Cry?' howled Tiny and was about to hit out at The Old Un again. 'Hell, I'll make you cry, you sadist!' He swung his fists in the air but the Little Legionnaire and Porta fell on him and threw him down.

The Old Un stood up, cut the umbilical cord and tied it off with the wool. He dried his brow.

'By God, this is the most evil birth yet. Not even in a spot like this can we avoid fighting.'

He started to wash the child. A shirt was torn to pieces to provide a bandage for the navel. Tiny sat on his haunches beside the mother hopefully reassuring her and murmuring threats of murder against The Old Un and the child's father. Porta and the Little Legionnaire broke a new bottle of vodka.

We all started when Tiny emitted an ear-splitting shriek:

'Another baby's coming. Help! Old Un come here and help! You're the only one who's had babies before!'

'Shut up,' cried The Old Un and ordered as before: 'Water, thread, knife, fire!'

We flew about like frightened sparrows.

'My God, a whole nursery's on the way!' said Porta.

Half-an-hour later when it was all over we sat dead-tired smoking our cigarettes. We celebrated the birth of the twins in vodka.

Tiny wanted to name them. He insisted that one should be called Oscar. When we protested we suddenly remembered we had forgotten to see if the children were boys or girls.

The Old Un was told off violently by Tiny and threatened with a beating when we found they were both girls, as The Old Un held them out to common inspection and proof.

'Hell's bells, you can't treat young women like that,' growled Tiny. He had suddenly become surprisingly prudish.

A couple of machine-guns barked in the night and reminded us of our whereabouts. Rapidly we started gathering our stuff together. Porta carried the infants to the tank and handed them to the Little Legionnaire who improvised a bed for them behind the driver's seat. Here the tank had a hatch in the side which meant we could quickly get the mother and her babies out if we were hit and set on fire.

The Old Un didn't want us to drive on. We protested violently.

'The after-birth's got to come first,' decided The Old Un shortly and started to massage the woman's abdomen.

When the after-birth came Tiny cried out in fright. He thought a third baby was on the way.

The Old Un examined the after-birth with a skilled eye and nodded satisfied. He then gave orders to leave. We carried the woman to the tank and placed her beside her babies. The hatch was shut.

With the darkness covering us we rolled westwards surrounded by hostile vehicles on all sides.

'This'll never do!' complained the Little Legionnaire. 'I wish I was in the desert! That was child's play compared with this rotten war.'

Porta laughed loudly:

'Got enough, eh, desert-nomad? You're not only a desert-nomad, but you're a fascist pimp and a stupid swine, and now you're a midwife.'

'Allah is great. Nobody's greater than Allah,' mumbled the Little Legionnaire and stroked his pockmarked face.

A column of Russian infantry appeared. The Little Legionnaire cocked his machine-gun.

'Nervous, desert-nomad?' grinned Porta and speeded up the tank.

'Not at all. I enjoy it,' the Little Legionnaire sneered.

Porta whistled:

'Wer soll das bezahlen?
Wer hat das bestellt?'

He smiled at the woman behind him.

'What a labour-ward this old sledge has become. The twins' friends will envy them their birth certificates at school.'

'I wish you'd shut up,' the Little Legionnaire said.

'Careful now, dear desert-nomad, or your face will have a few more decorations.'

'And who'd do that?' the Little Legionnaire drawled as he sucked in a sinister way at a hollow tooth.

'This one,' answered Porta and held his combat-knife out. 'Don't forget it, you Arab!'

The Little Legionnaire raised a blond eyebrow, slowly lit a cigarette and grinned his evil smile:

'Great man, very great man! As courageous as a big pig! But I—'

He got no further. Tiny who had been sitting half-asleep bent forward and hit him on the head with the handle of his bayonet. The Little Legionnaire promptly slid down unconscious.

'You uncouth new boy! I'll teach you to speak badly about Tiny when he's napping!'

He was just about to kick the helpless Legionnaire's head when The Old Un and I charged in and managed to calm him down.

Porta laughed loudly and heartily:

'That poor desert-nomad has a lot to learn. It must have been a sort of Sunday-school down there among the date-palms. He doesn't know any nice tricks. Fancy Tiny bashing his head in with that stupid bayonet. Allah is truly great, only he hasn't got eyes in the back of his head.'

The twins started crying. The mother was restless. The restlessness was contagious. Porta handed her a bottle of vodka. She pushed his hand away with revulsion and mumbled something.

Porta shrugged his shoulders.

'God protect me! I shan't annoy you, madame. My name is Joseph Porta, Corporal by the Grace of God, and midwife!'

The Little Legionnaire groaned and put his hands to his head. He sat up, lit a cigarette and bent his head back to glare at Tiny.

'Clever, eh? Don't forget to look behind you, big fellow. Maybe you'll get a quiet thump on the back of the neck.'

'Hey!' shouted Tiny and started to swing his gorilla-like arms. 'I'll make mincemeat of you so that even the Arab tarts won't recognize you!'

The Old Un slid down from the turret.

'Enough of that,' he ordered. 'If you must fight, jump out of the tank and do it quick. There are hundreds of our colleagues trotting along beside us and you'll soon have your fill.'

Tiny turned angrily to The Old Un.

'What the hell! That's no way to speak to us. Who do you think you are?' He bent forward, shook his enormous fist under The Old Un's nose, cursed and threatened.

The Old Un looked calmly at him.

'Don't get into a state now! Nobody's going to do anything to you.'

'Do something to me,' bellowed Tiny. 'Do something to Tiny? Let me see the bastard who'd do Tiny!' He bent sideways to the Little Legionnaire and nearly knotted himself in order to look the little fellow in the face. 'You wouldn't do anything to Tiny?'

'No,' the Little Legionnaire laughed. 'Unless of course you were tied up. Then I might cut your throat!'

Tiny was clearly relaxed at the word 'tied'. But still he questioned each one of us.

Porta cursed, and accelerated so abruptly that we beat our heads against the hull.

Machine-cannons and guns hammered at us. The bullets crashed into the steel flank of the tank. A road-block was forced and a few S-mines exploded under us without harming the tank.

One Russian infantryman tried to mount it but he misjudged his jump and was flung under the rollers.

Hand-grenades kept being lobbed at us. The Little Legionnaire fired some quick sweeping bursts with his machine-gun. Through the sighting mechanism I saw some confused Russian infantrymen running about. They took cover by the wayside. On the road in front stood a tank firing at us with its 2-cm. machine-cannon.

The turret engine purred. Figures danced in the sighting mechanism. The points met. A couple of quick orders. A thundering detonation. The 8.8-cm. shell tore the tank to pieces. Our flame-thrower cleared the road. Rapidly we disappeared into the darkness, leaving behind us for our remembrance a burning Russian panzer tank.

Instead of a fortnight's rest, each of us got two ounces of water-cheese from the quartermaster and orders to go back into the line. When all the cheese had been distributed we were given a coloured photo of Hitler. Then, we were marched to our fighting position without either rest or cheese.

But first Porta had a big job to do. He used five of the Führer's photographs as toilet paper.

22

The Refugees

The grey ghostly light of day emerged over the horizon.

Porta turned the tank in on a narrow forest-road. Everyone sat half-asleep. The woman cried. The children coughed and cried with pain caused by the sharp acid fumes from our guns.

Porta braked the tank. Frightened, we peeped out through the observation-slits. In front of us some vaguely-seen figures were running about. A truck had been put across the road. It looked like a road-block.

The Little Legionnaire swore and cocked his machine-gun.

'Take it easy, easy,' The Old Un soothed. A shot rang out. Panic took hold of us when we saw a 'stove-pipe' trained on us. The figures in the sighting-mechanism swirled in front of my eyes.

'Ready, guns clear,' came Tiny's automatic report.

A click. The little red lamp inside the tank blinked evilly. The cannon and the turret machine-gun were cleared for action. The 8.8-cm. explosive shell lay poker-still in the chamber. A knot of people sat straight in front of our sights. Our fingers tightened on the triggers.

'*Tac-tac-tac!*' rattled the machine-gun. The rolling death echoed through the wood.

A lot of them tried to find cover in the wood. Screams and cries reached us.

'Don't let them get into the forest,' warned The Old Un.

'Then they'll get us! They'll smash us before we can wink an eye.'

The turret swung round, the points on the sighting-mirror met.

'*Rummmun . . . !*' thundered the guns and sent a rushing fountain of fire, earth and bloody limbs skywards as the 8.8-cm. high-explosive shell exploded in the middle of the clump of people.

Two machine-guns, Mark 42, pumped ammunition into the scrub. The engine's growl rose to a roar as we rolled towards what had been a road-block.

Were we shocked when the truth in all its horror dawned on us? I don't think so. Rather relieved. Maybe a little uneasy.

The 'road-block' was a cart which had broken down. The hostile 'gunners' were refugees, women, children, old men, sick and exhausted. The 'stove-pipe' was the shaft of the cart.

The hatches were carefully opened. Inflamed eyes registered the destruction. Five pairs of tank-soldiers' ears listened to the death-rattle of the dying. Five noses sniffed the sharp stink of cordite. Steel rattled against steel as the hatches were made fast. Rocking on its tracks the large killer-apparatus curtsied to the dead and dying.

A tank with a handful of soldiers, a Russian woman and her new-born twins disappeared, cursed by the dying.

We sucked up petrol with the aid of a rubber hose. Three lonely Russian gunners had been killed before they knew what came growling up behind them.

In the distance we heard the rumbling of a heavy artillery barrage. We smeared the swastikas on each side of the turret with mud until they became indistinguishable.

The woman had a temperature. She talked wildly. The Old Un shook his head.

'I'm afraid she's dying.'

'What are we going to do?' asked the Little Legionnaire in despair, and twisted his hands.

The Old Un looked at him for a long time before he answered:

'You're a funny lot. By God, you're funny. You fire without blinking at everything which moves, and yet you fear for the life of an unknown woman just because she lies beside you and breathes in the same rotten stale air.'

Nobody answered.

It was almost dark when we halted. In the distance we saw a fire.

'It looks like a large town going up in flames,' Porta said. 'Maybe Oscha?'

'Are you mad?' replied The Old Un. 'Oscha is far behind us. No, more likely it's Brodny or Lemberg.'

'It doesn't matter two hoots which it is,' decided the Little Legionnaire. 'It's burning. A good thing we're not there!'

. . . Tiny saw them first. Two large diesel-trucks. Proper 'soldier-sledges'. They were German air force lorries. A dozen air force personnel were lying about sleeping. Farther away and half-hidden in the bushes lay about a hundred women and children.

We climbed out.

They jumped up panic-stricken as we approached them soundlessly in our black tank-uniforms. They stared paralysed at Porta's top-hat with its red-painted bands.

There were two German nurses among them. The hospital they had been at had been surprised and occupied by Russians. These were the only two who had got away alive. All the wounded had been liquidated in their beds or in the corridors. A large Russian infantry unit had come to the village where they had sought shelter. But they had been friendly and warned them to get away as those who were following them were really brutal.

The whole village except a few old people had run away. Day after day they had dragged themselves along. Other refugees had joined them, Polish, German, Russian, Latvian, Estonian, Lithuanian. People from the Balkans, yes from all directions, had joined in the refugees' wretched caravan. They had forgotten racial and regional emotions in their common terror: the rapidly rolling Russian tanks.

The air force men had brought them here. They had been fired at several times. Some had died and been thrown off. New refugees had fought for the spare places in the trucks.

When they had left the forest they had been fired at again. The soldiers had raced on and stopped where we now met them.

The air force men would not go on. They had quite simply given up: full of apathy they had laid down to sleep.

They stared indifferently at us with our machine-pistols under our arms. A sergeant lay on his back with his hands folded under his head. He grinned mockingly at us.

'Well, heroes, still racing for victory? Why not call Ivan, then you'd be able to use your pop-guns? Bah, fascist-dirt!'

'Hell's bells!' Tiny fumed. 'Are you fresh, my sparrow? Shall I let him have it, Old Un?'

'Quiet Tiny,' answered The Old Un and studied the sergeant through half-closed eyes.

'What are you going to do?'

The sergeant shrugged his shoulders.

'Wait for the colleagues, and shake their hands.'

'And the women?' The Old Un wanted to know and indicated the women and children with a jerk of his head.

'Give the lot to Ivan. That is, if you don't wish to take 'em along on your victory-chase. I've had enough and I'm thinking of myself. I don't care a scrap about what becomes of that lot. Can you swallow that, black brother?'

A terrible quarrel began between The Old Un and the apathetic sergeant. Several others interfered.

'Do you think we want to get away from Ivan just to be hanged by our own "head-hunters"?' asked the sergeant.

Suddenly the Little Legionnaire pushed himself forward with his machine-pistol ready. He pointed the muzzle at the sergeant and his men.

'You cowardly filthy dogs! What a lot of damned collar-and-tie soldiers! The whole war you've been sitting on an aerodrome far behind the front-line, and now when you hear a few bangs you're scared stiff. I'll shoot the lot of you if you don't take the women along!'

For a moment there was deathly silence.

We withdrew from the Little Legionnaire. He stood with splayed legs, his machine-pistol ready, his body tensed.

One of the air force men grinned.

'Well then, shoot. Why don't you shoot, you black monster? Did Goebbels teach you fat words? We're tired of waiting!'

Several others started to jeer at the Little Legionnaire.

'Careful now,' whispered The Old Un. 'Something's going to happen.'

Slowly we spread out with our machine-pistols ready.

'Will you drive?' hissed the Little Legionnaire. His cigarette bounced in his mouth and sparks dropped on his chest. 'For the last time. Will you drive the girls?'

'You're a hero,' laughed one of the air force men. 'A big hero from the steppes of Ukrania! Woman-Liberator! They'll put up a statue of this mannikin on top of the wash-house!'

Roars of laughter reverberated. Evil flames burst from the Little Legionnaire's blue-black weapon. The Little Legionnaire swayed with the recoil. The laughter changed into a rattle. Grey soldiers twisted about on the ground. One crawled on all fours to us shrieking like a lunatic.

Again the machine-pistol barked. Dead bodies trembled under the burst of steel.

Only three got away with their lives. They were pushed into the drivers' cabs of the three lorries with the help of machine-pistols. Muzzles at the ready.

Dumb and with dead eyes, the refugees crawled into the trucks.

With the tanks bringing up the rear we drove north-west. Away from a heap of bloody corpses in grey uniforms. Men who had given up hope, and so had been killed by their own.

The war rolled on.

Small groups of soldiers were dragging themselves along the road. One voice started to cry desperately:

'Comrade, take us along!'

But our comrades disappeared in a breath of petrol fumes. One truck collapsed. Its load of people fled on foot along the road.

In Velenski, a village like thousands of others in Ukrania and Poland, a river of people had stopped marching for a little rest and warmth.

'Hurry up!' The shout was repeated ceaselessly, but it was not necessary. The threatened collapse of the 3rd Panzer Army and the rapidly rolling Russian tank columns which crushed every living thing were more than enough to make the refugees race on.

German grenadiers and Russian prisoners ran about like confused chickens among the swarm of civilians. They flocked round our tank. Everyone asked the same question:

'Where is the Red Army?'

For days, disrupted military units and wretched civilians had travelled through Velenski. Panic had taken a stranglehold on everyone from the youngest to the oldest. The terror of the Russians racing behind. The shock of the total collapse of the front. Horror of the T34s which loomed up and crushed a whole column of refugees in a moment. The frightfulness of the 'butchers' and Jabos which made the road a sea of flames in a split second.

In addition came fatigue, hunger, gales, frost and rain.

Invocations to God rose to heaven in many tongues, but nothing helped. The tank-tracks ground along the blood-soaked earth of Ukrania and Poland.

One of the nurses had some morphia which we gave to the mother of the twins. We got hold of some milk and made ready to drive on. They stood round us, hundreds of them. Imploring hands were stretched to us:

'Take us. Don't leave us to die!'

They offered the most unbelievable things in exchange for a small corner in the tank. They sat on the turret, at the back and in the front. They hung by their arms from the gun-ports. Many sat on the long barrel of the cannon, tightly packed shoulder to shoulder.

We cursed and swore and threatened them with our machine-pistols to get them off the muzzles of the guns and flame-thrower, but they did not care.

The Old Un shook his head in despair.

'Heaven help us! If we get into a scrap, they'll go to hell, the lot of them!'

We took some children into the tank before we made the hatches fast. Then our death-march began.

A few miles on we met four more tanks. They belonged to No. 2 Panzer Regiment and like us they had lost contact with headquarters.

A lieutenant, 18 years old, took command of all our five tanks. He ordered all the refugees to get down, but not one obeyed. On the contary, more refugees plus some German stragglers crawled on.

He climbed, swearing, into the tank through the bottom hatch. So many people were sitting on the turret that he could not get through the turret-hatch.

Over the radio he announced that we had to pass under a railway line. We had been travelling parallel with it. The tunnel was so narrow that there was not an inch to spare.

We tried to explain to the refugees that they would be swept off if they remained sitting on the tank and promised to pick them up again on the other side of the tunnel. They pretended not to understand. Nobody dared give up the place he or she had won. Even mothers who had lost their children didn't move.

The first tank disappeared down the steep curve. It lurched about violently. Some refugees fell off, but managed to save themselves on the steep banks on both sides of the road before our tank came slipping on. Our grating tracks were unable to brake on the slippery road which had a decline of thirty-five degrees.

We stared desperately at the first tank as it entered the narrow tunnel. The refugees were crushed between cement and steel or swept off.

In despair Porta tried to brake, to put the tank in reverse, but the huge 65-ton Tiger rolled relentlessly on towards the crawling, screaming people who next minute were crushed under the steel caterpillar-tracks.

Many of the refugees on our tank jumped off when they saw what had happened, only to be crushed by the following tank which like ours came shrieking and slithering down the road. The refugees tried to make themselves small, but they were all mashed down to a red-grey porridge which dripped like paint off the tunnel's walls.

A small boy threw himself at our tank to stop it from running over his mother who lay unconscious in the road. His terror-stricken face disappeared beneath the tracks of our terrible juggernaut.

The tank bobbed up and down at regular intervals as if we were running over a large wash-board.

On the other side of the railway line we stopped. The lieutenant by now had lost his mind. He ran about in a circle, tore off the badges and decorations on his uniform and threw them in the air. When he had demoted himself, he grabbed his machine-pistol and started firing single shots at us.

Without a word Porta took his sniper's rifle and pressed the trigger.

The young lieutenant fell back, kicked desperately with his legs and beat out helplessly with his arms in a swinging motion. Another shot and he lay still.

The refugees who had got away alive and the others who had not been on the tanks came across to us threatening and screaming. We had seen what they had done to the gunners from one of the other tanks, how they had choked them with their bare hands.

They came at us swinging weapons and cudgels. The Old Un hurriedly jumped into the tank, but before he could close the hatch some were already on the hull trying to throw in hand-grenades.

A piece of shrapnel wounded The Old Un in the cheek.

We saw them flinging out the corpses through the hatches of another tank.

The Old Un shook his head.

'God in heaven, help me. What am I to do?'

Porta put his head back and looked at The Old Un.

'Hurry up, Old Un, what's your orders? You're in command of all these sledges now.'

'Do what you like. I give up,' sobbed The Old Un and sank down. Tiny's feet came out and pushed him away.

'Good,' replied Porta. 'I understand. Shut your eyes, old married man, then you won't see what we're going to do!'

He turned to the Little Legionnaire who was sitting by his radio to relay his orders to the other tanks:

'Brush off the refugees! Be ready to open fire! Shoot at any stray tank and anyone carrying firearms!'

The refugees and the desperate German stragglers evidently wanted to finish us off. The first handgrenade was bowled over our heads.

Automatically I sighted my gun on the tank pirated by the refugees. The points met on my mirror. The number on the large turret was visible in my sighting circle. Tiny reported laconically:

'Ready, gun clear!'

The red lamp blinked. A yard-long flame licked out of the muzzle and a shell burst through the air. The next moment the turret of the other tank went up in the air. Large flames shot skywards. Burnt limbs lay everywhere.

A furious roar rose from the civilians. A shell from a 'stove-pipe' crashed into the ground immediately in front of us. Another tore the tracks off another tank which immediately opened fire in return.

A terrific slaughter of people made insane by terror and despair began. Four 8.8-cm. tank-guns, four flame-throwers and eight machine-guns sent bursts of killing steel and fire at their defenceless targets.

After ten minutes it was over. The tracks on the damaged tank were repaired and we went on our way north-west. We carried one dying mother and her new-born babies and five bigger children whose parents we had very likely massacred.

Porta pointed with an expressive gesture at a tree from which hung the bodies of three German infantry soldiers. All the four tanks halted to study the victims a little closer.

'Hell and damnation!' the Little Legionnaire burst out when we read the text on the paper notices strung round the necks of the hanged infantry men: 'We are deserters and traitors and have received our well-deserved punishment.'

Their legs swung in the light wind like pendulums on some large clock. Their necks were horribly long. You suspected they would snap and leave only the heads in the ropes.

Mutely we travelled on.

Just before entering another village we saw several more hanged soldiers, among them a major-general.

'I have refused to obey the Führer's orders,' his label said.

In a ditch lay a whole row of infantry and artillery troops, also a single engineer, easily recognizable by his black shoulder-tabs. They had been executed by machine-gun fire. These had no labels.

'It's the head-hunters at work,' said Porta. 'Let us get one of these bastards in front of the muzzle of our "candy-sprayer". May the devil skin me, but he'll get so many acid drops in his carcass he'll die of indigestion!'

'Allah has granted your wish,' the Little Legionnaire said and pointed ahead.

There stood five MPs. They gave their stop-signal. They were armed to the teeth and their brutal, square faces looked threateningly at us.

'They'll hang us for sure, when they discover how far away from the regiment we are,' The Old Un said.

Porta braked and stopped a little in front of the gendarmes. The tanks behind us also stopped. The crews swung their machine-guns up and down and were obviously nervous of what might happen.

A sergeant-major and a sergeant with fists just made to knot a hangman's rope approached us.

The Little Legionnaire opened the hatch and peeped out.

The sergeant-major planted himself in front of our tank and shouted arrogantly:

'What fellows are you?'

'Tank fellows.' The Little Legionnaire grinned.

'Not funny!' said the sergeant-major. 'Your papers! Hurry up, or you'll be swinging, my friend!'

'11th Panzer Regiment,' lied the Little Legionnaire.

'What? 11th?' shouted the sergeant. 'You've had it! You're for the rope!'

Porta pushed the Little Legionnaire away and before the gendarmes realized what was going on, he had banged the hatch to. The tank leaped forward and hurled down both men. The tracks went over them. Both our machine-guns started to bark at the three remaining MPs standing a little farther down the road. One was hit immediately and fell. The two others took to their heels across a field, and a stream of bullets followed them.

We quickly radioed the other tanks that the gendarmes were disguised partisans who had tried to stop us.

Laughing fiendishly, Porta swung the tank into the field, accelerated, and, raising a dust-cloud behind us, we rolled at full speed after the two madly screaming gendarmes who had thrown away their weapons to lighten their steps.

The slower one stumbled. The next minute he was crushed under the tracks. The other one stopped, put his hands up and gaped in terror as the huge steel-giant rumbled at him.

Porta stopped when we were right on top of him and made the tank jog to and fro to mash him well into the ground.

Tiny cried out. He pointed to two more gendarmes. They had been placed as covering party in the ditch with a heavy machine-gun.

Porta whipped the tank round on its own axis, but before we could reach them one of the other tanks roared at them and crushed the machine-gun and the two gendarmes. Methodically its vast steel body like a film actress swinging her hips nuzzled to grind the gendarmes to an unrecognizable mess.

Later we joined the remnants of an infantry unit and harboured behind some hovels, where we were camouflaged with grass and branches to mask us from aircraft. The crews of the four tanks were billeted in the same hut. We placed the twins and their sick mother in a corner. Most of the time the woman was unconscious.

A young doctor from the infantry battalion which had absorbed us had a look at her. He let us have various pills to give her but Porta got mad and threw them away. We forced a medical orderly to give her an injection to reduce her fever. She often cried out in her delirium and tried to get up. We took turns to look after her. The Old Un pronounced that she would soon die. To the twins we gave milk stolen from the battalion quartermaster.

The other five children were still with us. One, a boy, kept completely dumb. He never answered our questions. He only looked at us with eyes filled with indescribable hatred. The Old Un was disturbed about him.

'Be careful he doesn't get hold of any weapons,' he said. 'That lad's capable of anything. His hatred's eating him up.'

When Tiny tried to play with the boy, he spat straight into Tiny's face. It might have had serious consequences but for Porta's and the Little Legionnaire's intervention.

The acting infantry battalion commander, an old major, looked on our four big sledges as the world's eighth wonder. He placed us as flank protection at the southern end of the village. He then lulled himself into the belief that he could counter any attacking forces successfully.

Large columns of fleeing troops arrived from different army units and were absorbed into the infantry battalion, which now took on the proportions of a regiment.

The major acted like a general determined to fight it out with the whole world. He strutted about and announced that victorious battles were soon to be fought.

Flocks of civilians built strong positions round the village. Heavy infantry guns were camouflaged and made part of the intricate defence system, but it was obvious that the work had been executed by inexperienced hands.

One old infantry sergeant who commanded an anti-tank battery was convinced that his two pathetic cannon would make the fast Russian tank units scuttle.

'You'll soon be wiser,' laughed a tank sergeant. 'Just wait till

Ivan comes with his T34s. He'll parade along your positions. The only thing which counts when T34s show up is how fast you can run.'

The infantry sergeant looked primly at the tank sergeant. He turned to his men and said loud enough for us all to hear, which was what he wanted:

'The Herr Commander has ordered that the positions must be held to the last man and the last bullet. If anyone withdraws without the personal order of the major he'll be shot as a traitor!' Smartly he strutted across to his two 7.5-cm. anti-tank guns.

Porta shouted mockingly to the nearest tank crew:

'Somebody here's got a bat in his belfry!'

We soon forgot the sergeant and his simple faith.

Porta started telling stories. He gave us a detailed description of a girl he had once met.

'You should have seen her,' he said rapturously and gesticulated expressingly with his arms. 'Her udders were the most luscious pleasure-buds you ever imagined. Real pets they were. Her legs were the loveliest pins you ever saw, real mare's form! Maybe she was a bit high off the ground, but, hell, you can't have everything! She was well-trained, too, lads; four times she'd been caught in the family way, but a medicine-man had fixed her up.'

Tiny stared open-mouthed at Porta who enthusiastically painted in every detail of his girl-friend.

'Oh, shut up,' groaned Tiny, 'it's enough to drive you crazy!'

'God help us, your breeding-pin is always restless!' Porta retorted. 'If you can't stand listening to me, run away!'

But Tiny stayed and suffered bravely. Porta raised one of his legs and made a full stop in his usual manner.

'Thank you! What a hell of a bird that was—'

'What the hell!' The Old Un burst out and suddenly jumped up. Simultaneously we spotted the Russians. First a scattered few carrying machine-pistols, then lots of them. Carefully they looked about. An officer waved with his machine-pistol. More of them appeared. At least a company.

Quickly we scrambled into our tanks, pointed our guns and sent a few killing bursts in their direction. That made them disappear for the present.

The tank engines were revved up and we made ready to flee if necessary.

Furious shooting started:

'Hell, Ivan must be behind us,' growled The Old Un and listened. 'Porta, get this coffin out of the hole. We've to get into the village to see what's going on.'

The Little Legionnaire radioed the other three tanks and together we left the position despite the threats and cries of the infantrymen. We drove down into the village in the valley.

Here hell was loose. Russians swarmed everywhere.

Our four tanks rolled snarling into the broad main street. A whole company of Russians was parading. Four machine-guns sent simultaneous bursts at them and they fell like nine-pins. A few tried to run away, but our automatic weapons soon finished them off.

A Russian tank of the small T60 type was literally pulverized as it appeared from behind a hut only twenty-five yards away from our 8.8-cm. cannons.

Tiny shouted from the hatch in the turret:

'Come on, you devils. We'll soon flatten you out like bedside mats!'

A bullet hit the edge of the hatch and ricocheted with a sharp whine. Tiny quickly shut the hatch.

In the next quarter of an hour we cleared the village of Russians. They had not the weapons to fight our large tanks.

The Old Un was sure it would be only a short respite before they got T34s and large anti-tank guns.

Darkness fell, nothing happened except some skirmishing in the distance, and we settled into our billets.

At midnight the mother of the twins died. We wrapped her in a thin blanket and decided to bury her at daylight. The Old Un sat holding the twins while Porta and the Little Legionnaire each held an improvised baby-bottle.

'What on earth are we going to do with these two?' The Old

Un asked. 'We can't keep them for good, and if we give them to the refugee-disposal squad what'll become of them?'

Presently we seemed to hear some movement outside. We thought it was probably some newly-arrived refugee column.

Suddenly the door was torn open. An enormous figure with a sheepskin cap above a flat, earth-brown face, dressed in a quilted coat and carrying a machine-pistol under its arm, stood in the doorway. The Little Legionnaire who by chance had been sitting cleaning his pistol fired at once. The large Russian fell without a sound. Porta grabbed his machine-pistol, Tiny extinguished the Hindenburg-candle with his large fist to plunge the room into darkness.

We ran from the house. The Russians swarmed round the tanks. We ran across the road and threw ourselves into cover behind another hovel.

The major was shaving in his quarters. He opened the door to see what the noise was that had disturbed him. He was probably thinking of the many good years he had spent as a lecturer at the University of Göttingen. He never knew what hit him. He fell with the shaving-brush clasped in his hand. A small blob of soap hit the door-frame. Some earth-brown men stamped carelessly across his body.

A couple of officers in pyjamas sat up in their beds. They were quickly dealt with by two machine-pistols.

The machine-guns rattled on between the hollow explosions of the hand-grenades. Yelling, indescribable shrieks came from women who had fallen calmly asleep with their children. They were brutally awakened by the Siberian infantrymen. Ghoulish laughter and screams mingled in horrible confusion. Women were wakened by clammy, cold, clawed hands tearing at their breasts.

In the middle of the road, in mud and rain the hysterical females were raped by the drunken Mongolian soldiers.

Threats and curses, yelling and terrible cries for help vied with the stuttering firing. This was the night's music in the village of Verbe.

In one hut where over fifty civilian refugees were sheltering a sergeant and ten men broke in. They pulled the women out one by one. The men and the halfgrown boys were forced up against the wall and shot. Then the women were raped.

An infantry lieutenant who was sitting in his company office with the sergeant-major and a couple of clerks was surprised by a Russian group. All had to kneel on the floor. A Siberian corporal grabbed them by the hair one by one, bent their heads back and slowly and precisely cut their throats.

A Ukrainian farmer tried to save his 12-year-old daughter from two Siberians. He was hit with a riflebutt and had his throat cut. From it the blood spurted like a fountain. Beside his blood-stained corpse they raped his daughter.

A naked woman with her hair flying ran screaming down the street, pursued by a roaring soldier. One of his friends kicked her legs from under her. They raped her there and then.

Porta half-rose. He aimed carefully as on a firing range. The soldier who had thrown himself at the woman sprang up only to fall again hit neatly in the temple.

The other one who was holding the woman by her feet looked about him, startled. Then he fell, waltzing his death agony, having been hit precisely in the middle of the forehead.

'A bull's eye,' Porta announced with his vulperine grin.

Tiny growled like a wild animal and fingered his pouch of hand-grenades.

The Old Un, taking a deep breath, signalled to some of our gunners lying behind another house and watching us.

'Forward and get 'em!' he shouted frantically.

Yelling infernally we jumped up and, shooting from the hip, stormed forward. Others caught our fury and followed.

The Russians were almost paralysed by the sudden attack of an enemy they thought was wildly fleeing.

The Old Un shouted to Porta:

'Save our children!'

A nod. Tiny and Porta raced for the hut where we had bedded down. Before they could reach it the Russians started a counter-attack.

Hand-grenades were being lobbed through the air. Furious bursts from automatic weapons swept the ground.

We jumped into cover in a shell-hole. Four dead Russians already occupied it. We rolled them up on the edge to serve as a breast-work. A light machine-gun was brought into position.

Porta got hold of a Russian 'stove-pipe' which had been discarded. He knelt quite calmly in the middle of the road and took careful aim before sending a rocket-shell into the attacking Russians.

Another swarm of brown-clad soldiers appeared. The door of the hut where we had left the children and the dead woman opened. The silent boy who had so clearly shown his hatred of us stood waving a piece of white cloth.

The Old Un placed his hand on the Little Legionnaire's shoulder to stop him firing. The boy came out to go across to the Russians. He managed to take only a few steps before he collapsed in the rain of bullets showering from both sides.

Tiny swore and wanted to jump out of the shell-hole. The Old Un took hold of him.

'Have you got brain-fever? They'd fill you with nails before you could say boo!'

A hand-grenade flew over and exploded right in front of the house.

The Little Legionnaire behind the heavy machine-gun at once answered with some long bursts. Another hand-grenade hit the house. We heard the children weeping and screaming. The face of a girl appeared at one window but disappeared fast.

A brown-clad figure popped up just by the house. An arm swung. A dark thing shot through the air and burst the window. A thundering explosion. Long tongues of flame. The door flew off its hinges. The crying and screaming ceased.

The Old Un hid his face in his hands.

'Let's get away. It's no use staying!'

Porta was the last to run away. He stood up with the light machine-gun in his hands, fired a salvo at the Russians and shouted:

'Can you see me waving good-bye?' Then he ran after us.

Tiny cursed and swore revenge because the Russians had thrown a hand-grenade at our twins, although it might easily have been a German hand-grenade which burst in on them.

A bemused Russian infantry soldier suddenly appeared in front of us. Tiny swung his machine-pistol casually, and the Russian's head was bashed in.

We heard the sounds of pursuers catching up with us. The Little Legionnaire was practically all-in, but he still breathlessly hung on.

In a narrow gorge we stopped. Silently we spread out waiting for the hunt to arrive. Porta laughed a little:

'You'll have your nappies to wring out, you red heroes . . .'

They appeared in a large clump, shouting in their arrogance.

When they reached the middle of the gorge we opened fire. They checked, swayed and fell. Some rose and tried to run, but they were lost. Bleeding they fell. One crawled off on all fours. Tiny threw his knife at him. It stuck trembling between his shoulder-blades. He crawled on. Then he collapsed. We threw a hand-grenade into the heap of corpses to bring down the curtain.

We ran on. Behind us shots still rang out. We heard the cries of the Russians chasing our fleeing soldiers.

After a minute's rest The Old Un stood up and said:

'Come on. It reeks of shots in the neck here.'

Breathlessly we raced on through thorny bushes and undergrowth, our hands and faces skinned and blood streaming down our cheeks and necks.

'Take it easy!' Porta said suddenly and halted. 'We're running about like flies to escape a one-way ticket to Kolyma! But it's no use!'

'What's the matter?' The Old Un asked.

'There,' Porta pointed. 'Just look. Or do you need a pair of eye-crutches!'

In the direction where Porta was pointing we dimly saw figures lying in wait in some hastily prepared trenches.

The Old Un quickly made his decision. We were to circle them in the darkness in a westerly direction.

'Fine,' Porta grinned. 'My conk can turn in only one direction at the moment: west. It's sick for the smell of Berlin!'

We had not gone very far before a voice from the darkness shouted excitedly:

'Halt! Wer da?'

Porta took a deep breath, blew his nose in his fingers and shouted heartily:

'Kiss me, comrade. We've made it!'

'That can only be our own lot,' said the voice from the darkness. It now sounded a little calmer.

'What the hell?' Porta shouted. 'Did you think it was reindeer in aspic?'

'Keep left,' warned the voice, 'and straight on, but be careful: we've laid mines!'

'God help me, really?' Tiny said with heavy humour. 'We thought you'd put out easter-eggs. Mines? What are they?' he asked Porta.

'Something used for making smoked backside with vegetables,' Porta grinned.

A hand reached out to help us into a trench. We saw silver glinting on our helper's shoulder.

The Old Un stood to attention and reported we were lost from the 867th Infantry Battalion.

A group of young cavalrymen suddenly shot out of the ground, staring at us in astonishment. Somebody mumbled something about coming from Verbe.

'Hm,' replied another. 'I always believed that where the German soldier stood he remained!'

Porta turned to him, jeering:

'Maybe you believe in the stork too – and Santa Claus?'

23

'When we were fighting in Morocco,' said the Little Legionnaire, 'we'd only one thing to do: turn our faces to Mecca and say: "Allah's will be done," and let loose. We can't do anything else here. So, forward, comrades! We shall die like animals.'

Cannon – machine-guns – machine-pistols – flame-throwers – Haubitzers – Stalin-organs – mines – hand-grenades – bombs – shells. Words, words, words! But what horrors they evoke!

Comrades, here we come!

To-morrow you are dead, YOU: death's vagabonds.

They storm forward. The sick, drunk, frightened, insane, persecuted, poor men and boys in uniforms.

Prey is beckoning you. Blood, women, food, booze.

Viva la muerte!

Long Live Death

'Here we go again,' Porta swore. 'No sooner have we found our gang again than we're back in the shit as a fighting-group.'

'As long as we're lying here nice and quiet there's no need to make a fuss,' The Old Un said.

Porta removed his top-hat, polished it with a rifle-rag, spat, and invited us to play pontoon.

Stege sneered.

'Any minute now we can expect Ivan. It would be wiser to get some shut-eye before we're at it again.'

But when Porta, Tiny, the SS man and Sergeant Heide started to play pontoon, Stege could not forbear to join in.

They sat at the bottom of the trench playing and of course quarrelling. Tiny had found an age-old bowler-hat and on Porta's advice was wearing it.

When von Barring innocently inquired what sort of head-gear he had introduced to the tank troops the Little Legionnaire announced to the apparently shocked battalion commander:

'It's a sort of mascot. An elephant's pessary. Tiny found it in an old-folk's home in Brodny.'

'Well, well,' sighed von Barring. 'I'd prefer you not to make clowns of yourselves. The CO doesn't approve of it.'

'But, Herr Commander!' Porta put in. 'The bloody caps we're issued with are bad for the hair, and the skull-muffs are too hot for the spring. That's why Tiny's introduced his air-conditioned topee.'

Von Barring shook his head and moved off along the trench, followed by his adjutant, Lieutenant Vogt.

Tiny touched the brim of his bowler and announced:

'Don't anybody dare say a word about Tiny's lid!'

Von Barring turned and looked inscrutably at us. Then he went on without a word.

We lay there for several days without being disturbed. The Russians on the other side had dug themselves in, and they kept quiet. All we exchanged was shouted words.

One German-speaking Russian was especially eager. He promised us unbelievable rewards if we would only throw away our weapons and go over to the other side.

'In Moscow thousands of the most elegant bitches' legs are waiting for you,' he shouted, and he naturally arrested Tiny's undivided attention.

'Do you believe that shoddy bastard?' he asked us earnestly.

'Why don't you go and ask him?' Porta suggested.

Tiny hoisted himself up on the edge of the trench, pulled his bowler over his forehead to keep out the sun, put his hand to his mouth and shouted:

'Hey, you whore-master! This is Tiny. What's this you're telling us about the bits in Moscow? If you can prove it, let's talk.'

A little later the Russian replied:

'Tiny, just come here and we'll give you a ticket for the Moscow express. It'll tip you out right in the middle of the biggest whore-shop there.'

Tiny turned the answer over in his mind and looked round at us, frowning solemnly.

'Sounds all right, what that grunting bull says, but it's too good to be true.'

Again he rose above the parapet and announced with a voice filled with contempt: 'You're full of bloody lies, you red shite!'

Little by little, we gathered that something was going to happen. Day and night, large concentrations of artillery were assembled on both sides.

Early one morning, we spotted high in the sky a small silver-shimmering moth-like plane. Every man in the position turned his face to it.

'Artillery-spotter,' Heide proclaimed.

'What the hell do you know about it?' mocked Porta.

Heide glared at him, but kept quiet.

Precisely at nine o'clock it started. One long concerted infernal howling, growling and thundering. Cannon and mortars of all calibres unloaded thousands of shells, rockets and bombs over the whole front.

We curled up like hedgehogs in our hollows. Over the entire trench-system was an umbrella of red-hot steel.

It lasted exactly two hours. Then an ominous silence shrouded everything.

We hardly believed our eyes that not a single man had got as much as a scratch, and that not one of our shell-throwers, infantry-guns or machine-guns had been hit. We were speechless. It was like a fairy-tale. Liberating laughter rose from each of our positions when we realized how lucky we had been.

Then the planes appeared just above the trees with howling engines and a hail of phosphorous and petrol bombs. Men who did not manage to take cover in a split second were finished. For a whole hour wave upon wave of the hated 'butchers' were upon us. After a short lull a new artillery barrage started.

Porta looked up and said drily:

'What a party this is! I didn't know we were still worth this lot!'

He was about to say something more when an organ-like

roar and a colossal explosion made him jump. Earth, steel and stone rained down on us.

Tiny started to say something but the Little Legionnaire, his ears muffled in his headphones, held up his hand.

'The battalion commander's calling, but I can't understand a word.'

'Try again,' ordered the company commander, Lieutenant von Lüders. Desperately the Little Legionnaire twiddled the knobs of his radio and listened eagerly. He grinned at von Lüders:

'Don't tell me I'm nuts, Herr Lieutenant, but the commander's nattering something about the corps commander coming right out here to our position. The CO is already escorting the rare animal out here.'

Von Lüders and all of us stared at the Little Legionnaire as if he were some peculiar apparition.

'God help us!' the lieutenant breathed when he realized just what the Little Legionnaire had said.

'What's going on?' Tiny asked. 'Are we getting some artillery?'

'No, just a full lieutenant-general!' Porta replied.

'God protect the nipples of our girls and their fair hair,' Tiny beamed. 'I bet the red-striped warthog is going to shoo us right across to Ivan. I wish I knew where the kitchen-staircase was!'

Lieutenant von Lüders received orders to meet the commandant and his party by a sunken road and to show the distinguished spectators the positions in order to convince them that we were conducting well-regulated warfare in the approved manner.

Swearing freely, von Lüders ordered The Old Un to provide the escort to meet the high brass.

'We'll be losing pounds in weight again,' Porta observed. 'Running, running, that's the only thing we're good at.'

'Good, we're off,' von Lüders laughed and started to run across an open space between the trenches.

'No, by God, we're not,' Porta answered breathing hard. 'But I wish we were. We'll have to keep a still tongue in our pants – no, I mean our mouths—'

The Russians at once had us in the sights of the heavy machine-gun they had sited on a mound right across from us. We practically flew down into a ditch as every evil spirit in the shape of small-arms ammunition hissed by us and hit the road with a rattle.

Crawling on our stomachs, we got across the road and went on, crouching behind a hedge. At least it hid us.

Completely breathless we reached the sunken road and threw ourselves into the ditch on the far side. Tiny put up his hand like a boy at school and asked:

'Herr Lieutenant, how well have we got to behave to be allowed to go on a trip like this next year?'

He got no answer. The general and his red-tabbed staff-officers came round a bend in the road.

It was an impressive party. Blood-red tabs, gold-lace and glittering Knight's Crosses lit up the landscape.

With the general and his staff came Colonel Hinka and Captain von Barring. Both appeared to be anxious and excited.

Lieutenant von Lüders clicked his heels together, saluted and reported:

'Herr Generaloberst, Lieutenant Lüders, commanding No. 5 Company, reports as ordered. The detail under Sergeant Beire will act as escort.'

The general eyed von Lüders coldly. Then without acknowledging the salute he turned to Colonel Hinka.

'Pay attention, Colonel, here's another one of your gangs. No discipline, no order. It looks more like an errand-boys' outfit than a military formation. A lieutenant reports to his corps commander with an escort straight from swimming in the ditch, smacking their lips like over-fed cows: Swine! A lot of filthy swine!' He pointed to Lüders who stood stiff as a tree in front of him.

'Where's your gas-mask? Where's your steel-helmet? Don't you know that you should carry your steel-helmet at all times when on active service? And you let yourself run round in a forage-cap!' He became dark-red in the face. Wild words poured out of his mouth. There was a trace of tears in his stuttering, excited voice. He pointed to Porta's and Tiny's head-gear. 'That bowler – and that top-hat! What's that for? What in the name of heaven have you got on your head?'

Porta straightened up very slowly. Leaning on his carbine he said:

'A cylinder, Herr Generaloberst.'

'So that's what it is, a cylinder! Throw it away! Take it off! Punish that man!' he shouted at Hinka. Then he turned to Tiny chewing a blade of grass and with the bowler-hat on the back of his head.

'And what is this kind of head-wear you've allowed yourself to be dressed up in?'

Startled, Tiny jumped up, tripped over his feet and dropped his light machine-gun. With much noise he found his feet and stood up.

'Herr Generaloberst, it's an elephant's pessary!'

(I'd better mention here that Tiny did not know what a pessary was. He truly believed it was the proper name for a bowler-hat.)

The general bared his teeth. The blood rushed to his puffy face. He turned to Hinka.

'That fellow will be court-martialled as soon as the regiment has returned from the front-line. I'll teach them to make fun of me!'

The Old Un whispered in prayer:

'Dear little Ivan, please bang a little! Only a teeny weeny little bang from your "organ"!'

But Ivan had no direct telepathic communication with The Old Un. Nothing happened.

Cursing and swearing the general ordered that he should be shown the battle positions. He jeered at a lieutenant of his staff who jumped for cover when a 7.5-cm. shell crashed on to the road.

'Did you drop something, Herr Lieutenant, since you're lying there?'

Red in the face, the lieutenant stood up and trudged confused after his great boss.

When the general had seen the positions, which he criticized severely, he started to cross a piece of open land where Ivan had a nice field of fire.

The heavy machine-gun on the hill immediately started firing. Three officers were wounded, but the general marched stiffly across the open space without even a glance at the wounded.

The road was hit by several shells. One tore out von Lüder's stomach and he died in a few minutes. Another officer lost his foot.

A few days later we were withdrawn from the line and to our delight Lieutenant Harder was appointed to be our new company commander. He had recently returned from hospital.

We were to rest for a fortnight, but on the very first night we had to turn out.

We had landed in a small village which had served as a recreation-centre for Russian commissars and later for German air force personnel. A dozen beautiful villas were sites for our heavy infantry guns.

In one room, which must have been occupied by women for it retained their female fragrance, Stege and I put up a machine-gun in a window embrasure to cover the railway line. In the attic Porta, the Little Legionnaire and Tiny put up another machine-gun.

Lieutenant Harder with the rest of the commando-group sat underneath us.

Tiny came down with a couple of bottles of vodka and a few herrings. He threw himself on the bed and rolled about with his nose to the sheet, like a retriever on the scent.

'Hell and damnation!' he shouted. 'It stinks of crumpet!'

He slid to the floor. Then he shouted wildly and disappeared under the bed. To our astonishment we heard women's voices, and bedlam followed.

Tiny's voice sounded as if he were speaking through an eiderdown.

'I've caught a couple of tarts!'

There was a violent feminine protest. Simultaneously two female legs appeared from under the bed.

Stege bent down and hauled out a kicking girl. Now Tiny dragged himself out with a second girl in his arms.

'Stupid swine!' she raged at Tiny who was showing off his catch with great delight.

Both girls were dressed partly in civvies. They could not disguise, however, that they were Blitzmädels from the air force.

Stege stood for a moment looking thoughtfully at them.

'Run away from the party?' he said, lifting an eyebrow.

'No, we haven't,' the blonde one said shortly.

'No?' Stege said. 'Well then we better get the OC. Tiny, call Harder!'

Tiny looked at him in astonishment.

'You must have caught an inflammation of the brain. Let's taste the roast first. Let the bloody officers come after. To hell with fetching them!'

The blonde dealt him a hefty blow on the face.

'We're not at all what you think! We're decent girls!'

'You're deserters,' Stege corrected. 'If we get Lieutenant Harder up here and he does his duty you'll be a couple of very long-necked girls!'

'You'd give us up?' gasped the dark girl, who was the younger.

'So you *have* left the treadmill,' Stege said and grinned.

'Yes, we stayed behind when the others left.'

'Left? That's a good one.' Stege laughed. 'We call it running away. Did they catch the express or the plane?'

'This is no time for cheap jokes,' the blonde said.

Stege shrugged his shoulders.

'What are your names?'

'My name's Grethe. My friend's Trude,' answered the blonde.

Tiny could not contain himself any longer. He almost fell on top of Grethe, but she cleverly avoided him.

'You're a good lay,' he shouted and ran after her. 'Just Tiny's number. I'll let you be my very own little tart!'

Stege grabbed him and said sharply:

'Let the girl alone, Tiny. She's no tart.'

'By God, she is!' Tiny cried and caught hold of her skirt. He nearly tugged it off. Frightened, she shouted wildly.

Now we heard thundering boots coming up the stairs.

'Get them away,' Stege snapped and the girls dived under the big bed.

The door opened.

Porta and the Little Legionnaire stood surveying the scene.

Tiny was sitting on the edge of the bed looking up at the ceiling in such a way that even a child would have detected he was hiding something.

Porta gave a long low whistle. He marched across to Tiny and lifted up his chin.

'Now be a good boy and tell Uncle Joseph where you've hidden her.'

'I don't know what you're talking about,' Tiny said.

Porta laughed and kicked a female shoe in front of Tiny.

'Do you know what this is?'

'Yes, a tart-sandal,' Tiny added piously: 'This is a disused whore-house we've landed in.'

'Where are they?' Porta suddenly shouted at Tiny making him fall backwards on the bed in fright.

'Under the bed,' Tiny gasped.

A minute later the girls were revealed. Tiny raged and swore that Grethe was his property.

How it might have ended is hard to tell. But just then a hostile machine-gun started to fire into the roof making the plaster drop on us.

We ran to our machine-gun and saw that the Russians were about to cross the railway line.

'The heavy mortar!' Lieutenant Harder shouted from the lavatory window.

Three men worked feverishly at bringing the large mortar into position. The rest of us tried to keep the Reds at bay with our machine-guns. But more and more Russians massed there.

Shells from a Soviet field-battery began to land on the houses round about and on the road. Harder desperately called the battalion asking for permission to withdraw; but we were ordered to stay put.

'We'll be surrounded!' Harder shouted down the receiver.

'Makes no difference,' replied von Barring. 'Corps HQ have ordered the position to be held. The other companies in the battalion are no better off than you. No. 3 is destroyed. Over.'

A corporal came running from the railway station. A shell hit the ground close by and whirled him upwards.

'Now we're trapped,' Stege shouted. 'Our colleagues have brought up heavy infantry-guns.'

The first shell was already with us. Stones, clods of earth, dust, plaster and shrapnel flew through the air.

We threw ourselves behind the wall for cover, but before the dust had subsided we were at our machine-gun again. Above us we heard Porta shouting and next we saw him sliding like an acrobat down the waste-pipe. He raced across to the station buildings, swiped a 'stove-pipe', knelt down covered by a wall and sent a rocket flying at the attacking Russians.

The effect at this short range was fantastic. Human limbs and firearms were blown into the air. The attack faltered, but a few Russian officers whipped their troops on with slogans from good old Ilya Ehrenburg. They gathered for a fresh attack.

The next rocket crashed with a howl and a smack into the tightly packed troops and scattered them.

Porta grinned up at us, removed his top-hat and bowed like a circus-performer. Then he tore back to the house.

'No more sweeties,' he shouted and started scrambling up the waste-pipe.

Tiny leaned out of the lavatory window:

'Did you notice if my tyres have got enough air? I'm going home by bike, I think.'

'I'll lend you my cycle clips,' the Little Legionnaire said, and laughed hollowly.

Ivan retreated behind the railway line. We loaded our ammunition belts to be ready for a new attack.

A little later a fierce firing came from the other end of the village where the Russians had launched another assault.

Both the girls had crawled under the bed when the fighting started. Now they came out, shaken and shocked.

'What do we do if the Russians come?' Grethe wanted to know.

Stege laughed without much amusement.

'You should have thought of that before you left the party.'

'All right, but what do we do?' Grethe asked.

'Get your pants off ready!' Porta cried as he entered the room.

'Cheeky fellow, you're worse than the Russians,' Grethe screeched.

'Sure, my little pet,' Porta laughed. 'But you'll soon have a chance of judging. Uncle Ivan's preparing his victory.'

He threw a piece of sausage at the girls who were now sitting miserably on the bed.

Tiny sat cross-legged on the floor, drinking vodka. He spat and wiped his mouth. Then he turned to the girls.

'Which of you'll play wild animals with Tiny? I'll pay of course,' he added and threw a 100-mark note on the bed.

'Get yourself some stockings or rose-water.'

The girls eyed him furiously. Porta laughed.

'You're warming up, Tiny!'

Tiny nodded.

'That's right. It's not every day we're fighting in a love-nest. Are you ready, girls, for Tiny? You can be served next.' He motioned to Porta and braced himself.

He bent over Grethe and tried to kiss her. She broke loose and cried hysterically.

'Just like the Russians!'

'Not quite,' Stege said, smiling cynically. 'It lacks a little something.'

'I prefer the Russians to this nasty animal!' she cried.

'You'll get your wish granted!' Stege shouted and flung a hand-grenade out of the window. 'Here they come!'

Ferocious gunfire broke out. The Russians had now almost reached the house. The mortar we had sited had been over-run by Russian infantry.

'Tanks!' The alarm came from the road, and across the railway line appeared the broad snout of a T34.

Lieutenant Harder shouted from downstairs:

'Come on, let's try to reach the cliff behind us. We'll take up a new position there. Bring along the wounded!'

'Now girls, go downstairs and give Ivan a nice kiss,' said Porta. 'Or else get your track-shoes on because we're going to run so fast the water will be pouring from us!'

Covered by the Little Legionnaire's machine-gun we withdrew from the house. As the wounded were hoisted from the lavatory window we were splashed with their blood.

Stege turned to the girls standing lost in the middle of the floor.

'What are you going to do?'

'We'll come,' they said.

They were quickly helped and received by The Old Un and Heide who stood in the back-yard.

'What the hell!' The Old Un burst out. 'Have you got girls up there!'

'Yes, they've been playing hide-and-seek with the head-hunters,' Stege shouted.

Porta and Tiny ran straight into three Russians but after a short scrap the Russians gave up and were taken prisoners.

One of them, a sergeant-major, said with feeling:

'*Waina nix karosch!*'

'Didn't you know that before,' Porta retorted. 'We've known it a long time.'

'*Nom d'un chien,*' the Little Legionnaire said and scuttled off bent under the weight of his machine-gun. The bullets were whining all around him.

Grethe gave a sudden scream. A thick column of blood spurted out of an open hole in her throat.

Tiny half-turned.

'She's eaten something that didn't agree with her.' He grabbed Trude, flung her up on his shoulder and ran off raising the dust with his enormous boots.

'*Quel malheur!*' cursed the Little Legionnaire and started to climb the cliff like a monkey. It towered almost vertically above the rest-camp.

The Russians stormed forward from both sides wildly shouting their '*Uhra!*'

Porta was half-way up the cliff supporting a wounded corporal, helped by the SS man. The Russian fire forced them to drop the wounded man. He fell with a hollow thump on the road.

Stege and I were firing our light machine-guns for all we were worth to keep the Russians at bay until the Little Legionnaire could place his heavier gun in position on top of the cliff.

It seemed as if eternity elapsed before we heard an angry rattling above us: the first burst from the Little Legionnaire's machine-gun hammering at the Russians.

Stege rose. As he climbed the cliff I received a violent blow in the stomach. The day blackened in front of my eyes and I felt I was falling into a deep, deep abyss. I just noticed Tiny handing Trude to Porta. Then everything disappeared.

When I regained consciousness terrible pains burned my whole body. I think I screamed.

Hand-grenades were exploding. Bursting shells flew like angry wasps. A flame-thrower hissed, glowing red. Shouts and cries battered at my ear-drums.

The Old Un was bending over me. He was smeared with blood and dust. He swung me like a sack of flour over his shoulder and with Tiny's help made for the cliff.

Another bullet hit me. 'A lung-wound,' was the thought that raced through my mind. Then it seemed I must suffocate.

THE END